Praise for *Drawing in the Dust*

An Indie Next List Notable Book

"Insight into the world of biblical excavation in Israel raises Rabbi Klein's debut novel from a Jewish *Da Vinci Code* to an emotionally rich story of personal and historical discovery. . . . Klein's most vivid passages depict the meditative tedium of digging, the exultation of discovery, and the intricate process of authentication and preservation, while love stories past and present—and a balanced, compassionate view of both Israeli and Arab traditions—add to the book's pleasures."

—*Publishers Weekly*

"Lively."

—*Kirkus Reviews*

"A suspenseful race against time."

—*Booklist*

"By turns philosophical, suspenseful, and passionate, this brilliant debut novel—in the bestselling tradition of Anita Diamant's *The Red Tent*—transports readers into a mystical world and takes them on a journey they won't soon forget."

—*IndieBound*

"A masterful debut by an author from whom we can wholeheartedly hope to read more."

—*San Diego Jewish World*

"A climax as incendiary as any Biblical prophecy. A satisfying, smart read."

—*Jewish Book World*

"A fast-paced modern adventure.... The plot is carried by a clear prose liberally interspersed with a poetic idiom."

—*Haaretz* magazine

"Challenges the ideas of relationships between academia and religion, of emotion and analysis, and of personal versus global achievement.... Klein's novel has a softness and a sweetness to its depictions of lovers' words and human emotion. An excellent book."

—Fresh Fiction

"Talented author Zoë Klein has crafted a must read.... The people and settings are so real you'll believe you've visited Israel and met new friends."

—Reader to Reader

"A magical and fully romantic read.... Breathtakingly beautiful.... Remarkable."

—A Journey of Books

"Klein is a master of images and descriptions, as her vivid portrayal of settings and reactions of the characters pack each moment with convincing realism.... Her depiction of life cleverly and plausibly comes alive regardless of the time period.... A profoundly moving story of emotional growth."

—Single Titles

"Sometimes you need a book that speaks to you. *Drawing in the Dust* makes you think and feel. When you're looking for a book that will touch your soul, this is the one to pick up. It is a masterpiece!"

—Readaholic

"Lyrical, transformative, and unexpected, *Drawing in the Dust* will keep you enthralled in the moment, yet racing to know more."

—Gina B. Nahai, *New York Times* bestselling author of *Moonlight on the Avenue of Faith*

"Archaeology is the most dangerous of sciences, fundamentalism the most insidious of religious beliefs, and fiction the most seductive form of writing. Mix all three together, and you have *Drawing in the Dust*. . . . Zoe Klein will rock your foundations! This is what fiction should be about."

—Kathleen O'Neal Gear and W. Michael Gear,
New York Times bestselling authors of *The Betrayal*

"A magically inventive archaeological expedition into love's psyche. Rabbi Klein's voice is enormously literate, politically sophisticated, spiritually captivating, and above all, unique."

—Lawrence Kushner, author of *Kabbalah: A Love Story*

"*Drawing in the Dust* is original in every sense of the word: creative, innovative, novel. It is an archaeological adventure that resurrects buried romance. With feeling intellect, the author reveals the secret of the heart."

—Rabbi Harold Schulweis, author of
Conscience: The Duty to Obey and the Duty to Disobey

This title is also available as an eBook

DRAWING
IN THE
DUST

ZOË KLEIN

GALLERY BOOKS

New York   London   Toronto   Sydney

Gallery Books
A Division of Simon & Schuster, Inc.
1230 Avenue of the Americas
New York, NY 10020

First Gallery Books trade paperback edition May 2010

GALLERY and colophon are trademarks of Simon & Schuster, Inc.

For information about special discounts for bulk purchases, please contact Simon & Schuster Special Sales at 1-866-506-1949 or business@simonandschuster.com.

The Simon & Schuster Speakers Bureau can bring authors to your live event. For more information or to book an event, contact the Simon & Schuster Speakers Bureau at 1-866-248-3049 or visit our website at www.simonspeakers.com.

Designed by Renata Di Biase

Manufactured in the United States of America

10   9   8   7   6   5   4   3   2   1

Library of Congress Cataloging-in-Publication Data
Klein, Zoe.
  Drawing in the dust / Zoë Klein.
    p. cm.
  1. Archaeologists—Israel—Fiction. 2. Scrolls—Fiction. 3. Bible—Antiquities—Fiction.
I. Title.
  PS3611.L453D73 2009
  813'.6—dc22
                                        2008046292

ISBN 978-1-4165-9912-8
ISBN 978-1-4165-9913-5 (pbk)
ISBN 978-1-4391-1744-6 (ebook)

For Rachmiel,
Rhythm of creation,

For Kinneret,
Queen of the mermaids,

For Zimra,
Our sparkle,

For my husband Jonathan,
My unending courtship.

I adjure you, daughters of Jerusalem,
Adore to weeping,
Love to laughing,
Desire to praising.
Tickle, giggle, kiss!
Adonai my God,
For one moment in love,
Let alone a thousand,
Let alone my life,
For the honor of raising and loving
Children in love,
Praise of You is ever upon my lips.

ACKNOWLEDGMENTS

In the back of an Italian nook on Broome Street in SoHo, I sat with my agent, Mollie Glick, and editor, Lauren McKenna, two of the most beautiful, intelligent women in Manhattan, to discuss *Drawing in the Dust*. We spent four hours discussing the manuscript over peach and basil salads with shaved parmigiano, balsamic- and vanilla-roasted figs with sheep's milk ricotta, lemon-scented potato gnocchi, and wine. Mollie is an extraordinary shepherdess. She had nourished my writing and continues to sustain me with her sageness, enthusiasm, keen insight, and persistent faith. Between antipasti and dolci, I was captivated by Lauren's transformative vision, sharp wisdom, and mastery of both the forest and the trees. I am grateful for the partnership of such luminous book lovers.

There aren't nearly enough Al Silvermans in this world, but I am grateful to know one well. Al encouraged me from a young homesick letter writer into an author. I remember visiting his office at Viking/Penguin, and even with hundreds of manuscripts piled around his desk, he received my first attempt at a book into his hands as if receiving a baby. My mentor, Rabbi Jerome Malino, who loved

Jeremiah as much as I, once leaped out of his car in Anatot, Jeremiah's birthplace, and started dancing. His spirit, I am certain, dances there still, as well as in me. Deep thanks to Michael Wilt for knowing how to take rough-hewn text and polish it to gleaming. I want to thank Dr. David Ilan, the director of the Nelson Glueck School of Biblical Archaeology, for being a generous resource. Thank you to the community of Temple Isaiah, for inviting me into the scrolls of your hearts.

People often thank their parents. That doesn't mean that anyone but my brother and I understand what it means to thank ours. As a child I would sit in a bin of fabric and watch my father work dawn to dusk, enjoying conversations about matters great and minute, which continue to be like revelations to me. I have spent most of my life seeking the kind of sanctuary I have felt beside my father's drawing board. There is nothing like my mother's garden in full bloom, except for her heart, which is endlessly giving. Her generosity, love, and strength must derive from a hidden fountain, or a divine sort of grace. Our parents, like most parents, worked hard to give us food and shelter. What is unique is that they worked just as hard if not harder to give us magic. I want to thank my brother, Zachary, and Nicole Grashow, and my nephews, Gavin and Nathaniel, for sharing it all.

Above all, I throw my arms around my husband, Jonathan, in praise and admiration, for filling our family's life with music and meaning, for extraordinary support, for eyes that sparkle and dance, for playfulness and profundity, compassion and camaraderie, for innumerable deeds of loving-kindness. At the summit of Mount Sinai, you asked me to marry you, and every day together we step closer to promise. And to our children, Rachmiel, Kinneret, and Zimra, for demanding of your tired parents new stories every night, and letting us know what you think of them, and for sugaring our whole lives with your sticky, gooey, smart-alecky love. Every verse in the scrolls of your days sings to us of hope and wonder. You amaze me.

You kids write good books too.

PROLOGUE

J ust above and to the left of the basketball net, across a gym filled
with dancing students, hung the clock, faintly glowing like a full
moon through a polluted night, calmly eating the seconds before the new year. I sat slumped on the lowest bleacher, my gangly
knees pressed together under pink tulle and my shoes pointing shyly
toward each other. The vapor from the fog machine grew thicker.
I didn't know anyone at the social except for my cousins Marilyn
and Grace, who had reluctantly invited me only because my father
had agreed to chaperone alongside my uncle. The clock was my only
partner at the dance. We had been watching each other, my small face
filled with braces, concave cheeks, and forehead fringed with wisps of
baby-chick hair, and the clock's big, round, benevolent face. When it
was swallowed by the fog, I was left alone.

The heat of bodies welded together caused the fog to rise to the
ceiling of the crowded gym, and soon water droplets began to rain.
The crowd was ecstatic, jumping up and down with their tongues
out to catch the condensation. I caught a glimpse of Grace with her
hands on a boy's shoulders. Two drops fell on my leg, another on my

hand, and I ran out of the gym into the hallway. My father was there, leaning against a locker, smoking a cigarette. I hadn't seen him smoke in years. His silhouette was framed by steely streetlight coming in through a large window zigzagged with wire. His hair was mussed as if his hand had just run through it. His silver breath spiraled in the air. I burst into tears.

"What happened, sweetheart?" he said, turning and reaching for me.

I buried my face in his corduroy jacket, big buttons pressed against my cheek. "I don't like it here," I said. "I don't know anyone. I want to go home."

"Don't you want to stay with your cousins?" he asked, his hand holding my head against him.

"They're too interested in boys to be with me," I sobbed.

"I'm supposed to be chaperoning this thing until two," he said.

I peeled away, keeping my arms around his waist. "You're just smoking in the hall. You're a terrible chaperone."

"I'm monitoring the hall," he defended himself, and then pulled a long drag off his cigarette. I could feel his chest expand as he held the smoke in his lungs. He added, "To make sure there are no problems."

I looked both ways up and down the hall. Even with the music thrumming through the cinderblock walls, the long and vacant hall felt abandoned. I looked up at him as he exhaled and I said, "Looks like I'm your only problem."

I saw the trace of a smile before he snuffed out his cigarette, scooped me up, and began running. My arms bounced against his back as he ran with me to the subway station, flying down the steps. "I'll get you home by midnight, princess."

My father was not a big man, but that night, he seemed giant, larger than life itself, bounding over the city blocks. I was twelve years old, and he made me feel like feathers. As he ran, racing the clock, I could feel his heart strong and healthy, the dark bristles of his face, his arms clutched around me like iron. A hero. On the subway I lay across three seats, my head on his thigh, as the train hurtled faster and faster away from that lonely gym. When we came to our stop, my father vaulted up the stairs with me to the street, running up to our building. He pulled off my shoes in the elevator. In the apartment he ran with me until he practically threw me into my bed. The clock radio read 11:59. He tucked my comforter all around me in a mad scramble, even though I was still in my starchy dress. I was laughing. My mother stood in the doorway, all smiles, shaking her head and saying, "What happened? What happened to the dance, you two?"

When the clock clicked to midnight, he kissed me right between my eyes and said, "I love you, Page. Happy New Year."

I sank blissfully into my pillow, marveling at him, and at the red square numbers hovering over his shoulder. Twelve o'clock. "We made it!" I exclaimed. The thinnest veil of a curtain fell over his eyes and then dissolved, and in that moment my eyes opened. I had known about the doctor visits, but I hadn't been paying close enough attention. Now I knew. He had in him the same thing that killed his father, my granddaddy, when my father was just a boy. He had inherited the broken gene with its malicious promise. A fatal fissure that could very well be in me as well.

Midnight is the most intimate of instants. The most hollow, superstitious, lost-in-the-woods, something's-in-the-attic moment of the day. Twelve is the knifepoint between the day's deepest darkening and the commencement of its lightening, the kiss between the kingdom of the moon and the kingdom of the sun. It is a razor-breadth's flash between despair and hope.

In that moment, for me, one day ended and a different kind of day began. A day made up entirely of midnights, each poised to tip into a new day but trapped, unable to wake to it, even after years under the blazing Mediterranean sun.

1

*There is no blemish on the glow which surrounds you like a metal
shield. But what good is a shield if the hurt is inside? . . . O Lord,
let his heart break and begin to heal rather than this perpetual and
terrible swell!*

—THE SCROLL OF ANATIYA 4:42–47

I always wake before sunrise, at least two hours before any of my
three housemates. I sit up in bed and stretch, kick off my covers. The polished limestone floor is cold, sending a shiver from
my feet all the way up my spine, and it delights me. The light sifting
through the window is soft and inviting, as if the house floats inside
a lavender cloud. I pull on shorts, a tank top, and slide my white bandana over my hair. I lather my face, arms, legs with sun lotion. The
air has the chill of white wine. I've seen sunlamps for people with
seasonal depression, so that in the long, dark winters when their sadness peaks, they can replicate bright days and feel healed. I'd rather
retire to a room with a gentle moonlamp, whirring metal fan, and
dewy humidifier. I pull on my socks, my sneakers.

I patter down the hall. The door to our supervisor Norris's suite
is ajar. He always sleeps with it a little open, as if tempting someone
to come in. I can see his jeans and belt hanging over the back of his
desk chair as I pass by. A picture of Mickey and Orna on their wed-

ding day hangs on their closed door. In the picture Mickey is wearing
a light brown suit and lopsided bow tie that look like they and the
groom had just arrived in Israel off a boat from Russia, which isn't too
far from the truth. He is bending his voluptuous sabra bride, Orna,
a little bit backward, her raven black hair wild with curls, and resting
his head just above her cleavage. Mickey always said he fell in love
with her because she had "the ripest breasts in the Fertile Crescent . . .
and a heart to match." A wooden plaque hangs from their doorknob
reading in Hebrew *birkat habayit*, "blessing of the home."

I am the house ghost, in a way, spooking my way through
the living room. Norris's leather chair, so out of place in a room of
institutional-style furniture, is opened in a reclining position with
a thin blanket spread over the arm and a rummaged newspaper at
its feet. I can imagine him sitting here, as he often does late at night,
drinking tea and watching reruns of *Baywatch* on Lebanese television.
In the kitchen I drink a glass of grapefruit juice. I make a sandwich,
roasted eggplant and turkey tucked into pita, and take a canteen of
ice out of the freezer, pack them in my knapsack along with my tools,
and head to the door.

There is a note pinned to the door that reads, "P—Dinner with
Jerrold March tonight at 8. Prepare to present on shaft tombs.—N."
I feel a tide of fury rise in me, not at the idea of dinner with Mr.
March, one of our most generous sponsors. I've met with him many
times whenever I've returned to New York, and he is always a perfect
gentleman from the tip of his mustache to his deftness with a salad
fork, harmlessly flirtatious after a few glasses of wine. It is easy to
melt into his luxurious world, and fun to bring him into the world
he funds, my dirty world of chamber pots and ceramic coffins. I'm
not angry even at Norris's directive, although I already knew about
dinner. I already have sketches to show Jerrold of official seals, basins,
statuettes, and ivories, maps indicating where we'd found the three
thousand infant burial jars. Norris knows I'm always prepared. We
have been working here together for more than a decade. It is that the
note is written on the back of the title page of my last book, an act

obviously intended to upset me. The page had been crumpled in his most recent fit, and then, I suppose, he smoothed it out to use it as scratch paper. To let me know how little he thinks of it, or me.

It's not worth spending the most beautiful time of the day fuming over him. He's been playing these games for so many months I'm practically numb to them. When I step outside, closing the door softly behind me, my anger dissolves in the wet, clean, and shimmering air. I love the early morning. Pine trees cast long shadows across the road and clouds stained deep grape and plum are strewn messily over the horizon, as if someone hadn't yet cleaned up the table linens after a giant party.

It is a two-mile walk to the tell. Every working morning I take this walk, leaving my old white Mazda in the driveway like a beached baby beluga. The air is tinged with rosemary, mint, and diesel. I try to drink in the coolness as I walk, knowing the sun will soon sizzle it all to chalk. There is a mist of sparkles over my clothes and my skin. The little hairs on my arms have been alchemized by the sun to fine gold. My naturally pale skin is gilded by exposure, despite my devotion to applying and reapplying lotion. I feel lean and able striding up the road, my mind clear. I enjoy the long stride of my body every morning before settling into a day of crouching in dirt.

The Judean Hills lie languid over the horizon and birds are winging between the pines. There is a Bedouin woman pulling up herbs down a stony slope. She is swathed in a long black robe, chanting in Arabic:

Fear not if you wander the barley fields after there has been a good rain
And you find an old lover who was slain long ago has risen to meet you
again.

I can see the museum at the bottom of the hill. I've been working in Megiddo for twelve years, in the heart of the Jezreel Valley in the north of Israel. Every year nearly four million tourists visit this very place. It is an extraordinary site. Megiddo is a hill that spans about fifteen acres, made up of thirty cities built one on top of the other over six millennia, beginning with the prepottery Neolithic period nine thousand years ago.

The wrestlings of my own heart should be overshadowed in this valley of death. At least thirty-four nations have battled in this place, with enormous slaughters. This is where Pharaoh Thutmose III fought the first battle known in recorded history anywhere in the world. The author of the Book of Revelation predicted that in the end of days, the battle between good and evil will ultimately take place here. In fact, the word *Armageddon* is a corruption of the Hebrew phrase *Har Megiddo*, Mount of Megiddo.

Modern Israel is no stranger to conflict, and one doesn't have to dig to remember. Every weapon created has been wielded here, and the newest generations, biological and nuclear, hang like Damocles's sword over the young nation. To stay ahead, defense systems scurry to evolve from the technology of tunnels and walls. I've spent my career here underground with the ancients, without emerging much into today's headlines. I've been less interested in the political and religious conflict of any century and more interested in personal practice, mostly studying Middle Bronze Age mortuary practices.

In the past, countless have lived, thrived, and then bled here until they became bone. Today, millions come to visit, including historic visits; the first visit of a pope to Israel took place here in Megiddo. Two hundred professionals dig here every working day. Norris directs them all, and I supervise twenty archaeologists and volunteers concentrating on the temples of stratum XV and the elaborate shaft tombs.

But each morning, like this one, there is just me. The generations below me are silent, and the tour buses have not yet rumbled in. In the half light, the site is empty. I cross the museum parking lot and begin to climb the tell. The land is perfectly still and mute, guarding its deep treasures of seedlings, cemeteries, and secret gardens. When I dig my callused hands into the cool, predawn earth, I feel all of her richness tingle through my skin. Before dawn the land always seems to yield, hinting that, with just the right touch, everything dormant in her might awaken, push through its black chambers, and Ezekiel's field of bones would drink the moist sky.

I walk through the remains of Solomon's stables, the rows of dark cold arches. I imagine the din of whinnying and neighing echoing through the ancient hall. Sparse, thorny grasses and sharp foliage poke through the stones.

As I emerge from the maze of stables, the horizon wears a crown. The sun is just rising. I kneel beside my most recent project, the three thousand and seventy-second infant burial jar we've unearthed. I put down my knapsack and unroll my pack of tools: a small pickax, a toothbrush, variously sized paintbrushes, and fine dental tools. The jar is shaped like a womb, the corpse inside curled toward the entry. How disappointing for them to be delivered not by some messiah to life everlasting but by me, to a mention in my field notes. I begin to gently dust the rim of the jar, thinking.

It is hard for me to believe that I am thirty-nine years old. Looking at the swollen shape of the jar, I involuntarily draw my hand over my stomach. I used to wonder what it would be like to be round and full like that instead of empty, flat. To carry life inside me. I don't think about it much anymore. I have never gotten myself tested to see if I have the Lou Gehrig's gene like my father, like my grandfather. I tremble at the thought of bequeathing my fear to another, if not my child, then his or hers, a Damocles sword over all my generations. And at the same time . . .

I sigh. The sky that had sagged so sweetly, as if the Kingdom of Heaven's doormat was just within reach, is pinned back into place by a fiery thumbtack. I labor over the jar and its crumbled contents. "You would be, I'd estimate, three thousand years old today," I say. Some scholars have written that these are the remains of child sacrifices from an ancient cult. It's possible, I shrug to myself. Infant mortality rates were astronomically high. Still are in many places. "I don't know," I say out loud to no one. "Either way, you probably weren't going to make it to your three-thousandth birthday anyhow." I begin to hear the buzz of insects as the sun climbs, doing their jobs as well. Diggers are beginning to arrive. Soon my team will assemble and I'll direct them. I pull out my notebook and lean in close to the jar, sketching the details.

"The early bird gets the urn, eh?"

I sit back. Norris is standing over me, eclipsing the sun. I squint a little. He's smiling, so I smile back.

"Get my note?" he asks, tilting his head. I remember the crumpled page of my book tacked to the door and the plume of heat it fueled in me. I used to stew over his mockery for days. I wonder for a moment if the fact that I've started to become used to it, that I can recover so quickly, is a bad sign. A sign I've accepted abuse as the norm. It wasn't always this way.

Norris, my professor of Levantine archaeology at Columbia, had been a great supporter of my first book, *Body of Water, Body of Air: Water and Theology in Ancient Israel*. My second book, *Up in Smoke*, was based on my thesis, a study of cultic theology and connections between altars found in Israel, especially at Megiddo, and altars found throughout the Middle East, tracing borrowed cultic practices throughout the region. The new manuscript, *Upon This Altar*, was a follow-up to *Up in Smoke*. I did so much research, imprinting my eyes with microfilms of altars, that I began to see them everywhere. In the shape of my desk there was an altar. A baby's pram was an altar. The park bench. I developed a new philosophy, which I tried to expound in my introduction to the book, exploring the idea that when there were no more altars in space, there would always be altars in time. That there are moments, precious and sacred, when something intangible but terrible is slain, and we are born into a new light. When it happens, the moment could be called forgiveness, or mercy, or even love.

I was delirious with confidence. I was ecstatic for its release. I had written it in a trance. It was, in retrospect, probably just a crappy little book. But it was important to me. I couldn't wait to hear what my peers would think of my multidisciplinary approach.

As it turned out, no one thought very much of it. In fact, if anyone bothered to read the introduction, they didn't understand it, or didn't like it. One critic wrote, "One has to wonder what sort of incense burned on Brookstone's own altar when she wrote her prologue." But the worst criticism came from the one person I'd come to depend upon for unconditional support.

So sure was I that Norris would love my "altarism" philosophy that I denied his requests to read the early manuscript and made him wait until the book was actually published. The day a box full of books landed on our doorstep, I came home to find Norris holding up a copy, the veins rising to the surface of his scaly neck.

He said, "What the hell are you talking about? What do you think you are—some kind of New Age theologian? You going to start wandering around Jerusalem with the other lunatics? This is scholarship? This is a dozen years at Megiddo?"

Norris had never raised his voice to me, and only once had I heard him yelling on the phone at his ex-wife when he was in his bedroom with the door, for once, closed.

He continued in a mocking tone, reading from the introduction, "What does this even mean, 'When you encounter an altar in time, you slip into serenity, just one letter to the left of eternity'?"

I tried to explain, bewildered by his anger, "The difference between *serenity* and *eternity* is that the *s* becomes a *t*, and *s* is to the left of *t* in the alphabet."

"What, now we're playing word games? You expect people to figure that out? You expect people to care?"

Norris fumed at me, crumpling the torn cover of my book in his fist. That afternoon, I felt as though my father had died a second time. I knew that his anger had little to do with the book and instead was about what had happened between us a few weeks earlier working in the pit—that unfortunate kiss—something I'd rather bury and forget. That was six months ago, and since then I've been walking on eggshells.

I look up at Norris. When I first met him he was in his late forties, and today, over a dozen years later, he still looks like he is in his late forties. He is tall and ruddily attractive, his arms and legs sinewy and brown, his dark hair salted, skin weathered. He looks like a man who has had many adventures. I had originally perceived him as some kind of golden emissary, rising up from the sacred rubble of the Holy Land, full of wisdom. His first lecture dazzled me. It was not until later that I discovered the streaks in his hair and the bronze of his face were less the distinctions of heroism and more simply signs of sun damage, his face sun-dried and preserved, the corners of his brown eyes bouquets of tawny creases. He was attractive, an eloquent speaker, a fine supervisor, and oppressive to the people he loved best.

"Dinner at eight," I answer. "Saw the note. By the way, I saw chicken in the freezer. Jerrold always orders steak."

"I've known Jerrold a lot longer than you," he says, laughing lightly at me as if I am a child.

My head is down over my sketchbook but I can see Norris's boots still planted nearby. I know he's not leaving just yet, so I put the book aside and stretch out my legs. We need to get beyond this.

I ask him casually, "Will the photographs of the mosaic be ready?"

He squats down, his knees popping. "They should be finished today. Oldest known church in the world! Astounding!"

Norris's pride is well earned. I have been meaning to send digital pictures of the recently uncovered mosaic to Father Chuck Oren, my family's priest, with whom I've remained in touch. He will be electrified to see the circular pattern in the center depicting two fish mirroring one another, an ancient symbol for Jesus that predates the cross by at least a thousand years.

It should excite me too, but for some time now I've been longing for something deeper, something more alive. I became an archaeologist because I thought that in drawing cities and remains out of the dust, I could bring a small part of them back to life. I conjured up the spirits locked in the bones and beads of the people who dwelled in this land millennia ago. I believed I could rub lanterns and set the dream of them free. I have been digging through graves looking for proof that civilizations, people, and stories don't really ever die, but what I've learned, over and over, is that they always do. Maybe I have to step back from it all a little, the way one looks at a mosaic, to be able to see how all the brokenness actually fits together into a greater design.

"You know, people would give their right arm to do what you do," Norris feels the need to point out, "yet you seem disappointed. What did you think you would find"—he guffaws lightly—"a photo album?"

"Maybe," I say, twisting my lips to the side in thought. "Or a diary."

Norris now laughs heartily. Then he sits all the way down. He picks up my sketchbook and looks at my drawings. All at once, he is my professor again, whom I admired so much.

"There is an Ugaritic epic in which the virgin goddess Anat avenges her husband-brother's death by searching for his murderer, Mot, the god of death," he says. He glances from the sketchbook to the burial jar and back. "When she finds Mot, she chops him into little pieces, grinds him up, and spreads him over the fields like fertilizer."

"Huh," I say.

He glances at me, then back to the book, and goes on, encouraged, "It could be argued that death may be the debt we owe to the earth, ensuring the earth's fertility. Think about sacrifices offered to ensure a grain harvest."

"*For dust you are and to dust you shall return,*" I say quietly, partly to Norris and partly to the 3000-year-old infant in the jar.

"Right, but the return is purposeful, no? The life of the child becomes the life of the wheat, fields and fields of it." He thinks for a moment. "Burial is a planting . . ."

A pretty idea, but I don't buy it. Still, I'm interested. And I'm curious, tentatively, about whether Norris is reaching out to me. "So she actually kills the god of death and her husband gets resurrected?"

"Alas," Norris sighs. "As the epic continues, with the death of death, Anat's husband-brother returns to life. But so does Mot.

And the cycle continues"—he gestures toward the burial jar—"to this day."

I'm disappointed but not surprised. "So the god of death's own death is annulled by his death."

Norris reaches out and pats my head as if I'm a puppy. "Aw, poor Page. What is a goddess to do?" He stands up and twists his back hard. I hear his bones pop again. I look up at him and find no tenderness there. He shakes his head slowly and pouts in pretend pity. "Always on the losing end."

WE SPEND THE early evening straightening the house for Jerrold's visit. We all share in the rent, but Norris as the supervisor, having served this dig for almost thirty years, keeps the master suite. The Bograshovs have the second-largest room, with private bathroom as well. My bedroom is the smallest, but it has the nicest morning light, as it faces east. I can reach my hand out my window and pick tomatoes right from our garden and often do—ripe yellow, green, and red tomatoes. The bathroom down the hall is understood as mine, and for guests. It is a modest limestone house, windows arched in the classic Middle Eastern style. Orna is in her midtwenties, and the rest of us probably seem, in varying degrees, beyond the age bracket for house sharing, although it is not unusual in this region. Financially it has made sense. Norris still pays hefty spousal support to his wife in California. The Bograshovs are saving, dreaming of starting a family someday. And I have maintained my apartment in New York City, which I try to visit at least twice a year, when I return to lecture and to visit my mother and my closest friend, Jordanna. It sometimes seems foolish to keep it, that empty cube filled with furniture quietly waiting all year to be used: the empty bed and desk in the one tiny bedroom, small empty loveseat, breakfast table with the leaves folded down, cold two-burner stove in the wall kitchen. But I've always felt that to give it up would be to become untethered in the world, utterly rootless. I love when I return there and collapse into a chair, looking at the beveled ceiling and listening to footsteps cross the floor above me. Sometimes I wonder, however, if the opposite is true, if maintaining it all these years has prevented me from taking more risks and finding a real place to call home, rather than a rent-controlled barrenness.

Jerrold arrives in a herringbone suit and a thin black cashmere turtleneck underneath. His silver hair is shaped and gleaming over his head like poured metal, mustache slicked into place. His presence is of prosperity, his skin tight over his face and appropriately bronzed, teeth surprisingly white. He is worldly, sophisticated. Older than Norris, he walks into our home with shiny shoes and a silver-tipped cane, carrying two bottles of Côtes du Rhône. I have showered, pulled my hair back into a clip, and put on a simple black dress. We all look nice but clearly underfunded.

Orna brings out chicken and stewed zucchini, apricots, olives, and pine nuts over a mound of couscous.

"Tell me, Mikhail," Jerrold drawls while Norris dishes out the meal, "what is your specialty? I've heard rumor you are a garbage man!"

"Indeed," Mickey says in his heavy Russian accent, which somehow always makes it seem as if he is reciting something. "Everyone should spend at least a year collecting and sorting garbage. Yesterday's dinners, news clippings, and junk can tell you more about human behavior and consumption than anything else. From an archaeologist's perspective, garbage is the great chronicle of life."

"Well said! Good man," Jerrold says enthusiastically. "Let's open that wine and toast. A toast to garbage!"

Norris wrestles with the wine bottle between his knees. He says, lest Jerrold should really think Mickey is a garbage man, "When Mickey emigrated from Russia, he had multiple degrees." He huffs a little and manages to pull out the cork. "Physical anthropology, paleontology, linguistics, and chem. He spoke six languages, but not Hebrew, at the time. The only work he could find in his early years was as a garbage collector."

"I met him when I was a docent at the Diaspora museum," says Orna. She has Moroccan features and sapphire eyes. "He was an Aladdin's lamp in a heap of trash."

Mickey puts his arm around Orna and says, "I only needed one rub."

Orna blushes deeply and Jerrold laughs mightily, lifting his glass to Orna, adding, "And then all your wishes came true!" He continues, "A toast . . . but wait, Norris my boy, you have no wine. You must! It is a nineteen forty-two bottle!"

"Yes." Norris clears his throat a bit nervously. "None for me, thanks." He looks to me for the briefest moment, and Jerrold notices.

"Ah!" Jerrold exclaims. "There are stories in this house! I see, yes, I've always wondered, an old dog like yourself sharing a roof with one of your former students." He slaps the table. "You bastard! Of course you had to hire the prettiest one!"

I laugh. "Thanks, Mr. March."

Jerrold hands his glass to Norris and then pours himself another and says exuberantly, "To garbage! Because it is messy!"

Glasses clink and Norris says soberly, "Yes, well, Mickey speaks of garbage with exaggerated romanticism."

"But he's right!" says Jerrold. "Ah yes, trash, other people's trash, it is romantic! Lost sandals and scandals and partially burned candles . . . it's poetry, you see?"

After speaking about the mosaic, which is far more interesting than my shaft tombs, and after a few more glasses of wine, Jerrold rests his face in one of his big hands, leaning his elbow on the table and looking across at me. "And Page, yes, the thing about Page is that I've never met a human being who knows the Bible better than this one. How is it possible that a girl like you knows the Bible so well? What a shame if it is because they sent you to waste your youth in a nunnery."

Norris answers, a little clipped, "Ms. Brookstone studied Christian theology at Harvard Divinity."

"Yes." Jerrold nods. "I remember now." He looks deeply into my face, and I can see he's a little drunk. "All those blood-soaked texts, the Levitical sacrifices, the blood on the altars, the blood on the doorways, *whoever sheds the blood of man by man shall his blood be shed . . .*" With his fingers Jerrold picks up a chicken leg out of the bowl in the center of the table. He points it at me and says, "You sucked the marrow out of the Bible until there was nothing but bone."

"Something like that," I say. I can feel the wine warming me as well, can see it creeping over everyone. Only Norris remains rigid.

Mickey says, "Every night, she filled her bathtub with Bible stories the way Countess Bathory of Transylvania would fill her tub with the blood of virgins, to achieve eternal beauty, to live forever."

Orna slaps her husband playfully against the arm.

"It looks to me like it's working," Jerrold says, eyes absorbing my face.

"But I left Harvard," I say, "after I heard a lecture by Dr. Norris Anderson. I remember it so clearly. He said, 'Archaeology is the place where the precision of science and the intuitive certainty of faith intersect.' I was so impressed. I gave up my pursuit of a doctorate in divinity for a master's in archaeology."

Jerrold's eyes sparkle and dance. "You abandoned armchair philosophy to pursue the philosopher's stone. A noble one you are!"

Norris laughs. "Actually, the thing Ms. Brookstone wants desperately to find more than anything else at Megiddo is a diary."

"Adorable!" bursts Jerrold. "A diary! Now that would be something!" He extends his head over the table toward me, closes his eyes for a moment, and breathes, as if inhaling perfume. "Now, I'll bet you kept a diary when you were a girl."

"No," I say, "but there was this time when our family's pastor, Father Chuck, got so angry at me."

"Yes, tell me," Jerrold croons. "I'd love to know where this leads."

"He had told us the Noah story, that a man could build a boat to fit all those animals, and I just couldn't believe it, so I said so."

Orna says, "Always challenging things, even as a child!"

"Father Chuck turned to me and smiled like a prizefighter stepping into a ring. He took his chair and brought it to the other side of my desk and sat down. He put his elbows on my desk, right on top of my illustrated children's Bible. He was very young for a priest, and he stared straight into me, as if there weren't fifteen other students in the room."

"Indeed, I'm sure." Jerrold nods vigorously.

"He said, 'Thousands of years from now, long after you and everyone you know are dead, someone will find the ruins of your house. They will pick through the rubble and sift through the sand. And you know what they will find?'"

"Trash!" Jerrold erupts. "Mountains and mountains of trash!"

"That's right," Mickey affirms, raising his glass.

I shook my head. "'Two books,' he said. 'And in one there will be all our records—school records, medical records, dental records, criminal records, growth charts, degrees, honorable mentions . . . and in the other book, they will find a diary. A diary of all the dreams of all the people.' Father Chuck said, 'Imagine that every night everyone rose at midnight and recorded their dreams, and all those dreams were compiled into a book of fantasies, longings. The other book would be the cold facts, but this book would be the deep truth.'"

"The Bible is the diary of dreams," Orna says, mesmerized.

"I'm in love." Jerrold heaves a sigh. "Ask me for anything, Page. Even half the kingdom and I'll give it to you."

Norris is glowering. I feel suddenly a little sad for him. When he hired me to come to Megiddo, Norris had just finalized a bitter divorce. He had a daughter just a couple of years younger than I who lived with his ex-wife and refused to speak with him, even though it was his wife who had left him for another man. I had sensed that he thought of me like a daughter, someone he could mentor who'd appreciate him. I thought we comforted one another. I knew very little about his ex-wife or the divorce. Whenever the subject delicately surfaced, he would bat it away saying, "My ex-wife is a lunatic," or "She left me for crazy."

I say, "That first time I heard Norris speak, he reminded me of Father Chuck. They are both so fluent and persuasive."

At this, Norris laughs sharply, pushes his chair away from the table with a screech, and begins loudly clearing plates. "Yeah, me," he says while making a racket with the dishes, "a fuckin' priest. That's how she thinks of me."

After Jerrold leaves, Orna and Mickey insist on cleaning up. I fill up a canteen to put in the freezer for work tomorrow and Norris brushes past me and scowls. "Enjoy yourself tonight?" He walks out of the kitchen and Orna looks at me and lifts her hands as if to say, *I don't know what his problem is.*

I pass his suite on my way to my room, and the door, slightly open, makes me uncomfortable. We cannot go on living in the same house this way.

II

It is an appalling and horrible thing to be an ancient scroll, filled
with stories and secrets, prophecies and truths, a tapestry of words
sewn together with golden thread, hidden in an earthen jar sealed
tightly, and buried deep in a cave, in a sheath of rock, where no one
can find you, or touch you, or know you.
— THE SCROLL OF ANATIYA 5:60–61

I was delighted after that first lecture when Professor Anderson
put his hand on my shoulder and asked, "Are you by any chance
the daughter of Sean Brookstone?"

We had coffee at a little café in the university bookstore. Earlier
in the day, when he read over the class roster, my name had caught
Norris's eye because he had had an old college buddy with the same
last name.

It was always intriguing to me to learn about my father's past.
He and Norris had lost touch over the years. Norris had only learned
of my father's death from a listing in the college alumni update. Norris was nothing like my father, not nearly as charismatic, but the fact
that they had known each other, even peripherally, made him immediately dear to me.

On the twentieth anniversary of my father's death, I found myself crying in the living room. Norris came and lowered himself onto

the ottoman in front of me, holding my hands in his. I felt comforted that he was there. We had already been working together on this dig for six years. My heart opened as we sat, leaning into each other, and I wept freely.

Norris pressed my head against his chest. He said, "I will help you love again," and I remembered how good it felt to have someone watch over and comfort me as my father had when I was a girl. I thought we had a quiet understanding.

But all of that changed six months ago. We had been amicably working and living together, and I thought that we'd go on like that forever. One night though, when Norris had a bit too much to drink, our steady relationship faltered. We were in the pit with our little sifting screens and brushes. The moon was already visible and everyone else had quit for the day. I could feel the sweat lifting off me as twilight drew over the sands like a cool satin sheet.

"Everything is in fragments," Norris said as he sifted a few chips of pottery, a dusting of sand falling over his shoes. He glanced up at me and I smiled. "When we meet people, when we talk, it's all incomplete. Even you and I, we've worked together so long, and yet everything is still in fragments."

"What do you mean?" I asked. The air shifted cooler and I began to feel a little anxious.

"We present ourselves to each other as if this is who we are. I talk with you as if this is the whole Norris Anderson. And you like to believe it is so. You don't know me, and I certainly don't know you."

I felt like he was critiquing me, but when I looked up from my sifting I saw that Norris was smiling. His gaze was loving, and he seemed eager for my response. "I don't think it's a bad thing, to present oneself in fragments," I said, lowering my head again to my sifter. I began talking nervously, trying to fill the space and distract Norris from noticing how pretty the moonlight was becoming. "The only thing that's really mine is me. That's the only thing that was ever really given me. Everything else I own is impartial. The money I earn wasn't minted for me; the land I buy wasn't lifted out of the sea and quaked from the continents just for me. Even a gift I've been given isn't really for me. The contents of a box wrapped with dancing Santas—it was manufactured for a seven-year-old kid, but not specifically me. The only thing that's really yours is you, so you have every right to keep it for yourself."

I looked up. Norris's smile had widened, and it took me back a little. "What did you get for Christmas in that little box when you were seven?"

I shrugged and looked back down. "A pair of ballet shoes." Norris hadn't taken a step toward me, but all of a sudden the space between us seemed to narrow.

"Did you take ballet?" he asked. I could almost feel his words on my cheek.

"For a little while," I whispered to his dust-covered shoes.

"You see," Norris said. "There are so many fragments of you to be found."

"I don't know," I said, taking a step back. "There are some cultures where the more you hide, the more intriguing you become. When you are exposed you become just like everybody else. Like those Bedouin women who passed through the other day, all swathed in gauze. They were so intriguing to me. But underneath the gauze, I am sure they are just . . ."

"Just what?" Norris's hand tipped my chin up.

"Just like everybody else," I barely said.

"Just like everybody else how?"

"What do you mean, how?" I slid back a little, but Norris didn't seem to notice. He put his hand on my shoulder.

"When you said underneath the gauze, you meant that they were just like everybody else." With his other hand, Norris began gently tracing a line down my neck. "A warm hollow just above their narrow collarbones, rough elbows, smooth bellies, just like everybody else. The whole point of the wraps is that the women beneath them become less intriguing. And yet you were imagining them naked."

"I was not," I said, waving his hands off me as kindly as I could. "You were thinking of me thinking of them naked."

"No, you were thinking of them that way. I just pieced together an interesting fragment of you," he said, letting his eyes run down and up my body.

"I'm not sure I like being thought of as an artifact, Norris," I said, startled. "It makes me feel like something those teenagers would put in a museum." I immediately regretted mentioning the teenagers who volunteered on our dig. Did I have to share my insecurities with Norris at that very moment? I turned to walk away, but Norris tightened his hand on my shoulder.

"Who? Those kids? They're easy to piece together. But you're much harder. You have little tiny pieces scattered over many years that need to be collected carefully, touched together bit by bit. You have little lost claws and long femurs. Why, they are just arrowheads and clubs, while you're a *Tyrannosaurus rex!*"

Before I could respond, Norris drew me into his chest, and his mouth closed over mine. It wasn't that it was a bad kiss: in fact, Norris had a somewhat sensual touch. But I couldn't get his image of me as a *T. rex* out of my head. It made me feel like Norris intended to pick me apart like a specimen, and Norris's tongue felt suddenly like a spade. I pulled away. His face looked pale.

"We're delirious," I said gently, while his face went from white to red to white again. "You know we're not compatible in this way."

He recovered himself and laughed it off, saying, "I know. I was just testing you."

The days that followed were awkward, but neither of us broached the subject. I figured that we had worked together for eleven and a half years and would work together many more—that time would devour this memory along with everything else. Eventually we recovered from the incident, or at least, we never spoke of it again. One time at dinner, Norris passed up a beer, saying, "We all know what that does to me," and I accepted that as an apology, or at least a dismissal of the whole thing. It wasn't until recently that I realized that he'd never really forgive me for turning away from him.

I PICK UP my pace and walk until I reach the northernmost edge of Mount Megiddo just before dawn. Ribbons of pink and orange sky tie up the world as a gift. From the center point of the dig, the landscape is like an unswept floor littered with labyrinths of rocks, a clump of date palms like upside-down brooms leaning against the sky. But here at the edge of the mount, I can look down to an olive grove of twisted silver trunks and long, slender leaves, beyond which the valley unrolls in a patchwork of greens, headlights gliding between the yellow-green of wheat fields and rows of citrus.

I stand at the end of the tell, looking toward the uncovered remains of Via Maris, the most important highway of the ancient world, connecting Egypt and Mesopotamia, the road that Megiddo guards. The air is pungent with eucalyptus and lavender rising from the valley.

I sit on a slab of limestone and roll my knuckles over my thighs, flexing my feet. I roll my head slowly from one shoulder to the other and breathe a deep draft of the freshly perfumed air. I look down at the valley, the dew beginning to burn off in mist, and I think about my father. The disease had seeped through his body swiftly, and over the course of one year, what had started as a tingling numbness in his feet and lower calves had crept up over his loins. The disease was on an unstoppable journey toward his heart and his lungs, his arms and shoulders, and eventually his neck and his chin and his tongue, leaving his fully functional, imaginative, wonderful mind as the perfect witness to his own slow death.

When the disease reached my father's groin, he told my mother that he was half dead.

"I am buried up to my waist," he lamented. "That is what it feels like. I am half dead. And everyone I know knows it, so they are all half grieving. They come and visit me and they know that half of me is stuck in the grave, and so they wear dark colors out of respect for that half, and they bend down and put flowers on the grave and weep. But then they notice the rest of me sticking up from the ground, and they say, 'How've you been? Nice day, huh? Too bad you're stuck here or we'd take you with us to the bar. All your friends are getting together there to drown their sadness and forget all about you.'"

"You are not half anything," my mother responded. "You are *everything* to us."

"Go ahead, Page, kick my leg, kick it! It is dead. I can't feel a thing."

Instead I punched him in his chest over his heart, where I knew he could feel it. I punched him again and again.

"Page!" my mother shouted, pulling me away.

My father winced and rubbed his chest. I was only fourteen but I knew I threw good punches.

While my mother held me, I said to him, "That's what your illness feels like to me."

My mother yelled at my father, "You carry on as if the whole world is your amphitheater and you're auditioning for Sophocles. But save it for your fans, okay? Your family can't take it every day. We just can't take it."

I rub my thighs while I sit on the stone slab, making sure they are not numb. Sometimes I also feel half dead. I am going nowhere but down, sinking. And what is there, who is there, to pull me out? Or punch me in the chest just to remind me I can still feel something there?

At his funeral, everyone who eulogized him kept emphasizing that the disease couldn't get him in the end. That he was so smart he even outwitted his fatal illness. And I suppose it was true. It wasn't the disease that killed him. He committed suicide. And ironically, he killed himself by asphyxiation, which is probably how he would have died anyway a few months later when his lungs and throat began to collapse. But I was never allowed to be angry that he committed suicide. Rather, I was expected to be amazed at what a survivor he was, that he was a survivor until the end and took his life with his own hand before letting the disease do him in. He was so brave. He was so independent. He loved us so much he wanted to spare me and my mother. He was so sharp-tongued he couldn't bear to lose his speech. That was what everyone said. But I wanted to be angry at him for committing suicide. Maybe it was true, that his pain was so great and he knew his death was imminent anyway, but I didn't buy it. I had still believed in my father's invincibility, and so for me his taking his own life wasn't courage at all. It was a cop-out. I don't think I ever really mourned him correctly, caught between my anger at his weakness and everyone else's celebration of his strength.

I think I see two figures moving through the olive trees, their limbs swallowed up by spears of sun beginning to pierce through the gray air. The ancient olive trees may be playing tricks on me, but as the two figures emerge from the grove and begin to climb the edge of the hill, I can see they are a man and a woman.

"Hello?" I call to them, but they don't answer, too busy helping each other find footholds along the steep path.

They reach the top just as the sun erupts. The woman is petite with a black bob of hair. Her eyes are long, like the ones depicted in sculptures of Sita, where the corners seem to disappear around the side of her face. Her cheeks are flushed from the climb, her lips the color of a bruise. The man seems more fatigued than the woman. He is slight of frame, though his build seems strong. His shoulders are slumped, but his eyes are bright, clear, and penetrating. He has a beautiful crop of chocolate locks, curled toward the sky as if caught in an updraft. The deep lines around his mouth and the fine lines around his eyes remind me of the languid writing one sees carved into the stone entrance of mosques.

"*Salaam*," I say, guessing they are Arab by the gauzy black tunic with colorful embroidery she wears over her jeans.

Once the man catches his breath, he answers in English, "We are looking to talk with an archaeologist. I am Ibrahim Barakat and this is my wife, Naima."

"You could have taken the road instead of hiking up the side of the tell," I say after introducing myself.

"Our car broke down," Ibrahim says, and points to just beyond the olive grove, a flash of metal and windshield.

I invite them to have tea with me in the tent where we usually take our water breaks and lunches and write our field notes in the heat of the day.

"That is nice of you," says Naima. She is, in many ways, the opposite of myself. Where she is dark, I am light. Where she is short, I am tall. I find her, and her husband for that matter, beautiful, and organic to this place, as if born of the groves out of which they emerged. Standing beside them, I feel awkward in my skin, giraffelike and out of place.

Her husband straightens himself suddenly, as if taking a stance. He says, "We will have tea with you after you answer one question."

Naima puts her hand on her husband's shoulder, steadying him. His tone has a note of desperation in it, and his eyes flash frustration. "We have time, Ibrahim. Let's have tea," she says softly.

He brushes her hand off his shoulder and his question, when he asks it, sounds more like a command, "Will you excavate under our house?"

I smile at them and ask why.

"Because there is something buried there," Ibrahim answers sharply. He already knows I will not come, and he does not want to waste time talking about it. He is ready to go back down the hill before I say another word. His hands are on his hips as he turns his angry gaze from me to the extensive dig behind me.

"This is Israel. There is something buried everywhere," I say in a soft voice.

Ibrahim immediately grabs his wife's hand, turns around, and marches to the edge of the mount. Skidding on the pebbles and loose rocks he starts down, helping his wife, who looks back at me apologetically. I watch them descend into the olive grove while the clang of shovels behind me announces that the diggers have arrived.

I hurry back across the dig to the tent where I stashed my knapsack. Norris is drinking tea and stretching, ready for the day. "Who were you talking to?" he asks.

"A strange couple. Hey, I need to borrow your car. Their car broke down and I want to drive down to help them. You got jumpers?"

"What were they doing up here?"

"I don't know," I say. "They said something about excavating under their house."

Norris's eyebrows lift. "I heard about these guys. They go to digs looking for someone to come home with them. I've heard they are insane." Norris sits down and begins breaking sprigs of mint into his tea. "Ramon told me they came to his dig yesterday talking about spirits haunting their house. Saying they see these spirits in dark corners at night leaning against each other like coeds sneaking kisses in a locker room. They see ghosts in the mirrors, hear them creaking along the floor. They see the dust from their footsteps come up with each step, even saw them in their bed. Supposedly the sheets were blowing around but the window was closed. Good stuff. Ramon got a real kick out of them."

"Can I have your keys?" I say. I watch him stirring the mint into the tea. "Please."

He reaches into his pocket and takes out his keys, handing them to me. When I reach for them, he pulls them away and says, "Tell them archaeology isn't a joke."

"I just want to help them," I say, and snatch the keys, hurrying out of the tent.

I climb into Norris's car, annoyed at first at how many papers he has stuffed over the dashboard. As I drive toward their car, I laugh to myself as I think about Ibrahim and Naima. I want to hear their ghost stories firsthand.

Ibrahim has his head under his hood as I pull up. Naima is leaning against the silver sedan.

I roll down my window and say to them, "Want a jump start?"

I pull Norris's car up to theirs, fender to fender, and pop the hood.

Ibrahim ignores me. I have the feeling that he is more embarrassed than angry.

I try to sound light and friendly when I ask, "You have ghosts in your house?"

Ibrahim bangs a wrench against the engine and curses in Arabic. Naima shrugs apologetically and says, "Yes. We are not the only ones who have seen them in our house."

"How many digs have you gone to looking for an archaeologist?"

Ibrahim slams down the hood of his car and barks, "We come to you people who are supposed to be interested in the past. You come with your Bibles and shovels. We happen to be very educated people. You think we like to sound like fools to you?"

"I never said you were fools." I try to soothe him.

Naima interrupts with her calm tone and kind smile. "There are two spirits that live in our house. Everyone who comes to our house is overcome with a feeling of love and desire. It has gotten to the point that we have to do something about it. We have stones thrown at our house by people in town. Our windows are broken nearly every week. Fathers think the house will take their daughters' virginity. Couples who have been entirely faithful come to our house and—"

Ibrahim bursts in with his rant. "You all think of yourselves as academics. We went to university. We are academics too!"

Naima continues, trying to deflect Ibrahim's frustration into a conversation. "Our parents blame all of this on university. Our house is in Anatot. We built it ourselves."

"But you are not academics at all," Ibrahim pushes on. "What we are trying to tell you, Miss America, is that we have had an *experience*. We have seen and felt and studied something very, very real. This is not a story. This is an experience that Naima and I and many others have had in our house, and we have mustered the courage to talk about it only to be met with mockery and insults."

"I am not mocking you," I remind him. "I am listening."

And I *am* listening, although I don't believe in ghosts as I once did. After a dozen years I have found every skull as empty as the next, the skulls of the Holy Land no more potent than the skulls of Mesoamerica.

Ibrahim fastens the jumper cables between our cars.

"What do they look like?" I ask Naima.

Ibrahim stomps around the side of his car to get in. He barks, "The last person we spoke to? You know what he said? He said, 'Academics don't go on psychic digs. We don't fiddle about and poke holes in people's backyards because they have a notion and no funding. Buy a shovel.'"

"Sounds like Ramon," I say.

Ibrahim drops into his seat and begins revving his engine.

I have to step toward Naima to hear her soft voice over the engine's grinding. "I saw the female one sitting on the kitchen counter when I was making soup. The steam from the pot was filling the kitchen, and it seemed to break apart around her, but there was nothing there. Only the outline of a woman. And the male ghost came moving through the steam. I saw the steam parting around him. I could see the outline of his fingers, his knuckles even, and he ran them up her thighs and around her back. Then he picked her up and their faces came together and they were gone. That was my clearest sighting."

The car kicks into gear and Ibrahim jumps out, pulls the cables off his battery, and bangs shut the hood. He leaves them dangling out of Norris's car and motions Naima to get in. As she gets into the car she says to me, "We live in Anatot. Come and we'll have that tea, and you will tell us what to do. Our house is not haunted, Miss Page. It is blessed."

I watch the Barakats speed away, throw the cables into the passenger seat, and return to the dig. I lift my tools onto my back and walk to the shaft tombs. The dig is now filled with people. I walk past all those nice Jewish girls with their long tan legs and little teenage hips, white bra straps and fizzy ponytails that look like root-beer cotton candy. And their male counterparts, rosy boys with fops of sun-streaked hair, baseball hats, and cut-off jeans, nodding to their favorite music downloads as they chip away indelicately with spades. They come from North America, South Africa, Europe, and Australia, as part of an "Israel Experience" tour. The dig is just part of their "experience," along with floating in the Dead Sea, climbing Masada, and rafting down the Jordan River.

My encounter with the Barakats will soon fade into history, along with all the mighty civilizations that lie in heaps beneath me. There are no ghosts, I think to myself.

I used to believe in them. In fact, most of my classmates in grad school secretly wanted to believe. We had studied psychic archaeology, or "questing," which is the use of psychic skills to locate dig sites and identify artifacts. It is scorned by experts in the field, mocked the way that astronomers mock astrology. The idea of being able to receive clairvoyant impressions from objects, to practice "retrocognition," seeing into the past, is absurd to a scientist.

I return to the three thousand seventy-second infant burial jar and unroll the green tarp I had laid over it at day's end. There are very strict rules concerning burial in Jewish law. Disturbing the dead is taboo. I blow into the jar and stir up a dusty gust that exhales back at me. The ancient Israelites didn't bury their infants in jars. This was a Canaanite tradition, so this skeleton is permitted for study. As I kneel here, I wonder how the mother of this one would feel about our cataloguing her child. "I'm sure your baby was very beautiful," I mouth to the buzzing heat.

I touch a brush gingerly inside the jar and dust the little bones. I think about my favorite biblical story, which is told all in one verse in the Second Book of Kings. Not long after my father died, I copied down the verse along with a drawing for Father Chuck. The verse tells how a family in the midst of burying a man suddenly spy bandits heading their way. They throw the corpse into the nearest tomb, which happens to be the tomb of the prophet Elisha, and they all rush off to safety. What they don't stick around long enough to realize is that when the body comes into contact with the magical bones of Elisha, it is immediately revived. In my illustration, I drew a man with a big happy face, black spiky hair, and a tie exactly like the one my mother had picked out for me to give to my father only a year earlier—green, with brown zigzags. The man was rocketing out of a grave. Hearts and glittery stars swirling around in his wake showed how joyful he was to be alive again. His mouth was half open as if he was about to sing a song of praise. But just behind him, there were three or four dimly crayoned men lifting bloody swords and hatchets, ready to butcher the reborn man as soon as he touched ground. Father Chuck kept it in a file he labeled "Page Brookstone's New New Testament."

I lay down the brush and reach into the jar with trembling fingers to lightly touch a jutting ossicle smaller than a popsicle stick, shamefully hoping that I might, in this very moment of contact, achieve perpetuity.

III

~~~~~~~~~~~~~~~~~~~~~~~

*I have wrestled the demons of the cliff. I have slept with a rock for
my pillow. I have shaded my skin from the swarthing sun, healed
my passion-wracked frame. But the instant I see you appear, out
of clouds of dust, I feel the sickness overtake me again, grab hold
of my heart, and steal my breath. I am sick for you! Sick in love!
I never again want to be numbly healthy. Rather, let me be filled
with hurt and longing. Let me burn.*

—THE SCROLL OF ANATIYA 7:10–14

What brought them to our little dig?" Mickey asks, holding a beer on his leg. His pants are patterned with wet
circles from where he rested his beer between swigs.
We are sitting in the living room with a plate of pita and hummus
on the coffee table. The slow ceiling fan helps little on this hot June
evening. Orna brings in two bowls, one of pistachios and the other
of cherries.

"Where's Norris?" I ask. I sweep my bandana off my head and let
my hair fall loose. A taste of my beer sends a low-watt volt through
me and I shiver and feel my shoulders relax.

Orna sits down and nestles into her husband. "Out with one of
his lady friends," she says.

I lean back in my chair and take another swig, allowing myself to loosen.

"They really wanted help," I say. I remember the slight tremor in Ibrahim's hand as he reached for his wife to get in the car. "They insisted that there are spirits in their house. They seemed so nice. I feel bad for them."

"A haunted house!" Orna says. She nestles into Mickey, and adds, "*Aizeh ta'anug*," how delightful.

"Naima and Ibrahim Barakat," I say, holding the beer against my cheek and rolling it back and forth. "They see these ghosts, basically, making love in their house. It would be one thing if one of them had an overactive imagination, but they both believe it. And they say they have university degrees. They seem like smart people, it's just that they see ghosts fondling all over their house."

"The ghosts went to university?" Orna asks teasingly. "What did they study?"

Mickey announces, "I have figured this out. You say they are Arab, and they went to university, so clearly they are caught and confused between the worlds of tradition and modernity. They have repressed upbringings and have been educated with a progressive mentality and now they are delusional with guilt. I'm telling you, that's what those ghosts are, manifestations of shame."

Orna says, "I think they're lucky! They have an overly active fantasy life. Were they attractive?"

"Very," I say. "He had these eyebrows that came together like a seagull against the sun, and these indignant eyes that were green as an After Eight Mint wrapper."

"Wow," Mickey says, "maybe you got zapped by one of their cupids."

"And she had very fine features," I continue, and while Mickey takes a swig I add, "delicate as a custard."

Mickey spits his beer forward in a gush and Orna leaps up, exclaiming, "God, Mickey, what the hell," while Mickey snorts with laughter, "Custard!"

Orna wipes herself off, shaking her head, and then she says, "*Rega*, wait. Ibrahim Barakat. That name sounds familiar."

I get up to bring my laptop while Mickey is talking, oblivious to who's listening: "Psychometry is the ability to receive memories connected with an artifact or a place. When a person walks into a house and knows something horrible happened there in the past, for example. There are people who say they can conjure the image of a person who had once lived in a certain room or held a certain object. They get the psychic impressions left there, even recall the thoughts of the person who had been there."

"That's bull," Orna says.

"I don't know, maybe," Mickey says. "Did you ever read about Frederick Bond? He was hired by the Church of England to excavate the ruins of Glastonbury Abbey? Bond employed the help of John Allen Bartlett, who practiced 'automatic writing.' Bartlett rested his pen on paper and cleared his mind, letting the deceased write through him. They invoked the spirits of the abbey, who transmitted drawings to them in Latin and English. They found everything exactly where the drawing directed them."

I sat back down, firing up my computer. "But Bond was an expert in medieval churches," I say. "He had already studied the maps, plans, and drawings of the abbey before consulting Bartlett. It's not as if he was a shoemaker. And when the church realized his methods, he was excommunicated . . . Hey! Here he is, Ibrahim Barakat! Sheesh, he's a human rights lawyer."

"Yes, that's right!" Orna says. "He was in the news years ago."

"Here it is," I say. "He represented Palestinian academics who were sentenced to life in prison for protesting the PLO. Here's a picture of him. How crazy could he be?"

Mickey continues his own line of thought. "The truth is, many people do actually use automatic writing and create great works of literature, music, and art. They claim that the spirits of great artists and composers were completing their works through them."

"Yeah," Orna says, "but just because they say it doesn't mean they are actually channeling spirits. They could just be meditating and tapping into their creative recesses. The same could be said of the power of tarot, that it allows us into the stuff we've buried in ourselves."

Mickey studies Orna for a moment and says, "That's where I know you from; you were that gypsy who lived on my corner, telling everyone's fortune for a ruble."

Orna twists the skin on his arm and he winces with pleasure and pain. "What," he protests, "she was exotic!"

"It says he was the lawyer in the Basil case in ninety-eight," I say, scrolling through pages. "Something about punitive house demolitions."

"That's where I heard his name," Orna says. "That was a big case."

"Psychic archaeology has been used to find sites all over the world," Mickey rambles, between crunching pistachios.

"But they've done tests, putting artifacts in boxes and having people guess what's inside. It's no different from guesswork," Orna argues. "And instead of widening the field, those methods just burden the rest of us."

I consider Orna's words and then muse, "But it was interesting. Out of the olive grove and the morning mist, these two people rose up to me. With no introduction, no real effort to persuade me, they demanded someone excavate under their house because they saw ghosts. With all this on the internet about him, he's got to be highly educated." I think for a second. "And honestly, every time a shovel strikes the ground, isn't there a bit of this-feels-like-a-good-spot, and isn't that feeling a psychic impression?"

"Or hopefulness," Orna says.

"What's the difference really between hope, intuition, and faith?" I ask.

"Hope is always positive," Mickey answers, rattling pistachios in his hand. "Intuition is objective. Faith is a combination of the two."

Orna suddenly looks at me as if she has made a discovery. She says, "You're looking for a way out of Meggido," and then blushes, embarrassed for speaking what she was thinking. Mickey looks at her, as if measuring her words, then looks at me.

"No," I say, staring at my laptop rather than looking at them. "No, definitely not. Meggido's great. Look, I found Naima Barakat, she has a degree from Oxford!"

"You are," Orna says more quietly, but this time with more conviction.

"Well, I'm not leaving to go poke holes in someone's floorboards because they have a hunch." I laugh and swipe some hummus with a triangle of pita. "Really!"

Mickey is still contemplating me. He says, "I think Mrs. Custard and Mr. Minty Eyes cast a spell on you."

Norris comes home. There are five bottles on the table, one on the floor by my chair. He unbuttons his shirt and sits in his leather chair, kicking up the feet. "Spoke to Ramon today. Man, you should hear the stories going around about that couple. You know they've visited at least sixteen digs?"

That fact makes me momentarily queasy. "If they are so certain, why don't they just do it themselves?" Mickey asks. "I'm sure it happens in people's backyards all over this country."

"That's what Ramon told them! He minced no words. He told them they had no right to come to our workplace and start talking of pornographic ghosts, expecting people to have some level of respect for them when they are through. What do they think? That one of us will drop everything, abandon a historically significant, well-sponsored, extensive dig and assemble a team to clean someone's basement? It's preposterous. *Museums* are fighting over our collections. They want us to come on a notion, with no funding." He laughs and points to me. "I guarantee you were too nice."

I think about Mickey's question, why don't they just do it themselves, and I suddenly wonder if it's not because they are unreasonable but because they believe in the collegiality of professionals; maybe they're asking for help out of respect for the field. "Maybe they just want a professional to come to their home, and if a professional says there is nothing there, then they will drop it. Maybe it's out of deference for archaeology that they come to us."

Norris throws his hands up into the air and at the same time pushes back on the seat to recline further. "Like I said, too nice! And a little dense," he taps his head with his finger. "It's just that kind of thinking that gets people more interested in mummies' curses than true history."

The sweetness I had felt sitting with Mickey and Orna moments ago begins to sour. "Wasn't it you who said, 'Miraculous happenings can't always be discovered by secular means'? Wasn't it you who taught me that science and faith were like a body and soul, and that biblical archaeology was a field essentially about wholeness?"

"You know, Page, you are an idiot sometimes. That was one lecture. One lecture fifteen years ago. Biblical archaeology is a lot of things to a lot of people, but one thing it is not is a damn séance. Jesus Christ, if I have to hear about that one lecture again, I'll go apoplectic."

"Take it easy, Norris," Mickey says. "We're all just drinking some beers and talking here. No reason to get riled up."

I get up and leave, aware of Orna studying me as I head out the door to my room at the end of the hall.

IV

Dear Lord, in Your wisdom You understand this girl, whose life is but a forgotten dream, whose heart is a shattered urn. Gather these pieces, merciful Lord! Fit them into a mosaic on the Temple floor, and let the high priests tread on my desire. I am but dust, my Lord. Sweep me up! Sweep me in Your kindness into Divine Evermore!

—THE SCROLL OF ANATIYA 9:17–19

It is Saturday morning, and the Bograshous and Norris will all be sleeping in. The sun hasn't yet risen when I step outside the house, pulling my bandana over my hair. I stand for a moment, listening to a bird hidden somewhere in the evergreens above me. I take a deep breath. I throw my rolling bag into my back seat and turn the ignition. The sound seems to fill the world before settling into a purr.

I roll down my window and tilt my head out as I drive. The wind ruffles my bandana and I smile. The sky is mottled purple and gray, and I can see headlights of a few other early morning drivers across the gently undulating fields. Rows and rows of sunflowers on either side of the road stand all facing the same direction, with their heads drooped down, like exiles marching away from home. Soon the sun will rise, and they will all lift their heads, golden manes gleaming, jubilant as exiles returning.

I drive to a beach in Haifa, park my car, and amble to the edge of the sea. I sit on the cool sand with my knees tucked up under my chin, looking out over the blushing water. The beach is empty. There is a helicopter half a mile off shore whose noise is drowned by the crashing of waves. It is shining a searchlight over the ocean. I wonder what they are looking for, and then I become frightened at the idea of being lost at sea. I imagine paddling, exhausted, over the waves, and seeing that searchlight scanning the surface of the deep, closer and then farther away, illuminating a coin of rough water in search of me. The mechanical angel tilts to the side in an exasperated shrug and peels off in a backward hairpin turn. I involuntarily think, *Who will find me now?*

I spend most of the day here. The beach fills with people, and the ocean air feels good to me. The hem of the Mediterranean Sea is delicious on my skin. By late afternoon, I still feel that I don't want to return to Megiddo. Do I imagine that the three thousand seventy-*third* infant burial jar I uncover will be the one filled with answers? The certainty that it won't weighs me with sadness. It seems I could tunnel straight through the earth, expertly drilling and nimbly sifting through the seven sedimentary layers of Dante's circles, coming out the other side an old woman, reporters gathering around me and asking, "You are the first person to tunnel all the way through the planet. What did you find?" and I would grimly hold up an oil lamp and a jug and say, "This is it. This is all there ever was under the sun."

I MAKE A reservation at a hotel in Jerusalem and get into my car, brushing the sand off my feet before shutting the door. It is the weekend. I can run away for a little while. I call Orna and let her know I'm taking off for a day or two.

I love Jerusalem deeply and irrationally. It is a small white-gold crown of a city. Like the taster who can detect in wine the faintest hint of oak, almond kernel bitterness, dark fruited overtone, and green-grass aroma, the sensitive archaeologist might detect in New

York City the hint of duped Algonquins, the signs of fossilized primate prints in the spire of the Empire State Building, or the crushed remains of lynchings under Washington Square Park. A sensitive archaeologist might barely detect this trace vibration beneath New York's rumbling arteries, but in Jerusalem, one needs no trained sensitivity.

One time, when I was in middle school and my father was still alive, my family vacationed in Jamaica. While we were there, we drove a jeep out to the bluest, most pristinely beautiful lake I had ever seen. It was small, but the guide explained that it was deeper than we could ever imagine. Miles deep, he claimed, because it was in fact the mouth of an extinct volcano. To swim in that lake was deliciously disconcerting, and I wondered what mythic or prehistoric creature might bubble to the surface and snap me in two. That's Jerusalem. Small, but crammed full. Its Roman arches and Herodian foundations reach deep into the earth where some molten lava once bled. Temples here once drew throngs of pilgrims, spice traders swept from every known direction, prayers were warbled in fire-breathing gutturals, wars raged, and maniacs and missionaries—all manner of displaced peoples—pulse and pant just a layer of dust below the feet of the teenage soldiers, young mothers, garbage collectors, and mailmen who inhabit the modern city. And then there's *me*, eating my giant spinach, goat cheese, olive, and sun-dried tomato salad under an umbrella in an outdoor café. This tiny mountaintop village always feels to me like the largest city on earth—the umbilical cord through which God feeds the belly of the world.

I call my closest friend, Jordanna, in Connecticut. Jordanna is well into her third pregnancy. I can picture her, lips sensually full and her dark coffee hair in full sheen. Her eyes are on the opposite end of blue from mine, hers closer to blueberry, mine closer to sky. Her glasses always make them look twice as large. I glance at myself in the rearview mirror and see that the sun has made my nose and cheeks pink.

"Boo," I say when she answers.

"Page, it's you! Hi! Where are you?" she says.

"I'm driving to Jerusalem. Wooshing up the road. I wish you were with me," I say. When I decided to leave divinity school, I had already taken away the two things that would be the most valuable in my life—my knowledge of the Bible and my friendship with Jordanna. She was a graduate student studying Hebrew and Aramaic at the time I was immersed in theology. We became fast friends and shared an apartment for two years, consistently ignoring our boyfriends of the month for late nights together poring over the texts we loved.

"Are you going to see Itai?" she says. She sounds as if she could be in the car with me.

I laugh. "You do remember that Itai and I broke up three years ago and that he is married."

"I remember," she says, "but some of your best stories come from when you have been with Itai." I think about the time I first saw him. He was strong, solid, and stocky. His eyes were set wide apart, and they were an almost black-green. He had a square jaw and deep jowls that parenthesized his mouth. His family was Yemenite and he had exotic olive skin and black hair that made me wish I knew how to paint. Back then he was an IT specialist working primarily with government offices. He hadn't yet become the director of surveys and excavations at the Department of Antiquities, as he is now.

"I recently learned that his wife studied linguistics at Columbia as an exchange student, the same years I was there," I share.

"He married an Israeli version of you," she says. "He was so in love with you. You should have fought for him." Jordanna rarely edits her thoughts and tends to share how she believes things should be done as if there is obviously no other correct way.

"It did feel like love for a while," I agree, and then remind her, "but he felt guilty that he was falling for an American, and a Christian at that, and started pushing me away. I always had this clear sense of Israel as the other woman in our relationship. As if she was stretched out in the back seat wherever we went, with long gold legs, a fashionable chain around her waist, gold skin. Languid as a panther. Her slick black hair in a Cleopatra cut. Her chin resting on the back of her hand, watching the scenery pass by, her jewel eyes bored by my blather."

"I see," says Jordanna expertly, "it was your *imagination* that got between you and Itai."

Our dynamic usually is that I fight back when Jordanna challenges me about my decisions, but I am tired. I just say, "I did cry a little for Itai," and then I shrug, glancing out as I pass the sparkling silver acres of a fish farm. "A few months, at most."

"You miss him?" Jordanna asks, with a twinge of hope.

"I do sometimes," I admit.

Jordanna shares, "I read a text the other day which taught that a heart suffering from depression is like an upside-down bowl. It cannot hold anything. But a broken heart is like a right-side-up bowl, only broken. It went on to say how much better it is to be brokenhearted than depressed, because even though there is a crack, the vessel still longs to receive and to hold." A group of young soldiers at a bus stop wave toward me, looking to hitch a ride. Some of them could be half my age. "So it makes me happy to see a heart move from depressed to broken."

"I wish I could say I am brokenhearted if that would please you," I say, "but I'm afraid I'm just bored. Numb and bored."

Jordanna laughs lightly but says nothing. I glance in my mirror at the bus stop receding behind me, the soldiers waving toward the next car.

"Are you upstairs in your attic?" I ask. I imagine the attic study where she works. It is painted white, and the beams of the ceiling are stenciled blue like the rim of a Staffordshire Willow plate. There is a daybed, jammed between the wall and the sharply slanted ceiling, upon which she lies whenever she faces a difficult text, letting the letters realign themselves into translations. Over her desk is a small round window overlooking a long ascent of forest.

"Yes," she says. "Sitting at my desk."

"Read to me the last thing you translated." Today her window would frame a plush carpet of green. In autumn the trees light up as if they are on fire. Winter, the forest attends a ball, draped in white mink, fingers full of ice.

"Mm, okay, it's a poem written by an ultra-Orthodox woman, Basya Kaplan. She expresses this unusual longing and sensitivity. So simple. Listen to this. I don't have the meter quite right, but I love the imagery: *If you are looking for God, don't bother. He is not around. He is not upon. He in not under, or in or beyond. He is not over, within, or beneath. If you are searching for God, talk to me. Look up from your psalter for once and see your wife. I know where he is, Mendel. He is between us.*"

"Interesting." I smile. I love when Jordanna reads to me. "I don't know how I feel about it. It's sweet. Translation is everything everyone thinks archaeology is. You enter inside the thoughts of lost poets and I only dust off their skulls."

Jordanna laughs. "Translation is so tedious. You don't always like the author you translate and sometimes I work for months on legal codes that bore me to tears."

"No dust, no hot and hungry hours, no dry, fruitless months, no begging for grants, no long-distance travel, no dirty fingernails."

"But you get to be tactile. Translation has been described as kissing a woman through a veil . . ."

"At least you can see the end to boredom. You have a certain amount of text to wade through and then you move on to something new. I have no idea where my work ends. At what point have I found enough pieces to finish the puzzle, and what is the puzzle anyway? There is no creativity in what I do. It's all just glorified mechanics. You actually partner up with these thinkers. You make active, creative decisions, and in that way, you immortalize yourself with the words you translate."

Jordanna laughs at me, but with affection. "You never change, Page," she says, and I wonder what I said that makes her say it. "I will never be able to convince you that what I do is all about restraint.

Creativity is betrayal in my work. In fact, most of the time you feel like nothing more than a stenographer."

My shoulders are starting to cramp. I squeeze them back and rearrange my hands on the wheel.

There is so much wonder in Jordanna's life, I think to myself. When legal codes bore her to tears, she bounds downstairs to be amused by the antics of her children. She doesn't end a tedious day as I do, alone, with no end in sight. Then I remember the Barakats. I tell her about their visit and their conviction that their home is haunted by amorous phantoms.

"Of course it would captivate you. You've always been searching for ghosts." I have grown somewhat accustomed to Jordanna's righteous assaults, but I am feeling raw from last night with Norris. Her comment makes me aware of my hollowness and hunger. I am quiet for a moment, then I say, "Maybe I am a ghost," looking out the window. The shadow of me in my car is lengthening across the road as I speed. "I'm running away from Megiddo for a few days. Maybe I'm trying to come back to life."

"Is it Norris? Is he still haranguing you for not being madly in love with him?"

I smile at the idea that she thinks my life is adventuresome, when the opposite is true. Her interest in my experience is deeper than a vicarious curiosity. As a Jewish woman with many family ties to Israel, she was the one who should have ended up here, while I should be living in the New York suburbs. "You have this way of translating my most boring of days into some kind of drama," I say. "The truth is, I'm miserable there. I'm burying myself alive. I'm just shoveling my own grave deeper and deeper, burrowing my tomb under the sediment. This is where I'll kick the bucket, under a stone slab with coins and bone fragments scattered about my body. Day after day, the sun's heat will melt layers of me until I am nothing but wrinkled leather hide with a ghastly expression."

"Ick, Page, stop. How can you stand to have that reel playing in your head all the time, it's awful. *You* have this way of translating everything into some self-pitying script about a poor lost girl with no daddy."

"Ouch, seriously," I say, bracing myself for her to launch into me.

"You are an incredibly powerful woman," she is saying. A watermelon truck slows beside me as she continues talking and the swarthy, gummy driver grins down his approval. My legs feel too naked. The truck passes. "You are one of the youngest supervisors of a well-funded dig. You are beautiful. You could do anything, have anyone. You could leave your job if you want! Leave Israel, in fact. Pursue something else if you're so disillusioned with it. What's keeping you there?"

"Uh-uh, go on. I'm sure you're not through." A yellow and black bumper sticker on the back of the truck declares in Hebrew that the Messiah is on his way. Three miles outside Jerusalem, just before the ascent to the city, I see a little green sign upon which the same word is written in both Hebrew and Arabic: Anatot/Anata.

"You have this way of devaluing everything you do. At your funeral I am going to tell it like it is. I am going to scream out from the back pew, 'Page Brookstone was a blond bombshell! She was beautiful.' I'm going to blow apart this myth you've created about yourself. I'm going to say it clearly, so no one can misunderstand me: 'Page had it all. And I loved her.'"

I have to laugh suddenly. I veer off my route, listening to Jordanna talk about me postmortem. At a stop sign a small white owl swoops just before my car out of an avocado tree where it spent the day.

"Did I upset you?" she asks, suddenly contrite, and I laugh more.

"No, of course not, you're probably right." We are quiet for a moment. "I want to be happy. I'm just not sure I remember how. I was very spontaneous as a child, and then I stopped. All throughout my life there have been these moments when I've asked myself, Should I or shouldn't I? and most of the time I've said I shouldn't and

I didn't. But every now and then, when I felt I've been submerged in my numbing waters too long and the whale of me needed to come up for one great and gasping breath, I've told myself I shouldn't, and I did."

"I remember some of those mistakes," Jordanna says. "Most of them were pretty cute. Especially Devon. Remember Devon, the art assistant? With the snake tattoo?"

I slow down at the Anatot checkpoint. I say, "Sometimes I felt that my very life depended on it."

"On what? On Devon's tattoo?"

"On coming up for air." A female soldier who could probably wear a bracelet for a belt waves me through.

"It does." And then after a moment, "Where exactly are you?"

"I'm going to visit the Barakats in Anatot. See if there are any ghosts or not. For fun. Out of curiosity. Just something different to do."

"Ghosts instead of graves, well, at least you're going up," she says, and then announces encouragingly, "Actually, I think it is a good idea. You *should* go to Anatot. Break out of your routine. And then, maybe you'll think about coming home? You have your apartment waiting for you here, a pretty nest with a good view. And your mom. And me."

V

O to be that docile lamb led to the slaughter unaware! . . . Better
contented absentmindedness than this slow killing thing wielding
its sword like an elusive sunbeam under our chins.
—THE SCROLL OF ANATIYA 15:24–26

Anatot, just three miles northeast of Jerusalem, is today considered a Jewish settlement. It has volleyed over the years between being annexed Jerusalem and occupied territory, settling for the past few years into the latter. Like many towns in the territories, the settlement is side by side with an Arab town of a similar name, both vying for legitimacy, and so Anatot, a town of 170 or so Jewish families living in apartment complexes and a few private homes, is separated by an unused road from Anata, a town of a slightly larger number of Arab families living in small private homes. I am familiar with references to Anatot in the Book of Jeremiah, naming it as his birthplace. I know also that there are other references to similarly named cities which are probably all one in the same, Alamet in I Chronicles, and Al-Mut in the Book of Joshua.

Anatot is greener than I expected. There is a beautiful stretch of vineyard sloping down from the apartments. As I crossed into Anata, everything changes. The houses are squat and square, homemade instead of subcontracted. The flaps of white sheets hanging on lines in Anatot and Anata wave to one another cheerfully over the border road, dumb to controversy.

I open my window and ask a man sitting on the curb if he can direct me to the home of Naima and Ibrahim Barakat. He looks to the side and doesn't answer. Driving a bit further, I see a boy playing soccer in his front yard with a younger sibling, and I call to him out my window. He tells me it is just at the end of the street. The house with the flowers in the window. "But," he cautions, "not good to go there." Then he puts his arms out with his fingers dangling down and *whoos* like a ghost. His little brother buckles over and laughs and the boy makes kissy sounds.

"Mahmoud! Hassan!" I hear someone call them.

I sit in my car across the street from the Barakat home. It is a small, two-story home built of hewn limestone with the typical flat umber roof. It is clearly well maintained. Pretty, well-trimmed ivy creeps up the front of the house, carefully trained to frame the little windows. Window boxes on both the lower and upper floors tumble with red, puffy geraniums. Low stone walls delineate a small treeless property from the lots on either side. It is by far the prettiest house on the street. It seems to be the prettiest house in all of Anata, a bit out of place next to the boxy dilapidated homes with missing window panes and herb gardens run all amok. A neat path through rounded tufts of fragrant rosemary leads to the front door.

I approach the Barakats' front stoop, looking down at the welcome mat, which reads Salaam in English letters. There is a wind chime hanging from the top of the doorframe, a jangle of rusted spoons, forks, and butter knives. I feel nervous, and then I think of Jordanna going downstairs to help her children get ready for school. In an hour the sun will leave this continent to lord over there. It comforts me that she holds me in her mind even from so far away. I knock twice on the door.

No one comes. I knock a few more times and call out their names, but it is clear no one is home. I am surprised by my own disappointment. It is probably better this way, I tell myself, although I feel a strange hunger to learn what's inside. I feel like a traveler who has a vague sense of leaving something behind, only to realize that it was, after all, the most important thing. But what is it? Standing by my car now, I scratch my head and stare up at the house. An unexpected breeze sweeps up from the vineyards and disturbs the geraniums, and they dance for me like the hems of a flamenco dancer. The ivy over the house shivers. The ruffling petals and the chinking of the wind chime complement each other, as if the soft breeze has spiraled sound and light waves out of their places into a ringing light. The gauze curtains swell out the upper-story windows and for a moment it is as if the whole house has taken a deep breath, and then all is absolutely still.

I get into my car and mosey toward the edge of town by a different route than I came. Crossing over into Anatot, I notice a little kiosk marked Falafel, Cigarettes, Fruit, Tours. I am hesitant to leave. I think, I might as well learn a bit about Jeremiah's home. He is by far the most interesting prophet to me. Sure, Ezekiel had the visions and Jonah had the whale, but Jeremiah knew how to brood, which makes him a kindred spirit.

"You give tours?" I lean over the kiosk and ask a man who is napping on a sack of grain underneath the counter. He snaps to alertness immediately.

"Yes, yes, of course!" says the old merchant. His face is as mottled and grooved as tree bark, and he has a friendly smile.

"Is there much to see here?" I ask.

"Oh yes, *arbeh lirot*! You want a tour? Nice day to walk." His accent is heavy. He comes around from behind the stand.

"What is there to see in Anatot?" I look around me.

"Yes, you know Torah? Torah?" he opens his hands pantomiming a book. "Anatot is everywhere in the Bible. Jeremiah was born in Anatot. I show you his tomb."

"Please. Show me his tomb."

"Fifty shekel," he says, shrugging like it's nothing.

"Thirty," I say, bargaining just so that he doesn't think I'm a fool.

"Okay, forty-five. Shuki! You watch store now." A young boy appears out of the house and jogs to the kiosk, head high with responsibility. The merchant turns to me and asks, "You want juice, dear?"

"No, thank you."

"Follow me then." He pulls two waters out of an icy bucket and we start walking. "You see that there? There is a quarry, you know, for stones. All of Jerusalem made from stones from *that* quarry. Old, old stones."

"*All* of Jerusalem?"

"Okay." He laughs, eyes crinkling. "So what are you, a teacher? So not all of Jerusalem. But much."

Quarries captivate me. I have seen quarries in Israel that unknowingly unearth stones and bricks from undiscovered archaeological sites, reshuffling them to be used in modern buildings. I love the notion that the polished wall of a bank was once the millstone or bench in a humble ancient household.

The short hike with my guide half a mile up a rocky road feels essential. We reach a stone mausoleum with a domed roof. There is a water fountain outside the door where one can wash hands and feet before entering, and an elderly woman hands out blue stretches of cloth that a woman can wrap around her legs, if she is wearing shorts, or use to cover her hair, preserving modesty in the holy site.

"*Shalom*, Edna," my guide greets the woman.

"*Shalom*, Elazar," she answers kindly.

I wrap the cloth around my indecent legs. Inside the mausoleum there are two nuns praying, four Jewish women reciting psalms, and six Jewish men praying and rocking their bodies like reeds in a windstorm, the ecstasy of faith clearly upon them. The women are on one side of the room, with a lace room divider shielding them from the men. Just behind the lace there is a large stone coffin draped in red velvet embroidered with sprouting twigs and verses from the Book of Jeremiah. I know that this cannot possibly be Jeremiah's tomb. The dome shape of the roof means that it is more likely early Muslim, but tell that to the faithful. I bow my head in feigned piety and utter a prayer that the Bedouin sheik most likely buried in this place be worthy of the worshippers who pay him homage.

Elazar and I walk back down the road to his kiosk. I can see that there are a few people sitting on the curb holding out small clear glasses. The boy is pouring coffee into them. As we come closer, one of the men looks familiar to me, and before I can register that it's Ibrahim, he leaps up to his feet.

"Hello! Yes, hello!" Ibrahim shouts, running up the street. He grabs me by both my wrists. I am jolted by his touch and his exuberance to see me. "Are you here to visit us? Are you hungry? Are you thirsty? Naima is at home. Don't leave without visiting. It will break her heart and mine." His green eyes dance in the late sun. I feel my heart race, pulsing up through my neck.

"Ibrahim, you invite her to have coffee too," Elazar suggests, relieving Shuki of the black kettle.

In a rush of gratitude, Ibrahim takes my two hands and lifts them to his lips, pressing a kiss on my bundled fingertips. He turns to the three men on the curb and announces proudly, "An American archaeologist," as if presenting a rare specimen.

One of the men says something in Arabic and the others laugh.

Ibrahim doesn't laugh. He says, "I know what I know," to them and me. They lift their steaming glasses to us and one says to me in elegant English, "Remember, darling, nothing he says is true unless he is under oath."

"I'm always under oath," Ibrahim reassures, swatting toward his friends to let me know they should be ignored.

I follow Ibrahim's car in mine. He keeps gesturing wildly out his window to me, afraid that I will turn away.

When we arrive at the Barakats' home, Ibrahim leaps out of his car and opens my door even before I have stopped rolling.

"Whoa, slow down," I caution, turning off the car. I can feel my cheeks are red.

"It is Page, right?" He asks as he tugs me to the house by my elbow. His shirt struggles against his strong shoulders. "Naima! Naima!"

Naima opens the door and as soon as she sees me, she shrieks in joy. I whisk my arm from Ibrahim's grip. "I knew it! I told Ibrahim." She rushes out to me and takes my hand between her two, shaking it vigorously. She is a full head shorter than I am. Without letting go, she says to her husband, "You see? I told you she was different. I knew it because you came to help us with our car. Ibrahim was in a bad state, he couldn't see. You came to help us, and then you asked us what they looked like!"

Ibrahim leans in and kisses her swiftly on the lips. His eyes flash with pride and he says, "You did tell me."

As we cross the threshold of their home, I suddenly feel sad that I came here. I feel sorry for them. They are so overjoyed to see me, their faces glowing. I am the only expert they have, and I have come just for a story, really. I don't believe there is anything here. I am not honestly going to excavate under a stranger's house. Maybe this is just their way of trying to meet people. To reach outside this lonely settlement and make contact with people who remind them of their friends in university. I suddenly think of my mother's father, whose veins were thin and hard to find. When he was in the hospital toward the end of his life, the nurses would spend nearly half an hour repeatedly stabbing him with those needles searching for one. He was bruised up and down his arms, big purple and yellow stains, but it was clear he enjoyed every minute. Being touched was more important to him than the reason for the contact.

I can hear Norris in my head saying with condescension, "You went to visit them? Have you completely cracked?"

The house is pleasant enough. It has a center hall leading to the stairs. To the right is a dining room, with a swinging door that leads, I presume, to the kitchen. To the left is a living room. I am immediately drawn to the living room.

"I tried to do a little on my own," Ibrahim explains.

The room is modestly furnished, an old couch pushed up against the wall beneath a crooked framed poster of an English garden and gate. Across from the couch against the opposite wall is a low oak cabinet with a television sitting before a bay window facing the front yard. What is remarkable, however, is that between the couch and the television, where a rug and coffee table should be, the floor is torn up. Someone has jackhammered through the boards and into the foundation. Splintered floorboards are jutting up all around the ditch, which appears to be three yards deep and about ten by ten feet across, with a black tarp lying across the bottom.

I walk to its edge. "Why didn't you dig in your backyard? It would have been so much easier," I say, and then bite my tongue.

"Two reasons, really," Ibrahim says. "One, I can work on it at night this way. Draw the curtains and no one knows. Two—well, we've never seen them in the backyard."

"Them?" I say, staring down, and then recall. "Oh right, them."

"Come into the dining room," Naima urges, still holding my hand. She senses I'm uncomfortable. I notice an ax in the corner of the room. "I'll put out something to eat. You like baklava? My grandmother made it."

I am only too happy to leave the living room. Seeing the floor hacked apart makes me a little afraid.

"I am on my way to Jerusalem," I begin to explain. I feel white as a ghost myself. But Naima is pleasant. She leads me to the dining room and Ibrahim follows. "I'm staying there for a couple of days."

"I am so glad you stopped by!" Naima says with enthusiasm, gesturing for us to sit. As soon as I sit, I feel weary, as if I've been carrying a heavy weight. She lays out a tray of baklava and a pitcher of iced tea. "We have been at our wits' end with this place. Your work is so serious and demanding, and to you we must seem like complete charlatans. But you came anyway. That makes you someone very special."

"What is it that you two do? I mean, besides that," I say, motioning behind me to the living room. God, that hole in there. The longer

I sit, the more horrible it seems. I have an impulse to turn around and see if it is growing, spreading over the floor to swallow me up. It is as if this cute little house, with its thin curtains and happy window boxes, is trying to scream, its mouth stopped up and muffled with black tarp. I don't turn around.

"Ibrahim is a lawyer and I am a teacher in the local high school. I teach history. We met when I was in university in London and Ibrahim was there studying law. We stayed in London for a number of years after we married, but we really wanted to use our training to assist the people from our home, so we came back. We still feel out of place. But we are committed."

"That"—I gesture again behind me—"must contribute to your feeling out of place."

"I know," Ibrahim says. "I regret doing it."

"You do?" I ask, a little relieved. I reach for a triangle of baklava and sink my fingers around the honey-soaked leaves of pastry.

"Yes, I do. If you had come last week, you could have stopped me. I only started last night. Your friend, you remember, told us to buy a shovel, and when we got home I was so mad that I did just that. I bought a shovel and an ax and a jackhammer, and I went to work," Ibrahim says. Then he immediately adds, "I wasn't mad at you. I was mad at how foolish this house was making us. I figured I'd take a look myself, and if I saw nothing within a week or two, then no loss. I would just put it back together; we'd sell the house, and try to move on. But you know what I learned? That I really have no idea what I'm doing. I'm just making a mess. It isn't as big a deal as it seems. We built this house. I know how to put it back together. You just give me the word, doctor. You're the expert."

Ibrahim is completely different than he was yesterday at Megiddo, struggling up the hill and then huffing and growling at me. Naima hands out napkins and takes a baklava dusted with sugar and crumbled almonds. Ibrahim is brushing crumbs off his fingers. In his home he seems easy and relaxed. It is the thought of his drilling through his floor that makes me tense.

"My instinct is to say this is crazy and you should patch up your house and move on. But I'll take a closer look, seeing I'm the only expert you have."

Naima smiles. "Will you stay for dinner? My nephew is coming from the north and I think you'd get along. He's seventeen. We are trying to convince him to go to university, but his parents are set against it. Now he has a girlfriend, and if he marries young, well, I think that's the end of his education. He is very bright."

"You two might not be the best ones to argue for higher education," I say. I hear myself speak as if through thick felt. My words seem to me muffled and slow. My tongue feels thick and my head heavy. I realize that I may have offended them. I feel suddenly dizzy but I exert myself to say, "I'm sorry. I didn't mean that. It sounds like you sacrificed a lot to return here and give back to your community. You probably could have been a big success in London."

Naima shakes her head. "We could never have stayed in London. Here we have less, but we wouldn't trade it for the world." Ibrahim reaches across the table and they braid hands, inches from my own. I am staring at the baklava, and the plate seems to vibrate.

"Do you have a family?" Ibrahim asked.

I blink my eyes. "I have my mother, who lives in New York." I feel as if the air is congealing, and I am sinking backward, away from the table, shuttling further and further away from the Barakats and their braided hands.

"Do you believe in love?" he says as if from a distance. I can't seem to get my bearings. I want him to reach out and hold me, and bring me back in. I want her to embrace me too.

"I don't know," my voice says, without me. "I believe in what I see. What does love look like?"

Ibrahim laughs and puts his hands up. "It looks like the blue is falling down out of the sky and the blue is flying up out of the sea and everything is upside down and different but absolutely the same and right."

For a split second I see my father in Ibrahim. My father, back before he was sick, stringing together words like a jeweler strings pearls.

"Something just happened to your face," Naima says, full of hope. "Did you see one of them?"

"No, no." I feign a laugh. "Do you mind if I use the bathroom? I think I have something in my eye."

"Why don't you take a shower before dinner? Relax. I'll give you a towel. Walid won't be here for another hour and we have to cook. He is going to be so mad at Ibrahim for digging up the floor. You two can laugh at us together. Come, follow me."

Why don't I leave?

She releases Ibrahim and reaches out to me. Her touch on my shoulder seems to steady the room. Her touch makes me feel as if I am exactly where I am supposed to be. It steadies me. Jerusalem seems as if it is far away, on a cloud. Megiddo, on the other side of the moon. New York on the edge of the galaxy. She anchors me here. I want to stay, but I don't know why.

Getting into my car seems a monumental task. She leads me up the stairs. I think of my mother's apartment, her brisket and mashed potatoes, so hearty and nourishing. The baklava layered and drenched in honey seems to unfold inside me, thickening my veins. With each step up the narrow staircase, my body becomes more and more leaden. By the time I reach the bathroom, a well of tears walls up behind my eyelids and there are anvils in my feet and hands. Naima squeezes my shoulder. She has a look of recognition on her face.

I enter the bathroom and she shuts the door lightly behind me. It flits across my mind that I have been drugged. There was poison in the baklava. I have to get out of here. That ditch, it is so unnatural. They are going to bury me in it. Pour the new foundation over me. When they are looking for my body, Jordanna will remember I am here. She is holding me in her mind right now.

I sit on the lid of the toilet and let my heavy head fall between my knees. *C'mon, you paranoid hypochondriac,* I command myself. *Get up. You haven't been drugged. Jesus. You are just depressed. Your heart is an upside-down bowl*. I wash my face with cold water and look into the mirror. I pull off my bandana. My hair spills down like lemonade just below my shoulders. I undress and sit on the edge of the tub.

I look at the bathtub. How much nicer it will be to drive into the night without my legs sticking to the vinyl seats. I can feel a thin layer of beach on me. There are lilac- and vanilla-laced salts from the Dead Sea on the tub's ledge. I fill the tub, swirling my fingers in the water. Why am I still here? My mind starts wandering. It must be nice to take a hot bath in London on a foggy day, I imagine, to open the window and watch the cool mist and hot steam meet in the heady, perfumed air. To be hot and cold at the same time.

These people are going to bury me under their living room floor, and I am stepping into a bath. "What is wrong with me?" I wonder absently. I slide into the water, which is as soft and warm as Israel's summer air. I tilt my head back and close my eyes. My neck feels so relaxed. The air is thick with steam, droplets rolling down the tiles, down the mirror. My eyes are dewy and sealed. I imagine I hear some-one enter the room. A soft squall of cool air breaks over me from the open door and I know I haven't imagined it. Someone has come in. I wonder who, even as I lift my head and part my lips to ask, but I don't say anything. I do not open my eyes. I feel perfectly safe tucked behind my eyelids. A bubble pops near my cheek.

"I thought you might need another towel," I hear Naima say.

I hear her leave, the door clicking shut behind her, and I slide lower into the bath. An old memory surfaces, one I've long forgotten. I was a child, maybe six or seven, and I had come into the living room in my nightgown. My parents were having a party. I had been woken by laughter.

"Come here," a woman said. She had Middle Eastern features, black hair pulled back severely from her face.

"Have a sip." She smiled. Her teeth were crooked. I could see down her sweater through the tunnel of her cleavage as she bent to me. She held the tiny pink crystal goblet, one from the set my parents had bought in Prague, to my lips. She put a hand under my chin and tilted the goblet. The sherry just barely touched my lips when my father said, "Page, go back to bed."

There is something strange in this house, something seductive. All sorts of feelings roll over me. The perfumed air makes me sleepy. I imagine waking to Itai's strong hands. He used to always take me in my sleep.

After some time I stand up and secure the towel around me, struggling to surface from the strange haze that envelops me. I can barely see my reflection in the fogged mirror. As the steam gradually dissipates, my mind too becomes clearer. Droplets roll down the mirror in silver ribbons. I can see thin slivers of my reflection. I squint. Between strips of fog I think I see another figure, standing behind me, just over my shoulder. I jump backward and lose my footing in the bath, crashing into the water with a tremendous splash. The steam spirals around me as I leap up. There is no one else in the room. I wipe the mirror with the back of my hand and there is just me. My heart pounds. I know I saw something, a figure. I dry myself and dress quickly, thinking, *They've drugged me.* But the form is becoming clearer in my mind. I touch the smooth walls of the shower. It was right here, appearing in the air like a plume of sea spray leaping off a wave. With arms, and the contours of a face. I look at the water slopped onto the floor from my fall.

I throw on my clothes and fly down the stairs. I am ready to run out of this house and never look back. My hands are shaking on the doorknob, trying to open it, when I hear someone say, "What's your hurry?"

I look to the living room. A young man is climbing into the hole in the middle.

"*Ahlan,*" he greets me.

I stop and try to collect myself, rubbing my forehead. I take a deep breath. What, after all, am I running from?

"Hi," I say, still a little breathless. "I was just . . ."

"I'm Walid," he introduces himself. His accent is much thicker than Ibrahim's. He is handsome and willowy, with brown eyes and diamond-shaped nostrils, wide mouth, and ruddy complexion.

"Where are Naima and Ibrahim?" I ask. My voice is brittle.

"Upstairs in their room. Don't ask." He smiles widely at me. Then he continues, "My uncle is crazy. Look what he do." Walid starts lifting up the black tarp at the bottom of the ditch. He looks like he is struggling a little.

"Let me help you," I say. I lie on the floor and let him hand me the tarp's edge. Walid's hands look soft, his skin a caramel suede. Together we pull the tarp out of the ditch. I am surprised: what had seemed only a few yards deep is actually much deeper in the center. The sheet has been covering a hole about five yards deep, with a wooden ladder going down.

"Jesus," I say. Curiosity gets the better of me, and I can't resist climbing in. I am after all, their only expert. Walid helps me down. I run my fingers along the sides, over a jutting rock. Maybe it hasn't been the house screaming, but the stones. I hate to see stones chewed up like this. I've always felt that stones have souls, and memory. They remember the creation of the world and foretell the future. "God. Look at how he butchered this place." If there was anything in the path of that jackhammer, it was surely chewed up. "He was *driven*," I say to myself, crouching down and sifting the earth in my fingers. What he is doing to his house seems so punishing. You could only get this far and deep in a single night if you were *attacking*.

"Get me a flashlight?" I ask Walid.

He scrambles up and returns a minute later, handing me a small penlight. He sits on the edge of the pit, leaning in and watching me.

"Thanks," I say.

It is hard to discern anything from the walls of the ditch, but on one side, something does catch my eye. Toward the bottom of the pit there are two broken slabs of stone sticking out, one above the other. Ibrahim has blindly torn through them, but enough remains for me to think that these may have once been steps. This would not be unusual. All of Israel is essentially an archaeological treasure trove. You walk up and down the uneven streets of Jerusalem and know that the undulating paths are layers and layers of rubbled cities, spanning forty centuries, one upon the other.

"Where do you think you're going?" I ask the slabs under my breath. I love steps—the way they suggest the possibility of going somewhere else.

"Have you seen them?" I call up to Walid.

"The ghosts?" he asks.

"Yeah," I say, measuring the slabs with handbreadths.

"I don't know," he acknowledges. "Something like they say. But I don't know what I see. I think they talk so much they make you think you see things."

I climb out. "Tell Ibrahim and Naima they need to stop. Someone is going to fall in here and get hurt. A kid could trip and fall in, get tangled in the tarp, and then they'd really be in trouble."

I hear a toilet flush upstairs. The chewed-up floorboards look sharp and dangerous. Walid is bent over the pit, readjusting the tarp. On the back of his black T-shirt there is white Arabic writing with a large exclamation mark on the end. I walk hurriedly to the door, saying I have to run.

"My aunt thinks you are staying for dinner," Walid says, leaping up. He has the incisors of a cat.

"No, no, I'm sorry," I say, rushing to my car.

I CHECK INTO the Jersualem Citadel. I go to the pool as dusk swallows the city, to chlorinate away the sweet residue of the Barakats' bath. There is a woman offering massages. I lie down on the terry cloth–padded table and she kneads my back.

"You have no knots," she observes. "A very relaxed and limber woman."

"Beaten taffy is relaxed too," I say through the hole in the table. "Tenderized chicken has been pounded with mallets."

I can feel the knuckles of her fists rolling into the small of my back. After the massage, I slip into the hot tub and sit holding my feet up to the jets. The pediatrician once told my mother that with my high arches I would make a great ballerina. Our family dentist once ran his latexed thumb along the roof of my mouth, commenting that it was "cathedral-like" with its high arch. I'm physically archaeological, I muse to myself.

I lean my head against the edge of the hot tub and stare up at the sky. I can barely detect the twinkle of the first stars, clinging to the sky like dew to a spider's web. What happened in the Barakat house had felt so strange. So inevitable. Norris will say that I left him for crazy, just like his ex-wife. If only I could be content sifting through the ancient dirt at Megiddo for the rest of my life. Marry Norris, let him read newspapers on the porch night after night. Make him tea in our neat kitchen. Wear a flannel robe. Slippers.

There is a woman in the hot tub with me, past her prime, but pretty. Her skin has that old suede texture of having spent half a life in the sun. I have been soaking in the water too long and feel myself becoming dizzy, seeing spots. I stand up.

She says, "Honey, your body's to die for."

"Believe me," I tell her, retying my bikini's strings, "I'm dying for it."

VI

⁂

And Jerusalem will spin slowly as a great wheel rising above the mountain, our spirits contained within it. At that time, Jeremiah, I am going to stand from my place. I am going to ascend before your eyes, and your ears will be filled with the sound of mirth and gladness . . .

—THE SCROLL OF ANATIYA 16:13–15

Itai picks me up in front of the hotel and we drive toward Beit Shemesh, a small city a few miles southwest of Jerusalem. We dated for three years, and it is easy and familiar to be with him. I look at his arms and his hands on the wheel as he drives. His skin is so rich I feel comparatively translucent.

He was a beautiful lover, experimental and passionate. When I was nestled in my deepest slumber, with the heat of sleep all around me, he would roll me over with gentle hands and shushing tones, the way a parent shushes their drowsy child while transferring her from car to crib. He would pull away just enough if I started to stir. He knew I slept deeply. Each time I would awake slowly in stages, and the first stage was the most beautiful. My body would feel him, but my mind would still be wrapped in some dream, limbs still numb, and out of that bizarre mingling of sex and dream would surface fantasies I never knew I had.

"Are you some kind of secret necrophiliac?" I would tease him.

"I can't help it. You sleep seductively."

I often think back to those nights, with their balanced sweetness. I hadn't given, I had been taken, innocently conspired against by my lover in cahoots with my dream self. What choice did I have? The ecstasy that my church might have called sin was met with instant absolution. No matter what we did at night—what I may have said as I came to—I always felt innocent with him by morning. In so many ways, Itai made it okay for me to be a child again. But a time comes in every relationship when your truths get dragged out into the light of day. You can't slumber through a relationship. Eventually, you have to wake up.

"Sharon and I got a puppy," he says.

I take a deep, satisfying breath. "I know someone who might be interested in initiating a dig beneath his home," I share.

"Everybody's fantasy here, that they are sitting above the Ark of the Covenant," he says.

"He's in Anatot. I visited yesterday," I say. He glances at me. "There are ancient stairs leading down."

"Anatot is complicated," he says. "A settlement just outside Jerusalem proper. There are entanglements when it comes to any kind of construction, or planned deconstruction in this case. Only a few months ago there was military activity outside Anatot; I know you don't watch the news, so you probably didn't know that. There was a small riot. The political climate is crazy right now. Cough up his name and I'll throw him into a Galilean dungeon."

"It's an Arab family," I say.

"An Arab family interested in digging in Israel? I've never had a request for digging permits from an Arab family. How bizarre. All right, I'm a little curious. I could find them in an instant, you know that." He thinks for a moment. "Wait a minute, you're not talking about that couple who think their house is haunted, are you?"

He glances at me and I nod, feeling my face flush.

"You went to their house?" he says, scrunching his eyebrows at me and then looking hard at the road. "I don't like them," Itai says. "I don't like people going around wanting to punch holes in my country at random, even if they are a talent in the courtroom."

There she was in the back seat again, Israel, reaching over and drawing circles on his chest. He was clearly hers. Itai had been a paratrooper and claimed he was afraid of heights, but he loved being with his army friends and would do anything, jump from any height, for them and for her. His faith also was simple and pure.

"How do you know God exists?" I asked him once.

"Because I didn't die in Lebanon," he answered.

"But you have friends who died in Lebanon."

"But we can't ask them about God now, can we?"

He is smiling, his hands lightly hooked over the bottom of the steering wheel. "You look good, Page," he says. *How much better it is to be brokenhearted than depressed.* My heart aches a little and I smile back at him.

"You are a lot like Israel," he says, as we turn off the highway. "You are full of internal conflict. You have this constant awareness of mortality. But there is so much more to Israel, and potentially so much more to you. Did you know that Israel has more companies traded on NASDAQ than any other country outside of yours? More than Japan!"

I nod and look out the window at the landscape. Israel's wardrobe is filled with gowns of gold and green, dotted with cactus flowers.

He goes on, glorifying, "People think of Israel and they think of ancient ruins. But Israel is the Silicon Valley of Europe. From cell phones and Instant Messaging to Smart Cars and heart transplants." The sun is shining into his eyes and he lowers the sun visor. His eyes continue marveling. "You could put this entire country into Lake Michigan and still have room for every American to wade in. Do you ever wonder how such a small country creates so much?"

"All the time," I lie.

"Because it's a culture that accepts risk. Because although she is realistically aware of the antagonism around her, she does not let fear rule her. She constantly creates and expands her mind. She thrives." He smiles and thinks back to younger days. "Sitting with friends with a hot glass of cinnamon *sahlab*, and warm, melting *rugeleh* from Marzipan bakery, after dancing all night at a club, *that* is my Israel." He glances at me. "You could learn from Israel about how to rise up out of the ruins." He reaches over and squeezes my hand. I melt a little, like the chocolate inside that rugaleh I remember sharing with him so many times. I think about him with his wife, Sharon, who is about as American as an Israeli can be, and wonder if this resembles anything like the conversations they have over dinner. I doubt it.

Itai parks and we get out of the car. The air is sweet with goldenrod. Itai leads me on a *tiyul*, sharing information on the aromatic and medicinal properties of every plant we pass. We reach the entrance of a cave. "You are going to love this." He smiles, taking my hand and leading me in. He lights a flashlight and we descend on wooden steps that have been built by some local spelunker.

"Look. Moses."

Itai turns the cone of his flashlight onto a stalagmite that has formed in such a way that it looks as if it has a beard. With imagination, there even appears to be two stone tablets. Our laughter echoes throughout the cave, chiming along with the constant pure *ping* of dripping water.

"But come see something else, over here. This you'll really like."

We walk along the wooden slats deeper into the cave and Itai spotlights a stalactite and stalagmite pair, each a good ten feet, which are only half an inch from touching one another.

He says, "They've been reaching toward each other for a million years. It may be a thousand more before they kiss, but there is no question they will. That is what they were born to do."

There is a tiny bead of water clinging to the stalactite. What will have changed in the above-ground world when they finally touch? Long after I die, they'll become a pillar. Tears begin to well over my eyes, and to stop them, I ask shakily, "How do you hold that flashlight so steady?"

He laughs and says my name. I can tell he sees right through me, but Itai is kind. He says, "Gun training."

Deeper into the cave, he squeezes my elbow and asks, "I can't remember, you like bats?"

"Not particularly," I say.

"I do," he says and cocks his arm back.

"No, don't!" I shout, and throw myself upon his arm, but the weight of me doesn't deter him. Itai's arms are so strong and beautiful, and with me hanging on like a koala he hurls a small rock to the ceiling of the cave. I fling myself down just as a great tide of small screeching bats rushes down over us. My heart is racing with sheer terror while Itai remains tall, a proud masthead cutting through a hurricane.

"I'm sorry," he says, laughing as he helps me up. "I know these bats, they're harmless."

Frightened and foolish, I fall into him and he holds me. He turns off the flashlight and kisses me just over my ear. I am grateful for that blackest of black one only finds in caves, because my tears are rolling freely now, and my whole body shakes, a sight I'd rather he not witness.

"You and I were good together," he whispers as he peels me off him. "I want you to love and be loved the way Sharon and I love each other." He flicks on his flashlight.

"I know," I say, punching him playfully and then wiping my nose with the back of my hand. "We'll see."

MY CELL PHONE rings while I am sipping wine on my balcony at the Citadel. There is a wedding in the courtyard below me and the music and laughter seeps up without tiring, promising to continue all night.

"Page? Did I wake you? This is Ibrahim. Ibrahim Barakat. I need to talk to you."

I am surprised to hear him and I stand up. "How did you get my number?"

He sounds breathless. "Online. I am sorry to wake you. Something happened," he says desperately. I'm not sure if he is telling me something happened or asking me if it did.

"I'm sorry I didn't say good-bye." I rub my eyes. I feel ashamed of running away. Hearing his voice makes me uneasy and embarrassed for how I acted. They had hoped I'd stay for dinner and talk with them about their project. "I had to run," I say unconvincingly.

"Oh no," he says, his voice a little calmer. "Something happened yesterday. I need to know what to do."

So this is how it is going to be, I think. They are going to track me down every time something happens in their house. I will never get rid of them. I think of the look that Itai gave me when he learned I had visited them.

"Ibrahim, it's the middle of the night. Let me call you back tomorrow."

"You won't call me back. Please! Let me just tell you." His urgency returns.

"All right." I sigh, sitting back down. I hear applause from the wedding.

"I went down into the hole yesterday with the jackhammer—"

"Dangerous," I mutter, but Ibrahim is undeterred.

"I was alone in the house and I started going deeper—"

"The thing could have slipped out of your hand and turned around and killed you."

"And suddenly, you won't believe this—"

"A ghost popped out," I interrupt him. Norris, Ramon, Itai, everyone will mock me for visiting them. His voice stirs anxiety all through me. "I've got to go, Ibrahim. It is the middle of the night. I should never have come to your house. Please." I finish my wine and put down the glass, looking at the lights of the city reflected inside.

"I'll talk fast," he says, and then his words pour out. I laugh to myself imagining him smooth in a courtroom as opposed to tripping over himself now. My heart softens. "I was pushing on the jackhammer and it suddenly fell through the ground. I fell forward onto my face, scraped myself horribly. It fell through the ground, way way down, it just pierced through and fell, it sounded like it fell two stories before I heard it crash. I looked through the hole with a flashlight, but I still couldn't see much. It looks like a giant room. I don't know what to do. It just fell away from me. I could have fallen in."

"It fell through the ground?" Suddenly all my senses are alert.

"Yes, yes!" Ibrahim is excited. He knows he has my attention now. "Is it a tunnel? What is it? When are you coming back?"

"A tunnel? Do you have a digital camera?" My mind begins to race. Where did those stone steps lead after all?

"Yes," he says. I think I hear him clapping his hands together. "Of course I do. I'm getting it."

"Lower in lights by rope, reach your hand in, and take pictures. Three hundred sixty degrees," I supervise. "I saw some slabs that looked like steps. Send the attachments to my email address. But be really careful. Tie a rope around your waist and have someone hold the other end, or tie it around a pipe or something. That ground is very unstable. Don't even think about touching a jackhammer."

"The jackhammer is smashed to bits down there, so you don't have to worry about that. I'll do it now. I send you the pictures as soon as I can."

"Don't hurt yourself," I say. I am pacing on the balcony.

"Will you come?" he asks.

"Let me see the pictures first."

My laptop sits open on my bed. I change into my nightshirt and climb into bed with it, waiting. When the emails arrive, I click open the first JPEG. It is a photo of the shadowy walls of what seems to be a very deep cavern. I can see even from the shadowy image that the walls of the cavity beneath the Barakats' home are smooth. *Well, would you look at that. He found a goddamn cistern underneath his house.* I open the next four attachments, and they only confirm what I already know. On the sixth my computer freezes, but I've seen enough.

I leap up and begin pacing quickly all over the hotel room, trying to manage my expectations. The walls of cisterns are rock turned

silk, the surface burnished to a creamy shine. A cistern deep and un-
disturbed like that could have been used for a lot more than water. A
storehouse of weaponry, art, or burial. And the existence of a cistern
means there once had to be a substantial village nearby. Homes. Forti-
fications. Ibrahim has found a cistern. He isn't totally crazy after all.

A haunted cistern! I laugh, open-mouthed and out loud, nearly
bringing myself to tears. I sit on the edge of the bed, bouncing and
clasping my hands together. For the time being, no other archaeologist on earth knows it exists, and I find myself savoring this fact. I feel
a tiny vial of happiness deep inside me uncork, a taste of joy washing
through me. It is like being in the parking lot of an amusement park,
where I can hear all the noise of elation just a shoulder ride away.
I want to play in there, in that cistern. Quiet and dank. Moist and
clean. The idea of returning to Megiddo is dreadful. I could take a
sabbatical. I am giddy. Perhaps this is what I've been missing for the
past few years? Something I could call my own. A cave of spirits to
call home. Anything more animated than bone.

I think about Naima and Ibrahim, with their baklava and Dead
Sea salts. I remember how I ran away from that house. How leaden I
felt in there. Then I think about returning to Megiddo, and to Norris, and I feel worse. A cistern, I think, and new sparks ignite in me.
He found me a cistern.

I AM RELIEVED when I return to Megiddo to see that Norris's car is
gone. He and Mickey have already left for the dig. Orna sits in my
room with me as I pack my things.

I express my concerns with Orna about how my colleagues may
view me for going to spend time excavating the allegedly haunted
grounds of an Arab couple's home. Orna reassures me, "We are all
risk takers in this house. I quit school to marry Mickey. Mickey left
Russia. We both took a chance moving to Megiddo." She pulls and
twists one of the fringes on my blanket and adds solemnly, "From
what I hear about Anata, however, I do think you are making a mis-

take. But"—she tosses the blanket aside—"you don't have a family. You are young enough to survive big mistakes."

"I'm almost forty," I say, stuffing clothing into a duffel bag. I am surprised at how little I've accumulated here after all this time. Barely enough to fill the trunk of a car.

"Almost forty?" Orna says, genuinely surprised. "I didn't even think you were thirty-five. But I'm Israeli. We age quicker than Americans. It makes me laugh, thinking about all of the antiwrinkle cream you Americans buy. You don't have the lifestyle that causes wrinkles in the first place! You have the luxury of water to waste, high-fat diets, low-stress environments . . ."

I look up at her. "Your skin is perfect." I say, and it is. She smiles.

"My skin is thick. Don't worry, Page, you're still plenty young enough to get it all wrong and then find a way to make it all right."

With everything in my car, I return to my room to check one last time. I reach out the window and pull a handful of small cherry tomatoes off a vine, popping them into my mouth. They burst with the flavor of summer and bring me courage to call Norris's cell phone.

I sit on my bed, now stripped of its bedding. I run my hand over the bare mattress. Norris answers immediately, as if the cell phone had been waiting, right by his ear.

"Why do you do this to me?" he sighs before I can say more than a few words. I imagine him rising from a crouched position, stretching, twisting his back so it pops.

"What am I doing to you?" I ask. "They found a cistern under their house. I have a lot of vacation time that I've never taken, and I want to explore there a little. I will delegate supervision of the shaft tombs to—"

"I brought you to Megiddo," he interrupts. He sounds disappointed. "I believed in you. I have always been good to you, supportive, encouraging. And I always thought I would get some return."

"Some return?" I feel myself sink lower into the mattress with a dreadful feeling we are talking about the kiss.

"I'm talking about friendship. Real friendship. I think I deserve at least that much. I have always been supportive of you—and of your work." *Always, except the time you crumpled my manuscript.* I stare out the window and think for a heartbeat.

"I have always been friendly with you, and grateful, and supportive." I try to sound matter-of-fact.

"I know you've been friendly, but you haven't ever really been a friend. Remember when I had a flu earlier this year? The same flu I get every year. I was in bed for a week. Orna brought me chicken soup. Mickey brought me the newspaper and sat by me. Everyone wanted to help me but you." I imagine him at the dig, walking now across it, waving amicably toward colleagues and volunteers until he finds a private place to talk.

"It was just a flu, Norris," I say, trying to think back to when he had the flu. I cannot remember.

"It is not that it was just a flu. It is that you never came into my room. You would peek your head in and ask how I was feeling, but you didn't really care. Maybe you thought I'd try to kiss you again." Something has entered his voice. A seething.

Suddenly I do remember his having the flu. I did peek in, and immediately thought about the story of Tamar in Second Samuel. *Amnon lay down and pretended to be sick . . . Tamar went to the house of her brother Amnon, who was in bed . . . but when she served the cakes to him, he caught hold of her . . . he overpowered her and lay with her by force.* Norris is right, I'd been afraid to enter his bedroom because I had worried he wanted more than a few soothing words.

"Believe me, Page, I would never make that mistake again." I could feel his anger swelling. "But then the truth hit me. You really don't like me at all. You tolerate me."

My eyes begin to well. I feel my strength leaking out of me. "Norris, you are breaking my heart. Stop it."

"I already have a grown daughter to worry about. And now you want to leave us for them. For those perverts!" He raises his voice a notch. He must be alone now, out of range of any eavesdroppers. Perhaps he is behind an olive tree, or ducked down in one of Solomon's stables. "Am I too commonplace? I bore you? Megiddo with all of its history, it means nothing to you?"

"Norris, I am that way with everyone," I find myself struggling to defend myself. Norris is right, I think. Thirty-nine years old and I only have one real friend—Jordanna. But I thought by now that Norris would have understood me better.

Norris is speaking slowly. Deliberately. "I have been by your side for twelve years. And like it or not, it's me who mentored you and brought you to Israel and made you supervisor over a dream of an excavation site, planning to hand this whole project over to you some day. I don't want you to become the laughingstock of our profession. I care about you, and I care about my work. I didn't put this much into you so that you could become a laughingstock." That's the problem with some mentors. They want to mold you into something you haven't yet chosen for yourself, and then they fall in love with their promised creation. He wanted a star and got a black hole.

As Norris speaks, I slide off the mattress onto the floor, leaning my head back. I can feel the static electricity between my hair and the mattress, thin gold strands lifting into the air. We had been able to move on from the kiss to a certain point. We had been able to move on from his tirade over my manuscript. But I am not sure we could ever recover from this conversation. All this time, I've treated him like a parent, and all this time I never realized who he really was. Have I been so self-obsessed, ruminating over my own loneliness, that I never noticed?

I interrupt pitifully, "I'm so sad because I've hurt you, Norris; you have been a rock for me. I never wanted you to think I haven't been a friend! I'm disassociated. But I can change. Take back what you said about me not being a friend!"

Norris laughs. "Take it back? Page, it's how I feel!" He sounds almost as if he is enjoying this.

A flame of frustration burns through me. "Well, what am I supposed to do? I can't rewind twelve years." I am lying on the floor now beside my empty bed, staring up at its metal frame, and past to the ceiling. My eyes are aching, my head pounding.

"I don't really care what you do. I mean, in terms of you and me. I have my own issues to sort through and, to be honest, you are the least of them. So don't flatter yourself. But I do care what you do when it comes to archaeology. That I take personally."

"You are being so mean to me," I barely manage to whisper.

"I am trying to save you. Is that mean? I have every right to be angry with you for abandoning this dig."

"I'm not abandoning it." I try to sound convincing. "I just thought I'd take some time off. You know I've been having a hard time lately, that my heart hasn't been in it. A change may refresh me. And it has been so tense between you and me."

"Don't kid yourself," he says curtly.

"I've given twelve years."

"And I've been here thirty."

"You make it sound like I've given nothing, like I've been horrible this whole time."

"You've done great work here and you know it, everyone knows it, but I am someone who is in it for life. And I thought you'd be there too."

"We're not getting a divorce, Norris." I know as soon as I say this that it is a mistake. Norris had just begun to sound calmer.

His anger now seems to swell up, over and around me like the sail of a giant pirate ship. "You are the one who is making a fool of yourself, Page! You! Not me! Am I getting through to you? Sometimes I think you have your head underwater! Those people probably went to every dig in the entire country telling their inane story and you are the only one—the only one—in this whole fucking country moronic enough to listen! How does that make you feel?"

"Please stop," I whisper, though I'm not sure the words are heard. "I thought of you like a father."

"Oh," he says with extreme sarcasm, "it all makes sense now: you think of me as your dead father. A fucking ghost! If you leave this dig, it makes me look bad too. Any archaeologist would give their right arm to do what you do, in a place as rich as Megiddo! I don't deserve that from you." He pauses, and then adds with difficulty, "You don't deserve that from yourself."

"But—" I start.

"You could stick a shovel anywhere in the world and find something! My God, that Bedouin kid who found the Dead Sea Scrolls? Or that kid who tried to pick up a pebble in a playground and it turned out to be the tip of some wooly mammoth tusk? People find things everywhere. Illiterate shepherds find things. So what. You didn't get a master's degree to become a commonplace shepherd. Am I getting through that thick head of yours? Knock, knock." I hear Norris bang the phone against something, a stone perhaps. "Can you hear me? Are you listening?"

I am silent.

"I wanted to mentor you. And I take pride in your successes. But if you leave this dig for that house of horrors, I swear I will regret bringing you here for the remainder of my days."

I close my eyes and hold the phone away from me, choking back the tears. I roll over onto my side. The floor under the bed is coated with dust.

"How can I come back, knowing how much you hate me?" I ask, and immediately regret it, because the minute I ask it I know that the real reason Norris is so angry is that he thinks he is in love with me.

"You are so blind! You see everything that isn't there and nothing that is. Hate you? I am furious with you! But hate? You don't know anything. You make me want to punch a wall."

I wipe off my eyes with the back of my hand. "I'm sorry for not knowing anything," I say, defeated, exhausted. What I don't say is, *It is not my fault you think you're in love with me, but I am sorry I didn't pay attention. I'm sorry I didn't see you for the person you are.*

"All right then," he says, his tone a bit softer now. I can imagine him rubbing his hand against his rough cheek, thinking.

We hang on the phone for a long moment. I imagine him staring up as well, at a cloudless sky.

"I'm sorry," I whisper.

"Yeah, I know," Norris snaps.

"I'm terribly sad," I confess, trying to reconnect with him.

"Good," Norris says, almost teasingly. We both pause, our breath hanging in the air.

"Norris?" I venture forward with hope. Maybe a friendship can be redeemed. We've recovered from disagreements before.

"What."

"I need you to believe I've been as much a friend to you as I've been to anyone. It's how I am. I'm poorly wired." As I say it, I believe it.

"Page?" Norris says, his voice stiffening again.

"What?" I wait meekly, now lying limp on the floor.

"Fuck you."

When I shut off the phone, I lie very still. I close my eyes and imagine I am on a subway, speeding under the earth. My body begins to relax. It is done, I think to myself. I will never allow him to speak to me that way again. It is over. I imagine we are hurtling through space, my father and I, racing the clock. We are going to make it. Norris will convince them all that I'm out of my mind. I know he will. But I'm okay. When I finally lift my head off the floor, the ends of my hair pull a train of dust like a long antique mantilla from under the bed. I see myself in the mirror and stare for a moment before pulling the dust off me. That's the last time, I think again. It's over.

Orna walks me to the car. She has loaded the back seat with extra equipment, a loan that she says Norris will never notice. I embrace her and feel safe and comforted wrapped in her arms.

"There will be an archaeological field day featuring me on a spit for everyone to roast," I say as we release each other.

"People have their demons," she says, as if sharing her secret wisdom. She smiles at me tenderly. "As well as their ghosts."

"I know," I say. I get into the car and take her hand through the window.

"Anyway, you're still a landsman, right?" she says perkily. "You're not leaving Israel any time soon? We can get together." I smile, give her hand one last squeeze, and pull away.

VII

*Someday someone will uncover these, my words inscribed, and my
name her lips will murmur, summoning up my sleepy spirit . . .
I believe with perfect faith that she will release me, that she will
speak me, resurrect me, and save me . . . We must live and record,
brilliant interpreter, lest the libraries be stacked with scrolls of war
and not one leaf of love.*

—THE SCROLL OF ANATIYA 17:1–9

I feel different. I feel ignited, youthful, and vital for the first time
in a long while. In grade school I traipsed to a special spot in the
front office a few times a year to retrieve a jacket or a notebook.
They called it the lost and found, although it was just an old mail bin
stuffed under the receptionist's desk. This place, right here, beneath
this house, I suspect, is the real lost and found.

It is early afternoon and Ibrahim helps me lower a long ladder
into the cistern. I am the first to climb down the rickety rungs, with
a lantern tied to one of the belt loops on my shorts. On the last rung,
a verse from the Revelation of Saint John the Divine comes to me:
*I saw a star fall from heaven unto the earth, and to him was given the key of
the bottomless pit.* When I was immersed in Bible studies in divinity
school, verses seemed to materialize to me wherever I went, scripted
into brick, bark and the migration of birds. Sacred words would fall

into my lashes like snowflakes. However, there has been so little for a long, long while, until this moment, and I am washed with gratitude. I feel that a part of my heart that had been sealed with silver battlement, a chamber of enchanted ancient prose, has been opened again to me. That I've been presented, in this cistern, with a key.

At the bottom of the pit I see the outline of a rectangular object, lying on the ground, a few feet from the smashed jackhammer. My heart starts to pound. Even as I walk toward the thing, I am sweetly aware of the dank, delicious smell of earth. I have penetrated a pocket of air that hasn't been breathed in over a thousand years. I walk toward the object, squinting. It is a book. I pick it up. A Koran.

"Ibrahim!" I call up. "I thought you said you hadn't been down here!" My voice reverberates. I feel a pang of disappointment. I want to be the first.

"I haven't." I can see his little face peering over the ledge down at me. "When I broke through, I was so frightened that Naima told me to throw a Koran in, chase away the bad spirits."

There are no bad spirits here, I think to myself, smiling and looking around. I walk the perimeter of the space, running my fingers along the wall. It is like entering the ventricles of my own heart.

At the first light of dawn, the king arose and rushed to the lion's den . . . Daniel then talked with the king, "My God sent his angel, who shut the mouths of the lions so that they did not injure me." All the lions of my fear are being shut up. There are no bad spirits here. Angels in this den, perhaps.

This is a sacred space, I think. A healing space. The walls feel to me deeply loved, incessantly caressed to bald, rubbed of nubs by water, smoothed the way a much-loved toy is effaced of texture from the child's constant sleepy massage. Cisterns are magic cradles, all of a city's purity humming deep inside the earth.

There are nooks in the wall where oil lamps once shimmered. Rooms usually have fours walls, but caves are really composed of one wall, winding in and around itself like a Möbius strip. There is a ledge all around the perimeter, clearly built after the cistern was no longer in use. The cistern floor is teardrop-shaped, forty-one and a

quarter feet at its longest diameter, and twenty-three at its widest—
about a thousand square feet total. The steps are located at the single
southern point.

Looking up, I see the living room light seeping into the hole. I
feel like a genie, frolicking at the bottom of my big-bellied samovar.
When I stand just below the hole, I can see the ceiling fan with its
four protruding lights. I can be happy here, I marvel. I wonder to
myself if I have this feeling simply because I am away from Norris.
Sitting in the middle of the floor I shake my head. I don't think so.
It is beautiful here. It is so beautiful here, no wonder the Barakats
were driven mad to find it. I hear them talking far above me. She is
calling to him, asking him to be sure to pick up eggs and lamb. There
is something so lovely about a dig that traces itself to pure intuition.
Its origin is in trusting oneself, therefore any discovery is inevitably a
self-discovery.

I spend the day taking measurements, noting the places where
the rock seems disturbed. Along with the eggs and lamb, I've given
Ibrahim a list of equipment to buy including long electrical cords
and floodlights. I asked him if Israeli hardware stores sell Christmas lights. It would be nice to illuminate the ceiling, if possible. He
looked at me quizzically and I laughed and said never mind.

Naima has given me the small room upstairs that Ibrahim
uses as his study. Two walls are lined with chipboard bookshelves,
which lean ominously, filled with heavy volumes of law. Boxes and
stacks of books make a maze of mesas across the burgundy and
gold Persian rug. There is an old metal school desk in the corner of
the room with a big eggshell computer, and more stacks of books.
A comfortable bed, tucked tightly with army-style blankets, is opposite the door, and Naima's left a pitcher of iced tea on a beat-up
nightstand. A stained-glass floor lamp dapples the room in amber
and red diamonds.

Each morning I wake early, slip out of the house in jeans and a
T-shirt, and walk, retracing my steps past Elazar's *Falafel, Cigarettes,
Fruit, Tours* stand and up to Jeremiah's tomb. I don't enter with the

worshippers, but Edna, still handing out modest wraps at the entrance, greets me. I pause at the top, taking in the quilted landscape, the same way I would survey the Via Maris and olive groves from Megiddo's summit.

Verses of Ecclesiastes spill over the horizon, flooding the vineyards with light. *What profit has a man of all his labor wherein he labors under the sun? One generation passes away, and another generation comes: but the earth abides forever. The sun also rises, and the sun goes down, and hastens to its place where it rises again. All things are full of weariness . . . and there is nothing new under the sun.*

I stretch my arms out, as if gathering clouds, and close my eyes toward the sun, which hovers over the distant hills, the warmth making pink spirals behind my lids. Maybe there is something new under you, I think. Maybe there is more than weariness to this world.

I head back down the slope, my heart pumping, lungs full. I stop at Elazar's stand and have a strong shot of coffee, practice my poor Arabic with the workers who sit there each morning. Then I return and descend into a cradle of earth, surfacing around lunch and again for dinner and to go to bed.

Two days after I move in with the Barakats, I invite Itai to come, hoping to acquire the necessary permits to make the dig official so I can bring in a small crew. I have some money saved up, and I also consider contacting Mr. Jerrold March.

Itai brings his puppy to Anata. I stand at the end of the front walk and see his car coming up the road, with him swatting at the dog in the passenger seat. I am nervous about his coming here, nervous that he won't help me legitimize it. I look behind me at the house. The sun-bleached stone and dark windows, which had seemed so pleasant and inviting the first visit, now seem to grow out of the dusty ground like Goliath's skull. Itai's car pulls up, kicking a light spray of gravel at my calves.

"Cute house. Nice flowers." He smiles. He holds up a poppy to me. I take it and thank him. Naima is at the door, and Itai's puppy immediately dashes into the house.

"*S'licha*," Itai apologizes and dashes past Naima after the dog, shouting, "Mazal! Mazal! *Bo alai!* Mazal, where are you?"

I stand on the threshold, the mobile of glinting butterknives just over my head. I grimace while I listen to him inside. I know what is coming. "Mazal? Mazal? What the . . . *oy va voy, aizeh ketah!*"

I hurry in to find Itai with Mazal in his arms standing in the living room before the pit. Ibrahim and I have done our best to clean up the gouged-out foundation. Wires have been dropped in and the lights are set up so that out of the punctured bottom of the chiseled pit rises a promising shine. I imagine it from Itai's perspective. It looks as if a glowing marble of a meteor struck someone's house, just missing the TV and the couch to make a neat little crater where a coffee table should be.

Itai's eyes skim lightly over the edges of the torn-up floor. Mazal is in Itai's arms, her nose powdered with concrete dust. When he sets her down, she sniffs the surroundings, her tail beating the dust out of couches and chairs.

Ibrahim enters the room, stopping in his tracks when he sees Itai. Itai just stares at the punctured floor, addressing it in Hebrew. "Ibrahim Barakat. The Arab human rights lawyer. Isn't that an oxymoron?"

Ibrahim's face darkens. He also keeps his eyes on the mouth of the pit. Perhaps for my benefit, he responds in English, "A pleasure to welcome you to my home, Mr. Harani."

Itai, now also speaking in English, continues addressing the pit as he paces around it slowly, testing the floor before committing to each next step. "No freedom of the press. No right to criticize government. No freedom of speech. Arrests without trial. When a man murders his wife or daughter, it is an honor killing. You practice human rights in a society that encourages their children to kill themselves, tells them if they commit suicide and take a few lives with them, they will be praised. How can you speak of human rights within a community that doesn't even love its own children?"

"Suicide killings speak more of hopelessness and desperation than of the love or lack thereof between a parent and a child." Ibrahim's tone is lawyerly, his anger restrained. I look at the jagged edges of the living room floor around the hole. It seems to be participating in the conversation as well, its mouth opened wide at their feet like a mass grave waiting to be filled, and I am suddenly afraid I'll be drawn in. I reach my hand behind me and grab hold of the pretty yellow curtain that lines the window.

After living the better part of twelve years in Israel, I am no longer surprised how quickly strangers engage in arguing politics. In America, religion and politics are pools people wade into gradually.

"I have a friend. His uncle was buying flowers for his wife for Shabbat when he was killed. How would a human rights lawyer explain that to his four children? Why a nineteen-year-old strapped explosives and nails all over his body and then blew himself apart. And then, to see Palestinians in Gaza dancing and celebrating his death, carrying posters of the homicide bomber like he is some kind of a hero."

Ibrahim speaks softly. "I was not dancing. Nor were any of my friends. We wept. Not only for your friend's uncle, but for a world that teaches a boy that he can serve his people best not through education and social justice but through death. What a terribly hopeless world, if this is what a boy thinks."

"No," Itai says, looking up at Ibrahim for the first time. "You didn't have time for dancing. You were busy preparing to defend the bomber's family because the government demolished their house. You were trying to get compensation for them."

"Questioning punitive house demolitions does not mean I condone murder," Ibrahim says, holding Itai's steady stare. They remain locked this way for a measure that may be a heartbeat or two but that creates a vacuum that I fear threatens to swallow everything up.

I let go of the curtain and speak quickly, unnaturally upbeat. "I read about you, Ibrahim, on the internet. How you represented three men who were suspected of selling land to Jews. One had rebuilt a fence and was accused of rebuilding it one and a half inches short of his lot's perimeter, and his neighbor was a Jew. He was accused of ceding more than an inch to Israel. I forget what the other two had done. All three were sentenced to death, right?"

Ibrahim blinks and looks at me. Itai's hand goes to his hip. Ibrahim says mournfully, "They were peaceful men who were executed. Everyone knew them as peaceful."

I look at Itai and continue, "And I read that you represented eight Palestinian men who had been accused of criticizing the Palestinian Authority. A couple were sentenced to death. Some were sentenced to life at hard labor, some have their trials pending and have been waiting for years. And, their admissions were extracted under torture—hammer blows to the head, threats to rape their sisters."

Ibrahim sighs. "There is very little in this world as futile as a human rights lawyer in an authoritarian regime supported by dictatorships."

"Like chasing ghosts," I point out.

Itai is pressing his lips together and holding his stomach, trying not to laugh. We both look at him. I am angry, and Ibrahim looks deeply insulted, but Itai points at me and says with wonder, "Look who is suddenly interested in the above-ground world! Page talking politics." He slaps his head in disbelief. He cranes his head over the pit and says, "You sure you haven't unearthed the Messiah down there?"

I laugh too, and Ibrahim loosens. He nods at Itai as if they have reached an agreement. Then Itai points down into the hole and says with a voice full of humor, "The leading spokesperson against house demolition, and look at your own living room." He crouches down to scratch Mazal under the chin and looks back up at Ibrahim. "How do you defend this, the demolition of your own house?"

"This is a calling, and I confess, it may have no logical defense."

Itai walks the small perimeter of the pit one more time. He kneels and gingerly touches the edge of a torn floorboard. Then he rises and looks at me. "You are something else, Miss Brookstone." His eyes dance over me. My senses tingle and my pulse quickens. Then he informs me, "Israel, on the other hand, respects human rights. She introduced the concept of civil liberties to the Arab world," and I remember *her* beside him, sneaking her leg up over him, reveling in her eternal youth.

Itai invites me to come to the department to fill out some paperwork. He says, "There may be some technical loopholes since it's inside a private abode; I'll do my research. But since people are talking, I want to make sure it's all *kasher*." At the door we embrace, and he touches his lips to the corner of my eye. Withdrawing a bit, he lets his eyes settle for a moment on the hollow of my throat. I feel heat rise up my neck, reddening my cheeks.

"*B'seder*," he says, pulling away quickly. "I have to get home to Sharon." Releasing me, he gives me a lingering sympathetic smile and then gestures to his dog, "*Boi Mazal*, time to go," and the pup bounds to his side. After Itai's car door shuts, Ibrahim picks up a broom and begins sweeping the foyer, even though the floor is clean.

I watch him for a moment, finding his repetitive motions calming. "Are you okay?" I ask.

He says, "He's right, and I know it. Israel has taught us about human rights as only a democracy can. I have stood up in Israeli courts. I know the difference when I can't get a Palestinian judge to allow any medical examining of detainees. No impartial exam. I do feel like an oxymoron," he says, and lifts his eyes to me, and I see that they are unfathomable wells of sadness. "Why try? But every now and then, a heart is turned, a prison cell gets opened, the violent world cools by a fraction of a degree, and hope breathes . . ."

He laughs ironically, leans on the broom, and looks toward the living room. "Those men who were executed? They *haunt* me," he says. Naima is standing at the entrance to the dining room, her arms lightly crossed. She watches him from behind while he looks toward the hole. He continues, "I begged for their lives in Palestinian courts. They were good men. Smart men. Professors. But I was as much an idiot to the officials as Naima and I were to you and your colleagues. I couldn't get them out and nearly got myself killed many times trying."

I follow his gaze toward the pit and imagine the souls of all the men he has tried to represent trapped in there. I look at him, his sad eyes and brow set with thinking, and it dawns on me that he is as desperate to unspool death as I am.

I say, "You have learned from Israel, but there is a lot she can learn from you as well."

He turns slowly toward me and half smiles. "From you too," he assures me, and I feel a sweet pleasure embrace me. Naima and I look to each other and smile in a way akin to sister-wives who share a generous love for the same man.

VIII

Your flesh is white-hot and fine gold. I want to sear my body against it. My thoughts turn from all that is holy. I want to ravage you like Ruth on the threshing floor. I want to lie at your feet while you sleep . . . I want to bite into you, tug at your hair in clumps, beat that vicious God out of you, thresh out intrusive visions and leave only skin and pulse and want. I fall to my knees before a stream's muddy bank and choke on tears as hard as diamonds.

—THE SCROLL OF ANATIYA 17:10–16

I stand just before the long Moorish-style reflecting pool in the cloister garden of the Rockefeller Archaeological Museum looking toward the main building, whose central tower rises up like a well-structured octagonal wedding cake. The pool is fed by two underground cisterns, and the thought of those living bellies of water pleases me. The Department of Antiquities is housed here, and I decide to take the long walk toward its wing, winding through the museum's extensive collections. Rows and rows of pottery greet me with mouths gaping like giant puffball mushrooms after releasing spores. I admire the Crusader stonework, the ornamented Persian columns and Islamic tablets. Gods and goddesses in classic profiles stare at me, one-eyed, from detailed Egyptian ivories. I pass through stone arches from the Iron Age to the noble statuary of the Romans. I lean over one of the long display cases housing leaves of the Dead Sea Scrolls in a long, bright hall. I try to read it in its ancient script, and I'm able to pick out a few verses.

There is an Orthodox Jewish man in the same hall leaning over another case, running his finger over the glass as he reads. The sun streaming in from one of the tall arched windows ignites the rim of his black hat like a dark halo. In his long black coat he stands in stark relief against the white walls. It is hard to ignore him, even in this giant room. I try to focus on the verses before me, the miraculous survival of these letters, and meanwhile in the corner of my eye he moves like the shadow of a shark.

I am uncomfortable and abandon the parchment, slipping into a smaller room whose cases glint with jewelry and coins. There is a display featuring a number of bullae, little dollops of clay impressed with a seal; they were generally attached to documents to identify the scribe. I admire the ones here. Four of these bullae caused quite a stir not too long ago, and one in particular. All four are impressed with the names of scribes found in the Book of Jeremiah. Two have the name Baruch son of Neriah impressed on them, the scribe who accompanied the prophet. I lean in to look at the most famous of the bullae and the magnified photo beside it. On the upper left of the bulla is the clear impression of a fingerprint. The fingerprint of Jeremiah's scribe.

I straighten up when he walks in. The room is so small, I feel as uncomfortable as I do when I'm in an elevator with a stranger, when neither knows where to look. I am staring at a beaded necklace on the wall, rather unremarkable, when I hear him say, "Excuse me, are you *Geveret* Brookstone?" I turn around.

His black hat, tipped awkwardly back on his head, looks out of place atop hair the color of straw that has been steeped in a tea of strawberries. It is closely cropped—he has no sidelocks—but still unruly, as if it wants to mutiny against that hat and grow wild. His face is clean shaven. The top two buttons of his white shirt are unbuttoned. His clothes and pants don't seem to fit right. It is as if I am seeing two men, one superimposed upon the other. One is lit with honeyed hues and bright blue eyes. The other is dark and piously morose. It is as if a handsome American farm boy has been crossed with an Orthodox Jew. He is creepy, and I feel the air thin in the room, which suddenly seems littler.

"Yes," I say politely. "And you are?"

"Mortichai Masters," he says, and I automatically extend my hand to him, expecting to shake hands as is the way of the world when meeting someone new, but he only looks down at my outstretched hand as if it is one of the ivories on display, and I feel my neck become flushed with embarrassment. I have forgotten for a moment that the Orthodox Jews don't touch any woman besides their wives.

"Nice to meet you," I say, dropping my hand and stepping toward the exit. "I have to go."

"I attended a lecture of yours at Tel Aviv University," he says. "The Tombs of Faith."

"Thank you," I say, and the redness creeps higher up my neck because I realize he hasn't complimented me.

"Your heart wasn't in it," he notes, his voice as monotone as a radiator.

A shudder runs down my back. "Um, all right," I say, backing out into the hall. Before I leave him, I can't help but ask with sarcasm, "And who are you again?" I walk away swiftly before he says anything in return. I visit the Byzantine collection, glancing over my shoulder to see if he's followed me, until I am able to relax and enjoy the miniatures. The collections are all rich, and yet all I can think about is my cistern. Even if it contains nothing but the caresses of water, I think, it is precious. I drift through the rooms a little longer.

I enter the big walnut doors to the Antiquities Authority, where Itai works. I immediately sense a low-decibel hum of people talking about me. I hear whispered snippets in Hebrew: "She's leaving Megiddo." "A little crazy." "An Arab family." "Ghosts." As I approach the waiting area, I see Itai's secretary. She is plump and wears her top stretched below her shoulders. She wears glasses studded with rhinestones. Even though he is dressed basically like every other Orthodox Jew, from the back I recognize Mr. Masters immediately by the way the cuffs of his pants are too high on his long legs, the way his coat sleeves barely reach his wrists, and the way those wisps of rose blond curls are trying to escape for dear life.

I hear Itai's secretary saying to him in Hebrew, "His next appointment is with a ghost hunter." Her eyes widen, looking at him over her specs and nodding. Then she notices me and bolts upright, exclaiming, "Page! *Shalom*, he's on a call, but I'll let him know you're here."

I sit down and Mr. Masters turns to me. I look down and snatch a copy of Israel's archaeology publication, *Atiqot*, off the side table.

He speaks to me as if he hasn't noticed that I backed out of the room clearly uninterested in talking with him only a short while ago. "I was saying that your heart wasn't in it in the same way that it is in your writing."

I glance up at him, shrug and half smile, then look back down at the publication. He says more, as if he is talking to himself. "I understand there is a cistern in Anata."

I slap the publication down and snap, "Who told you that?"

"*Gever* Anderson posted an article on *Hadashot Arkheologiyot's* website. I called him and he confirmed it."

I laugh. No wonder I find him creepy. "Aha," I say, "a friend of Norris's. I'm sure he also told you exactly what he thinks of me."

Now Mr. Masters looks down at his feet. "I wouldn't repeat what he said."

"Right," I say, opening the publication again. What is taking Itai so long?

I can feel the strange man still looking at me. I feel him like a shadow looming over me, the same way Norris would stand over me, criticizing and mocking, while I crouched in the sand. He drones, "Jeremiah the prophet lived in Anatot."

"Oh really," I say without looking up from my pages. I make my voice as flat as his. "I had no idea. I wonder if there is a book or something where I could find out more."

Mortichai Masters doesn't seem to pick up on sarcasm. "Yes," he rambles. "It says, *So I bought the land in Anatot from my cousin Hanamel. I weighed out the money to him, seventeen shekels of silver.* More significant for you is the verse in that chapter, *Take these documents, this deed of purchase, the sealed text and the open one, and put them into an earthen jar.*"

Does he think I need a lesson on biblical history? He claims he attended one of my lectures. Doesn't he realize that I know this stuff better than anyone, even when my heart isn't in it? I say, "Yes, I know chapter thirty-two. And it follows: *The Lord said unto Jeremiah, 'build ye a cistern twelve cubits deep that the waters of justice may never run dry.' And the prophet did so, using only a flint, and he kneweth that some day to be sure, a woman would descend into that place where her reputation might be marred-eth for life.*"

"There is no such verse," he says drily. I can detect no humor in him at all. He says, "Is it possible that it is the same cistern from chapter forty-one where it says—"

"I know what it says," I interrupt, looking at him sharply. "*The cistern into which Ishmael threw all the corpses of the men he had killed.*" I am flushed with anger at myself, astounded that with all the verses of light and redemption that have been flooding me the past few days, this one about a cistern, potentially in Anata, so obvious, never appeared.

He looks back at me steadily. I realize he is not much older than I am, perhaps forty? Forty-two? His face is freckled with faint clusters of dots. His skin is like a cream drizzled with maple syrup. The pupils of his pale eyes widen, an inkling that maybe he's finally figured out that I'm being rude to him. "*You* are the ghost hunter they are talking about," he says, piecing a puzzle together.

"Sue me," I say. The secretary is watching us while she types emails.

Mr. Masters turns to her and says, "Let *Gever* Harani know that I dropped by. Here is my card." He hands her a card from inside his long black coat and then turns to walk out. However, he pauses to say to me, "If it is the same cistern mentioned in the Book of Jeremiah, which was filled with corpses, and if it is haunted with the spirits of those men who rotted there, unavenged, then I'd be concerned you have some pretty hostile ghosts you're dealing with, *Geveret*." He tips his hat at me like a cowboy and walks out.

"Who the hell was that?" I ask the secretary after the door closes.

She looks at the business card and says, "I don't know, but it says he works for CROSS." She squints at it and reads, "Christian Remains Salvation Society."

My eyebrows lift. "He works for an organization called CROSS?" I grunt to myself and say, "Well, isn't that one mess of contradictions."

She looks at me over her glasses as if to suggest maybe I am not one to judge anyone else. Still, she suggests, "Probably a bone hunter."

This makes immediate and clear sense to me. The attorney general of Israel ruled many years ago that human bones are not covered under the antiquities law, so the Antiquities Authority cannot keep the contents of graves for study but must send them to the religious authorities. Often times, despite pressure, remains can sit in labs for years before being handed over to be reburied, which infuriates the faithful. Aside from the historical value of these archaeological finds, DNA extracted from the bones of remains provides vital data about the history of genetic disorders. The loss of access to these ancient remains places a large stumbling block in the path of research.

Personally, I appreciate having respect for the dead. I really do. But I'd have more respect for them if they'd get up and do something. Lending themselves to science allows them to continue contributing long after their names have been forgotten.

But in Jewish law, respect for the dead is of critical importance. The very sanctity of life hinges upon respect for the dead. Therefore, graves cannot be disturbed, and when remains are discovered in an archaeological site or construction zone, the holdups can be severe. I know archaeologists who have received death threats from ultra-Orthodox sects for disturbing gravesites, and three years ago there was an arson case at the Antiquities Authority's main office. A couple of years after I came to Megiddo, there was a gathering of thirty or so black-hatted protestors blockading our way to the vertical shaft tombs.

In actuality, the religious authority only has a mandate when the remains are clearly Jewish. Burial jars were a Canaanite practice, so the thousands of infants I've discovered buried in them do not require such strict attention. I can deal with them as I see fit, which means I keep the finds covered and protected when I am not work-ing and I photograph each stage. After everything is documented, I call my physical anthropologist, who takes over, bringing the remains to the lab and reconstructing this person's life and death, looking for evidence of pathologies and disease.

Itai's secretary buzzes me into his office. Itai stands up and wel-comes me from behind his thick oak desk, and we sit across from each other. His window overlooks Sultan Suleiman Street in East Jerusalem, and I can hear the clatter of cars and commerce below. A long, crackled leather couch sits against a wall of books. I remember that couch when it was in his apartment. Sharon must have made him take it away. I remember that couch well. I bite my lip.

"Your new secretary was blabbing to some kooky bone hunter about me," I say.

"I hate the bone hunters. Violent toward the living to protect the dead. Did you know the construction of this very building was delayed because of an ancient graveyard? Practially every construction site in Israel gets delayed because someone finds something which usually turns out to be the thigh of a Paleolithic mule."

Before he can add something along the lines of "But my Israel, she keeps right on reaching for the sky," I jump in. "Why are they all talking about me? What do they care what I do?"

"That's what we do here." He laughs kindly. "We care about what archaeologists unearth. Anyway, Norris blew through here like a storm yesterday while I was visiting you at Anata. He was cursing about spirits and demented Arabs and homosexuals and cisterns, so you can't be too shocked if people are talking."

"Homosexuals?" I ask.

"Honestly, I don't know what he was talking about. He ridiculed you. The point is, word has spread about it, less because it is controversial and more because people always need something to take their minds off their own problems. You probably should go back to Megiddo and ride it out."

I pale listening to Itai. The idea of Norris leaping into his car and tearing like a tornado through the department, spinning tales about me, makes me feel invaded. "He called me yesterday," Itai continues. "He told me about the dig and asked me to put a stop to it. I told him that you had already spoken with me about permits, and he blew a fuse. He huffed, 'Well then, that's that,' and hung up." I turn white. I feel my eyes widen, and my breath becomes shallow.

"I'm excavating this cistern," I say, mustering courage. "I am not returning to Megiddo."

Itai sits back in his chair and it squeaks. He is smiling widely. "I know that already." He pushes a folder across the desk for me. The tab reads, "Excavation: Anata." He says, "I've filled most of it out already."

I sigh deeply. I feel the color return to my face. "Thank you."

"As you know, we generally like to assign an Israeli to help supervise any digs in our country. At some point, it may help keep things kosher if I send someone to assist you."

I nod. "Of course. Can you give me a little time though just to soak it in on my own?"

Itai puts his hands behind his head and studies me. He says, "Norris always hated me, because I had you." My eyes linger on his mouth. The leather couch seems to swell. I remember lying on it with him. I remember that with my head on the armrest it holds me comfortably, even with my legs straight. He says, "Tell me something else about your life. You know, we once shared something much more than work, *motek*."

When I leave through the front of the museum, I see Mr. Masters sitting on the edge of the reflecting pool, looking down at the sky. I hurry past him and say nothing, and he says nothing to me.

IX

"If you have no respect for the void and its immense power," the potter revealed to us, "then you cannot understand." Jeremiah bowed his head and whispered, "I understand . . . that the breath of God is in man before he is ever formed from the clay."
—THE SCROLL OF ANATIYA 18:12–13

Excavating, at its best, can be meditative. My hands revisit steady motions again and again, like a bodily mantra. Alone in the pit, I am certain that I've made the right decision in coming here.

I've been at the Barakats' home for a week. Before that, the idea of my colleagues laughing at me would have been terrifying, it would have been a death. But now I realize that my fear was only the cowardice of the partially committed. When you put your toe in the pool, the water is cold and immersion seems impossible. But if you forget the toe dip and just dive straight in, shooting through the water, your skin shouts *hallelujah!* as if a year has just been added to your life.

I am relaxed. I can imagine so clearly the faint glimmer of the ancient oil lamps on the walls of the cistern. I recognize it as a kind of hope. Only at night, as I lie on an unfamiliar bed, looking across the room, the stacks of books make an eerie forest, and I remember what the Orthodox bone hunter said. I remember the story from

Jeremiah. The king of Ammon sent Ishmael son of Nethaniah to
assassinate the governor of Judah. It had been a time of relative peace.
Governor Gedaliah had been sent warnings that Ishmael intended
to murder him, but he didn't believe them. Ishmael slaughtered him,
and all the Judeans with him. A fourth-century bloodbath. *The cistern
into which Ishmael threw all the corpses was a large cistern which King Asa
had constructed . . . that was the one which Ishmael son of Nethaniah filled
with corpses.* I blink my eyes and for a moment the stacks of books are
bodies dropped into twisted shapes. "I'd be concerned you have some
pretty hostile ghosts you're dealing with, *Geveret,*" he said. I remember
how agitated I was the first time I visited this house, dragging my
leaden legs up the stairs while that deep hole in the living room cried
out for help. It was very cruel of Mr. Masters to plant that thought
in me. I am angry at him and hope he and Norris have fun spreading
tales about me. I turn over in the bed and sleep facing the wall.

IT IS MORNING and I am laying out my equipment on the floor of the
cistern, continuing the process of planting stakes and sectioning off
the space into a manageable grid when Naima calls down to me.

"You have visitors," she calls cheerily.

Begrudgingly climbing the long ladder, emerging out of the living room floor, I see two Israeli women in their early twenties standing awkwardly in the front hall. They are a cacophony of clashing
colors. The tall one has a shag of brightly dyed red hair, and her petite
friend has long stringy purple locks with two inches of black roots.
They have leather wristbands and neckbands, silver bangles up to
their elbows, and hoops and piercings crowding the rims of their ears.
The redhead's nose is pierced with a small silver stud, and the other's
eyes are sullen and sunken, painted with so much black she could be
courting raccoons. I dust off my hands and introduce myself.

They ask me if they can volunteer; they shift their weight from
hip to hip, ready to defy my response. They want to work as assistants on my dig.

"How on earth did you learn about this dig?" I ask, searching their ghostly faces. They could have been living underground for years, these two. Their skin looks like it's never seen sunlight. The redhead introduces herself as Meirav and her silent, purple-haired friend as Dalia. Naima offers everyone tea.

Meirav hands me a printout of a recent posting to the online edition of the *Journal of Eastern Archaeology*. The article is titled, "Is Page Brookstone Too among the Prophets?"

I motion for the girls to come in and sit in the dining room while I wander toward the living room reading the piece. The title was a play on 1 Samuel 10:11. After King Saul was gripped by the spirit of God and began speaking in ecstasy, the people began to ask each other, *"What's happened to the son of Kish? Is Saul too among the prophets?"* In other words, they thought he had gone insane. To be among the prophets means that you've lost your mind. The article is written by Norris.

He speaks about an Arab couple who claim to have seen ghosts, and about the archaeologist who has agreed to assist them. "What kind of academic discipline is this?" He wants to humiliate me. He writes about the danger of validating psychic quests, and even tries to examine the particular psychology of otherwise successful archaeologists who prefer to hunt phantoms. "By celebrating the happenstance discovery of any archaeologist following a psychic lead, we commit gross disservice to that individual, whose emotional instability and desperate cry for help we reward rather than appropriately treat." He wants to be sure that if anything of value is discovered here, it should be dismissed because the ends shouldn't justify such unstable means. His tone sounds so sincere, as if he genuinely cares about his colleagues instead of his own wounded ego. I am grateful he doesn't mention the cistern, and that he doesn't include Naima and Ibrahim's names or the location of the dig.

I return to the shifty punks, who sit uncomfortably on the dining room chairs as though they are afraid they might contract mediocrity from them. "There are no names in this article except mine. How did you find where I was?" I ask, sitting across from them. Naima joins us with glasses of tea mixed with so many mint sprigs they look like little cups of pond.

Dalia speaks, "We asked Professor Anderson. He told us there was a cistern and you might need some help with it." Her meek demeanor contrasts with her spiky appearance.

I can imagine that Norris would be only too happy to point these girls in my direction. They are freaks. Laughable, just like he hopes I will become. "Do you have any experience with this kind of thing?"

"We study archaeology at Hebrew University," Dalia says.

"Otherwise, you think we'd be reading stuff like this?" Meirav says, leaning back so her chair teeters on two legs. "*The Journal of Eastern Archaeology*?" She juts her tongue into one of her cheeks to look rebellious.

"I read your book, Mrs. Brookstone," ventures the gentler Dalia. "*Body of Water, Body of Air*. You theorized that where there is water, there was always worship. That the Hebrew word for Heaven also means, 'there's water.'" She blushes and adds, tucking her head down so I can hardly hear her, "I thought that was very interesting."

"Thank you," I say, watching her. I fold the printout and then tear it into two.

Dalia looks up and continues, a bit hesitantly, "If where there is water there is also worship, then isn't it logical that there would be ghosts where there is a cistern?"

I cannot help laughing out loud and blurting, "Logical?" How Norris would love this.

Meirav bangs her chair to all fours and says tartly, "We're not the ones who are among the prophets."

I like them. I like the way their bored eyes suddenly light up when I bring them down into the cistern. Meirav stepping with her long legs over the gridlines looks like a psychedelic flamingo. Dalia just stands in one place, drinking in the cool, sweet space with her black-rimmed eyes.

I welcome them and give the girls brushes and picks, instructing them to clear around the steps. They immediately fill the cistern with banter about overbearing parents and boys. In spite of their careless talk, they are careful and attentive to details. I enjoy their chatter. It chips further away at the wall I've had around me.

WE'VE RECOVERED SEVEN fragments of a small jug—peach-colored ceramic, short-necked. A water-collecting vessel. Meirav and Dalia have excavated two entire steps. The second step has a layer of mortar a quarter of an inch thick, unlike the other steps, which are stacked one upon the other without mortar. It's possible someone was beginning a fortification process.

Today we are concentrating on the southeast edge of the cistern, three and a half feet to the left of the corner of the lowest step. There is a roughness to the wall here, suggesting there may have been some tampering or silt collecting. Meirav and Dalia are trying to excavate a full five steps before we begin clearing the area around them. For three days they have shown promise of being a strong little team, but today their concentration is wavering. This afternoon we were joined by a new volunteer.

Ibrahim and Naima's nephew Walid has come to join us. He is fascinated with the two firecrackers underneath his uncle's house, while Meirav and Dalia tighten their clique against him, although they cast an occasional flirty leer in his direction. I have him measuring, photographing, and numbering the nooks where oil lamps once sat. He wears the same black shirt, exclaiming something in Arabic, as when I first met him. He keeps looking over his shoulder at the girls crouched beside the jutting stone steps.

Meirav says loud enough for Walid to hear, "Some of them may be decent, but I refuse to forgive all Arabs."

I can see Walid's back tense, even as he continues laying out his measurements. After a moment he straightens up, pauses, and turns in their direction. He says steadily, almost mechanically, "Who would want your forgiveness anyway? A girl with no respect for others, or for your own body. *I don't forgive* you."

Meirav bolts upright and her eyes bore into Walid, who visibly takes a step back. "You leave my body out of it, you hear me? You are not allowed to look at or think about my body."

Walid looks a little wobbly, holding his tape measure extended about a foot. He is at least three years younger than the girls. He takes a breath in resolve to not back down and says with the breathy vowels and clipped consanants of an Arabic accent, "And you are not allowed to think about *my* body."

Meirav's crosses her arms in front of her chest and Dalia, still crouched down, tries to stifle an eruption of laughter. Meirav shoots her a look and Walid turns back to the wall, lifting his tape measure, and I can see from where I sit that he is smiling.

I am studying the rim of the ledge that is built all around the bottom of the cistern, one and a half feet high. The ledge was built later by some sensitive hands that smoothed it into the wall's texture. Perhaps someone lived here for a time. I can imagine people worshipping here and, if so, there is probably an altar or an ark buried somewhere nearby. I hear muffled excitement from the girls, when Dalia leaps up excitedly and calls out, her voice ringing through the cistern, "There is something here between the steps!"

I spring up from my squat. Someone should write a fitness book, *The Archaeologist and the Deep Knee Bend*. Walid dashes over, his eyes wide. I dust with my soft brush and tip my dental probe in between the slabs, scraping at the mortar beneath the second step. When I am sure what it is, I cannot help but smile. I love my team of misfits gathered around me. I love sharing this moment with them.

I sit up, "It is a beaten gold earring. I've seen that style before. It is Egyptian, from the sixth century BC." I grab my finest-tipped tools and work at dislodging it.

"A gold earring? I found an earring!" Dalia jumps up and down.

Meirav is leaning against the wall, unimpressed, "What's another earring? You have seventeen." But Dalia dances over to Walid and grabs him in a big hug. "Won't your uncle be excited?" she says to him. She is sweet and childish in her enthusiasm. Walid is startled to be in her arms. He doesn't know what to do with his own, and his hands dangle down at his hips. She releases him and skips around the cistern until she comes back to where we are. She leans in close to me and says, breathless, "Maybe the ghosts in the house are an Egyptian prince and a princess!"

"That would be logical," I say with a smile.

Meirav is still unimpressed. "We wanted to work in a haunted house," Meirav says, apathetic, "because the world of the living sucks."

I murmur as I tunnel around the earring, "Ecclesiastes says, *I accounted those who died long since more fortunate than those who are still living.*"

"Exactly. Exactly that!" Meirav agrees, suddenly ignited. "The living suck. They're murderous and judgmental. So much fighting and killing. But no one who dies is imperfect. Everyone remembers the dead as if they were all heroes. Like it's any great feat to die. To live is what kills you!"

As she speaks, Meirav squats down next to Walid. "Up there, I would never talk to you. An Arab boy. And you would never talk to me. You would sooner throw a stone at me. Right? But down here in the underworld, we can make our own rules." He looks dazed, like he still has a lasso of Dalia around him.

"Down here I could even do this." Meirav grabs Walid by the back of his head and crushes her blue-glossed lips against his. When Meirav pulls away her cheeks are flushed as bright as her hair and Walid, a bedazzled cherry, stumbles back on his haunches. "And it wouldn't even matter." Meirav shrugs, wiping her mouth with the back of her hand. She looks at Dalia. Dalia shrinks a little lower and says nothing.

I enjoy being with them. They are really no different than the excitable teenagers who would stop at Megiddo on their Israel Teen

Tour, except at Megiddo I took no pleasure in watching them. In fact, their vitality made me jealous.

I hold up the earring. It is a hammered gold drop hoop. The gold is tinged orange, but the most marvelous thing is that it has five turquoise beads dangling from its bottom rim. It took a special craftsman to create this piece. Dalia is now dancing at the far end of the cistern to a rhythm no one else can hear. I smile watching her. Seventeen earrings around that petite face. And Meirav, with her little flashing nose ring and take-no-prisoners attitude. They both think themselves so countercultural. I look at the earring in my hand and think of Rachel from Genesis who was adorned with golden armbands and a nose ring, and of Shulamit in Song of Songs draped in heavy necklaces and makeup. I look at my little team and think, There have always been girls just like the two of you. I clasp my palm around the earring. And sometimes they became matriarchs and changed the world.

I lie back and rest the earring on my stomach. I used to lie like this in the field with my parents when we visited friends in Connecticut. We would stretch out on scratchy mats and stargaze. I remember watching the shower of Perseus streak the sky. I'd lie just like this, with my hands behind my head, making wishes as fast as they'd come.

"Don't move," my father once said. "A star landed on your belly."

I lifted my head slowly, slowly, and saw a firefly had landed upon me, on my overstuffed ski jacket, blinking its lime bulb.

And now this earring, lying upon my dust-smeared white T-shirt, rising and falling with my breath. This star isn't going to fly away. If nothing else, this damn psychic dig has yielded an earring.

I turn around to see what new mischief my assistants have gotten into and am struck with a wonderful realization. The mortar under the step isn't fortification. Someone wanted to keep something from being found in there. If the mortar was scraped away, the slab could be lifted.

I climb out of the pit and lay the earring on the dining room table with my sketchbook and graph paper. Naima's brow furrows.

"I never saw her wearing earrings," she says, looking at the hoop quizzically.

"Oh," I say, laughing to myself.

Ibrahim comes in close and considers the piece critically. "It must have been given to her as a gift," he says as if it is a matter of fact.

I cannot contain myself and I laugh out loud. "Yes, sure! A gift!" I wipe tears from the corners of my eyes. "I'll put it in my field notes; the lady of the house was way too down-to-earth for something so fancy."

They both nod as if this makes perfect sense.

The girls emerge out of the living room floor, followed by Walid, who looks strangely tipsy and glowy. The girls beg me to let them stay the night so they can start work first thing the next morning. I tell them no, and Meirav says, "You are not our *mother*."

"True, but I am your boss," I respond.

"What could happen?" Dalia asks innocently. Walid grins with those incisors like a cat. I glance from his mouth to Dalia's long pale neck.

"Fine, stay," I say. Walid looks like he might implode.

With the point of our spades, we work on digging out the layer of mortar beneath the second step. Meirav sits with her hand resting casually on Walid's thigh, and Dalia is scrunched near the wall, each one of us gently chipping away. Meirav talks. "Occupation is as bad for us as it is for you," she is arguing to Walid, who seems to have much interest in her but little interest in her words. "There is no solution," she says. "Occupation doesn't work. That's the death of the Right. Working for peace doesn't work when our peace partner wants to kill us. That's the death of the Left. Two-state solution? We gave you Gaza and you respond with an endless barrage of missiles. That's the death of the Center." She curls her fingers around his belt. "I guess there's nowhere to go but down," she says, running her eyes seductively over him. He grins and leans into her. She nips his ear.

"Or up," Dalia says shyly, and we all look up at her. She is diligently scraping at the mortar as if she hasn't said anything.

"Excuse me?" Meirav asks as if she's been insulted.

Dalia says softly, "Up. To the sun, which is so kind and impartial. Unlike oil, which makes people fat, lazy, and cruel."

"What does the sun have to do with anything?" Meirav snaps, annoyed.

Dalia lifts her tire-ringed eyes. "If we all climb out of our silos and realize we can share the sun . . ."

"It's a nice idea," I say, smiling at her. Her smallness and sweetness tugs at me.

"*Pshh*," says Meirav, batting it away.

Coming to Dalia's aid, Walid blurts, "Or the Dead Sea." Meirav looks at him like a specimen and he continues, "We all share the Dead Sea, you, me, the Jordanians . . . We could realize we share the Dead Sea." He stops, caught between Dalia smiling at him through purple wisps and Meirav now clutching his thigh.

Dalia sits up straight and announces, "The air at the Dead Sea has the highest oxygen content in the whole world!" She takes a deep, exaggerated breath. "We can all share that!"

"We share sadness," I say, "we share yearning . . . We share joy, as well, and love."

"I have borrowed Palestinian eyes and what I see is much sadness and yearning," Dalia says, her own eyes wide and gleaming from deep in her face. Walid's face is melting toward her.

By early afternoon we have cleared enough that with a little exertion we'll be able to slide the slab out. Naima has come home and makes us tea and beef kabobs. While we labor, she makes at least five trips up and down that ladder in order to bring down a large copper tray and a stand to rest it on; a hot kettle, which she carries in a basket, and five porcelain bowls, not much bigger than eggcups, which sit in copper rings with handles; a large flaky sheet of spiced flatbread, which she carries down draped over one arm; and a basket of the savory kabobs. She sits cross-legged in the center of the cistern with her little table set up, steam curling toward the hole, sipping strong tea. She looks so small in this space—a little mouse in a concert hall. I know Ibrahim is due to return around three and though I know I have enough adrenaline flowing to shift the slab with an extra push from one of the misfits, I feel that it is right to wait for him. Our team sits with Naima, eating and talking. Walid is tearing pieces of bread, soaking up juices from the kabobs to feed Meirav, and she is licking his fingers whenever Naima looks away. The steam curling away from the kabob is heady and intoxicating.

Dalia reaches out for my chin and turns my face from side to side. "You are one of those women who don't need eyeliner," she observes.

"You don't need it either," I say lightly.

Ibrahim comes home and nearly slides down the ladder in his rush to join us. There is a true intimacy forming among all the inhabitants of this house. I imagine that this is what it would have been like to live in King Solomon's harem, lolling with the women.

I stand up and motion everyone over to the slab. Dalia turns on the video camera. Ibrahim climbs into the little cavern we have scooped out around the step, wraps his fingers around its edge, and pushes while Walid and I pull from the front. The slab whooshes so wonderfully, I lifted my head and say to Dalia, "Did you get that sound? That's the sound of the End of Days."

"I got it. Now I'm doing a close-up of Ibrahim's eyes." She giggles. "He is bugging out!" I see Ibrahim's hand reaching into the rectangle of dark that has been beneath the slab.

"Don't touch anything!" I arrest his hand. "Meirav, Walid, bring me lights, bring them closer."

Meirav hands me a lantern. I dip it down, and in the Cimmerian cavity, objects that have not been touched by light for thousands of years glint in the beams. My eyes rush from one shiny thing to the next like two pinballs run wild, ricocheting from elastic band to silver bell, all the buzzers in my body sounding at once.

I photograph the cavity and sketch the location of each object before extracting them. We redeem the objects out of the hollow with ceremony and solemnity. There is a black metal chest filled with jewelry, most notably one earring to match the one lodged in mortar, a nose ring, and a gold pendant designed with pharaonic features, a large cuff bracelet of burnished brass imbedded with a small stone upon which is etched in Hebrew "I love you," and a signet ring of braided gold with a flat bead engraved on one side with the image of a quill and on the other, an eye. We extract an intricate ivory sphinx with grooved plumage and smiling lips. There are four scarabs. We carefully lift out a clay model of a female skull, carved with thousands of tiny flowers all around, even inside the eye sockets. There is another cube-shaped metal box, which contains the broken fragments of a small jug. There is a figurine of a pregnant woman seated upon a rock and an alabaster jar that had contained ink.

In spite of all the things that I've found at Megiddo—the basalt vessels, cylindrical seals and javelin heads, the lavish proto-Ionic capitals and limestone altars—it has been years since anything has made me tremble with delight. But the careful placement of the treasures in the cistern is impressive. Someone did this with intense deliberateness. I feel so alive at the bottom of this well, all the treasures standing around us. I can feel the energy of the earth's radiation seeping up into me, strengthening my pulse and sharpening my thoughts.

One by one my team rubs their eyes and ascends into the house until I am alone with my treasure. It must be very late; I climb out to go to bed, yawning as I pause in the middle of the ladder. A flicker catches my eye toward the ceiling of the cistern, as if a firefly has blinked and disappeared. I rub my eyes and yawn again, not thinking more about it. I go to my room, and from there I can hear Walid and Meirav in the adjacent bedroom. The thump suggests to me she's thrown him against something. When I approach the bathroom, I see through the crack in the door Naima brushing Dalia's two-toned hair, talking softly. Ibrahim is leaning against the windowsill watching them. I hurry back to my room, grab my pillow and two blankets, and retreat back down into the cistern.

I arrange the objects in a circle and cocoon myself in my blankets in the center. *Come ghosts,* I think, *seep out of your walls and claim me.* I smile to myself, glancing around in the shadows of my lantern. There are no signs of spirits here. I think of the nightmares Mr. Masters has given me. This cannot be the same cistern, I think. I cannot imagine it filled with murdered corpses. Still, the feeling of cold liquid comes over my spine. I will stay here, I resolve, and dispel the nightmares for good.

I stretch out on the floor, brushing against the edge of the metal box filled with fragments of a rotund jug. What was someone saving it for? Sentimental reasons? I settle into my pillow and turn out the lantern. It is a perfect darkness. I strain my eyes through the ink air, but there is nothing for my eyes to settle on, nothing that interrupts the darkness, even from the hole above. I feel as if I am floating. I have an inkling that there could be something here much bigger than myself. I stare into the unknown distance, perhaps short of a wall, perhaps farther. The walls are smooth. Imperceptible. Here, darkness all around, I feel somehow filled up. Maybe I'm not just a dried-up little thing in the dust. Maybe I'm here for a reason. I had taken a risk leaving Megiddo. I came here against everyone's advice, and now I am teetering on the precipice of a beautiful mystery. I smile to myself. In this dark and deep cave, I feel as if I am in the right place, on the right track. All at once, I see that strange little blink again, although it is bigger this time than the blink of a firefly. It is more like the smoke wisp of a candle just extinguished. My chest seizes a little, and my heart starts to race, but I am resolved to lie still. There is nothing here. It could have been a floater in my eye. It is gone as fast as it came, like a luminescent jellyfish disappearing into dark waters. I close my eyes and regulate my breathing. My heart slows down. No, it wasn't like a smoke wisp. It wasn't like a jellyfish. It was a woman. A tiny liquid-glass woman rushing in and out of the black in a rippling of thin shrouds.

I open my eyes. The space is perfectly black. And then there is movement in the darkness. The air itself ripples as if it has become a black sea. I blink my eyes hard, thinking, I'm tired, nothing more. But as I clutch my blankets closer to me and glance about the pitch-black space, it happens again. The whole cistern ripples, as if it is filled with water, and though there is no light source at all, I see the shadows undulate across the walls for an instant, and a gleaming arc as if from a large bubble wand. God bless my overactive imagination, I think nervously, almost frantically. I close my eyes, remembering the prophet Daniel, who saw a hand appear out of thin air to write upon a wall. Brookstone too is among the prophets. Brookstone too has lost her mind. I gather my senses and calm my nerves, saying to myself, "When you open your eyes, everything will be as it should."

I open my eyes slowly, and my heart nearly stops. The room is oscillating with shadows. I scramble to my feet as if trying to swim up out of a pool, flailing my arms about, trying to chase the impression away. Panic seizes my chest as I grope about for the ladder. My throat is closing with fear. I am going to drown on dry ground! I fall to my knees and pat the ground frantically for my lantern, knocking over artifacts.

Finally I grab hold of it and turn it on, and a wash of yellow light floods the floor, instantly dispelling the illusion. I hold the light toward each of my treasures, pausing on the figurine of the pregnant woman. To reassure myself that I am not floating in space or drowning in water, I lift my lantern to the solid walls, and then I gasp out loud. In the hoop of light I can see pictures, drawings emerging from the dust. All around me, the walls are painted. I leap to my feet. There are figures, chariots, and horses. I draw the lantern over the walls. There are murals everywhere. From just above the ledge to the ceiling, the walls are painted. How is it possible that none of us noticed? Am I dreaming? I have studied these walls. I have admired these walls. It is as if a layer of dust has just shaken itself loose. My head throbs and my heart pounds.

Suddenly there is a great crash outside and I scramble up the ladder as quickly as I can just as Ibrahim is rushing down the stairs.

"They are throwing stones again!" he says, opening the door.

"Ibrahim, no!" I rush to stop him. I am afraid of someone's hurting him.

He yells into the night in Arabic, "Show your faces, you cowards! I will have each of you arrested!"

A cluster of four men stand on the road in the dark. They shout back, "Traitor!"

Ibrahim runs at them roaring and they disappear back into the darkness.

At the top of the stairs Walid stands with his arms around Meirav and Dalia. Naima calls the police. Ibrahim comes back in, his brow sweaty and his face red. He looks up at Walid with the two girls, and then looks at me and says quietly, "They know we have Jews in this house."

The police don't come. I help Ibrahim nail a sheet of plywood over the kitchen's broken window, and then we retire to our rooms. I lock my door, fold up some of my sweaters as a pillow, and get into bed. I don't want to go back down into the cistern until daylight breaks.

FOR THE FIRST time, I am the last one in the house to wake up. Ibrahim is cleaning up glass on the kitchen floor. I come downstairs—still wearing the leggings and T-shirt I slept in, my hair a mess—and climb right down into the cistern. Meirav, Dalia, and Walid have straightened the circle of artifacts but have not touched my tumble of blankets and pillow in the center.

Dalia laughs when she sees me. "Did you sleep here last night?"

"Yeah," I admit. Remembering what happened, I glance around the walls. They are the same as always, bald and blemish-free. I rub my eyes and walk toward the western side, to the place where I first shined the lantern last night. I pick up a soft-haired brush and step up upon the ledge, yawning sleepily. I brush the wall lightly, and there before my eyes, not two inches away, in the tiny window swept free of dust, a face peeks back at me. It is a woman's face, no bigger than a thumbnail, with little elfin ears. "Hello, you," I whisper. I blow upon the wall and small clouds of dust billow away from the face and there she is, hands held high, steadying a large jar upon her head, green robe tied with a dark cord. She is straight-backed, feet pointing ahead of her. I contemplate her for a moment. A part of me considers covering her back up until I am alone, but after all their hard work, I know I have to share her with my team. I send Walid to get Ibrahim and Naima while I stand guard, making sure no one sees her before the mistress and master of the house arrive.

When they have all climbed down into the cistern, I motion to Naima to come to me.

"Is this our spook?" I ask, and move aside, revealing her.

Ibrahim, Walid, Meirav, and Dalia all rush up close. Naima's hands come up over her mouth and she gasps, "She's beautiful!" She throws her arms around Ibrahim. Dalia exclaims, "It is the princess! The one with all the jewelry!"

I pick up the video camera and begin to document. I instruct everyone not to touch the walls. We are going to need a team to do this. A chronologist to secure the dates, a preservationist to protect the mural, a geologist. But I am hesitant to bring any outside witnesses into this sacred space. I don't want this rabbit's hole disturbed before I confront my own red queen.

X

There was a time when this land was uninhabited. Yellow insects hovered close to the ground, nectar glistening on their bellies. Migrating flocks alighted upon its bristling slopes and sang to
God new songs. The sand was not a scorching sudden death but
endlessly patient. We shall never see the land this way. Our soft
footprints have left scars.

—THE SCROLL OF ANATIYA 22:15–19

We set about systematically brushing the walls of the cistern. My team proceeds with utmost care, as if we've
been working together for years. Everyone struggles to
maintain precision in their trembling hands. No one speaks. Beginning at the stairs and working counterclockwise, a pictorial story begins to unfold all around us, a new mural in between each of the
nooks where the light of oil lamps once danced.

"Just give it a light dusting, so we can get a sense of the scope,
and then we'll return to each panel and clean them slowly, top to bottom," I direct.

The artist has an exquisite hand, far more sophisticated than
other art I've seen from this time period. His lines are thin and fluid,
and not every portrait is in profile. Enough color remains to trigger
our imaginations: how rich the mustards, greens, reds, and even the

rare blues must have been, how the white paint must have sparkled here in the dancing light. Who was this artist who spent hundreds of hours in this space, transforming a cistern into a gallery?

First we uncover a picture of a young boy standing in a field of stones, looking up at a clear sky. The edges of the sky are tinged with color, and a black, foreboding storm threatens to cut through the bright day.

In the second mural, the boy is crying, weeping into his hands, and over his head, dark chariots emerge from the torn sky.

Lunchtime comes and goes. Dinnertime too, but none of us wants to stop to eat. We continue working in reverent quiet, until well after midnight has passed.

In the third mural, a young man stands upon a slab of rock in the courtyard of the Temple in Jerusalem. His hands indicate that he is passionately addressing throngs of people who seem otherwise occupied in their various trades. Over the young man's head there is a smudge of black that seems to follow him throughout the story, like an ominous cloud.

In another mural, he is in a prison filled with prisoners, and he has the black smudge over his head, only it has grown larger than in scene 3.

In the fifth, there is a landscape suffering drought, and the man is imploring the sky.

By the time we retire, a fine powder coats us all, sticking especially to Dalia and Meirav's painted faces. I enter the bathroom to take a shower. I turn on the faucet and undress while I wait for the water to heat up. I look in the mirror and straighten up, staring at myself. I feel beautiful. In fact, I've never felt so beautiful, which is ironic, I think, because objectively, I look terrible. I am covered in dust, smeared with dirt and sweat. My hair is greasy from being pressed under my bandana so many hours. I can taste dust in my mouth. I remember when God cursed the snake in the Garden of Eden, God said, *On your belly shall you crawl and dust shall you eat.* The dust I taste doesn't taste like a curse. In fact, I remember a poem

Jordanna once shared with me by Li-Young Lee: "Peaches we devour, dusty skins and all, comes the familiar dust of summer, dust we eat. O, to take what we love inside, to carry within us an orchard." All my life I've been clearing dust, pushing it away, trying to rescue things out of it. But this dust—I wish I could draw it in. This dust, which has protected those murals for so many centuries like a thin, fine blanket—I want it to protect me too. It is beautiful. The stuff of fairies. The Book of Daniel says, *Those that sleep in the dust shall awake to eternal life.* I have been not only sleeping in dust. I've been sleeping, kneeling, toiling, drawing, digging, weeping, dreaming in the dust. I step under the showerhead, and my skin emerges from beneath its gentle coating. I feel, all at once, *awakened.*

I RETURN TO the Rockefeller Museum with Ibrahim to deliver our artifacts to a secure location. We have packed them carefully in wooden crates bungeed to two metal dollies. Together we roll our loot through the cloister garden. We are both quiet and contemplative, slowing down instinctively as we approach the front door. Ibrahim pauses at a large antique sundial and I find myself glancing into the reflecting pool, down at the sky. We both feel hesitant about revealing our finds, which have been such a sweet little secret the six of us alone have shared. We agree that we aren't quite ready to expose the murals, but the artifacts should be stored safely. We will do a little more dusting of the murals before inviting in the Antiquities Authority, and the press.

We spend three hours with Itai and two of his specialists unpacking and discussing the artifacts. They will be dated, studied by an Egyptologist, and written about. We spend the most time talking about the clay skull carved with hundreds of tiny flowers. "I've never seen anything like this," Itai says, and none of us has. Ibrahim is happy. While archaeological terms are batted around, he just stands, staring at the treasures all standing on the table before us as if readying for a parade. His mouth is set as he listens intently, but his eyes cannot suppress that he is smiling. At one point Itai pats Ibrahim on the back and nods at him, and without a word I see a special kind of bond form between them.

After our delivery, Ibrahim takes time to explore for the first time the collections along the corridors of the Rockefeller Museum, and I excuse myself to the library to see what I can find about clay renditions of skulls. The library here is the most important archaeology library in the Middle East. The magnitude of its book collection is dwarfed by the fat white pillars that hold up its fantastic arched ceiling. It is so quiet, one can imagine hearing the shafts of sunshine dappling like keys of a celestial organ being played. The soft cork floor absorbs my footsteps as I wind around a fat pillar. Just behind the pillar, between two shelves of books, I see Mr. Masters leaning over a large open folio on a desk. I don't see his face, but his ill-fitted pants identify him well enough. His hat is on the table before him. His black overcoat is hanging from his shoulders like a cape.

I duck back behind the pillar. After a moment I peek at Mr. Masters again. His head turns a bit as he reads, but he doesn't see me. I half expect to see fangs to go along with his capelike coat. I find myself watching him for a moment. His white shirt seems so old and thin, I can almost see the faint pink of his skin through the fabric. His sleeves are pushed up. His arms seem cut of gold and amber and the pale pink of trembling hydrangea when they just begin to yellow. From here I can see, washed in sunlight, tiny diamonds of sun clinging to his lashes. His hair blazes like a sunrise. The black yarmulke sitting on top of him seems to me out of place, like a barnacle. For a moment, all the best colors of the world are reflected upon him. He straightens up and his head emerges from the slant of sun into shadow. He notices me.

He reaches for his hat and puts it back on over the yarmulke. He says in a monotone as he closes the folio before him, "You look different."

I find it to be a strange comment, and yet eerily observant, because I feel very different. I come out from behind the pillar. "I'm happy because we found some beautiful relics."

His eyebrows go up. "Anything Egyptian?" he asks. His lips are thin but beautifully shaped, the color of leaves of Japanese maple.

"Four scarabs, jewelry, a sphinx," I say. I come forward and tentatively touch the back of a chair at the desk. "Why?"

"Jeremiah spent time in Egypt," he says, adjusting his too-small hat. He seems frustrated with it and yanks it down so it awkwardly squeezes his head.

I come around the chair and sit down. His eyebrows knit and then unknit. I say, "You know anything about clay skulls?"

"Clay skulls?" he repeats. "Huh. No. I know a lot about skulls, but not ones made of clay."

"I'm sure you do know about skulls," I say to him, as if I have just found him out as a bone hunter. "We haven't found any remains, if that's what you're worried about."

His eyebrows knit again and then he looks down at himself as if he has just remembered what he is wearing. "Oh, this, you think I am worried about bones," and for the first time he smiles the tiniest hint of a smile and huffs in what one might interpret as a laugh. He swoops off his coat and lays it on the table beside the closed folio. He takes off his uncomfortable hat and puts it down on top of the coat. The pile looks like all that remained of the Wicked Witch after Dorothy melted her. He looks at me as he pulls a chair around and says, "I'm not."

"Now *you* look different," I say. His shoulders swell out against his shirt, which is also too tight. He looks strong. I fidget in my seat.

"I know I don't look like your typical black-hat," he says. "My father was Irish and my mother was a Russian Jew. They met on a kibbutz while picking avocados. They fell in love, he converted, and the rest is history. But"—he fingers the edge of his hat—"not the kind of history anyone would be interested in."

I think suddenly that perhaps I might be interested. "This skull is carved meticulously with flowers," I say.

"I would very much like to see that," he says. A moment stretches between us.

"And who are you again?" I ask, cocking my head. I find myself intrigued by this second meeting.

This time he really does laugh. I like seeing the solemness of his face crack open even briefly. He points out, "It is nice to hear you ask that and mean it, instead of being a jerk."

"Me?" I ask, stunned. "You had just told me I had no heart."

"No, I didn't, I said your heart wasn't in that lecture, that's all." He rolls his head on his neck and looks up at the window and arched ceiling. "You spoke Torah with the speed and precision of a missile launcher," he says admiringly, "but without much heart."

I am not sure what to do with this, to take it as a compliment mixed with an insult, or to accept it just as observation. I decide to move on. "I heard you work for an organization called CROSS," I say, trying to encourage him to speak.

He looks at me and says, "You really don't remember when I came to hear you? I even spoke with you after the lecture. Well, it's all right. I wasn't dressed in these clothes in those days. I've only been wearing the hat, the fringes, and the coat for the past two years." Mortichai pauses for a moment. He seems to be considering how much to tell me.

"You weren't born Orthodox?" I ask, curious about him.

"Oh, I was born Orthodox, believe me. I had an older brother, Menachem," he says. "I have five younger sisters and three younger brothers. For the women in my community, it is as if the whole Torah with its six hundred and thirteen commandments begins and ends with the first two."

Be fruitful and multiply, I say.

"Bingo, those are the two," he says. "I have twenty nieces and nephews with at least three on the way."

"Can you name them all?" I feel suddenly very comfortable with him. I hook my foot around the leg of my chair and relax.

"It helps that there are four Menachems, named after my

brother." He laughs again. He seems relaxed as well. Then his tone changes, "But with eight other siblings, my biggest rival was him. I could never be as good or as smart as my mother was sure he was destined to be." He pauses and then says more softly, "Menachem the first died when I was five."

Mortichai grows quiet, and I am about to say how sorry I am when he continues, "The one time my mother was proud of me was when I became engaged to a girl named Fruma. She was the rabbi's daughter." I sense that he is watching me carefully when he tells me this, though I am not sure why.

"That's prestigious," I say, feeling suddenly awkward that our conversation has become so personal.

Mortichai nods. "I broke it off. I didn't know her. I wanted to study secular things. Science. Literature."

"Archaeology is not entirely secular," I say.

"I know. It was actually our rabbi's idea. I thought he'd be angry at me for breaking his daughter's heart. But he told my parents to lay off the matchmaking and understand I had a different destiny, that my destiny would serve our people the same as if I stayed home, married, and had children."

"Sounds like a wise rabbi. I think my priest had a lot to do with me getting into biblical archaeology too."

"Priest?" he asks, surprised.

"Red-blooded, yellow-haired Catholic," I say proudly, and then despite myself I find myself adding almost apologetically, "Not meet-the-parents material, I suppose."

He doesn't respond to that comment and I shift in my seat a bit. But he is still looking at me, eyes interested. "Tell me about this priest," he says, moving to the edge of his chair.

Suddenly I hear my own mouth volunteer what I rarely say to anyone, "My father committed suicide," and once I say it, I realize that it feels good to tell him, it feels safe to speak to him, and so I continue, "Actually, he was going to die anyway, but he hastened it and killed himself. He was forty years old." I wait a moment, pondering, and then I add lightly, "Neither my grandfather nor my father lived past forty."

"You can do a lot in forty years," Mortichai says matter-of-factly, still leaning forward to hear more. I can't help but smile widely. He hasn't said, *That's a tragedy*, which I already know.

"Then I was hit by a car and fractured my neck. Father Chuck visited me in the hospital. He drove all the way down from his meditation cabin in the woods just to see me. A hundred miles! I had these bruises on my neck, and my mother said that my father had saved me, that I should think of the bruises as lipstick on my collar." I lift my hands in exaggerated exasperation. "Kind of a confusing metaphor, huh?"

"I'll say," he agrees, thinking. "For one thing, did your father even *wear* lipstick?"

I laugh. I feel my eyes twinkle. "So Father Chuck came to my bedside at the hospital," I say, remembering how I had moved my legs over when he sat on the bed. I remember the weight of him indenting the bed, my legs rolling toward him, till I drew them up to my chin so as not to touch. "I told Father Chuck that I felt that I was supposed to have died, that from this moment on I should be dead. That I didn't really own my life anymore." I haven't considered this moment in my life in many years, and I wonder why I feel so fluent with my past with him. Is it because of the religious clothing? Have I somehow placed him in the same category as Father Chuck? I continue, "He said to me, 'But you are not dead. God did not take you. In God's opinion, there is much more you have to offer.' Then I wondered out loud to him whether, in his opinion, my father had had nothing left to offer. And he said, 'God didn't take your father. Your father took your father.' And you know? He was the first one who really acknowledged that my father had killed himself. Everyone else talked about him outsmarting the disease. I said, 'But he was going to die anyway in a matter of months, maybe weeks.' And he said, 'It doesn't matter. There is eternity in every second.'" I feel my eyes moistening and swipe the corners with my fingertips. "He said that my father may have been destined to meet his Maker in a matter of days, but by rushing, he left a lot still undone. He said he left me undone."

"That's a wise priest," Mortichai says. His eyes narrow a bit as if he is trying to look deeper into me.

"When I stepped out of that hospital, I couldn't wait to get back to school, especially to my history books," I say, as if I am in a confessional. "I was all too happy to continue foraging further and further into the safe and sterile records of the past rather than focus on an uncertain future. I stepped out into the hopeful sunshine looking only as far forward as my mom's scrambled eggs and bacon—sorry." I smile at him and he shrugs it away. "But if I had had the foresight to look further, I would have seen the years of my life stretching forth from that moment like a desert of sand as far as the eye could see, and the sizzling horizon would be barely obstructed by any mile markers at all, nothing to speak of. I would have seen myself graduate from high school, from college . . ."

I look into the darker depths of the library as I think about the past. "I would have seen myself pursue my graduate degree, hours and hours in the library's labyrinths; disappear into divinity school a stone's throw from a nunnery; and then finally climb down into the yellow pits and remain there, sifting for something, for Jesus or joy or any elation, for decades. I would have seen myself numb and unignited, the fantasies of my youth frying into vapor under the sun, and I might have realized that what may have started as the pursuit of recovering the lost had ended with my finally finding a place where I could totally and completely lose myself in the depths of the dust of the long, long dead, where no one would never find me, and in this place, despite the inertia and the ennui, inside I would be more frantically afraid than ever."

"Wow," Mortichai says genuinely, and I shift my eyes to him. "I see. I am really grateful you shared that with me." He seems moved. He rubs his palms over his knees. "No wonder your heart wasn't in it," he says carefully, with gentleness. "Until now there were no mile markers, until the cistern."

"It feels that way," I admit, and I am suddenly overwhelmed and embarrassed at having spilled so much of myself. I need him to share, to even the field, before I turn completely and permanently red. I feel meek and a little desperate when I ask, "What about you?"

"Me," he says, sitting back. "Like I said, not a history anyone would be interested in. But, *hm*. I wanted to join the army, which is mandatory for the rest of my countrymen, but the ultra-Orthodox community is exempt on religious grounds. My rabbi convinced my parents to let me do this. So at eighteen I traded my coat and hat for fatigues. I trained and served as a medic for three years. My rabbi also convinced my parents to let me study abroad, at Indiana University, so I went to America when I was twenty-two and stayed there for my bachelor's and master's degrees. I was pretty secular in those days. I dated. I experimented. It was there that a professor of biblical archaeology, Yeshu Abraham, took the time to mentor me. He was the founder of CROSS."

"Christian Remains Salvation Society." I am listening to him, and also trying to picture him twenty years younger, dressed as an American college student, backpack slung over his shoulder. Dating. Experimenting. I am surprised how easy it is.

"Right. It worked out perfectly for me. They wanted someone they knew and trusted to scope out new sites in the Holy Land, and I wanted to return home. I never cared that it was a Christian organization. I never really cared how the reports were used. Yeshu was a born-again Christian. He's become increasingly erratic over the years, but his checks always come in on time, and I am grateful to be doing what I love." He pauses, as if weighing whether or not to say more. I am disappointed when he decides to conclude, "And that's pretty much my story."

"Why did you tell me I might be dealing with hostile ghosts?" I ask him. All the nightmares he caused!

"You're not?" he asks wryly.

"No," I say. "The cistern is filled with an energy that is life-affirming. It is beautiful."

"I mean your own ghosts," he says. "You were kind of being a jerk to me and I didn't know why. I figured you must have some hostile ghosts hanging around you."

"No. I mean," I fluster, "I did, maybe, for a long time. But not anymore, I hope."

He nods and we are sitting quietly for a moment when Ibrahim finds me. "Page!" He acknowledges Mortichai with a wave and says, "I've seen it all, every collection in this place, nothing compares. I want to get back home to it."

I widen my eyes at him to signal him to say no more, and I push my chair away to get up. I notice Mortichai's eyes have narrowed more. "Home to what?" he says observantly.

"The cistern," I say, and add for emphasis, "The cistern. The one that has never been filled with corpses."

XI

If you were a signet ring upon my right hand, I would press you into the wax and seal each of my scrolls with your sign. I would press you into the heels of my feet that every step I left would bear your mark, indicate that you had touched me. Have you touched me? Some mornings I wake with the distinct feeling, just shy of a surety, that you have touched me in the night, spirited to my side on tiptoe and laid your hand along my neck, my arm, my belly. I wake with that part of me raw and alarmed.
— THE SCROLL OF ANATIYA 22:42–45

The sixth mural depicts an exile, people in chains bound and bent. There are taskmasters with whips, and some of the prisoners are strapped and pulling heavily loaded carts. The man with the black cloud over his head is separate from the rest, wearing an ox yoke.

The seventh mural is at least twice as big as the previous ones. It is a portrayal of the Israelites marching through the Sea of Reeds. They march with timbrels held high, exuberant. Their heads are thrown back in song, their feet lifted in dance. In the distance the artist depicts the Egyptian armies following, their general waving them to follow after the Israelites. The man is not in this one. It's a breathtaking mural.

In the eighth mural, people are building houses and planting vineyards. Jerusalem is on a hilltop in the background. The man with the black cloud is among them, sitting under a tree with people gathered about him, presumably listening to his teaching.

After another long day dusting, I lie, freshly showered, in my bed. I think about Mortichai's hand resting on the well-worn folio as he spoke with me. How the veins on the back of his hand made an *H*. I think about the exquisite brushstrokes on the murals in the cistern. How long it must have taken someone to decorate that large space! To the tiniest detail.

The man is clearly Jeremiah. The dark cloud that trails him like a kite must be his gift, or burden, of prophecy. Jeremiah's prophecies are usually dark and dire. The murals illustrate his story, beginning with him as a young boy receiving the call of a prophet, then his vision of the attackers coming from the north. Then, of course, the prophet expounds to the people at the Temple Mount. In the next scene, he is thrown into prison for treason. Then, of course, drought, followed by exile to Babylonia, the long lines of people in ropes. And then the people replanting the land. Only the splitting of the sea is jarringly out of place. And yet, in many ways, it is the most beautiful painting of all, each wave tipped with a silvery white foam, each face crossing the sea different from the next.

I cannot sleep. I get out of bed, slip on my cut-off jeans, and head downstairs to have a cup of tea before descending into the pit for one more late-night look-around. It is after midnight and I assume everyone is sleeping. The house is quiet. I boil water with mint in it in the tiny kitchen, barely bigger in square footage than the couch in Itai's office. As the sweet steam starts to rise, I sit upon the windowsill with the lights out. Moonlight comes through the top and bottom of the window. The rest is still nailed shut with wooden boards. I inhale the perfume of mint. I remember Naima saying that she once saw a vision of the ghosts in the steam of her soup pot. The swinging door to the dining room is closed, but all at once I hear movement in the other room.

"Midnight snack?" I hear Dalia's voice.

"Can't sleep." It is Walid.

I am about to leave the kitchen and say hello—my hand already placed on the swinging door—when I hear Walid say, "You are going to break that table."

And her, "Come here."

I withdraw my hand from the door as I hear the table scratch against the floor. I do not want to disturb them, but I also don't want them to know I have been listening from the kitchen. I figure I will enjoy my tea here until they go back to bed, and then sneak back to my room. I turn off the stove and pour a cup. Suddenly the idea of one of them getting a glass of water and finding me standing here with my cup of tea is horrifying. I crouch down and climb under the sink, scooting the household cleaners aside and tucking my legs up. I hide there, my knees jutting up around the pipe. I reach out of the cabinet and pull in my cup of tea.

I hear Dalia moan. This should end soon, I tell myself, blowing on my tea. "Cheers," I say quietly, and click the pipe.

I hear a chair get kicked out of someone's way. There is a pause, and then the two of them start laughing and the scraping resumes. Soon, I think, the Barakats will have a hole in their dining room floor as well.

I resign myself to being stuck under the sink for a while. I stare at the metal pipe in front of me. I wonder what has been dropped down here. There is a painted cistern under the living room, so perhaps there is a Hope diamond in the drain. I start quietly unscrewing the pipe with my tea placed under my knee. I find a thin refrigerator magnet and hold it in the tiny sliver of light from between the cabinet doors. It is a business card, written in Arabic. The letters are faded. I smile. Maybe it's lucky. A tiny parchment with ancient illegible script. I contort to squeeze it into my pocket. I start to put the pipe back.

The banging moves from the table to against the wall adjoining the kitchen and the dining room.

I reach my arm up out of the cabinet and put my now-empty

teacup in the sink. Just as I pull my arm back in, Walid and Dalia fall through the swinging door onto the kitchen floor. I can see them through the slit between the cabinet doors. I close my eyes.

I try to imagine being somewhere else. Anything to distract myself from the thought of the two of them so close to me. I open my eyes a little and see them through the sliver between the doors. Dalia's hip is inches from where I hide. Pale skin with a thin red strap, like a trickle of blood. Walid reaches up toward the counter and I hold my breath, afraid he will knock open the cabinet and they'll see me here, but he reaches straight past where I am hiding and brings down the gallon of olive oil Naima uses for cooking.

He pours some of the gallon over her. I almost gasp out loud. The oil drizzles out of the bottle over her arched body, over the linoleum floor. The air tastes of olive oil.

I try to press myself as far from the cabinet doors as I can. I squeeze my eyes shut again. I imagine myself in a different place, a different time, but I can't. They slide into the cabinet, I open my eyes, and the doors bounce almost all the way open and then settle. For a moment I can see them entirely. The moonlight sifts around the boards of the kitchen window, illuminating their skin with pearly sheen. Walid's hands are on either side of Dalia's face, and they are kissing. Her hair spirals out on the floor as if she is floating on water.

They don't see me. The doors are shut again. In the cramped cabinet I suddenly feel as if I am in a tiny coffin, curled up the way corpses are buried in the Levant. I am cold. The pipe is cold, and inches away Walid and Dalia are clutching each other and sliding over the floor. I am nearly numb, and they are ecstatic, hot and alive.

I think of Mortichai. In his coat and hat he seemed so asexual, and then, sitting in the library, he seemed so different, so easy to talk with. In my mind I can put myself right back into that library. I can picture myself rising from my chair and walking the short distance to him, and having him pull me into his lap. I can imagine his arms around me, his mouth closing over mine. I can imagine slipping my

hand under his shirt, unpeeling all the articifial layers of him until I
find the core.

Walid and Dalia are lying still now on the floor, breathing heavily. I realize, I want that. I want to experience that again. I am beginning to feel a fragile goodness about myself again. I would like to be
in love.

When Walid and Dalia finally leave, I creep out from under the
sink, stretching my cramped body, hearing my knees click. I mop the
oil off the floor so no one will slip in the morning. All throughout
the next day I look for signs in Walid and Dalia. Don't they wonder
who cleaned up their oil spill? Aren't they at all curious? They act
as if nothing has happened. For a moment, I wonder if I saw Walid
and Dalia at all or if perhaps it was them, the spirits. Then I laugh at
myself. Even if I wasn't harboring romantic delusions, this house has
made its imprint on me as well.

NAIMA, WEARING A summery flowered dress, has joined us in the
cistern this morning. Meirav is carefully uncovering detail work
with one hand while the other is hooked onto Walid's belt. She
is taller than he is when she is not slouching, and although he is
muscular, beside her he seems like a pet. I am certain Meirav doesn't
know about her boyfriend's late-night tryst on the kitchen floor,
anointing her best friend with olive oil. Dalia works quietly on her
own, although she is clearly happy. She and Walid steal glances at
each other across the room. I feel the cell phone in my back pocket
vibrate. I wipe the sweat and dust off my brow with the back of
my arm and answer.

Mortichai says, "The flowered skull, *Geveret* Brookstone, is magnificent. The scarabs too, as well as the other things. I would love to
have a look at your cistern when you are ready to accept visitors."

"Why do I suspect that you are already on your way?" I say, hearing the sound of highway and wind.

"So supervisors of psychic digs do have psychic powers," he says.

"How do you know where we are?" I balance the phone between my cheek and shoulder and begin to climb out of the cistern.

"*Gever* Harani, your ex-boyfriend," he says. My heart starts to race. Has he been asking about me? It is strange to me that at first his voice sounded as dull as a radiator, and that now there is a hint of music in it. I am trying to figure out what holds all the incompatible parts of him together and feel there are big pieces of the puzzle missing.

I balance the phone between my cheek and shoulder and climb out of the cistern. I sit on the couch; my muscles ache. "It was nice talking with you, and hearing your story," I say. "*A word aptly spoken is like apples of gold in settings of silver.*"

"Ah," he says happily. "Who doesn't love Proverbs. I must reciprocate with a verse, but will the effervescent Bible scholar forgive my predictability if I pull a verse from Song of Songs?"

"Please just don't compare my breasts to two fawns, twins of a gazelle, and I beg you do not talk about my mount of myrrh. In fact, just about everything from chapter four would be inappropriate at this stage."

I hear Walid singing inside the cistern and I smile listening to his song resonate up into the living room.

"Chapter six is safe, no?" he asks. "*Who is she that shines through like the dawn, beautiful as the moon, radiant as the sun?*"

I laugh, flattered. "I'm not sure it's so safe," I say. I think of him bathed in light in the library and consider the verse from Ezekiel: *There was a radiance all about him. Like the appearance of the bow which shines in the clouds on the day of rain.* But that, I am sure, would be too much.

"What have you found today?" he asks.

"We struck oil earlier this morning," I say, thinking about Walid and Dalia. "And I have been cleaning it up ever since. It has gotten over everything, including me. It may not be the best time to visit." As much as I want to see him, I am serious. No one has seen inside the cistern except for my little core team. Why should I trust him so much? Because he is cute? Because I already confided in him, and in less than twenty-four hours he hasn't deceived me? Maybe I should be more protective of our project. Reveal it how and when we all have decided it is time.

"I understand," he says. "It's okay." After a heartbeat, "I have another call. I'm sorry, I'll call right back."

I walk to the kitchen to get some water. I am halfway finished with my second cup when my phone vibrates again. I put the glass down quickly, spilling water down the front of my shirt. "Hello?"

"It's me," he says. "It's all right, I don't have to come over to see the cistern. But can I at least come in for a drink?" There is a knock at the door.

"Jesus," I think, realizing I am filthy and now also all wet. Still, I open the door. My eyes take a moment to adjust to the bright daylight that engulfs him. He seems taller and broader than I remember from the library. He is not wearing his hat, only the yarmulke.

He glances at my shirt and says drily and with a smirk, "Looks like you got it all out."

"Got what all out?" I ask, crossing my arms in front of my chest.

"The oil," he says.

"Listen," I say, trusting my instinct rather than my better judgment. "A quick look around. Just promise me that you won't disturb anything and you won't talk about this with anyone yet. We want to be deliberate about revealing it."

He puts one hand over his heart and raises the other in the air. "I do," he says.

I usher him into the living room. As he walks past me, his jacket releases an aroma of citrus and clove and, for a moment, I think I do remember him from long ago, but as soon as he steps away, the memory is lost.

I bring him to the edge of the cistern. Soft Arabic music is pulsing up from Naima's radio.

I tell Mortichai that he is to make no reports for at least two weeks. That he can tell no one. He agrees again and steps onto the ladder gingerly but without fear. He descends slowly, while I lie on the living room floor, resting my chin upon my folded hands, watching. "We have a visitor," I call down to my team. "No bad behavior."

"Too late," brags Meirav.

Mortichai's eyes widen when he sees the colors on the walls, but his body remains relaxed and controlled. He does not study the walls, however, as I would have expected. He does not rush down to gawk at them. He only glances all about, as if it is enough for him to know exactly what it is that I have found. And then, amidst all the splendor of the cistern, he does the most unexpected thing. He lifts his eyes to me. I find myself wondering where he could have gotten such blue eyes, unless somewhere in his ancestry a lamb had strayed off with someone like me. Then I remember his Irish father. Meeting his steady gaze, I can tell that he knows why I need to keep this discovery a secret. That whatever story is scrawled down there is also scrawled inside of me. He seems surprised and for a moment he looks at me as if I am something amazing to behold. And you thought the scarabs were exquisite, I think, pleased with myself.

Mortichai does not go any further into the cistern. After descending a third of the way down, he climbs right out, brushing the gray dust from his black wool pants.

"It is the story of Jeremiah," he says after he emerges and sits on the couch. "It really is. I can't believe it." He looks at me a moment more and then says, "You told me all about yourself, *Geveret*, and you didn't even mention this!"

"Please call me Page," I say.

"I want to help you. If you need any help, I will help you. I'm a certified forensic archaeologist. I can bring you a résumé, whatever you need."

I laugh lightly. "I don't need any help."

"I'm sure you don't need anything, but I am offering myself to you for two weeks anyway. Itai told me he needed to assign an Israeli to this dig to legitimize it. Let it be me, please. No wonder you look different. No wonder you say you've dispelled your hostile ghosts." He jumps up and peers over the edge. "You've found a garden, in full bloom, underground!"

"You came in for a drink. What can I get you?" I ask him, and he answers, "What's a drink?" We laugh. I get him and myself iced tea. My shirt is practically dry. We sit in the dining room together, and he is thinking out loud. "The next mural, it is either going to be Jeremiah in prison again, or the Temple walls being breached." He is talking through me, I feel. I think about Itai and being jealous of Israel's constant seductive presence with us. I wonder if I could become jealous of my cistern. I bite down on a piece of ice. Who am I kidding, I think to myself. He has four nephews named Menachem, for God's sake. He's a black-hat, even if the damn thing is too small for his head. There is no chance he'd be serious with a girl like me. I spit the ice back into my glass and stir it with a spoon.

"Let's go down and I'll put you to work," I suggest to the twirling ice, and he lights up.

Meirav takes her petulant stance upon seeing that Mortichai is joining us. Hands on waist, hip jutting out, belly button spike glinting like a knife. She snorts, "W' the hell?" eyeing him up and down. "I refuse to work alongside some holier-than-thou army evader." Mortichai's sole has hardly left the last rung. "What, you think your blood is more blessed than mine? You think just because I have sex with whomever I please and dye my hair, I can die defending Israel but you can't?"

"Cool it, Meirav," I say. "He was a medic in the army, and furthermore, wasn't it you who said, 'Down here in the underworld we can make our own rules'? I think it was right before you smashed your lips against Walid. Hm?"

Dalia and Walid both laugh, and Mortichai seems unaffected by any of it. He walks straight to the mural of the Splitting Sea and says, "Extraordinary." Naima is on a ladder dusting the top of that mural and she welcomes him, asking him if he'd like a drink. "No, thank you," he says, "Page poured me iced tea upstairs. Wow. What I'd really like is a brush, or a feather."

Mortichai and I work together on the ninth mural—a beauty of a painting. The whole panel is up in flames, and in the midst of the flames is a burning scroll. The top of the panel swirls with black and gray smoke. I stand back, looking at the artfulness of the flames. I watch Mortichai's repetitive brushstroke from here, his white sleeves pushed up. The painted flames engulf him in the shadowy light. I admit I am pleased that Mortichai's prediction that the mural would either be a second prison scene or the walls being breeched is wrong. I want to know my walls better than he does. Then again, I think, as my eyes scuttle all over his shoulders and back like beetles over sacks of flour, I would also like him to tear my walls down.

He joins me to look at the panel, getting perspective on our work. He points toward the top and says in a reverent whisper, as if no one is supposed to know, "There are faint Hebrew letters in the smoke." I look to where he is pointing. He is right; it is as if the letters of the burning scroll have been released and are flying up.

"Chapter thirty-six," I say, "the scroll that Jeremiah wrote which the king burned in his palace."

"Of course," Mortichai says, like a man who already knows something.

XII

─❧❧─

See the gnarled olive tree, hollowed out by lightning and by rot.
Even so, and without much effort, it raises up a true branch
feathered with long green leaves that ruffle silvery in the wind.
It manages to nourish, with its body utterly cored, a dangling
of olive-fruit, rich as the coins dangling over a wealthy bride's
forehead.

—THE SCROLL OF ANATIYA 23:9–11

The next day we discover that Mortichai's predictions are
right. The tenth mural is the second prison scene. Jeremiah
with a cloud over his head is looking up from a deep pit
and it seems that people are lowering something to him with a rope.
There is an angry mob off to the left of him.

In the eleventh mural there is a battle scene, in the center of it a
general being speared. Jeremiah and some others, including a woman,
are in hiding underground. I think this is the same woman as the
original woman I found in the green dress, and I suspect that a couple
of faces in other scenes may also be her.

Mortichai is ecstatic and I am secretly a little perturbed, but
at the same time impressed. It is my second day working alongside
him. The citrus and clove scent of him intoxicates me even as I try to
ignore it.

Dalia asks him as she dusts why he chose forensic archaeology. She says, "I tried taking a class in it once, but I dropped it after two sessions. The slides the teacher showed made me ill."

As he brushes the mural of the Temple walls being breached, Mortichai answers her. "I love bones and the story they tell. I love the sheer mechanics of the body, the music of joints."

I am at the other end of the cistern, sitting on the ledge sketching. I pause in my work to listen in on their conversation.

"I look at the skull of an adult and trace the fontanels of his infancy. The breastbone branching into ribs. The bones of children, like finding flowers minutes before blooming, when their petals are all curled up into themselves and you just know something beautiful is inside, locked there forever, never exposed to the viral air." I have noticed that there are times—in fact, most of the time—when Mortichai speaks as if he is talking to himself, as if it doesn't matter if anyone is listening to him. Which is why when he does focus on you and speak directly to you, it feels as if something remarkable is happening. Now he is speaking to the wall, and himself, as if we are just witnesses.

"Doesn't it scare you?" Dalia asks. "The vacant sockets and ghoulish jaws?" She turns her own vacant sockets to him, still thickly painted.

"No, they are beautiful," Mortichai says gently. "You probably see bones and see stillness and death, so you become as petrified as they are. I see all the motion they once had. Bones are not hard. They are spongy and yielding. Flowers sometimes weave their roots straight through them. Bones speak. There is a song that still sings from deep in the marrow."

"Bones don't speak," Meirav says sharply.

"Of course they do," Mortichai continues, his back still to us. The attitude of the listener never deflects his course. "The breadth of shoulders tells a story of command. Sometimes I meet a skeleton and I know I hate this person. Though the bones are ordinary, there is a record in them of something crooked, a swagger in the legs, false pride in the chest. Other times, I meet a skeleton and praise heaven that I have a chance to meet this individual. I love the dance of the two bones in the forearm, and the two bones in the calf, partners for life. And why are there two? It is only so I can turn my wrist like this, or my ankle like that. Their sole purpose is to make us graceful. Bones are amazing. Lower ribs in the north, hips protruding in the south, gates to a forbidden city."

Meirav turns away from Mortichai, muttering, "You might look pious but you're a *freak*."

Mortichai continues, "Have you ever seen how elephants caress bones, how they recognize the remains of their relatives and weep? I love elephants. But dogs bury bones and kick up dirt between their hind legs."

While Mortichai is talking, I find myself putting my sketchbook aside and listening to him very carefully, trying to will his words to me like a child trying to attract butterflies. Then I murmur, out of the blue, "Norris once called me a *T. rex*," and am immediately ashamed. I hope he and Meirav haven't heard me, and I dread any response.

"He doesn't know bones," Mortichai says quietly, without turning around to see my face burning red. I am grateful.

"How would you describe my bones?" I ask, feeling safer talking to his back.

He answers instantly, "*Shacharit.*"

"What does that mean?" I am embarrassed to ask. My Hebrew is excellent, but I do not recognize that word.

"It means 'morning prayer,'" he says with the same even voice. "It is the prayer service we traditionally recite every morning."

My whole body relaxes as I lean back against the wall. I hope he never turns around, and yet I'm longing for his eyes.

"I've dug up hundreds of skeletons," I confess cautiously, "and I've been disappointed every time."

"Why," Mortichai asks, still brushing the mural. "Are you looking for Elisha?"

I am silent and he doesn't say anything more for a long while.

When he turns around, he sees me sitting staring in front of me. I am in a distant place, another time. As he walks toward me he says, "I'm sorry. Very obscure reference in Second Kings."

"Thirteen twenty-one," I answer. Then I add while looking at my lap, "I've been looking for Elisha for a long time." I am bewildered that he mentioned Elisha, the prophet whose bones brought a dead man to life. Whenever I uncover bones, I cannot help being struck with the horror that someday this will be all that will be left of me too. Even still, I've kept digging, kept uncovering more and more tombs at Megiddo, in the hope that someday I would come face to face with death and for once not be afraid. Not see myself. That someday somebody's bones would heal instead of frighten me. That I'd find Elisha.

"That is very sad," he says.

"That's me." He stands in front of me now. He is talking to me. Meirav, Dalia, and Walid are debating something else. It is just him and me.

"I didn't mean it is sad for you," he says. "I meant it is sad for the bones you find. That they are trying to tell you their story, and you are mad at them for obeying God's order. They still have magic, Page. You only have to be open to meeting them on their terms."

I want to respond. I want to say thank you for putting my fears into a new setting. *Apples of gold in settings of silver.*

Suddenly the cistern is filled with the sound of a loud buzzing. It comes from Mortichai's belt. He scrambles to shut it off and says abruptly and apologetically that he does some volunteering at a hospital. A determined look comes over his face and he furrows his brow as he looks down at me. Before I can ask what is wrong, he turns and races up the ladder. I imagine him grabbing his coat and hat off the couch. I listen as he runs out the front door and his car speeds away.

After Mortichai leaves, I don't feel like working anymore. I call Itai and tell him, "You don't have to assign an Israeli to supervise along with me, I found one. Mortichai Masters is assisting. Know him?"

"Mortichai, yeah, interesting guy. I'd trust him."

ON MY MORNING walk I think about Mortichai's face as he rushed off. A part of me feels that I may never see him again. That the buzzer was the sound of my time with him being up. When I return, he is not there. As the day progresses, my cell phone remains deathly still.

Late in the day we are all getting tired and a little frustrated. Our arms are sore from being held up for so many hours. Meirav complains, "If life is a bowl of cherries, archaeology is the pits." Everyone laughs and drops their arms in relief.

"It is a pity," contributes Dalia.

"*He who digs a pit will fall in it,*" I offer, reciting Proverbs.

Then I hear Mortichai's voice. Coming down the ladder, he takes up the challenge with, "*The mouth of a strange woman is a deep pit.*"

I am elated. I watch him descend. I see the flutter of Naima's skirt up above. She must have let him in the house.

Mortichai reaches the bottom. He looks in my direction, and his face cracks open into that smile and I feel myself transform into a young girl.

We reveal the twelfth mural, which depicts a group of people entering into Egypt. We are able to identify the Nile and the giant structures in the distance. It is remarkable to discover a mural of the Egyptian landscape here in Canaan. I am very taken by this panel. I am certain the artist must have been to Egypt, the images are so accurate. Is it possible the artist was a disciple of Jeremiah himself?

I hear Ibrahim return from work upstairs, and I know that it is night. Walid and the girls are leaving the cistern, and I am wiping my hands on my shorts. Reasoning that the worst that can happen would not be that bad, I ask Mortichai if maybe he wants to go out with me and celebrate the murals with a drink. Braced throughout the long moment it takes him to respond, I nearly fail to register it when he says, "Sounds good."

"I'll just wash my face?" I ask when we emerge into the living room.

He says, looking down at himself, "I have nothing to change

into." I laugh and sail upstairs, certain that we are going on a date. I rush into my room and shimmy out of my dusty clothes. I pull on jeans and a clean black jersey. In the bathroom I wash my face, peering into my blue eyes. I do look different, I think. I'm happy. I sweep off the bandana and brush through my hair. For a moment I wish I weren't so blond. I feel like my straight hair shines its message the same as if I were wearing a gold cross around my neck.

I bound down the stairs, and he is waiting just outside the front door. His coat is slung over one shoulder, and he looks contemplative. Unsure. "I'll drive?" I offer, and he snaps out of his mood and says, "No, no, allow me." He has a black little Subaru with tan seats. When he turns the ignition, the dashboard lights up with smoldering reds, like lava rising through cracks. I fold my hands nervously between my thighs, sensing that he is nervous as well.

"So," he says, while the squat houses of Anata roll by. Dark laundry in a nighttime breeze.

"Hey," I say to break the awkwardness, "isn't your name misspelled? Shouldn't it be Mordechai with a *d*?"

"My parents were not great spellers," he says. He is smiling, but barely. My eyes rest on the curl of his hands on the wheel.

"My parents were great spellers," I say. "In fact, they were Scrabble fanatics. They played every day with chesslike intensity. For fun, they composed an incredibly long song that contained, they claimed, every two-letter word in the English language plus their definitions."

"Sing it," he challenges.

"No," I say. I can feel my eyes gleaming.

"C'mon, sing it. I'm sure you heard it growing up," he glances over at me. "Or maybe you are lying."

I gasp exaggeratedly. "Lying! What do you take me for!" I almost slap him playfully but remember when I first met him, my holding my hand out awkwardly and his not taking it. "All right then," I say, and then after a breath begin, "*Xi* is a Greek letter, *ox* helps us plow better, *ye* is old English, *oy* is old Scottish, *it* is a neuter pronoun."

He laughs, "All right! I believe you. They were fanatics!"

"Yeah," I say. We cross through the checkpoint to Anatot. "My parents thought it was sacrilege to clear a Scrabble board unless you were starting a new game, so there was always a finished game sitting ceremoniously in the center of the coffee table. When my father died, my mother took the last game they had played and lacquered it. She framed it behind Plexiglas and wrote below it, 'Suicide Note.'"

"Suicide note," he says. "What did it say?"

I watch him watching the road. He is turning toward Jerusalem. "I can't tell you how often I would sit and stare at it, trying to glean some sort of message or explanation from it."

"Maybe I can help," he says.

I tell him what it said, pronouncing each word as if it is forbidden, a family secret locked with hidden meaning. "Breeze, zither, chimney, yowl, wiggle, landau, quack."

He is quiet for a long while. I watch him thinking, listening to the steady hum of the highway. I am expecting him to put it all together. I am expecting him to translate my father's unfinished game into the message I've been waiting to hear.

He glances at me minusculely and then back at the road. Then he nods and says, "Wow."

"What?" I ask, eagerly.

"Your parents really *were* good at Scrabble. I mean *zither* must be worth at least eighteen, right?"

I explode in laughter. I am laughing so hard that I have to wipe tears from my eyes. Mortichai is laughing too, and I can see him relax.

Catching my breath I say, "I never liked the name Mordechai anyway."

"Call me Jack," he says, and we are laughing again.

I clarify myself, "I mean I never liked it before, with a *d*, but Mortichai with a *t* changes everything. It is a perfectly balanced name. Like a menorah with four lit letters on each side and one in the middle."

"Now, what do Catholics know about menorahs?" he says to the road.

"I've lived in Israel a long time," I say. We are ascending to Jerusalem now. "On the left is *mort*, which is French for 'death,' and on the right is *chai*, which is Hebrew for 'life.' And in the middle is *I*, the ego. Front and center. It's perfect."

"I never thought about that," he says. "I always thought of it as More t'chai. More to life. I like your perfect balance better." He thinks for a moment. "I've never really been crazy about my name. Thought about changing it when I lived in Indiana. My roommate called me Mor, and that was all right. Isn't your name missing an *i*?"

We pull into a restaurant bar called the Colony. Another thing I love about Jerusalem is that its austere religious reputation is all but shattered by night when its cafés and clubs teem with jewel-eyed fillies and stallions. The Colony is crowded with Israelis and tourists, most of them younger than us. A few of them glance at Mortichai with his black yarmulke, white shirt, and black pants but pay little attention. We go to a two-top on the deck. A flat-screen television angled above his head shows a European soccer match on shimmering green. The patrons at the bar erupt in cheers now and then, and we sit oblivious. I order a lemon drop martini, he gets brandy on the rocks. I am giddy before the drink touches my lips.

I lean forward. His hands are open, on either side of his drink. I could drop my head into one of them and breathe in his palm. I say, "When you were speaking about bones in the cistern today, you didn't speak like a person who doesn't believe in ghosts or fairy tales or monsters under the bed."

"I don't," he says. "I'm into bones, not ghosts."

"When you talk they don't sound too different," I add, "to me."

He takes a deep drink, spinning his glass on the table between us when he puts it down. He says into the glass, "Bones are intimate. Even your lover never touches them. They are an ivory relief of an actual life, a physical record of journeys braved, wars fought, loves entangled. I love bones." He adds quietly, still to his drink, "Yours too."

"Mine?" I say, and he looks up, embarrassed. It is clear he regrets saying it, but I am perked up and encouraging.

He says, "How your face is all angled toward your mouth." I feel my blood racing on a course all over my body, rushing through my neck, down my arms, into my legs, every part of me coming alive.

I say, "I've always thought of bones as a mockery of desire and dreams. But skin, you know." I bite my lip. I blush. I'm falling apart.

"Skin's okay." He smiles, watching me. Then he laughs. "It changes color, that's for sure."

I laugh and dive into my drink. He says, "Especially the belly button. The body's only scar from when we were torn from our universe of softness. You don't have any weird piercings like those two girls who work for you, do you?"

I laugh and shake my head. Then I burst into giggles.

"What is funny?" he asks, smiling.

"The way you talk sometimes," I say. "You always surprise me."

He smiles widely as he shrugs and says, "There are worse things." He takes another drink and then speaks so softly I have to strain to hear him. He is shredding a napkin as he speaks. He seems nervous. "Remember when I told you that I was engaged?"

"Mm-hm," I say, drink to my mouth. I put it down. "The rabbi's daughter."

"Right," he says, thinking. Then he takes a breath, sits up, and scratches his head. His voice is stronger now. He says, "You tell me something. Tell me how you became such a rebel, chasing ghosts."

I laugh. "I'm no rebel, believe me, seriously. I am boring as a stone." I think for a moment and then say, "There was this one time when I was in grade school, and the teacher showed us these three sheets of colored cellophane, saying that these were the three primary colors. That all color came down to these—red, yellow, and blue. I just couldn't believe it! That's all there is? I was confounded. This reductive logic infuriated me. My hand shot up and I said, 'It can't be true, I've *seen* what paint can do!'"

Mortichai laughed. "You've *seen* what paint can do?"

I say, "That's exactly what I said to her! I was hoping I'd heard wrong. I had these sheets in my hand, and it didn't make sense. So I started throwing out the names of all my acrylic paints, firing them at her like those Wiffle ball machines, you know? Periwinkle, ochre, russet, eggplant, taupe, salmon, fawn, fuchsia, *fluorescent orange!*"

Mortichai is laughing. I continue, "And to each one the teacher barked, 'Yes, yes, yes, I said *all* the colors.' I kept going and going until the class could no longer contain its hysteria, and she yelled at me to stop. But the thing is, I wasn't asking for the sake of the class's amusement. I wasn't trying to be difficult. I really was troubled by the notion of three primary colors. I sat there while the lesson went on, my hands crossed while I pounded out colors in my head, growing more and more desperate. I knew purple and yellow made brown. And purple is blue and red. So if blue and red and yellow make brown, how do you make black? There is nothing left to add when there are only three: how do you get to black? And what about hue? Hues of red: crimson, canary, cherry. There has to be more to color, there just has to be more. It can't all end there. Suddenly it was as if I had stepped outside myself, because my actions were like those of another person. I slapped my hand onto my desk and stood up."

"No, you didn't," he says.

"I didn't lie about the Scrabble song, did I?"

"Touché," he says.

"The whole class turned to me and the teacher put down her chalk. Boiling in malice, I seethed at her through tightly clenched teeth, 'Silver.'"

"Fantastic!" Mortichai exclaims.

"She kicked me out!" I say.

Mortichai lifts his glass and proclaims, "To the priestess of silver. The world is your chalice!"

We clink our glasses. I say, "Father Chuck told me that the three colors represent the Father, Son, and Holy Ghost."

Mortichai says, "You know what's interesting? In the world of paint, the physical world, all the colors mixed together make black.

But in the world of light, the world of the spirit, all colors combine to make white. In the world of paint, it all may come from three. But in the world of light, the whole spectrum's refracted from only one." He holds up his finger and repeats, "One."

I am quiet for a moment, and then I burst out laughing. When I finally calm down, I see that he has emptied his drink. I say, "I've just always felt that there has to be more. You know? More to color. More to life. More." We both laugh and I say, "That's your name, right?" I am looking at him adoringly now. "Mor?" *Mor*, I practically purr.

"Oh, Page," he says, shaking his head. "You are something else." He pays the bill and says gently, "Let's get you home."

XIII

*Rather let my left hand take my right hand captive than witness
one nation enslave and demolish another. Rather let my heart drag
my feet away in chains than witness one ruler flex at the expense of
another. Let the flags of the nations be white and blank, and lifted,
in the great surrender of humanity . . .*
— THE SCROLL OF ANATIYA 25:34–36

All of us, Ibrahim and Naima, Walid and the girls, Mortichai
and I, are sitting in the living room around the entrance to
the pit planning out the assignments for the day and having
coffee when a brick comes crashing through the window. A cloud of
glass hangs over the pit for a fraction of time like a giant crystal chandelier, and then drops.

Mortichai instantly throws himself over me to shield me. Everyone else throws themselves onto the floor as well. A slew of stones
follows the brick.

I feel my breath, which was shallow and fast from fear, shift underneath him to desire. His body feels large, warm, and strong around
me, and I am a sugar cube dissolving into him. It is the first time he's
touched me. He lifts off me, and before I can feel ashamed of touching him, despoiling his religious purity, or ecstatic for myself, I catch
sight of Dalia and scream.

"Dalia! Are you all right?" Dalia is rising to her feet. Bright red blood runs in rivulets through her purple hair. Her eyes roll back and her legs begin to crumple, her body falling toward the pit.

I lunge toward her and grab her forearm, twisting her toward me. Mortichai grabs me around my waist before I tumble in with her. We all fall back. Dalia is unconscious.

Mortichai lays her body out and kneels over her. Naima rushes to call the paramedics. I massage Dalia's hand while Mortichai assures us she is breathing. Walid is pressing his T-shirt to Dalia's head to slow the bleeding. After five minutes Dalia suddenly gasps deeply, although she remains unconscious. Mortichai and I carefully remove all of her earrings. We hear a siren. Meirav says, "The sound of one ambulance is good. It means someone is going to get help. The sound of two means there was a bombing and people are probably dead. The sound of three or more ambulances and you can be sure a lot of people are dead."

Mortichai and I get into the ambulance with Dalia, each of us holding one of her hands. The paramedics put an oxygen mask over her mouth and nose and we race to the hospital. I think about what would have happened had she fallen into the pit and I instinctively cross myself.

I regret it when I realize Mortichai has seen me. But he doesn't seem to mind. He just nods to me as if he understands.

The rest of the team is following us in two cars. At the hospital Walid is particularly upset. He is visibly shaken by what has happened in the house; he's frightened and pale.

Dalia has a concussion and will be monitored in the hospital for a couple of days. When she is made comfortable in her room, we all come in and smile, petting her hands. She speaks weakly and her eyelids seem heavy. Walid sits on the chair beside her and says softly, "Ahlan," hi in Arabic. She smiles warmly at him and takes his hand in hers and says, "Ahlan." Walid bursts into tears and lays his head upon her belly and she smoothes his hair in tired strokes. A nurse comes in and asks us to leave so that Dalia can rest, and when we all begin exiting we find that Walid has fallen asleep.

I linger with Mortichai in the waiting room while the others go to the cafeteria. Mortichai sits beside me on the scratchy sofa picking at the frays on his left sleeve. I feel slumped and defeated, the fluorescent lights sapping my spirit.

After we sit for a long while I ask him, "Is this the hospital where you volunteer?"

He says quietly, "I don't volunteer at a hospital."

"But when your pager went off you said—"

"I am a volunteer for the Orthodox community. There is a small group of us who are specially trained in forensics and mortuary practice who are among the first to arrive when there is a terrorist attack or suicide bombing. I'm part of a volunteer group called ZAKA. We comb the crime scene for flesh and fragments to be sure that it all gets a proper burial. So that a child's fingertip or a grandmother's cheek won't rot in a gutter or get ground by tires into the street like it was trash."

He sits with his head in his hands. He looks extremely tired.

"What do you do with what you collect?" I ask softly.

"I bring it to an Orthodox mortuary, to Eternity Mortuary, outside the city. I've been working with Eternity for a long time now."

We sit for a long time in silence. Other people come into the waiting area, sit for a while, and then leave.

Mortichai lifts his hat for a moment to run his hands over his hair. Then he straightens and speaks while looking straight ahead, "I have seen the most terrible things, Page."

"Tell me," I urge.

He puts his head back into his hands and speaks, "I have seen bodies torn in half. I have scraped pounds of human remains from floors, walls, tables, and chairs. Digits blown fifty yards from their hands. I have picked up eyes, ears. I have found shreds of flesh in the sidewalk, a thimbleful of flesh, cold and soft and bloody, and I've scooped it up as gently as I could and laid it in my collection box. We each carry a collection box. And then we go to a morgue, and we try to sort out the pieces. It is better to bury an arm with the body that lost the arm, if the clothing or skin tone can help us match, but most of the parts can't be matched. We clean each part. We say a prayer. We bury it in a special section of the cemetery outside Jerusalem with no marker."

He turns to look at me. I don't say anything. He continues, "It is morbid, I know."

Mortichai gets up and walks away from me, out of the waiting room. I have the feeling that he may be crying and doesn't want me to see. I hold myself very still while I wait, and a few minutes later he returns, stuffing a napkin into his pocket. He sits back down and continues talking. "Once I found a little foot. I picked it up delicately. It had a little scrape on the ankle. The scrape was not from the bombing, it was older, from at least a week before. It had scabbed over. This was a perfect little boy's foot with a perfect little boy scrape on it from running, sliding, and playing tag. I can't even comprehend the pain that his family went through. All I know is that I mourned for his little foot." Mortichai pulls the napkin out of his pocket and presses it to his eyes. "They lost a whole child that morning. I only knew his foot."

After a few moments Mortichai says more. "I think of that as my job. To mourn the little parts. I mourn this little patch of skin that no one is thinking about because they are busy grieving the whole person. A person is not finite, Page." Mortichai turns and his eyes meet mine. "He is a galaxy. I could study a fragment of a person for a hundred years and would still only know a tiny speck in the whole of a person. I could study a fragment for a hundred years, or I could love a whole person, and never take the hundred years I would need to study that person's little finger, so how could we ever say we know anything?"

"I don't know," I manage to say in a whisper. Listening to Mortichai I feel lulled by the steady cadence of his voice.

"If you ever found bloodied flesh as I have, you would never be disappointed excavating bones again. Bones are always at peace, even if they are broken. A patch of flesh is an unfathomable physical and emotional hurt."

That night we take a cab back to the house. Mortichai leans forward in the back seat trying to listen to the news on the driver's radio. I sit back trying not to hear it.

WHILE THE OTHERS are in the dining room having lunch, Mortichai and I take a walk. We walk to Elazar's stand and buy falafel sandwiches and then continue up to Jeremiah's tomb. We walk down and detour into a sunflower field, sitting between the giant stalks. We unwrap our sandwiches. I stare at him. He looks sad. His head is down, his sandwich on its wax paper at his side. He is picking at a fallen sunflower head, tracing its seeds. He is holding in his two hands the golden spiral, Fibonacci's sequence that repeats itself in conch shells and unfurling roses and hurricanes. I am wondering if I have to marry him in order for him to touch me. I am wondering if I have to convert to Judaism for him to marry me. Looking at the galaxy in his hands, rimmed in joyful yellow petals, like a playful floppy crown, anything seems possible. He glances up at me.

He says, "I have misled you."

My mouth is full of falafel. "How?" I manage to say, cheeks puffed out.

"I didn't tell you everything about the rabbi's daughter," he says heavily.

"Mor, what did you do!" I say playfully, throwing a little pebble at him. "Did you take her chastity?"

Mortichai smiles faintly. He looks at me long and hard. I try to hold his gaze but become nervous and lower my eyes, digging into my sandwich. He says no more about the rabbi's daughter, and instead we talk about the cistern, and our plan to invite in the Antiquities Authority Tuesday. The site needs to be protected.

When we rise to leave, I lift myself on my fingers and groan, "Shoot, my nail." Examining my finger, with a chip of nail hanging off, I say, "When I was young, I had this little calcium deposit in my fingernail, in this fingernail. I never covered it with nail polish. I liked it. It was a little cloud. And every week it would move up as my nail grew, a cloud moving across the sky. My tiny firmament. And I let my nails grow long because I didn't want to lose it. So stupid, right?" I look at him. "To feel that way about a calcium deposit? And then my mom made me cut my nails. And when I saw that clipped nail, upon the table, severed from my finger, with its distinctive mark, I completely panicked. My mother couldn't understand what had happened to me; she thought I had cut myself." Mortichai is standing quite still. I feel uncomfortable all of a sudden. This is the sort of thing I never talk about with people.

"It's just that passage-of-time thing, I guess," I say. "Like St. Vincent Millay I am not resigned to the shutting away of loving hearts in the hard ground."

"Give it to me," he says with deep seriousness.

I laugh. I drop the nail into his palm. It looks so small, a tiny silver-gray fish arching in his large palm. He shuts his fist and starts walking through the sunflowers. Soon he is practically jogging. I dash after him. When I reach him, I start skipping in tight circles all around him like an excited child, saying, "What are you planning to do with that little piece of me? What are you going to do?"

"I'm going to put it in a locket," he says and laughs.

"No! C'mon, it is me! What are you going to do with me, what? What?"

Then he stops and says, "We are going to bury it and make peace with it. We are going to eulogize it, and then move on from this little death."

He kneels down and scrapes the soil, laying the little piece of me, my tiniest arch, into it. I kneel next to him, still laughing and giddy.

"Oh little piece of Page Brookstone," he says, "You were good at whatever you did. Thanks."

"How you twirled my hair so well," I chime in.

"All right, you want more. We say thank you. We know, little nail, that death is a part of life. Every time we blink we slough away millions of cells. We lose pieces smaller than you every moment, hair and skin, blood and tears, gone to feed the roses, and we don't even pause to say a prayer or blessing. And so you, little nail, represent all the pieces of us that we shed. We appreciate you all. You will always be a part of us. Amen."

"Amen! Amen!" I leap up and skip through the stalks.

"You see?" he says. "Part of us dies every day, but part of us skips away."

I stand still. "But one day, all of me will stop," I say, eyes wide with the truth of that.

"No," he corrects me. "The best of you will always skip away." We begin walking toward the road.

"I thought you loved bones," I say, tentatively.

"I do," he says, "but I love your bones the least of you." Then he quickly wipes his mouth, as if what he just said was distasteful. "I'm sorry," he apologizes.

"For what?" I ask, but we walk on saying nothing more.

XIV

If I could spirit that yoke away, if I could heal what ails you, if I could whisk you far from Judgment and close to Mercy, I would do anything, Jeremiah, but God guards you so tightly, and clasps His hands around your neck the way a fire clasps brightness . . .
—THE SCROLL OF ANATIYA 27:18–19

It is Saturday, and Mortichai is not with us. Meirav has gone to spend the day with her friends. It is just me, Naima, and Ibrahim, and we sit together at the dining room table. Naima has made a large salad. I ask them what they think of Mortichai, and she tells me that she had been talking to him yesterday after our walk, when I was down in the cistern.

"He comes from a big family," she says. "Lots of brothers and sisters, like me."

I push my carrots and cucumbers around with my fork. Ibrahim is eating, lost in his own thoughts. Every now and then he raises his head from his plate and looks past me, over my shoulder toward the living room.

"What's his story?" I ask Naima, seeing she is not volunteering information.

"You like him," she observes. And I surrender and nod. She says,

"I know he goes to biblical sites all over the country and makes reports for an American organization."

"I know," I say. I see something in her eyes, and I want her to tell me what it is. "What else did he say?"

"He studied at Indiana University," she offers.

"I almost applied to Indiana," Ibrahim says, as if he's just returned from some faraway place to land right in the middle of a conversation.

Naima shrugs. "He seems like a smart person," she says, and pushes her chair out. She goes into the kitchen to get bread out of the oven. I say to Ibrahim, "She knows something and she's not telling me."

He says, "She knows a lot of things."

Naima comes back and rips a piece of hot bread off the fresh loaf and tosses it on my plate. She blows on her fingers and waves them in the air.

"Did you burn yourself?" I ask.

"It's okay," Naima says. We go back to eating. I have successfully separated out the carrots from the cucumbers and now I mix them all together again.

Naima wipes her mouth. "Page, he's getting married at the end of the summer."

I look up at her. "At the end of the summer?" I ask. "It's July!" She waits and watches me. "Who is he marrying? Why didn't he tell me? I have been acting like such an idiot!" Shame and anger are vying for position inside me.

"He's marrying a widow. A rabbi's daughter. She has two children." Naima pinches a wad of salad with her bread and takes a big bite. With her mouth full she adds, "And one grandchild."

"He's going to have a stepgrandchild?" I ask. I am feeling sick.

Naima takes a drink of water. She asks me why I'm not eating and frowns, always a little insulted if the food she prepares isn't devoured. I feel a headache coming on and only want to lie down.

"I don't understand," I say. I want to throw all the plates against the wall. Throw the glasses so she doesn't take another stupid drink. *Just tell me.*

She says slowly, "He was engaged to the same woman when he was barely seventeen," she said. "But the engagement was called off."

"That was like twenty-five years ago!" I say, almost hysterical.

"After her husband died, I guess their romance was rekindled." Naima stuffs her mouth with bread, and I feel positively murderous. I look at Ibrahim and say, "What about you?" His mouth is also full of bread and salad. He says, "What about me? I think he's fine!"

Then Naima says, "His fiancée's probably no older than you are."

He is marrying the wife of his youth. That's what he's doing. What a fucking coward to not tell me. I am truly exhausted and I feel filthy from being underground so long. Filthy for being in love with him. Furious.

Ibrahim leaps up when the front door opens. It's Dalia coming back from the hospital. Walid has spent every day at her side, and when she returns through the door, they are hand in hand.

I disappear into my room without welcoming them. I curl into a ball on my bed and call Jordanna on my cell. Her husband, Nathaniel, says it's amazing I'm calling at this moment, because they think she may be in labor, it's wonderful.

"Oh," I say, "is Jordanna okay?"

"Yes," Nathaniel assures me, "it's still early." I burst into tears. "Please put her on!" I tell Jordanna, in between sobbing uncontrollably, my breath heaving, and once or twice shrieking into my pillow, that I met this man, and yes, it's been less than two weeks, but he's just—and then, there is no one left, I've waited too long, they're all gone! No one loves me, no one will ever love me, he let me imagine being in love with him, worse, he let me imagine he was in love with me! He was flirtatious, he was poetic, he was *beautiful*, it-was-as-if-he-was-composed-of-the-stuff-of-my-dreams, except his hat was too small (maniacal laughter), what am I going to do? What am I going to do? I yell at her. I curse him. I curse myself, I am so ugly, I am so stupid, I acted like such a *moron*. Blushing and giggling and tossing and turning! And on the other end of the line, I can hear Jordanna breathing short tight breaths, and Nathaniel saying urgently, "Hang up the phone, hang up the goddamn phone, *we're going to have a baby*," and her, "Just a minute, just a minute, the contractions are still far apart. I'm fine. She's falling apart."

SUNDAY WE ARE all in the pit. I am livid at Mortichai. He must know I know. He accepts my coldness and works. I am deciding when and how to confront him. I want to kick him out of this space. I want to hold him accountable for my heart's being shattered. My cell phone vibrates. It is Jordanna's husband. They have just delivered a baby boy whom they are naming Eli. I express my congratulations and excitement for them. When I get off the phone Meirav announces that she hopes she never has a child. The world is too dangerous and mean. She says that her new boyfriend, Shrag, also doesn't want kids. She points her spade at me and asks, "Have you ever regretted not having children?"

I am self-conscious about her question. I imagine what Mortichai must be thinking. His fiancée is a mother of two. His mother had ten children.

"It is hard to answer that question," I say to Meirav, wishing her to shut up.

In Mortichai's community a life like mine must be viewed as a dead end. I don't want to look at him, but involuntarily I glance his way. I remember that he also has not had children of his own. Even through my anger and humiliation I find myself wondering how he feels about becoming a stepfather, and a stepgrandfather. He says to me, "That's a good way to answer it." It makes me fume.

"Don't talk to me," I snap. Dali and Walid turn around and Meirav says, "Well, w'the hell's between you?"

"You don't talk to me either," I say to her. "We are opening this place the day after tomorrow. It is going to be a zoo and there is a lot to do."

Mortichai looks pale. He puts his hand over his eyes and rubs them. He says, "Page, I'm . . . ," and I point at him and say slowly and deliberately, "Don't you talk to me, do you understand?" as if he is an imbecile. He looks at me, almost helpless, his eyes pleading. Dalia and Walid are watching with their fingers interlaced. Independent Meirav just stands and waits. I say, "And congratulations, *Mortichai*. I am sure you *observed* that *this time*, my heart was in it."

"I know," he tries to say, but I shout, "Shut up! All right? How much more clear can I make it? Maybe in Hebrew you'll get it. *Shtok!*"

The hours roll by and everyone is working in silence. The only noise is the sound of equipment being moved and Naima's footsteps overhead, straightening and preparing a meal. I want to cry, but I concentrate on the mural before me. The Temple walls being breached.

After nearly three hours, there is a loud buzzer. Mortichai's pager goes off. He looks at me, his face blank as a ghost's, then climbs up the ladder.

I listen from the pit as Mortichai rushes out and the front door slams. Then something suddenly switches inside me. I remember what Jordanna once told me, when we were talking about my relationship with Itai. I loved him, but I didn't want to compete with Israel. I couldn't. Jordanna said, "And then you take hold of that little thread and pull it gently until the whole thing is unraveled." No, I think to myself. I am different now. This cistern has made me different. I am not going to spend the rest of this life, whether measured in minutes or decades, down here, underground. I remember Itai peering over the edge into the pit saying, "Look who is suddenly interested in the aboveground world! Page talking politics . . . You sure you haven't unearthed the Messiah down there?" I want to be in the open sky. I want to be with Mortichai. I want to understand him. I will not let this unravel.

I drop my tools and fly up the ladder. I hear the slam of the car door as I race through the living room, and when I burst out he is already off. A mania descends upon me and I take to running as fast as I have ever run, my arms pumping and my legs flying in long arches, my heart breaking at the possibility that he won't see me as I pound with all my might through the air. I know that he'll be stopped at the Anatot checkpoint. There is a slim chance I can catch him there. I run and run, my heart pounding so hard it feels as if my rib cage might break open. The wind fills my throat. I feel my legs slowing as the road begins to incline and I hate them furiously for it and pump them harder, the checkpoint just around the bend. Oh God, please let him be there. I turn the corner skidding upon the pebbles in the road but righting myself in a flash and there he is, just leaving the checkpoint, pulling away. "No!" I try to shout, but I have hardly a breath left in me. I just about give up when I see Mortichai's head tilt upward and turn a quarter inch to the right and there are his blue eyes in the rearview mirror. The car shoots over to the side and I sprint the final stretch and leap into the passenger seat, slamming the door shut and hunching over, holding my abdomen, gasping for breath and praying my heart will not burst.

Mortichai takes a canteen from the glove compartment and hands it to me.

I motion with my hand that I need a minute before I can talk. I take the water and settle into the seat, concentrating on restoring my body's rhythm, its breath and beat. I start nursing the canteen slowly, the water healing my constricted throat. My head is against the glass.

"Thank you for chasing me," he says.

I keep my head pressed against my window and say, "I don't want to talk to you right now."

"Can we go?" he asks. I wave him to drive.

As we approach the center of Jerusalem we see the ambulance lights flashing between the low buildings. I leap out of the car and follow Mortichai. The closer we get, the louder is the sound of wailing. The police there recognize Mortichai and wave us through. Mortichai makes a beeline for the other two members of the human remains collection team. They wear neon yellow vests with ZAKA written on them. I flatten myself against the smooth edifice of a bank and sink down to the sidewalk. There is a group of women with white cloths over their heads holding one another and sobbing. Their trembling hands come up to their mouths and then fly down and then up again. After watching them for some time, I realize there is a young woman in the center who is upon her knees holding her head and wailing.

A man not far from me is kneeling with his body arched back, his fists raised to the thick sky, and he is shouting. A group of young students in green plaid skirts and white blouses with black ribbons stand huddled together with their teacher, who is trying to hug all of them to her, while her eyes scan them frantically, counting. A policeman urges her to take the students away from the scene. High above me I see the smudge of black smoke still rising from the explosion.

People are being evacuated. Four people are on stretchers, shirts and pants drenched in blood, husbands and wives throwing themselves upon them and kissing their faces. And in the middle of the square there are two bodies, each with a white sheet draped over it, through which the blood of the lifeless continues to seep. Soldiers are barricading the perimeter. I cover my ears and press my back harder against the wall. I hope it will swallow me up.

The crime scene is similar to a dig, with all the experts piecing together the evidence they gather, posing hypotheses. I try to understand it this way, in order to be present, in order to look. Then I see Mortichai moving toward something. He walks across the charred stone of the courtyard. He is carrying what looks like a white dustbin hanging off his elbow and a white tin box in his hand. As he walks he bends down and, with white gloves, bright red at the fingertips with blood, he picks up large nails that have been shot from the bomb and he examines them. If they have blood or flesh upon them, he puts them in his box.

I watch him; how graceful he is. The other members of his team have thick and fuzzy black beards and mustaches, long black coats under their vests, and black hats. Mortichai's face is so smooth and clear. His brow is peaceful, as if he is comfortable here. *There was a radiance all about him. Like the appearance of the bow which shines in the clouds on the day of rain.*

A man on a stretcher is moaning terribly as he is lifted into the ambulance. Soon four ambulances are gone and only one remains. People are still screaming and crying. A family is huddled together close to me. The daughter has blood speckled across her face and her neck, but it doesn't appear to be her own. She is in shock. The family of four with their arms all around each other move to leave, to go home. When they shift, I can see the thing Mortichai is moving toward. It is a hand.

It looks like a man's hand from where I crouch. I turn my eyes away and then I turn quickly back. I want to understand what he sees. He moves toward it delicately and kneels down. He looks at it lying on the cobblestone, empty and upturned, as if it is asking for something, or offering something.

How is it that he is able to touch that hand without even a tremor in his body? He cups the hand between his gloved palms, lifting it from the street. He carries it as if he is a servant carrying a crown. His mouth is moving as he walks. He is uttering prayers. He walks to the remaining ambulance and speaks to the paramedics for a moment. Then he brings it to the hearse that one of his team has driven and lays it inside.

We stay for five hours. Long after everyone has left, Mortichai and the other collectors comb and inspect around every cobblestone and along the walls and the gutters. Two people died in the bombing. One of them had been a surgeon, the other was an eighteen-year-old suicide bomber. The hand had belonged to the latter.

When we get back into the car, a wash of shame comes over me. I have just crouched there against the wall hugging my legs for five hours. I have been paralyzed. As we drive away, tears well up and I take a deep breath and suppress them mightily. We are quiet in the car. How small my broken heart seems compared to what we have just seen.

And yet, it is the only heart I have.

And so I ask him to tell me.

Mortichai pulls over smoothly to the side of the road and the car comes to a gentle stop. He turns to me. He takes a deep breath and looks at my hands folded in my lap.

"The rabbi's daughter, Fruma," he says her name delicately, and I am not sure if he is protecting her or me, "got married soon after I left for the United States. There was no dearth of candidates. She was the rabbi's daughter, after all."

I show no understanding. He continues, "A kind, wispy man with soft eyes married her. A Torah scholar. Anyway, they had two children, a girl and a boy. Very proper, dainty and dutiful. And, well, her husband died of heart disease a year ago."

He waits a moment. I don't stir. He goes on, "And, you see, she called me, out of the blue. I hadn't spoken with her for years and years. She said, 'You know, I've never stopped thinking about you since I was sixteen. Especially on the anniversary of what was supposed to be our wedding day. We would have been married twenty-two years tomorrow.' And of course, I did not know that, nor had I thought of her much at all in all of that time. Well, we got together and had lunch a few times, and then dinner, and then Shabbat dinner in her home with her kids, and I found her to be very smart and gentle, and even worldly, even though she has never left Jerusalem. Maybe her husband's death did that to her. I don't know. And there was no pressure to marry her, we were just meeting as friends. Walking in the park. Taking in a lecture. I found myself buying her flowers once in a while for Shabbat. There was no pressure, but there was the allure that this was the woman who had been intended for me since we were children. That her children could have been my children. And I guess with all of that combined, well, it seemed inevitable that I would ask her to marry me, this time actually ask her myself, not have my father ask her father. I was forty-two years old. I had been traveling this land up and down for almost twenty years. It seemed like . . ." Mortichai's voice breaks for a moment. He clears his throat and resumes, "It seemed like enough. I wear the hat and the coat for her. To prepare to be a good husband for her."

"To be a good husband for her or to be like her old husband?" I ask.

Mortichai looks sadly out the window and says, "He was good." I know he is talking about Fruma's deceased husband, but for a moment I think he might be referring to his deceased brother. Mortichai's face reddens and he squeezes his eyes shut. He looks ashamed of what he is about to say. He opens his eyes and looks at me. I can see his eyes are moist. He says, "The clothes I wear were his. She was going to give them away to *tzedakka*, but I said, 'We are about the same size. Why give them to a stranger? I'll wear them.'"

"Do you love her?" I ask.

"I like to take care of her," he says. "She is loving and docile, and at the same time creative and strong. She is very different from the women in our community. She has reason to hold her head up very high."

"*Find joy in the wife of your youth.*"

"And then, I ran into you."

"Do you love her?" I ask again.

He says softly and with shame, "The instant I stepped into that house, I stopped knowing the answer to that question."

"You should have told me," I say. "You made me act like an idiot."

"Oh no," he says, looking at me closely, "no, you were never an idiot. Page, you are so exquisitely beautiful. You are so magnificent. You were never an idiot. I was. I still am. I am sorry I didn't tell you. I cannot understand why every time I tried, I stopped. I am so deeply sorry. You'll never know."

I nod almost imperceptibly. "Take me back, please," I say, and he puts the car into gear.

When we arrive at the Barakat house, we sit for a moment in the car. I say softly, "It's a shame you chose Indiana and not Columbia."

He turns to me and smiles. His shoulders relax. "I might have met you," he says, his swimming eyes holding mine for a moment.

Tonight as I lie in my bed, I imagine how high that black smudge of smoke has reached by now. I imagine it dissipating into the air, darkening the world. I can feel the height of the sky, the emptiness that goes so far.

XV

I buried my face into my hands and concentrated on breathing the scent of Jeremiah's hair, a scent of apples, and oil, and melon, and high, distant breezes that rustle the tips of the Lebanon cedars.
—The Scroll of Anatiya 27:44

We are in the cistern photographing the walls. We set up bright stage lights and umbrellas in order to put together a documentary to bring to the Department and the press tomorrow. It is time to open up this cocoon.

We have finished the northeast section and I am adjusting the tripod to shoot the southeast, where the picture of the woman in the green gown waits. She has been dressed for nearly two thousand years waiting for this moment, her lipstick still holding its shine.

"Oh, damn, stop that!" Meirav shouts, pointing toward a thin trickle of water that has run down the entrance to the pit and is continuing along the slanted ceiling, winding and zigzagging its own unpredictable path.

"Do something before it damages the mural!" she shouts, looking about.

For a moment we are all frozen, watching the silvery line snake along the ceiling.

"Where is it coming from?" I ask.

"Up there in the bath," Meirav says.

"Somebody stop them!" I make for the ladder but Ibrahim beats me to it. I can only imagine Walid and Dalia, sloshing the water all over the floor.

Naima says as if in a trance, "We had a leak once, a long time ago, but Ibrahim fixed it."

"Christ," I say looking around. "Go get some towels somebody, and a bucket. Detour the flow from the living room!" Meirav is already halfway up the ladder. Naima follows her. I turn and see Mortichai has taken off his shirt and is walking underneath the trickle ready to leap upon the ledge and swab it before it damages our walls. A few moments later, four towels are thrown down and I catch a pail tossed in. The trickle of water has come as close as a foot from the wall when it hits a ridge in the ceiling and begins to drip down. The trickle stops coming in from above; Naima and Ibrahim have detoured it with blankets and a mop, and I can hear them squeegeeing the small accumulated flood out the front door. I am watching the remaining water still skittering along the ceiling to that one ridge where it drips down, *plink-plink*, into our pail, when a minuscule clump of powdered dirt loosens from the ridge and comes down in barely a dusting, a poof of pixie dust, small but significant enough to let a thin trickle of water through to continue its short course to the wall.

"There, there!" I shout to Mortichai, who leaps upon the ledge with his shirt in his hand to swipe it away as soon as it comes. His bare back, paler than the skin on his face, against the painted walls, the chariots and spears flying around him, seems an open canvas reserved for the artist's crowning piece. What would I paint there? I would dip my hands in gold and press them against it. Looking at the naked slope of his spine, his sinews and muscles moving under his skin, I am filled with mourning for something that never happened, for the happiness I am sure we could create together but never will. He stretches his arm up to swab the wet, but somehow there is an unexpected indention in the wall that allows a few drops to free-fall past his swipe and land on the mural, washing a slow, thin stripe through the art. I climb up beside him with a towel in my hand.

"Wait," I say, "We don't want to smear it." Mortichai stops with his shirt held inches from the wall. "You're right," he says. We both leap down and we stand side by side watching the water roll slowly down, pausing here for an instant, veering to the left and the right according to the texture of the wall, until it slips into a very shallow, straight crevice, which channels what is left of the thread of water. Mortichai and I look at each other. He quickly puts his shirt back on. We both bring our faces closer to the crevice. It is on the very edge of the depiction of the wall of water from the splitting of the Red Sea.

"What is that?" Mortichai asks.

"Look," I say, and outlining with my finger, I show that the long crevice is actually the side of a large rectangle. The center of the rectangle is the center of the Sea of Reeds, a crowd of Israelites marching through. Because of the enormous detail in this scene, we have not realized that the clay is actually different here than the clay of the walls. This is not really part of the wall. This is a large brick that has been carefully sealed and painted over.

I suddenly think of the spirit I thought I'd seen standing behind me in the same bathroom where Dalia and Walid are making waves. I haven't been sure if the vision was male or female, but at this moment I can picture her distinctly, standing behind me in the mirror, her face radiant, her cheeks high and her eyes wide and beautiful. I can make out each of the silver strands of hair on her head as the steam breaks around her, as if she is standing before me this moment.

"We have to open this," I say.

For ninety minutes we scrape at the four grooves in the wall. Ibrahim documents our progress with the video camera and notebook. We don't want to destroy the painting, but in case it is damaged, we photograph it thoroughly. After an hour and a half we have scraped the grooves with tiny trowels until they are almost two inches deep. The piece is less of a brick and more of a large plaque. It tilts outward. Mortichai and I gently lower the piece, holding it with the awe of new parents. We lay the baked clay plaque upon the two towels. Inside the piece, we find a brick wall. I press my hand against it.

Mortichai picks up a pair of picks in order to hammer out the center of the wall and hands one to me.

I grip it and say, "The key to the city of the dead."

Mortichai strikes the wall first, and at the very moment his pick hits, we hear a deep moan from upstairs. He strikes it again and we hear Dalia shout out, *"Aiwa! Aiwa!"* Mortichai holds up his pick, looking at it for a moment.

Meirav says with lips pursed, hip out, "Quite a stroke, Mort." We all laugh, with the bare enthusiasm that Ponce de Leon hoped to rekindle every time he lowered his lips to a Floridian fount. We fill the underworld with peals of our laughter.

We resume the hammering together, Mortichai and I, hearing nothing more from upstairs. Only the echoing clop of our striking the wall. I feel a sense of calm unfold in me. It is as if we are all swept up in whatever afterglow the lovers are feeling upstairs. As we chisel the inner wall, my mind keeps repeating, "I am here. Don't worry. I am coming for you." I have this irrational feeling that the thing I will find inside this wall is myself. A trace of me waiting to be retrieved and reunited with the rest. At 1:30 p.m. we break through, dragging out some of the crumbled brick with the back of our pickaxes.

I feel a prickling all over me.

I look at Mortichai, and his face is as serene as the full moon sailing above the quarreling tide. We have parted the Sea of Reeds. I don't care what happens between us right now, I realize. For now, this is paradise. This, maybe, is heaven. While everyone is praying with their eyes searching up, we've found it way down here. Here, with him, outside of time, maybe this is enough. If for the rest of my life this is the past I live in, this moment full of eternity, okay.

I bring a lantern into the space and narrate into the camera. It is deeper than I expected. A room, maybe ten feet deep. There are three large jars inside, all sticking out their round bellies like chubby kindergartners gathered in a semicircle for story time. The jar on the left is tinted red. I feel that they have not been waiting for just anyone. I feel that they have been waiting for me. I ask everyone if I can have a little space, a moment alone.

Mortichai, Ibrahim, Naima, and Meirav immediately step back. Walid and Dalia are fast asleep in each other's arms upstairs. I do not realize that Ibrahim is continuing his taping when I kneel upon the ledge in front of the shrine, staring straight ahead of me into the dark space. I want so desperately to pray, but no prayer comes to me. I rock and rock, waiting for some verse to come, when the prayer Jonah prayed from the belly of the fish rises to me in full out of the darkness and I begin to repeat it to myself over and over. *In my trouble I called to the Lord and he answered me; from the belly of the grave I cried out and You heard my voice . . . the bars of the earth closed upon me forever. Yet You brought my life up from the pit.* As I am praying, I peer into the cavern, studying the jars. They are over two feet high. These are not kitchen jars. These are not jars to hold oil and grain. I can tell because the necks are so wide. These are the kind of jars that hold documents. As I pray and rock, I begin to see past the jars, my eyes becoming keener in the dim light. I begin to see the outline of something behind the jars. The cavern, I realize, is very, very deep.

"There is a coffin in here," I say suddenly. "Egyptian, I think."

I climb into the crypt and bring two of the jars out, handing them to Mortichai and Ibrahim, who set them in the center of the cistern. They feel about thirty pounds, and they are thirty inches high. The air inside is beautiful to me. More beautiful than ocean air, forest air, meadows-bursting-with-wildflowers air. In the crypt the air is buoyant, vibrant, pulsing, and alive. A textured warmth.

I gesture for Mortichai to climb in to help me with the third jar, which is at least twice as heavy as the other two. He climbs in and for a moment in that small space I think about being cramped under the sink while Walid and Dalia had sex on the kitchen floor, how I sat there and wondered if I'd always be alone.

We manage to extract the jar. Then we measure the coffin. It is seven feet long and forty-nine inches wide, very wide for a coffin. It is chiseled from a single enormous block of limestone. The coffin is covered in designs. None of the coffins I've uncovered at Megiddo were carved or ornamented quite like this. The sides are etched with what looks like parched trees, silhouettes of trunks and branches entwined and reaching upward. It is beautiful and simple. On the top there is a sculpted relief of a crane or a long-necked swan, swooping in graceful flight. It is carved with a languid hand, haunting and full of motion. The coffin is not painted except for one feather that is gold-leafed on the wonderful lifted wing of the bird. The feather is a long and luxurious gold plume sculpted higher than the rest of the bird, and its tip is painted black.

"It is a quill," I say to Mortichai,

He opens his mouth but doesn't speak.

We leave the coffin and open the lids of the jars. Looking into the mouth of the first jar we open, I see a golden spiral inside, the same spiral that repeats itself in conch shells, hurricanes, and the galaxy. I feel like I am floating in space, but the spiraled galaxy below me is the edge of a tightly wound scroll. As I tip over the first jar, the parchment softly slides out into my gloved hands. We open each scroll partway to ascertain what the document is about, then return them to the jars so they can be properly studied in a controlled environment.

Gently bending back the ancient parchment of the first scroll, we can read the clear, crisp, and familiar Hebrew words, "The words of Jeremiah son of Hilkiah, one of the priests at Anatot in the territory of Benjamin." It is the Book of Jeremiah, traditionally dated around 585 BC. The condition is excellent.

The second jar contains a small scroll that begins with the words, "Alas! Lonely sits the city once great with people. She that was great among nations is like a widow." It is the Book of Lamentations, which traditional Jews have ascribed to the prophet Jeremiah, and scholars have dated it circa 550 BC. The handwriting matches the handwriting of the first scroll.

"Could this have been Baruch's cistern?" I wonder aloud, thinking of Baruch, the scribe mentioned in the book of Jeremiah. I remember the bulla with the fingerprint. "If these are the possessions of Baruch," I add, "there may be a way to prove it."

"Fingerprints," Mortichai agrees. I look around the cistern, imagining what it would mean to be able to identify the artist of these beautiful walls. Of course, I think, it would be a scribe, a man who drew fluid, beautiful lines.

When I reach toward the third jar to open it, I pause. I suddenly think of the last discovery I had at Megiddo, the infant who had been buried inside a jar twenty-five hundred years ago, its head resting toward the mouth of the jar as if waiting to be reborn. My fingers resting lightly upon the lip of the third jar, I am a midwife again. The infant had been silent. I look at the trinity of jars on the floor of the cistern, each one pregnant. I imagine that unlike the skeletons death incessantly coughed up to me in my work, what will be born of this jar will at last speak.

It is difficult to open. The lid seems baked onto the body of the jar, which is tinted a dark umber, as if a red dye has been mixed into the clay. When we manage to chip it open, we find that inside the thin jar there is another jar. With a nail and a miniature hammer we chip at the belly of this jar and it breaks apart to reveal a third jar. Again we chip apart the belly of the jar to find a fourth jar. Inside the fourth jar is a fifth jar. Inside the fifth a sixth. As each jar opens, our excitement mounts. Behind the camera, Ibrahim is nearly delirious with anticipation. Inside the sixth jar, we find a very unusual container. Thin strips of clay have been woven into a basket-weave pattern and painted red. This small jar has a lid that is sealed. We are able to remove it without damaging the intricate innermost jar, surely the work of a highly skilled artisan.

It contains a scroll that begins (my poor translation): "The words of Anatiya, daughter of Avigayil, one of the servants at the temple at Anatot in the tribe of Benjamin. She fell deeply in love with Jeremiah when she was thirteen. Her body was weak with love for Jeremiah and her throat closed up and she was mute all her life."

The handwriting is distinct from that of the other scrolls. This is a new scroll that none of us recognize. Its meter is remarkably similar to Jeremiah's; however, the linguistic style is entirely unfamiliar to me, and distinctly feminine.

I text Itai, "3 SCROLLS AND A COFFIN. GET HERE NOW."

He texts back, "Scrolls? Can you identify them?"

I reply, quick as my fingers can type, "Jeremiah and Lamentations."

"You said 3."

I call him. "I'm getting a crew together," he says. "We'll be there within the hour. For God's sake, Page, stop touching things," he says, pretending to be playful. "What is the third scroll?"

I read the first few lines to him in Hebrew.

"Anatiya?" he says, his voice escalating. "*Anatiya?* Who under God's earth is Anatiya?" I hear him shout, "Get my preservationist on the phone! Keren, I want a chronologist too. Whoever is in the building, I want them to come now." He returns to me. "You have Jeremiah, Lamentations, and *Anatiya?* Who is that? A woman? Did you say there is a coffin?"

Less than half an hour later, Itai arrives, accompanied by his entire staff of fourteen coworkers including experts, historians, and archaeologists. Itai descends into the cistern first, and when his head is barely below ground, his hands clench the ladder as if he might fall off. He swivels around at the mural. In his expression I can see, accompanying his awe and amazement, a flash of anger at me for not sharing this earlier. But then he looks down at me standing there with my hands folded together and my shoulders shrugged, admitting my guilt and begging forgiveness, and his anger seems to melt away.

"Page, you selfish, sneaky girl," he says.

I am ready. I have kept this to myself as long as I could, and now I am thrilled to rush to the ledge with it and leap. I feel inspired, renewed, youthful, and dreamy. The jars stand like three wise men greeting a messiah. The coffin waits in its dark wing.

Equipment is ordered to extract the artifacts from the cistern. A bulldozer to knock down the wall of the living room. A crane to lift the coffin. Archaeologists begin to filter in from other digs. Orna and Mickey come in one car. Police and soldiers unroll fencing around the house to keep the growing crowd at a distance. A small military vehicle stands at the end of the Barakats' street, keeping watch. The media arrive.

Inside the cistern, Mortichai and I stand back while a group of workers struggle to lift the coffin and work a tarp underneath it. A dozen reporters and their cameramen are filming inside the cistern. The Egyptian rulers upon their thrones, in black and gold with streaks of amber, serve brilliantly as a backdrop for the Keshet anchorwoman when she says in Hebrew, "We are here, two stories beneath the living room floor of Naima and Ibrahim Barakat. Ibrahim Barakat is the lawyer who handled the Basil case, which closed in his favor two years ago September. Naima, I understand you've seen ghosts ..."

The olive grove with dark green leaves against a star-splayed night sky make a wonderful impression behind the BBC reporter in his black shirt who is saying, "We are here, in the house of a Palestinian family, where an American Christian has discovered three ancient Jewish scrolls." I am surprised when Meirav grabs me and kisses my cheek, exclaiming, "An underground carnival! Isn't this fun?" She practically skips into the BBC camera's shot.

With a great rumbling sound the coffin is slid to the lip of its crypt, and the workers lower it to the ground. I stand before the coffin and answer the reporters' questions concerning the origin of the dig and the discoveries thus far. I try to sound professional. I try to explain that most burial sites native to this region and this time period don't use coffins such as this but rather use burial slab benches. The coffin represents a practice borrowed from Egypt. I walk around the cistern, followed by cameras as though I am pulling them on leashes. I walk them through the scenes of the mural, ending at the crypt itself. I point out the trail of water that led us to discover the crevice. I move aside to allow each cameraman a close shot. I introduce them to each of our jars, announce what is inside, and then bring them back to the coffin, which still waits, with its sweeping trees, its beautiful swan or stork or crane, and glinting, golden quill. The cameras roll as four men from Itai's staff remove the lid.

When I see what is inside, I gasp. Naima enfolds herself into Ibrahim's arms and cries with emotion, "It's them! It's really them!"

Inside the coffin there is a male skeleton, about six feet tall, and a smaller female skeleton, and they are wrapped around each other. Their ribs nearly overlap. The man's right arm is around the woman's shoulder and the fingers of his right hand and the fingers of her left hand are entwined. Their skulls are gazing each at the other, her skull turned up to look into his face, and his skull tilted a bit downward. Her right leg is bent and comes up slightly over his legs. They are stunning. They are beautiful, locked in their eternal embrace. They must have been very important to have been buried like this. Someone must have loved them so very much that they wanted them preserved so well. Their bones seem radiant, alive beneath the dazzling lights. Her jaw is so delicate. Her back arches toward him, and his arm embraces her lovingly.

I hear Mortichai whisper behind me, "Are you thinking of Elisha?"

"No," I say, and turn my head to him, tears welling over my eyes and spilling down my cheeks. I walk over to Ibrahim and Naima and merge into their embrace. Naima is nestled into Ibrahim's neck, and he draws me close as well, kissing the top of my head and stroking my hair. "You listened to us. You listened and you came," he says, lips pressed to me. Naima moves her head from Ibrahim's neck to nestle into mine. "We love you," she says, and we stand this way, braided together for a long, sweet moment.

Just then I hear Walid. I peel away from the warmth of the Barakats. The man in the black shirt is interviewing him, asking him about working with Jews and Christians. Walid, overwhelmed with the attention, responds exuberantly in his broken English, "We all get along. What's the big deal? In the end we just men and women, right? We all make love here. Ibrahim make love with Naima. I make love with Meirav, I make love with Dalia, Miss Brookstone make love with Mortichai, and we all Christian, Jewish, Muslim. We're all just men and women in the end. Man falls in love with woman, right? Man cleaves to woman. It says in all our holy books."

By now all of the reporters have turned to capture Walid. A strange mix of emotions washes over me. Embarrassment, for one, and for some reason the other is a sense of freedom. It doesn't hurt me, I realize, to hear stories spread and spun. I feel free. Mortichai on the other hand doesn't look so happy, and for a moment I feel a flicker of pity toward him.

"Wait a minute, everyone," commands Walid with his enormous smile. He grabs Dalia and pulls her toward him. "This is my Dalia. She is a nice Jewish girl from Ashdod." Walid gets down on one knee and he takes Dalia's hand. Dalia with her electric hair beams like an interplanetary princess.

Walid says to her in Arabic, "Will you marry me?"

And she answers in Hebrew, "In a heartbeat."

Whoops of hooray erupt from the camera crew and staff. Walid plants a deep kiss upon his bride while the women in the cistern clap for them, and the skeletons continue to gaze into each other in a stare unbroken for centuries upon centuries.

Itai bounds up to me.

"You slept with that Orthodox guy?" he asks, thumbing toward Mortichai, his voice a pitch higher than he intends.

"No." I laugh. "Of course not."

"This is totally unfair," Itai jokes. "You know I was the best lover you had."

"Now everyone does." I point out a camera that is aimed in our direction. "Sharon is going to kill you."

Itai directs the team that removed the lid of the coffin to now replace it. First I look at the skeletons again. There is some evidence of shrouds, fragments of textiles upon them. The bones are still hard, and they even look manipulable. As this is clearly their primary burial place, they are in terrific condition. With a tremendous heave-ho the team lifts the stone lid, and rests a corner upon the coffin. They are preparing to slide it back into place over the mysterious couple when I have an impulse to dive down and see the underside of the lid. On my back, I slide beneath while a few men support the lid's weight. Drawing my penlight over the underside of the lid, I see an inscription. It appears to be in the same handwriting as the Scroll of Jeremiah and Lamentations.

"Get a camera down here," I say, and half a dozen materialize.

The cistern is as silent as it has been for thousands of years as I decipher the words. Finally I read the Hebrew inscription.

"Here are buried the Prophet Jeremiah, son of Hilkiah, and Anatiya, daughter of Avigayil of Anatot."

The cistern fills with gasps, and not ten seconds later there comes a wild cheering from a small gathering of my colleagues in the front yard.

XVI

Thus spoke the child: "Restrain your eyes from shedding tears. You are a little bit Rachel when you cry, weeping for her children. But there is reward for your labor. For you are not only the heart of the prophet, Anatiya, Jeremiah's unwed bride, but you are yourself a prophet of the Lord. And this you must remember. Your disciples are many: the orphans in the street, the desert trees, nymphs and spirits."

—THE SCROLL OF ANATIYA 31:29–32

When all our finds have been safely secured, and I finally step out of the house, I am overwhelmed by the hundreds of people who have assembled. Many of them are rocking in prayer circles. I see the old woman Edna. She has her basket of cloth and she is moving through the people, encouraging women to cover their shoulders and legs. There are many taking pictures and others just watching excitedly. As I walk out the door, the assembly applauds me, and my tears run without restraint. I sit among my colleagues, and even those who have expressed leeriness about the origins of my dig cannot diminish the enormity of the discovery. Have we truly discovered the bones of the prophet Jeremiah? This possibility, awaiting verification from carbon dating and in-depth analysis, is unprecedented. There are tombs regarded by the pious as the graves of biblical heroes all over Israel's countryside, but not one has been archaeologically or scientifically substantiated.

Among the people there, I catch a glimpse of Norris. I am struck by how small he seems to me now. He is talking with his friend Ramon. I want to approach him and thank him for having taught me so much, but when he sees me take a few steps toward him, his jaw clenches, so I turn away. A colleague grabs my arm and says boisterously, "Norris was right, you really are among the prophets!"

The wall of the living room is torn down in order to make room for a crane to lift the coffin out of the cistern. The crane rolls over the tufts of rosemary, and the air fills with the perfume. The coffin is lifted. As the bed of the truck is prepared to receive it, the coffin is momentarily suspended in the air, a red strip of sunset beneath it. Gently, it is lowered, steadied, and secured in order to be driven to Jerusalem. The gaping hole in the front of the Barakats' lovely home makes it appear as if an enormous animal has rushed out of it, bursting through the wall.

People start abandoning the site as night falls. The army leaves five guards outside the Barakat home. Walid and Dalia go to a hotel to celebrate. Meirav has gone home. Mortichai has left as well. Naima and Ibrahim are in their room, and I go to mine, where I snuggle into my pillows with a warm bliss upon me. I remember when I first saw the JPEGs of the cistern. I wanted to savor every moment of its being known only to me. This gold mine of mine. Now I feel completely peaceful to let it go. To be a mediator between prophet and people. Now it is all in their hands, guaranteed to be studied and adored, safe and sound. I am done. The cistern will become a museum, a necessary tour stop. I imagine a giant foyer will be built upon the house extending from the hole in the living room wall, and people will make a donation which will be used to maintain the place. I imagine the Barakats will give their share to charity. That is who they are. What I have done is good. What is good is done. I sleep deeply.

In the morning I wake with a delicious stretch and open my eyes to the flood of light through my window. For an instant I worry that yesterday was a dream, and a blink later I am soaring. In the Book of Jeremiah there is a character named Ebed-Melech, an Ethiopian servant of the king. When the king tells him to take Jeremiah out of the terrible pit in which he is imprisoned, Ebed-Melech throws rags down to the prophet so that the ropes used to pull him out don't chafe him under his arms. I think, How wonderful that the text took the time to note this act. And now I am counted, along with Ebed-Melech, as one of the few people to have rescued the prophet from the pit. As the slave took care of the delicate skin of his arm, I think to myself, I shall take care of his bones.

Of all prophets to have discovered—Jeremiah! I have always wanted to find Elisha because I wanted the healing wand of his bones. But of all prophets it is Jeremiah whom I would most want to meet. He is the most tragic and gripping prophet, so deeply mournful and passionate. For forty years he pleaded with the people to change their ways, all the while hating the outcast he'd become. He prophesied disaster, foreseeing the destruction of Jerusalem by the Babylonians and the exile of the people. Living with the knowledge that calamity would strike, he saw death all around him and his own life became hateful to him, so much so that he wished he had never been born. He wished his mother's womb had been his grave and that the person who brought his father the news that he had a son had been killed on the spot. That is how much he hated his life. So to find him, in the end, in the arms of a woman, is the most hopeful message from the other side I can imagine.

Jeremiah was very brave. He preached defeatism, calling for surrender, and was scorned and hated by his people. Tormented by various kings under whom he prophesied, and beaten by their loyal subjects, he was forced to wear a yoke around his neck. He was humiliated at every turn. He tried to convince the people that Babylon was only a tool being used by a wrathful God to punish them for disobeying the commandments. His artful scrolls were burned by the king's scribes. He was considered a traitor and was jailed during the reign of Zedekiah until Jerusalem was destroyed by the armies of Nebuchadnezzar. He lived to see the assassination of Gedaliah, whom the Babylonians had appointed to rule over Judah, and the dispersal of the remnant of the Jewish community.

But who was Anatiya? The way her body is nestled with his, I wonder if she was like Avishag, the young girl who was chosen to warm the old, dying body of King David, someone to console the king as he breathed his last. But no, my first impression of Jeremiah and Anatiya together was more like Adam and Eve. Isis and Osiris. Krishna and Radha. Jeremiah's life was unbearably lonely and exhausting. To find him in death, restful and loved, seems miraculous, heavenly.

In the car today, every radio station is talking about some aspect of the discovery. On television they play clips from the coffin being opened, clips of the mural and the jars, as well as interviews with Naima and Ibrahim about the strange particulars. I hear them play and replay excerpts from tapes we made. I hear myself say over and over, "Did you get that sound? That's the sound of the End of Days."

On television they repeatedly show me kneeling before the crypt, muttering to myself in prayer like Hannah at Shiloh. A shaft of light streaming from the mouth of the pit hits the back of my head so that my hair gleams yellow as a buttercup. The pious Christian archaeologist finding the Jewish prophet Jeremiah in the house of a philanthropic Muslim couple. There is always humor in the reporting, but just underneath the humor, barely veiled, a growing sparkle of hope, that love is stronger than death, that our common past transcends the warring present.

Back home, my mother has already been interviewed, along with some of my professors and many of my colleagues. Even Father Chuck has been interviewed by at least two networks. He sends me a long, flourishy email about what a discovery like this should mean, saying that he is not surprised. He knew, he writes, that I was destined, "that's what I told you in the hospital so many years ago."

I have been assigned a press agent, who books an American talk circuit over the next three weeks. Everyone tells me that the field can use a scholar's voice with a pretty face. I don't want to leave Jeremiah and Anatiya, the cistern or the scrolls. I don't want to leave Ibrahim and Naima or venture too far from Mortichai's wobbly orbit, but I arrange to be on a flight in a week, thinking that will give me at least some time to see how things unfold.

When I arrive at the Rockefeller Museum, I find it armed all around. Tanks and soldiers stand guard, and beyond the soldiers there are hundreds of tourists sitting on the sidewalks and filling the courtyard around the reflecting pool. Many are studying Jeremiah and Lamentations. There is also a large group of Orthodox men and women who are praying, teetering back and forth like metronomes. As I come closer, I can hear that they are wailing and sobbing. They are praying for the prophet to be protected and returned to the ground. I wonder if Mortichai regrets his role in exhuming the couple.

As I am escorted by a soldier to the entrance, a flutter of photographs are taken of me. The soldier who escorts me whispers into my ear, "My name is Yermiyahu," which is Hebrew for Jeremiah. And then for some reason he adds, "Last night I got back together with my girlfriend. We broke up because she cheated on me while I was serving in the West Bank. But I really love her, and I don't want to punish myself any longer, so I called her. She cried on the phone and told me she loved me. What do you think of that, Miss Brookstone?" I don't quite know what to say, so I just smile.

Past the walnut doors of the department, the front office employees stand and applaud when I walk in. I remember just weeks ago coming here and hearing their muffled snickers. Now a secretary and Yermiyahu the soldier lead me downstairs to where the skeletons are being prepared for dating. As we walk down the hall, the secretary's beige mules clopping along the linoleum, she says to us, "This is the most exciting day in my life."

"Me too," I say. And it is, one of them. In fact the handful of most exciting days of my life have all been gathered into a bouquet during these last few weeks.

She clarifies, "It is exciting because the bus driver finally asked me for my phone number this morning. I have been taking that bus for four years, and every day I prepare something sweet to say to him. Something that will make me stand out from all the others who just say 'Good morning' and 'Hi.' I say, 'The bus looks great,' or 'Last night I dreamt you picked me up and no one else was on the bus, but there were no seats on the bus; instead there were couches and a TV and it looked just like my apartment on wheels.' Isn't that a clever thing to tell him? This morning he asked for my number. I said, 'I thought you'd never ask.' Do you think it was too forward of me? Here is the place."

In the large, climate-controlled room Itai and a number of scientists are leaning over the coffin. I imagine them clustered around a large bassinet, cooing over a baby.

Itai strides toward me and tugs my arm excitedly. "Come look in the coffin," he says, yanking me.

The female's upturned chin seems so coy under the prophet's stern skull. I scan the outside of the coffin, that forest of thin, interlacing trees, a design so different from other art I've seen in this region. It is a pattern that seems more likely to appear on a painted silk kimono than a Middle Eastern sarcophagus. I crouch down to look more closely. I expect to find a signature of some sort inside, but I find something simpler and more profound. The inside has been lined with clay and then glazed. The clay has been patted down, rather than smoothed with an instrument. There are handprints all over the clay.

A smile spreads across my face. I glance into the eye sockets of the female, and those phantom orbs hold me steady for a moment. *Teach me something*, I think. *Show me something about how you were buried, about how you died, and I will unravel your story backward from there, untangle your life. A unique artisan created this coffin for Jeremiah. Of course, he is a prophet, and his resting place should be unique. But why trees? Jeremiah was no naturalist. And the hand that carved the outside with such spare and careful strokes, each one precisely placed, was it the same hand that painted the detailed walls of your cistern? Why would that same artisan so crudely pat down the inside of your coffin? Why wouldn't he paint or carve a coffin fit for a prophet?*

They say the eyes are the window to the soul. I've imagined eye sockets to be no more than the windows to the skull. But as I gaze into her eyes, a vague question forms in my mind. I study her face. *Is it possible that the prophet Jeremiah is a guest in your tomb instead of you being a guest in his?* I feel as if a lantern has been switched on in my chest. I wonder, *These crude handprints—were they the artist's way of touching you? Someone buried you in the arms of a prophet and then surrounded you all around with his own hands.*

Itai is standing next to me, motionless but full of anticipation. "We are analyzing Baruch's seal," he says. "Judging from what's been scanned into the computer, I believe we have a match."

An ancient hand, long disintegrated, and yet here, the imprints of a ghost. Baruch existed then, and now again, he exists! I am as dizzy as a newly dead soul the moment she realizes that heaven exists, that the nothingness that hounded her all her life was nothing to worry about after all. I am too giddy to do any significant work. I just want to watch and soak in all the words around me.

Scientists are gathering around the coffin. Thousands of years ago this prophet stood on stone slabs preaching until his voice gave out, and now here he is, in his stone slab, with no more voice to condemn peasants but plenty enough to say. They are working quickly to measure and document. They know that any moment the pressure from the Orthodox might force them to rebury the remains and that will be the end. They understand that the government is not stepping in immediately because they too want the research completed. The skeletons are in extraordinary shape—complete and unbroken. They remind me of the Christian saints whose corpses, I was taught, have the perfume of flowers, and whose bodies never decay. Snow White preserved in her glass coffin.

"Like the faithful at Mass," I say to myself, watching the kneeling scientists. I am in a place, mentally, emotionally, and spiritually, that I have never been before. If there is love in death, then certainly it must exist in life. There is nothing that can shatter my peace.

There is a deafening crash that rattles the whole building.

People dive under desks and chairs. I don't move. I barely notice. When everyone hits the floor, it seems as if all that is left in the room is the coffin and me, each one of us heavy and real, while every other object is swallowed by the white walls, or disappearing into the white floor. Only the coffin and I are still in color. People's mouths open, but I hear no sound, no scream. All I ever wanted was to be reassured that death is not the end. I've studied my Scriptures faithfully, letting every verse weave itself into my living fabric. There before me in that coffin is a key. I know it. There is an answer in that golden quill.

I am vaguely aware that something terrible is happening. A bomb, an earthquake. There is panic on the floor around me, but I am inside a cloud. And yet my mind is unclouded, vision becoming clear. I see nothing but that rectangular box in a white undifferentiated space. I walk toward it. It is an altar. The Ark of the Covenant. I tilt my head. A woman sits up from it. She is naked, her hair falling in dark, earthy tumbles; her skin seems hot and warm, alive; her breasts perch like birds, their beaks lifted to sing. I step toward her, and a man sits up beside her, his arm slipping around her shoulders; his hand is large, her skin reddens where his fingers press in, and he has white hair rolling down his head like a melting glacier, rolling down his face, his chin; his eyes gleam like coals. I feel the lantern in my own chest turn up, a brightness increasing inside me until it feels my face must be glowing. They are alive. They smile at me, and with glistening full brown lips she mouths a word to me. There are goosebumps on his broad chest. Yes, they are so completely alive. I step toward them as they turn toward each other. He wraps her hair in a great thick rope around his hand as he kisses her. I see the artery of her neck, her pulse fluttering under the corner of her jaw like moth wings. They are alive. I am this close to them. I reach out my hand to touch her.

A hand reaches up and pulls me to the ground. It is Itai. My ears open to the sounds around me. I look toward the coffin and it is as it was before.

A soldier bursts through the doors and asks, "*Kulam beseder?* Everyone okay?"

"What happened?" people ask, rising to their feet. "Was it a bomb?"

The soldier continues in Hebrew, "A car was sent full speed into the building. It got through the security gate. We were afraid it was going to be full of explosives. Someone leapt out leaving bricks on the gas pedal. The car nearly ran over Uri Golan, our chief commander. Luckily, no one was hurt." The soldier looks over to the coffin and then back to the rest of us. He laughs a little and says, "I'll bet there were no explosives because no one wants to damage the remains of a prophet, so I guess we have those bones to thank." He turns to leave, pausing to observe, "These people are crazy. They care more about the dead than the living."

A group of us follow the soldier up the stairs, into the lobby to see the damage.

I don't want to go outside. Although I heard the soldier say no one was hurt, I am halted by memories of the suicide bombing and that upturned hand. The wall a few feet to the right of the front door has been punctured by the impact of the car, plaster cracked and curved ominously inward. There is a great commotion of people outside and the lobby is filling with soldiers and people who work in the building. It is too crowded. I have to get out of the mob, be alone to try to recapture what has washed over me in the past hour. I do not want my feeling of peace to disintegrate in the nervous bustle of the people around me. I want to think about Jeremiah and Anatiya. I saw them. I think I saw them. I am dizzy. I speed to the stairs of the tower, up to an octagonal conference room on the second floor. There are great light-flooded windows and on each of the eight sides there is a seating niche.

I climb onto the banquette in one of the niches and peer down at the street. There is a chaotic din. A white car is sticking out of the building. Cameramen are trying to get past the police barricade. There are hundreds of civilians filling the front courtyard of the museum and about two hundred Orthodox men vacillating and praying together near the reflecting pool, their faces expressing great pain as they daven. There is a group of about twenty Orthodox boys who don't look older than twelve. They are hopping up and down chanting, "House of death! House of death!"

I unlock the panes of the large window and push them open like a gate. I look back down at the car. Through the windshield I can see there is a body in it. "I thought no one was hurt," I say to myself, straining to see. I can now see that there is blood splattered on the windshield, and squinting my eyes to look harder, I can see the pink skin of a person. It looks like a small person, a child. I cover my mouth with my hand. I feel sick.

I lean out a little. I am surprised to see Mortichai on the sidewalk below me, and I blink hard, as if the light and a headache are playing tricks on me. But there he is, and even in his black hat and coat he stands out, like a rose dropped into a bowl of cereal. I hear a police officer shout to him, "Hey, Mort, see that he gets a proper burial, will you?" Then the officer laughs.

Mortichai goes to the car and pulls out the body. I sigh in relief. It isn't a person. It is a pig. Where would those Orthodox boys, or Muslims for that matter, get their hands on a pig in Israel? I remember Itai telling me about a time his troop was doing night maneuvers in the Negev desert, when they found themselves unexpectedly knee-high in mud. They had stumbled on an unmarked pig export farm. Mortichai handles the pig with the same tenderness I saw in him when he picked up that hand.

I glance again at the ultra-Orthodox group standing in a thick mass. In their midst a man turns over a milk crate near the group of chanting boys. He flips on a little amplifier that hangs off a strap over his shoulder. He has the white-hot hair and burning eyes of a zealot.

His voice thunders over the chanting of the boys. *"They have defiled my land with the corpses of their abominations, and have filled my own possession with their abhorrent things.* You kneel down and pray to the corpses of your abominations, so let your doorways be filled with the stench of death! Let the filth of unclean offerings clog your nostrils!"

Soldiers move to surround the man, but still he rants. Looking down from my watchtower, I feel as if he is speaking directly to me, and I begin to tremble. Without my making a conscious decision to speak, my voice comes channeled from some faraway place, and I lean out the window with my hands upon the ledge and call down to him.

"Liar! You are the spreader of abhorrent things. You promote death as something unclean. You want to keep people afraid!" I don't recognize my own voice. Faces turn to me. The pious in their broad hats and heavy wigs. I see other archaeologists. Soldiers look away from the preacher and up to me, waiting, unsure.

A flare of recognition rises up in the eyes of the preacher, and a flush of wildness comes over his face. He points at me. *"The beast shall ascend out of the bottomless pit! It is the beast that shall ascend out of the pit! And the ten horns which thou sawest upon the beast, these shall hate the whore and shall make her desolate and naked and shall eat her flesh and burn her with fire."*

I lean farther out the window and counter, sarcastically, "Revelations seventeen, very colorful. But *you* are the beast, preaching venom and spilling blood."

The madman's hair is whipped into a meringue, his eyes wild as he sweeps his arm around to the large crowd of captivated onlookers. "Behold, Israel," he cries. "Behold your Jezebel, enemy of the prophets of the Lord."

I am enraged. "Enemy of the prophets?" I scream. "Enemy? Ezekiel thirty-seven, *The hand of the Lord came upon me. He took me out and set me down in the valley full of bones. He said to me, 'Can these bones live again?' Suddenly there was a sound of rattling, and the bones came together, bone matching bone. The breath entered them and they came to life and stood* up on their feet. He said to me, 'I am going to open your graves and lift you out of the graves.' Who lifts the people out of the graves? I do! I lift them out of the graves!"

The people in the streets are frozen. My face is moist with passion. Deep within the thickening crowd I can see the blazing hair of Meirav. I am suddenly rocketed into the present, suddenly conscious of what I am doing, what I am saying.

"Behold," the preacher repeats. "The mistress of Megiddo, your Jezebel. Let her fate be the same as that of the Jezebel who tormented the prophet Elijah. Let her fall from her window and be devoured by dogs!"

To my horror the boys all begin chanting, "Jezebel! Jezebel!"

One of them cocks his arm back and throws a stone my way. It falls far short of the window, but it startles me and I draw back. For a moment the preacher's words penetrate me and I fear I might actually be pushed from the window. A spray of rocks and fruit are launched toward me. My heart is pounding. My body seems locked and moving too slow. The door behind me opens and two soldiers rush toward me to pull me from the window. The instant their hands touch me, I scream, thinking they are going to throw me out to be trampled by horses and devoured by dogs, like Jezebel, who was betrayed by her own guard.

I press my face against the chest of one of the soldiers, trembling, my eyes squeezed closed. He is holding me. I worry the soldiers will be mad at me for escalating the situation. I let myself spiral out of control, acting like a prophet, spouting smoke and fire. Perhaps I am insane. I think about Anatiya and Jeremiah, sitting up in their coffin, smiling at me. I begin to cry. Maybe I am. If a straitjacket feels anything like this young soldier's arms, bind me in a dark room and leave me.

When I lift my head from against the rough gun strap, I see that both soldiers are smiling. The one holding me lets go and says, "You are okay now, relax."

I nod meekly and wipe my eyes with the back of my hand. How

did Jeremiah manage even one day speaking out against an angry mob? Just a few moments of it, and I am exhausted.

The other soldier laughs and stomps his heavy boot. "My God, Miss Brookstone," he says. "How does an American woman get to know Scripture like that?"

I am surprised to realize that they are not mad, nor do they seem to recognize that I am crazy. They are not mocking me as the onlookers mocked King Saul when he was seized by ecstasies. They are looking at me as if I have done something great.

The first soldier says, "All right, you're okay. We have cleanup to do down there. Go take it easy somewhere, but stay in the building. Things are chaotic down on the street. We'll be guarding the place."

The soldiers head for the door and I watch them walking away in their green uniforms. As they leave, Mortichai arrives, squeezing between them through the doorway to get in. He has lost a layer of clothing.

"Where're your hat and coat?" I ask him, slumping into a niche and wiping my eyes.

"The soldiers weren't going to let me in, so I took them off and tried again," he says. He pulls a chair around and sits across from me. He shakes his head, but he is smiling. "The speed and precision of a missile launcher," he says.

I am embarrassed.

He keeps looking steadily at me. "Who cares?" he says. "Forget it."

I laugh. I feel the tremor in my body begin to subside. "Do you know the people across the street?" I ask. I cannot imagine Mortichai among them.

"Some of them," he says. "From my neighborhood. But none of them are family."

The soldiers are working to clear the crowd outside.

"How do you feel?" Mortichai asks.

"I feel like I lost my mind, in front of a lot of people," I say, wanting to forget. I pull my knees up and hug them, putting my head down. I say into my knees, "What are you doing here? You are engaged to be married."

I peek at him from behind a knee and then duck my head back down.

"I wanted to see if you were all right," he says, a little too flatly. I lift my head. I am relieved to see that his face does look pained. I have the feeling that there is a big knot inside him, and if I tease it apart, he could come undone.

I want him to know how deeply I do understand. I remember how profound it was for me the day he asked if I was looking for Elisha. I want him to know that I can do that too, that I can see inside him and read the verse fastened to the core of him.

I say, "You know what it says in Deuteronomy, right? *I have put before you life and death, blessing and curse. Choose life . . . by loving the Lord Your God, heeding His commands, and holding fast to Him.*"

Mortichai pulls a handkerchief out of his pocket and presses it to his eyes. He takes a jagged breath and says, "Page, I wish you could understand what I feel."

I feel angry. I say, "Here is what I understand. You don't know what it means to choose life. Whether choosing life means to honor the dead or to honor the living. Whether choosing life means *loving the Lord* and *heeding His commands*, which in your narrow mind means caging yourself in a repressively religious community, marrying the wife of your youth, whom you like to take care of but don't really love." I can see I am hurting him. I don't care. "Or whether choosing life means . . ."

"Means what?" Mortichai asks, waiting. Servile.

Choosing me, I think to myself. *Choosing me, you fucking idiot.* I think for a moment and try a different approach. "You believe man is made in God's image?" I ask, lowering my knees. I cross one leg over the other and bounce it angrily. I cross my arms too.

"Yes," he says placidly. He looks ashamed.

"So," I say. "So there. You don't know whether choosing life means following a religious code laid out by *men* in the name of God, or whether choosing life means loving yourself, loving yourself as made in God's image, and heeding the commands of your heart."

We are both very quiet now. Mortichai looks drained. I clutch my arms against my chest. My heart is beating faster than when I chased him in his car. Blood rushes to my face and my hands are hot, clenched into fists tucked under my arms.

He says confessionally, reverently, "I have been wrestling with this since the day you allowed me to help you in the cistern."

I stand up. My body feels shaky, but I steady myself. "Good luck with that," I say and walk out of the room, resolved not to cry.

I hurry down the stairs to the basement, where Jeremiah and Anatiya lie. I want to be with them. I imagine my eyes are rimmed with red. Itai is there with two other members of his staff. I look at Jeremiah and Anatiya in their bed. I am so tired. When Itai turns to me, I see the concern in his face.

I tell him that I need to lie down and he walks me to his office. My head hurts so much. I feel cold. I lie on the couch and ask him for a blanket. I feel comforted being surrounded with Itai's things. They are familiar. He says he'll get me a blanket from the other room. I am asleep before he returns. I stay there until Ibrahim wakes me and takes me with him back home.

XVII

I stir up love into roaring waves. I cast a glisten into dull eyes. My love is a great river that bursts its banks and gushes from the portents of the sky, a flood that none can hold back, washing over towers and walls. Love's matriarch! Untouched by my own lover, my desire overwhelms and spills from me in torrents. My love cannot be measured, nor can its foundations ever be fathomed. As I contemplate the infinity of my love, a great miracle is mustered out of the depths of my musing—the sky rains! Great ropes of rain descend, in a great splashing rush!
—THE SCROLL OF ANATIYA 31:61–64

When we return in the morning, the chanting outside the museum is louder. The Orthodox pressure is increasing. They believe we have committed the highest sin, and every moment we keep these skeletons exhumed, we are continuing to commit it.

I go down into the basement to check on Itai's progress. I find him with at least ten other professionals. As soon as he sees me, he walks quickly to my side and offers me a cup of coffee.

"The preacher they questioned yesterday is named Elias Warner," he says. "He is an American evangelist who has been charged with disrupting the peace on a few occasions. It concerns me that he knew you."

"How do you know he knew me? Because he called me mistress of Megiddo, or because he called me a jezebel?" I jest, feeling healthier this morning after having slept well and showered.

Itai laughs. "Of course at this point anyone would recognize you, you are all over the news, but everyone knows you from what you did in Anata. He knew you from Megiddo."

"It doesn't seem strange to me," I say, shrugging. "He's an archaeophile."

Itai continues, "There was a bumper sticker on that white car that said Faithful and True."

"*Faithful and True?* Like the name of the rider on the white horse of Armaggedon in Revelation?"

"I thought you'd appreciate his attention to detail," he says. "Come with me."

In the basement of the Department of Antiquities wing, adjacent to the artifacts room, is a great cold room called the scrollery. Its walls are stacked with shelves of brown fragments, brittle as leaves salvaged from a forest fire. There, a group of specialists are working on two of the scrolls, Jeremiah and Lamentations. Both lie upon a long table, still rolled. They are so stiff that they will need to be cut into strips before being laid out.

I ask to help with the Scroll of Anatiya. It is exquisitely preserved, like the skeletons, so it does not have to be cut. It makes a crackling sound as we unroll it, hand over timorous hand. I hold my breath as each new column of text unfurls. I feel like we are unhooking the corset of a queen, slowly revealing band after band of her skin.

"Is it sheep or goat?" I ask a preservationist who is scraping flakes off the edge for carbon dating.

He gives me a bemused look, making it clear that he thinks it is a silly question—the least of the mysteries laid out before us.

"I would imagine goat," he says dismissively. He takes a digital camera and begins documenting the scroll. He puts the digital camera in a drawer at the bottom of the file cabinet, then he starts setting up a tripod and taking out more sophisticated equipment.

As I study the newly revealed segment, a word catches my eye, as if it is hovering, like a mosquito about to land on warm skin. *Mizbeach*—the Hebrew word for "altar." Scanning the passage before me, I notice that the same word is scattered throughout this segment of the scroll. I'm not a particularly talented translator, but the Hebrew in the passage is crisp and clear. I am grateful to be in the only country in the world that reads the ancient manuscripts they unearth in their own language. I am able to make out most of it. I read the verses of the panel, and suddenly I am caught up in another time and another world.

> *I threw myself upon their backs and they instantly shoved me away, as though I contained the impurity of a corpse. I could not break through to you. I scratched and ripped at their skin but they would not let me through to their prisoner. And so I did the only thing I could think of in my madness and my fear for you. I flew to the altar, past the guards who were turned toward the scene, and I took hold of the silver fire pan. I had intended to swing it against the priests, clang it against their heads like the walls of a bell. But when the instrument was in my hand, I was overcome with a fury, the likes of which I have never known . . .*
>
> *At the summit of the altar I threw my arms up, the shovel up over my head, and I slammed it down into the sacred fire. I slammed the shovel into the flames to extinguish them. To put an end to this burning. Smoke collected in my eyes, lifted the tresses of my hair. I could not put it out; I could not diminish the fire. I began to scatter the flames all about, tossing shovelfuls of flame over the sides of the altar. The flames died within moments of leaving the altar. Visions arose out of my madness: Moses, Nadav and Abihu, and Lot's wife; all those who had ever borne witness to fire raining from the sky. And I kept shoveling. I was twirling with shovel-*

fuls of flame and ash and scattering them in wide circles about the altar. Circles of fire. A guard turned to me and I saw him see me before he could shout. I leapt off the northern side of the altar, leaping over the rings that were used to fasten the heads of animals to the ground. Romantic words entered my mind on a misplaced ribbon of thought: "Hurry, my beloved, swift as a gazelle, to the hills of spices!" While you were defending yourself before the people and officials, I was ducked down and hiding in the chamber of the lambs.

I lift my head up. Yosef Schulman, a renowned interpreter in Israel, has just arrived with a black case of wonderful glass spectacles and magnifiers. My eyes are glistening from what I've just read. A woman scattering the fire on the Temple Mount, and she lived to tell her tale! I am brimming with awe. I can picture her swirling hoops of fire, trying to extinguish the sacral fire in order to save her prophet. In a way, I imagine, that sacral fire was like an energy conduit. She saw her love being electrocuted by God, and she was trying to unplug him. Yosef is beside himself with excitement over the chance to look at a never-before-translated scroll. I sit on a stool beside him as he studies the text's opening. I am warm with centuries-old afterglow from Anatiya's rings of fire. Yosef is a small man with an oily complexion and a messy black comb-over that makes it seem as if there is a permanent wind blowing at him from the left. With small eyes, he seems the type to have spent his life exactly like this, hunched over books and fragments, making notes. I can picture him as a child, engrossed by a flip book on bugs. He has an unattractive but earnest presence. I feel warm and happy. I feel that the scroll is safe lying between us.

Yosef looks up at me over his thick spectacles and says, "What you have found is astonishing." He dabs his forehead with a cloth. The preservationist is fastening glass casing over the table to protect the scroll. It is nearly all in place.

I reach over it and put my hand on Yosef's forearm and say, "Are you all right?"

"Yes. Yes, absolutely." He swabs at his eyes and then his whole face beams into a wide grin. "This is the story of a woman, Miss Brookstone. This is not the mention of a woman in the context of the story of a man. This is her own voice, describing her own love. And she lived during one of the most tumultuous times in this region's history. It's a perspective entirely missing from all our collections." He shakes his head as he looks at the length of scroll that awaits him, like a yellow brick road. It stretches nearly ten feet.

Yosef straightens his spectacles and leans over the text, his breath moistening the glass. He begins to translate the text out loud.

> The words of Anatiya, daughter of Avigayil, one of the handmaids at the temple at Anatot in the territory of Benjamin. She fell deeply in love with Jeremiah in her thirteenth year. Her body was so faint with love for Jeremiah that her soul caught in her throat and she remained mute for the remainder of her days.

I watch Yosef bent over the scroll, his fingertips resting tenderly on the edge of the table. I wonder if he has ever known a woman in the flesh. At the next table a paleographer and a scientist are arguing over the accuracy of script analysis. It is clear they are dating. The paleographer, discussing our scroll, places the text between 600 and 550 BC.

"Ah!" I say out loud, and laugh. Yosef gives me a strange look and the preservationist walks away. *Ah*, I think, *it is you, the two of you, prophet and paramour, doing this, making everyone fall in love.* I laugh again, lightly. *You've intoxicated us all, I am certain.* They have been seeping their love potion up into that house for years. I felt it in the bath. Naima and Ibrahim knew it. Walid and Meirav, Walid and Dalia. Mortichai. I sigh out loud. I have opened Pandora's lingerie drawer.

I recover myself and rejoin Yosef. After a half hour leaning over the scroll, I leap off my stool with excitement, saying, "Stop."

"What?" Yosef looks up, startled.

"Wait," I rummage through my knapsack and pull out my dog-

eared copy of the Bible with all of my penciled notes from seminary.
I look first at the scroll, at Anatiya's words:

> *I saw you surrounded with God . . . but I heard your brave little*
> *voice as a clear glass bell ring out: "Ah, Lord God, I don't know*
> *how to speak!"*
>
> *I lifted my eyes, I could not help myself! Your voice stirred me*
> *so. I looked up and saw you standing at God's very core, and you*
> *were not consumed . . .*
>
> *I thought I might die, but I lost my voice instead of my life.*

I compare it with verses from the opening of Jeremiah:

> *I replied: Ah, Lord God! I don't know how to speak, for I am still*
> *a boy . . . The Lord put out His hand and touched my mouth, and*
> *the Lord said to me: Herewith I put My words in your mouth.*

"Look at this, Yosef," I pant, astonished. "At the moment God
said to Jeremiah, '*Herewith I put My words in your mouth*,' God *took* the
words from the mouth of Anatiya. One becomes overwhelmed with
prophecy while the other grows mute. Oh, Yosef, this was not a commentary on Jeremiah, it was a parallel experience!"

Yosef caresses his pen and looks pensive.

"I wouldn't be surprised if this scroll could be broken into fifty-
two chapters just like Jeremiah. They mirror each other," I say.

"I would not say 'mirror,'" he says. "The texts may be parallel, but
this scroll reflects nothing I've ever seen." My heart flutters for him,
precious man.

I ask Itai for something to cover the parts of the scroll we have
not reached yet, and he brings me a pile of white cloths. I don't want
so many eyes staring at the naked text. I feel better covering it, protective. Now Anatiya's story can unfold in its own time.

I call Jordanna while Yosef continues to translate.

"Send me digital pictures! Please!" she says. "I have seen everything. I saw you exhuming on television. I saw you shouting from a watchtower like a maniac. I've seen photos of the skeletons, but they won't release anything about the scroll. You know this is driving me crazy!"

"I know," I say. "I want you to be here so much. You *belong* here with her. But you know from your work that stuff like this doesn't see the light of day sometimes for years."

"I know, they're all afraid it might say something heretical in there, something that will knock out the foundations of the great world religions. Like, 'the animals came on by threes.'"

We laugh. I love the sound of Jordanna's laugh. It tickles me from my head to my toes.

"Wait," I say, "let me read what Mr. Schulman just translated. *When God put out a hand and touched your mouth, God put out another hand, and touched the tip of a finger to my lips, whispering, 'shh . . .'*"

"Yum!" Jordanna exults. "Does it actually say 'shh' in the text? My heart! It is so wonderful, I wish—"

I tell Jordanna I have to go.

Yosef continues to translate with me beside him, my notebook and Bible in hand. Itai is buzzing by the door excitedly. He is carrying on about something. He rushes back to me and spins me on my stool to face him, his hands gripping my shoulders tightly. He gives me a little shake; his face is an explosion of happiness.

"What is it?" I urge him, putting my hands on his shoulders and shaking him back.

"Baruch's fingerprint"—he is breathless—"is a match."

I imagine his team rushing to construct an ornamented palanquin, putting the bulla inside on a silk pillow, and parading it through the streets of Jerusalem with banners and trumpets. "Baruch the scribe," he says, "he built that coffin. He probably painted those murals." He releases me and rushes back to the people gathered around the coffin. I look back at the Scroll of Anatiya. *So you both were scribes,* I think. *And you both followed Jeremiah.* I look toward the people all gathered and gabbing excitedly around their coffin. I feel an understanding unfurl throughout my mind. *While you were loving the prophet, he must have loved you. He must have modeled that clay skull and carved it with a thousand flowers. He must have loved you very deeply.*

Naima and Ibrahim arrive and are led directly to the coffin, to share in the liveliness of the Baruch discovery. I do not even rise to greet them. I do not want to leave the translator's side to miss a single nuance. Even Mortichai, thankfully, seems far away.

I continue to copy down the first chapter of Anatiya.

Where Anatiya writes, *I lie awake on my couch,* I am about to write in my notebook, "Here Anatiya is making reference to Song of Songs," but find myself hesitating. Who is to say whether the phrase originated with an outside source or with Anatiya herself? Who is to say that Jeremiah, Proverbs, the Song of Songs, and Job aren't all quoting her?

ITAI IS BECOMING frustrated with the number of people hovering around the department. The photographers, the experts, the reporters flow in and out. The guards struggle to manage the constant pressure outside. There are tents along the sidewalk across from the building with students having powwows over Jeremiah and Lamentations, studying and discussing, fueled by the excitement of being so near the source. In the meantime, we continue to translate the scroll.

> *Even as a youth, before the flower of my maidenhood had bloomed, I have been devoted to you; your secret bride whom you did not know. When my desire pierced me like a wreath of thorns around my head, and when the pain was sharp behind my eyes, I escaped into the wilderness and filled my arms with nature's harvest. I stretched out in beds of blossoms until my skin was pressed with petals. I tromped barefooted, plowing the soil with my toes. At the height of my sickness for you, Jeremiah, I threw my arms around a sturdy tree and my legs over a stubby branch, and, O God! Let my*

piety remain intact! I assure you no man has known me, my dear,
but that tree did break my virgin seal. I kissed its wooden heart.

"She has a tree fetish," I marvel out loud to myself. "An ancient dendrophiliac." I flip through my Bible and continue, "But if you read this alongside Jeremiah, same chapter, you will see that he writes, *On every high hill and under every verdant tree you recline as a whore . . . look at your deeds in the valley, like a lustful she-camel snuffing the wind in her eagerness whose passion none can restrain.* Throughout Scripture, Israel is compared to a maiden wantonly lusting after foreign gods, and the foreign gods are often referred to as wood because idols were carved of wood. It is a metaphor for idolatry."

"It doesn't sound like metaphor to me," Yosef says quietly, surprising me.

I think about it for a moment and agree. "In Jeremiah chapter one, he refers to a steaming pot as a metaphor for the lands to the north. In Anatiya's parallel verse, she refers to an actual steaming pot with which she cooks for Jeremiah. There in chapter two, Jeremiah talks of Israel reclining, metaphorically, as a whore. And in Anatiya, she implies she actually wrapped herself around a tree. Wherever he is metaphorical, she is literal."

He says, "As if she is the body and he the soul of one story, or one life." We look at one another across the table.

"Maybe you are right," I say. "In this passage she inadvertently becomes the perfect metaphor. What complicates matters is reading it alongside Jeremiah where it is written, *Your love as a bride, how you followed me in the wilderness,* and *I brought you to this country of farm land to enjoy its fruit and its bounty.*"

He wonders aloud, "Could Jeremiah have been watching her and drawing his metaphors from her?"

I nod, imagining. "Yes, he must have been watching her."

XVIII

Out of the heap which was Jeremiah, I saw a bony arm reach out, and a near skeletal hand extend. I heard Jeremiah whisper, "Come, O Jerusalem." I rushed to my love in a flurry of robes and tears, and threw my arms around him.

—The Scroll of Anatiya 38:76–77

I return to Jerusalem Sunday with my bags, feeling bright and free. I dress casually, in a light T-shirt and my cut-off jeans. I want to check in on things and then hit the road to Tel Aviv, planning to spend the night in a hotel by the airport. I walk in, full of breeziness, my knapsack with my notebook and laptop over my shoulder. But when I arrive in the Department of Antiquities, Itai tells me they are halting the translation.

"Why?" I demand, feeling storm clouds roll over me.

"There needs to be an international team. This is completely unprofessional. It has to stop."

"An international team? Are you crazy?" I am stunned. I can't believe Itai would want such a thing. Yosef is a renowned translator. I thought we were doing everything right, and it has been going so well!

In the 1940s an international team was selected to oversee the translation of the Dead Sea Scrolls. Well funded, the team had the leisure to take all the time in the world, and it proceeded with exclusivity and elitism. In 1991, two scholars from Hebrew Union College in Cincinnati managed to reconstruct the texts and get them published by the Biblical Archaeology Society. The international team was enraged. The *New York Times* said, "The committee, with its obsessive secrecy and cloak-and-dagger scholarship, long ago exhausted its credibility with scholars and laymen alike. The two Cincinnatians seem to know what the scroll committee forgot: that the scrolls and what they say about common roots of Christianity and Rabbinic Judaism belong to civilization, not to a few sequestered professors."

I am baffled by Itai's willingness to slow the rapid progress we are making and risk material's being lost. And then I see the elevator open. Norris steps out, and I know he is behind everything. A group of men walk behind him. The letters suddenly seem pale as watermarks on the scroll, reminding me of tearstains. I have a flight scheduled for tomorrow to New York and at this moment I wish I am on that plane already, racing far from Norris and his smirk. At the same time I dread leaving the scroll, with no one to defend and protect her from him. How he hates that I discovered something! I know it would give him pleasure to see it all destroyed. I wish I could gather the scroll into my arms, all ten feet of her, and run with her over the sea.

One of the men who steps out of the elevator into the scrollery with Norris is a stout, fuzzy man whom I recognize as Charles de Grout.

I have heard of de Grout. He looks exactly like photographs I have seen of him in journals. He has a bushy black mustache and a beard that hides his neck, making his body seem like a large oval. He is a lecturer on biblical archaeology and an enthusiastic supporter of digs. He was involved in Megiddo years before I arrived and sponsored and supervised digs around the country, as well as in Egypt and Jordan. I am immediately terrified of his involvement in the translation of the scrolls. There is suspicion that he made most of his fortune through participating in the illegal trade of antiquities, but this was never confirmed. He translated hundreds of religious texts from Hebrew, Aramaic, and Latin, but from what I've read, always with an emphasis on Catholic themes. It is his financial donations to the field more than his intellectual contributions which have earned him his prestige. I don't trust him to be true to anyone's voice but his own. He is just the type to suppress Anatiya's lyricism, burden her verse, and mute her, this time for good.

I glare at Norris. Yosef slips off his stool beside the scroll. He looks wounded. I want to protect him as well as the scroll, which seems so vulnerable before this group of men.

I try to sound respectful. "As you can see, we've been making wonderful progress in redeeming this story. Yosef Schulman is highly regarded all over the world, and I see no need for the process to be ground to tedium by committee." Yosef backs up to the desk he's set up. He is already gathering his things.

Charles de Grout holds out to me a photocopy of Yosef's translation of chapter 3. One column is Hebrew and the other English.

"As you can see," he says, "the need for discussion and careful procedure is imperative."

I take the paper from his hand and scan Yosef's writing quickly, trying to see it from Charles's eyes.

Josiah was eight years old when he became king, nearly twenty years before my birth . . . You found a companion in Shaphan the scribe. He delivered you a message from on high. He proclaimed: "I have found a scroll of the Teaching in the House of the Lord!"

He read, "These are the words that Moses addressed to all Israel on the other side of the Jordan." You did not stir, you barely blinked all the while he read, all through the night by a dim oil lamp. Your heart leapt when he read, "O happy Israel!" and a moment later you wept when he read, "He buried him." As he ended the scroll, in that tiny moment, the Lord showed the whole land to you. It was cringing and crying to you. You tore your garment, wept and stood . . .

I glance up from the paper I am holding only for a moment. At that moment I hate them all. I hate Itai for losing his nerve. I hate Charles for his selfish agenda. I hate Norris most of all, for punishing me in this way. He stands there, gloating, a sadistic expression in his eyes. I feel suddenly ashamed at what I am wearing. I am dressed like the teenagers on our dig, not like a supervisor. Not like someone who has any pride in herself. I lower my crappy knapsack.

"We cannot keep the Orthodox out of this forever," Itai is saying. "These texts belong to everyone."

"That is just the point," I say, struggling to retain composure. "If we create an international team, this text will never reach anyone. It will be manipulated and lost."

I understand exactly the problem with this chapter and why everyone is so concerned. There is a long-standing controversy among biblical scholars as to whether the Book of Deuteronomy should be included as one of the Five Books of Moses, or if it was actually written at a later time by a completely different source. Some have argued that Jeremiah actually wrote Deuteronomy, and that Deuteronomy is the scroll described in Second Kings 22:8–11.

The verses say that the servants had melted down the silver that was deposited, as if there had been a secret trade, a payment made by royalty, accepted clandestinely by the priesthood. Suddenly, after the payment, a scroll appears, seemingly out of nowhere. Many scholars believe that this scroll was Deuteronomy, the last of the Five Books, whose style is drastically different than that of the four previous books, and that it was created to enforce King Josiah's desire to return a corrupt land to theocracy. The problem with suggesting that Deuteronomy is not an authentic part of the Five Books of Moses is that it challenges every Torah scroll ever created.

The Scroll of Anatiya could be used as proof that the scroll Josiah read was indeed Deuteronomy. It begins by quoting directly from the opening of the book, *These are the words that Moses addressed to all Israel on the other side of the Jordan.* And then it continues to quote from the end of Deuteronomy, *O happy Israel!* and *He buried him.* Anatiya wrote, *The Lord showed the whole land to you*, in the same way God showed the whole land to Moses at the end of Deuteronomy.

"So what?" I say, looking up.

"You must understand the degree of sensitivity with which this must be handled," Charles says.

"No, actually, I don't understand," I say. "It is my understanding that religion is about truth and not about deceiving people. What exactly are you afraid of? How strong is a person's faith in the first place if this is all it takes to rattle it? How strong is your faith? According to Genesis, it's been less than six thousand years since the creation of the world, and the people who believe that aren't threatened whenever the bones of a *T. rex* show up." I look at Norris. He is stoic.

"To the secular world it makes a difference," Itai says solemnly. "To the secular Israeli world there is a lot of weight placed on the deeds of ownership that are in the Torah; the Jewish right to return to the land is based upon it. To call into question the legitimacy of the text's origin . . ."

"The legitimacy of the text's origin?" I try to remain calm. "The secularists unanimously agree that the text didn't appear out of heaven on Mount Sinai the way the Orthodox believe. They already question the origin. They already know it had to come from somewhere, so what difference if it was commissioned by King Josiah or written by the descendants of high priests?"

"The Torah is a sacred document; whether a person is secular or not, its stories are the fabric of our lives," Itai continues.

"So you are willing to halt the translation of this scroll because secularists feel sentimental over Scripture?" I say, trying to maintain control, "Don't you understand, Itai? They are using you!" I point at Charles. "He is counting on your believing that this is in the best interest of both secular and Orthodox Israel, when in fact it has nothing to do with you, it has nothing to do with the text, it has to do with his wanting to put his handprints all over history." No, I thought to myself, it has to do with Norris wanting to put his handprints all over me.

This is Norris's big opportunity. "Listen, Miss Brookstone. I understand that this is your discovery and so you feel protective, but you really don't have much choice in the matter. These scrolls do not belong to you alone, just because you lifted them out of the grave. You are being as elitist as you accuse others of being."

In the same flat tone he used when he told me as his student, "God must be kept out of science," he now says to me in front of my colleagues, "Emotions must be kept out of our work."

That infuriates me. What he is doing is all about emotions. In fact, he is punishing me precisely for *not* showing emotions toward him in all the twelve years we lived together at Megiddo. But there is nothing I can say about that without making myself look even more foolish. I decide to try another tactic. I collect my thoughts. "In the late eighteen hundreds Moses William Shapira bought a scroll that was said to be an ancient version of Deuteronomy but with several key differences from the canonized text. Although it was authenticated, one of his enemies accused him of creating a forgery. Shapira never recovered from the accusation, and he shot himself. The scroll, a tremendously important work, was lost. It is exactly in conversations like these that scrolls, and even lives, get destroyed."

The men are silent, and I continue, desperate to make my point. "We are all aware of how lucrative and underhanded the underground scroll trade is. That there are people who maintain intelligence networks with Bedouins and chase every hint and rumor of a find. Here we had an Arab couple, openly seeking archaeologists all over the country, and it is a miracle that no one from the underground scroll trade followed this lead before I did. We know how far the antiquity traders will go. We know that when they find a site, they will buy or rent the land, even construct a large Bedouin tent over it and dig only by night so as not to raise suspicion. Or in Jerusalem, where there is so much archaeological richness underneath, how people will drill through the bedrock under their cellars. I could have easily hidden this from the authorities. I could have pursued this on my own, dug up three scrolls, and sold them to a private collector for an unimaginable price. I could have kept them all. But I didn't. Specifically because I don't think this find belongs in the hands of the elite." I turn to Itai and resist falling to my knees. "Please, Itai, you know what is happening. If you stop the translation, this scroll will never see the light of day. If you create an international team, it may be lost forever."

Itai is genuinely pained by my distress. He says, "I understand your fears, Page. I want to keep you involved all the way. But I have to stop the translation. It has been out of control here. We have to follow a procedure."

I storm out of the scrollery. I know that it is primarily my own actions that will lead to my being shut out of the process of translating. Still, I vow I will not let what happened to the Dead Sea Scrolls happen to Anatiya.

IN THE ARTIFACTS room I pause when I see that no scientists are hovering around Jeremiah and Anatiya anymore. A lone artist is set up with a giant cube of clay on a stool in front of him. I stand for a moment considering him. He is something beautiful and Godlike in his long white smock, molding and pinching the creation. On the other hand, it is cruel, the way the focus is taken off the bones. The clay interpretation of them wouldn't bear the traces of change, pockets of time and aging, a record from infancy through death. That is exactly what they are going to do to her story, I think, watching the artist. They are going to prod and pinch it into the shape they prefer.

I walk over to the coffin and stare long and hard at the couple. I ask the artist, "Who are you sculpting first?"

He twists his face a bit as if the answer is so obvious he isn't sure I am serious. "Jeremiah, of course."

"Maybe the face of the one you love reflects you better than your own face," I say, more to Anatiya than to him.

I stand alone in the room with the sculptor. I can hear raised voices coming from the scrollery. I slump into a chair beside the artist.

"Tell me what you are thinking about as you work," I say, trying to hold myself together.

He smiles mischievously. "Actually, I am thinking about Giovanna Rusutto. The girl I worshipped back in high school. Her parents were Sicilian, but she was born here. In the army, I sculpted her from memory." With a wooden knife he peeled a wedge of clay away from what would become Jeremiah's neck. He continued, "We were encamped on the border of Lebanon. A Katyusha missile destroyed the sculpture. I had studied anatomy in school. I was intrigued by cadavers. I learned to use computers and clay to reconstruct a person's face. I worked with the Israeli police sometimes, sometimes with archaeologists around the world. Whenever I came across a female skull, I worried that what would emerge from my clay would be Giovanna's face. Last week, believe it or not, I saw her in a restaurant in my neighborhood and I almost spilled my wine."

"Did you speak to her?"

"No, it was enough. I never imagined I would ever lay eyes on her face again. And I did. I know what she looks like now. That is such a gift."

Everyone around me is dizzy with love. I looked back down at Jeremiah and Anatiya. This is your doing, I think. And then I look long and hard at Anatiya. Let him preserve Jeremiah, I think to myself. I will protect your story myself.

By five o'clock, when most people have cleared out, I sit with Itai in his office. We are both silent. I am afraid that if I speak, I will explode. How can you hand over poetry to wolves? Why didn't I do this all by myself, without involving you? Do you remember how much you once loved me?

"It is better that I am returning to the States so that you can do your job without me stirring things up," I say, finally.

"No, it is not better for me," Itai says apologetically. "But it may be better for you."

"I'm handing over everything I love to people who don't love it nearly as much," I say, sinking low into the couch. "So can I ask you just one favor? Can I spend the night here on your couch? I don't want to talk to anyone. I don't want to go to a hotel or drive back to Anata. I just want to be here, with the skeletons downstairs sleeping in their coffin. That would make me feel better. A chance to say good-bye."

Itai considers this for a moment. "I would love to let you stay, Page. I know I can trust you, but I would get in a heap of trouble. We just can't allow that, you understand. You are not saying good-bye. You are always welcome to be involved in this. I want you to. We all do. You need to be on the committee. But this has to become more organized, or else it will be thrown back at me, at all of us, in the worst way." He watches me and sighs. "We are locking up in an hour."

"Can I say good-bye to them before I leave?" I ask.

Itai stands, taking out his ring of keys. "Pretty much everyone's left. I'll take you down there."

We walk together down the hall to the steps, pushing through the heavy door. Clanking down the metal stairway, he says, "Don't be mad at me for doing my job, Page. I think this will all work out. It is not the forties anymore, it is a new era. The Dead Sea Scrolls were discovered over sixty years ago. You cannot compare the mistakes of sixty years ago to us today. We are much more professional. Anatiya won't be lost."

I loop my arm through his. "I'm not mad," I say. My heart feels like it's been hollowed with an ice-cream scoop.

At the bottom level, I reach for the handle of the door to the artifact room, and Itai says, "It's locked." He unlocks it and we enter. I walk over to the coffin, and the slow-closing door shuts with a click and heavy metallic bang. The two skeletons lie peacefully. A pedestal with a half-completed clay bust of Jeremiah, the foundation for the face to come, surveys the space. I stand over them while Itai leans against a wall, watching me watching them. *Help me think of something,* I mouth to her. My mind is racing frantically. I rest my hand on the edge of the pedestal with the clay. *Give me something. Give me something.* My fingers brush against the tools on the pedestal. I glance down. What look like little dental instruments sit in a pile like pickup sticks. Next to them is a business card. I pick it up and look at it. "Dror Katzenov. Forensic Art and Facial Reconstruction." I stare at it, thinking. My back is to Itai. I fold the card lengthwise and unfold it. Fold it again the other way. I remember another business card, the old refrigerator magnet with faded Arabic letters that I found under the sink the night I encrypted myself while Walid and Dalia made love on the kitchen floor. I thought that maybe it was lucky. I put my hand in my pocket. It is still there. I pull it out. I smile at Anatiya and mouth, *Thank you.* Then I add, *I'll try my best.*

I turn to Itai and he says, "That's it?" I nod and walk to him. He puts his arm around me as we walk toward the door and jabs, "You always were quick with the good-byes."

"You could have held on to me tighter," I retort, and he squeezes my shoulder. We exit the door. My heart is pounding so much I feel it in my eyes. We are on the first step when the door clicks and bangs shut.

"Oh," I gasp, "Jesus, I think I left something, hold on a sec."

"Let me open it," Itai reopens the door. I have the magnet in my hand. I rush over to the pedestal and take Dror's business card. I don't even steal a glance at the couple in their eternal cradle. Itai is standing outside the room, his arm reaching in to hold the door open for me. I step into the doorway, and while I quickly fit the magnet over the striker plate in the door frame, I wave with my other hand behind me, saying, "Make sure they take care of you, Ana!"

Itai laughs. "We will," he says, and I link arms with him. On the second step the door closes with a bang but no click. Itai doesn't notice.

"What do you need that guy's card for?" he asks as we ascend.

I say, thinking quickly, "I want to send him some stuff about Jeremiah. He should know more about the prophet he is reconstructing, don't you think?"

"See?" Itai says, pleased. "I know you'll stay involved."

In Itai's office I lightly kiss him good-bye. "If you wait fifteen minutes I'll walk you out," he says. I thank him and tell him I said good-bye and I think I'm just going to hit the road. Get to Tel Aviv. He settles into his desk and I heft up my knapsack from beside the couch.

At his door I turn back and ask him, "Do you think I'm crazy, Itai?"

He answers vaguely but kindly, "Not really. Listen, if I was digging through a house and bumped into the face of Moshe Rabbeinu, it might send me off the deep end too."

I walk casually out of the office, through the waiting room, and into the hall. There are office doors open along the hall. I can hear a few of the last remaining employees gathering their things. I slip through the door to the stairwell and rush down the stairs. I reach the metal door to the artifact room, utter a one-word prayer, *Please*, and gently push. The door opens. I peel off the magnet and put it in my pocket, then soundlessly close the door until a light click tells me it's locked.

I'm alone. Tears spring to my eyes and I want to scream with happiness. A sudden thought hits me and I scramble to turn off my cell phone. Then I sink to the ground and sit there, looking around me. It is so dark, except for a faint glow from an exit light. The silence around me is thick and heavy. Shelves and shelves of artifacts are used to the silence, sitting like tombstones night after night. I clear my throat and the sound echoes as loud as a train to me. The coffin is like a small planet, and every other dusty thing in the giant room rings it. I sit for a long while, feeling strangely safe. I get up and walk to the coffin; I lie down behind it with my knapsack under my head. I will wait here, I think, until everyone is gone. Until the hour is late enough that I can be sure they've all left, and it will be me and the night guards. They wouldn't come down here, I think. I trace one of the trees carved into the side of the coffin with my finger. "Oh, Baruch," I sigh. "What a beautiful hand you had." I stare into the dark and pray.

After at least two hours have passed, I walk to the scrollery. There are no windows here. The materials need to be protected from the sun. Still, when I snap on the light, I am afraid someone might see me. Regardless, I am compelled to do something before all this is locked away. I pull off the sheets that cover the scroll.

Running down the center of the room, under the glass casing, lie the ten feet of her, undulating under the amber lights like a desert path. My hands are trembling and feel terribly weak. I am searching for the camera I saw the preservationist use. I rummage over the desk in the room, under papers, in the crowded bookshelves. I open the desk drawers and dig. C'mon, I saw him put it here. I take a breath and tell myself there is no rush. I am here all night. Going more slowly, I find it in a black bag in the lowest filing drawer. I pop out the memory card and open my laptop so I can upload the pictures and take them with me. My back suddenly ripples with anxiety. I know it must be just a minute, but the computer seems to be taking an eternity to warm up. Finally the computer is open, and I insert the memory card. "C'mon, c'mon," I whisper. On my computer a window opens filled with thumbnails of the pictures on the card. "Damn," I say, scrolling through. They are all pictures of various digs, people holding up relics like proud fishermen with impressive catches. There are no pictures of the scroll. I pop the card back into the camera and rush to the beginning of the scroll. I try to hold the camera steady as I photograph the first panel of text, then review the photo in the viewing screen. The flash made a glare on the glass. I try again from a different angle and this time it is perfect. I store the first photo and hurriedly begin to make my way along the scroll. As I photograph panel after panel of text, my hands grow weaker and my arms are trembling. I try to hold the camera still, checking each image after I take it and sometimes taking it a second time, trying to fix my muscles so as not to shake.

I am snapped out of my reverie by the sound of footsteps clanging down the metal steps into the basement. My heart races. I still have nearly half the scroll to photograph, and the remaining panels are more important than the earlier ones, which have already been translated. I should have started at the end.

The footsteps grow closer, and I grimace when I realize that I am, in fact, at this moment, a thief. I have to get these images out of Israel before anyone knows I've taken them. I rush and shut off the light. My computer glows in the dark. I whisk it into a file drawer and duck under the desk, waiting. I find myself gnawing on my wrist. I hear the door of the artifact room open and shut loudly. I hear the heavy footsteps clomp through the artifacts room, pausing here and there. Then, all at once, the room I am in is flooded with light. I hold my breath, biting my lips shut. The footsteps thud closer. My pulse is a relentless mallet in my ear. His knee bumps the desk. I clench my fists, holding rock-still. He is also still for some time. I can see the shadow of his shoes from under the desk. Then he turns and his footsteps retreat. The blessed darkness returns. He walks out of the artifact room and, once again, I am gratefully alone.

When there are but four panels left, the camera indicates it has maxed its memory. Nearly dropping the camera, I erase earlier images of various digs and rush to photograph the end of the scroll. A verse from the passage I'd read last week rings inside me: *Hurry my beloved, swift as a gazelle.* At the same time, I tell myself, You have all night, just do it right. I take out the laptop and put in the memory card, uploading the images. I scrutinize each image to make sure it is clear. There can be no ambiguity. No glare. I retake photos of a number of sections. When they are all uploaded, I erase the pictures I took from the memory card and put the camera back where I found it. I pack my computer, back away, and walk into the artifact room. I wander carefully through the dark maze of artifact shelves until I feel sufficiently hidden and I lie down, passing the night dreaming, with eyes wide open, of how best to get this discovery to the public. I tell myself that her story has to be redeemed. Has to be told, why? Because it just has to. That's why. But deep down I know that I want to live to see it. And what if, as for my father, as for my grandfather, this year is my last?

XIX

Your eyes were the only eyes, the only eyes that saw everything.
They drank in visions like quills drinking ink . . .
—THE SCROLL OF ANATIYA 41:29–30

My cell phone says 7:45 a.m. I know the building opens at eight, and I want to get out before anyone comes down here. At exactly eight I gather myself and spirit up to the first floor. I slip into a bathroom. Standing in front of the mirror, I smooth my hair with my hands and take a deep breath. It's going to be okay. I wait until 8:15 and then walk in a swift beeline to the lobby. The wall that was damaged by the car is already repaired. Employees are coming in the front door. I don't see anyone I recognize, but I am concerned about their recognizing me. I walk quickly past and out the door and through the courtyard. The air is cool and fresh. When I reach the street, there are a couple of clusters of students reading Jeremiah texts on the sidewalk. Coffee canisters lie around them, along with candles that sputtered out some time ago. I turn the corner and run to my car, laughing and praising.

In the car I turn the radio up, trying to sing along to Israeli rock. When I don't know the words I make them up. At the airport I feel wonderfully, terribly conspicuous. Travelers whisper and point as I walk by. I see myself on the television monitor, kneeling in prayer before the crypt with a saintly light pouring over me. I see myself on covers of papers people are reading, my face flushed and dirty and my hair matted. I look happy. I see myself coming out the door of the Barakat home and everyone applauding. I see Jeremiah and Anatiya locked in eternal embrace.

People ask me to sign their newspapers, and I scribble my signature over my photograph, across my neck. A group gathers around me and starts to ask me questions. As I talk to them about the discovery, I begin to notice that every one of them is touching someone else, that the group around me is a mesh of arms and legs. A few of my admirers are holding hands, leaning against each other's shoulders. I excuse myself from the group. A man reaches out and grabs my elbow and says, "I am going to my son's wedding. He picked up a hitchhiker in Ashkelon and she turned out to be his second cousin. Now they are getting married. Isn't that a great love story?"

"Yes," I say, and wiggle myself away.

I give a quick smile and turn, and that's when I see Mortichai. He is standing in his black coat, black pants, hands in his pocket. He has no hat and his hair, barely eclipsed by his yarmulke, is a muss of hay and sunshine.

I am as surprised as if I'd seen Anatiya here, in the flesh, come to send me off.

"What are you doing here!" I beam.

"Wanted to see if you needed help with your luggage," he lies, and smiles. "I wanted to see you before you left."

"Coffee?" I ask him, and he laughs and says, "Nothing would be better."

We find as private a table as we can in Ben-Gurion Airport, where everything is glass and gleaming brilliantly and there is nowhere to hide.

"How are you?" he asks. His shoulders are stretching against that coat that isn't his. He looks so *constrained*.

"Good," I say. "How are you?"

"Good." He is smiling with his lips pressed together. We are waiting to see who is going to speak first.

I can't help myself. "I'm sure you know we started translating the scroll. Yosef Shulman finished three segments." I don't want to tell him about Norris and the international team. I just want to enjoy the fact that he is here.

"That's great," he says. "I can't wait to read it. Truly." He hasn't taken his eyes off me.

"Did you have a nice weekend?" I say, blushing.

"Not really," he says with a little smile.

"Why not?"

"I had a lot on my mind." I blush more deeply and then hate myself for doing so.

"Did you spend the Sabbath with your stepchildren?" I ask, trying to recover and ground myself.

Mortichai is quiet for a moment and then says, "Do you even know what the Sabbath is?"

"Yeah," I say, acting insulted, "the day of rest. *Sheesh*, who doesn't know that?"

He laughs. "Did you also know that it's the day of ultimate rest? In a way, every Sabbath is a rehearsal of death. We act like we are spirits moving through a material world."

"You spend almost as much time thinking about death as I do," I point out. I want to reach across the table and take clumps of his hair, pull him to me, and kiss him. He is adorable.

"Why do you think that is?" he asks. Hundreds of travelers bustle about. Ben-Gurion Airport is actually one of the most wonderful places in Israel, artistically desiged and lively. I feel so intimate with him, in this wide-open public space. The natural light floods us, bouncing off the polished stone floor so it is like we are floating in light.

He says, "At the end of the Passover meal we sing about God slaying the angel of death."

"Then what?" I say.

"Death only works inside of time, but in the messianic age, when every day is the Sabbath, we will live in eternity, outside of time. Death has no power but in time."

"But meanwhile," I say, "trapped in time, what do we do?"

"Drink more wine," he suggests.

"Ah, you see?" I say. "That's the answer to death, it turns out."

Mortichai thinks for a long time. The airport is bustling with people, but I find myself only living in his rich silence, waiting while his thoughts churn. Waiting for him to say the words I want to hear.

"Listen," he says, and I already am listening. "In the Garden of Eden, God says of the tree of knowledge, *When you eat of it you will die that very day.* Adam and his wife, who has no name at this point, eat of it, but they don't die that day. So what did God mean when he said *you will die*? God meant that when they ate from the tree of knowledge, they would learn that they were mortal."

I watch the contour of his hands around his Styrofoam cup.

He continues, "They had been going along playing in the garden, being children, invincible. And then they eat some fruit, and all of a sudden they know they will die one day. The first man and woman. Can you imagine the terror? They didn't have the benefit of centuries of poetry, art, and theology to deal with this, and so what did they do? That is your question, right? Trapped in time, what do we do?"

"Mm-hm."

"You know exactly what they did. You're a Bible scholar," he says happily. "Adam turned to his wife and he named her Eve *because she was the mother of all living.* He did not plead with God. He accepted that God made him mortal, and instantly put all his hope and trust in his partner. He saw eternity in her. Not just because she might bear him children someday—that is too literal—but because she was the *mother of all living.* Remember, this is before she has had a child, so what 'living' is she the mother of? It has to be life itself. Because . . ."—Mortichai's look deepens while he chooses his words carefully—"her love is in him and his love is in her, and that is something that lives forever. That is the heart of life. That is why one cleaves to another." He coughs. "So, to answer your question, love is what we do."

"Ah yes," I say, "even more intoxicating than wine." It is getting time for me to board. I decide to take a risk. I say, "I am happy for you that you are finding joy in the wife of your youth. I really am. I think it is a great story. Good symmetry." I watch him. He is waiting. "But I get the feeling that, even with all your death talk, you are a particularly fun guy. And you know something? I have been stuck in graves for most of my adult life, and I'm ready to get out, to skip through sunflowers, and break the law, make up my own rules, and enjoy being alive. You know?"

"Break the law?" he asks, eyebrows raised.

I wave that off and continue, "And I think it would be really great to do that with you." I let him see me run my eyes over him. "In fact," I say, "I think there is a big part of you that wants to take off the clothes that don't fit you and try someone like me on."

He laughs and shakes his head. "Wow," he says.

"Yeah," I say. "Wow."

"A big part of me, eh?" he says, and all at once I can picture us in a cafeteria in an American university, full of vitality and potential.

I get up and pull the handle out of my rolling bag. "I have to go," I say, and he gets up too. "Seriously, Mor," I say. "You have to get something new for your wedding. You can't wear a dead man's clothes. I don't mind the black and white thing, but all your seams are busting open. C'mon, it really looks horrible."

"You'll hear from me," he says. It pleases me that his face is red.

XX

Bring me a scroll, Baruch, quills, and a bottle of ink. I shall gather all these scraps. I shall arrange all these notes I have taken from the beginning and record them in a scroll as a testament of my life and a chronicle of how it is to love a prophet.
—THE SCROLL OF ANATIYA 49:15–17

For the first time, I do not feel as if I am home when I walk into my New York apartment. I miss Israel. I miss the Barakats. There is a package leaning against my door, and since my arms are full, I kick it gently into the apartment. I change into flannel pajamas, even though it is mid-July. The fabric is so old it is ready to disintegrate. I turn on all the metal fans. My answering machine is blinking frantically—its memory maxed out with messages.

I walk into my small living room, which is also my small dining room at times, and also my small kitchen, a blanket wrapped around my shoulders like a cape, and squat on the living room floor with the package. It is large. I am tired, and for a moment I become disoriented, thinking someone has packed up one of the scrolls and sent it to me for some reason. The return address says Department of Antiquities, but then the street address is all wrong. The package is very light.

It is an entire roll of paper towels. I begin to unroll it over my floor. In large graceful letters I read the words carefully transcribed onto the soft paper. It is the last few verses of the first chapter of the Scroll of Anatiya.

> I might kiss you never, but if I could save you but once, if I could be there one time to throw my body before a poisoned dart, if I could be there one time only to eat up your depression and die of it in your place, it would be sweeter to my soul than a kiss, no treasure could match it.

I read the passage over and over, looking at the paper towels unrolled in a great spiral around me, filling my living room. There is no name on it, but I know without a doubt that it is from Mortichai. My head feels light. I laugh a little, but not because it is funny.

There is a toy store on the block where I grew up, and they had these little mirrored magnets with metal ballerinas on top. I bought one because I loved how it seemed to be in perpetual motion. The ballerina's legs were shaped exactly like a 4, her head thrown back. Sometimes she'd spin so fast she'd fall. Like that little ballerina, I am spinning, but also dancing.

I imagine Mortichai on the floor with a felt-tip calligraphy pen, marking carefully so that he doesn't rip the delicate fibers, carefully writing so as not to bleed through onto the floor, all the time thinking what my expression will be as I read it, how I must be imagining him imagining me imagining him, two mirrors facing one another. I feel reflected in him exactly the way I want to see myself.

I can imagine him standing up and surveying the mess he created, washing his hands of ink spots so he won't leave any prints, drying them with a towel, then hunching over and carefully rolling it all up. Oh, Mortichai. Have it put in my will. When I die I want to be mummified in paper towel!

I call him on his cell phone.

"Shalom?" In Mortichai's voice I feel I can see the colors of his skin, feel its warmth.

"Hi," I say.

I hear him sigh as if relieved. "Hi."

"I found scrolls in Anata," I say. "And today, in New York, a scroll found me."

"Yes. I exhumed it from the back of a cleaning supply closet. I believe it is from the late Ironing Age."

I laugh. "It was very nice of you, Mor."

"I thought you'd miss Anatiya. I wanted to send a little bit of her to you."

"I liked the verses you chose."

"They reminded me of you."

"Would it be . . . ," I begin, and then shy from my own question.

"Sweeter than a kiss?" he finishes my thought for me. "How would I know?" Then he adds, "But to save a life, to sacrifice yourself, to save someone you admire so much, yes, I would imagine it would be sweeter."

"But then that is choosing death over life, isn't it?" I said slowly. "To say *to eat up your depression and die of it would be sweeter than a kiss*—isn't that choosing a noble but cold death, over a warm"—I pause, worrying that I have already said too much; I am afraid of what I am saying, afraid he won't understand—"life-affirming"—and I am also, equally, afraid that maybe he will—"kiss?"

"Yes," Mortichai says, with great solemnity, and then he repeats it quietly to himself, as if unable to say anything else, as if this is part of a conversation he has been having with himself for a very long time, "I know. Yes."

"And?" I ask.

I look at the paper towels all around. They are beautiful. Beautiful as the poetry of an ancient prophetess on parchment, which waited thousands of years to be found. I have been hiding behind so many fears, but Mortichai has been hiding too. He has been hiding in a dead man's clothes. But I have found him.

He says, "I miss you, *Geveret* Brookstone."

"Fruma," I remind him, though saying her name hurts. "Does she love you?"

There is a long quiet. "It's not about love in my community. At least not in the beginning. People marry and then fall in love, if they're lucky. But they don't marry because they are in love. They marry for love of God, I guess. To be able to fulfill all the commandments around having a home, raising children."

"Do you feel loved by her?"

"I feel that she and I could care for each other. I feel that her children honor me. She makes my parents happy."

"Your parents?" I can't help but laugh. "You are forty-three years old!"

Mortichai continues, "She and I have a rhythm together."

I almost ask him if he's had sex with her, if that's the rhythm he is talking about. But I realize he must be talking about the cycle of holidays. I rub the edge of the paper towels. *I might kiss you never, but if I could save you but once.* There is so much beauty in him, all tightly rolled up. Hidden. I think of him in the constraints of his too-tight clothing. My voice is gentle, unchallenging, when I ask, "If people don't marry because they are in love, does that mean that when an engagement is broken, their hearts remain intact? Would she cry over you," I add, even softer, "like I did, when I learned you were engaged?"

"Oh, Page," he says, exhaling sharply, "my God, you are . . ." He draws in his breath and collects himself. "She would remarry, there is no doubt. She is the rabbi's daughter, and he is very beloved. Oh, I know it's not fair of me to ask you to give me time to think. I think you can see how I feel. I'm struggling, because I had left the fold for so long, and I've just come back. I want to be sure, somehow, but how, I don't know."

"All right," I say, "it's all right. I have a lot to do, and I may lay low for a little while, so if you don't hear from me for a couple of weeks, don't worry too much. I don't blame you for struggling with the right things, Mor. You do what you have to do."

When we disconnect I feel peaceful with myself. I feel a love in my heart that is generous and not greedy. I reroll the paper towel and prop it on my bedside table, so it is that last thing I see before I go to sleep.

STEPPING OUT OF the shower, I hear a newscaster announce from the living room, "She's been called a 'psychic archaeologist,' and she has found the discovery of a lifetime—the bones of Jeremiah in the arms of a strange woman, as well as a brand-new scroll. The author of three books, Page Brookstone will be joining us tomorrow, and she'll be surprised to learn we've done some digging ourselves Just wait until she finds out what we've unearthed about her!"

When I show up on the set of *Good Morning America*, I feel radiant. I wear a gray silk button-down top and my best black slacks. I field questions with a smile, and during the first commercial break, a handsome man leaps up in the studio audience and shouts, "Page Brookstone, will you marry me?" It sends me into peals of giggles. There are twinkles in my eyes, and they don't fade even when one of the hosts asks me about my father. Two of my books are on the coffee table before me like old friends, *Body of Water, Body of Air* and *Upon This Altar*. They roll tape of me sliding out from underneath the lid of the coffin and announcing that these are the remains of the prophet Jeremiah. Later they show a clip of me shouting from the second-story window. I find it easy to laugh at myself.

Toward the end of the interview the host says, "There seems to be a lot of love in the air."

"Yes," I agree. "It's a spell that should never break."

After the show I step outside to the sunshine and glistening pavement. With my laptop bag in my arms, I hail a cab. I leap into the back seat giddy and high. I say to the driver, "You are in love with someone, right?"

He says, "Same woman, thirty-eight years."

"Take me to Trumbull, Connecticut," I say. The city rolling

by outside my window is bathed in sunlight. The buildings are almost platinum. A couple of times I glance through the rear window, imagining that perhaps someone knows what I have, what my plan is, where I am going. I am almost disappointed that I am not being followed.

Halfway to the Connecticut border, I pick up a *New York Post* from the floor of the cab.

Orthodox pressure in Jerusalem is increasing over the disruption of the grave of Jeremiah the prophet. Angry groups have been barricading archaeologists from working at their digs. Employees at the Department of Antiquities left work yesterday to find their cars smashed. Many have said that they are afraid for their lives.

Jewish Law forbids tampering with cadavers for any purpose, strongly discouraging autopsy and cremation for the violence they commit to the body.

Rabbi Yisroel Cohn wrote this letter to the Israeli Embassy on behalf of his community: "'Kavod hameit,' respect for the dead, is at the heart of our tradition. The body for us is not a prison the soul longs to escape. The body is the soul's partner, and allows the soul to bring deeds of loving-kindness to the world. At death the soul leaves a trace of itself in the grave with the promise that the rest will return someday.

"Resurrection is the ultimate love story between body and soul. They long for each other so desperately that their love is stronger than death, and they rise up reunited.

"It is a desecration to dig up a body to prod and poke for the sake of those voyeurs that call themselves scientists. A body in a grave is not just an empty shell in the ground. It is a sacred vessel in an ark. The Hebrew word 'aron,' used for the Ark of the Covenant, is the very same word that we use for coffin. A coffin is an Ark of the Covenant, and its contents, whether prophet or pauper, are no less sacred than the stones inscribed with the Ten Commandments. It is an abomination to exhume any body. No grave must be disturbed until God Himself opens them all."

I tip the driver amply and say, "Buy her something she's always wanted."

He thanks me and laughs, saying, "What more could she want? She has me!"

After he drives away, I stand looking at Jordanna's house and remember standing outside the Barakat home, daring myself to knock. I had no idea what I would find in Anatot. Now Jordanna has no idea what I am bringing for her. Her house is a beautiful Tudor. The sprinklers must have just finished their job because the walk is wet and shining, and the grass looks bright and pampered. I ring the bell, and Jordanna opens the door holding the baby. Her two older children are at camp and her husband is at work.

"I saw you on television this morning. You looked amazing!" she says, elated to see me. "You are wearing the same thing, you must have come here straight from the studio!"

"Let me see that baby. He looks just like his daddy." The baby, three weeks old, is scrunching his face at me.

We coo over Eli in the living room. There are toys strewn all over the floor and a tuxedo cat lounges in a patch of sun on the rug. I ask Jordanna about her life. She wants only to talk about the new scroll. Do I have copies of what was translated so far? What is it about? Could I recite some of it for her? Would it be months or decades before it is available?

"That depends on you," I say. The cat stretches and rolls over.

"What do you mean?" Jordanna asks. She has put Eli down in a bassinet and stands poised to go to the kitchen. "Do you want coffee?"

I shake my head no. "I'd love to see what you are working on."

I follow Jordanna up the stairs to her attic. The room is just as I remember, like being in a tree house. Through the window over the desk I can see the waving tips of maples and evergreens. Blue and white toile curtains match the quilt on the bed. Neat stacks of paper are organized beside her computer, along with a pretty lamp with a lacy shade. There is an electric swing for the baby in the corner.

Pale light sifts through the lace curtains over a small window. Jordanna goes proudly to her desk. Her skirt swings around her fuller hips, and she puts on her glasses.

"Still translating that book of Israeli poetry. Here." She holds up a piece of paper and clears her throat.

"Paint me. The canvas in the back of your studio, the one you return to when you have the time. Late Sabbath afternoon, add another speck. Oh to remain ever unfinished! My incompleteness creating a compulsion in you—to touch up, to layer your paint upon paint. May messianic days bring glorious finish to the world but let me ever remain your work in progress, the canvas upon which you imagine the worlds you've yet to create."

Her cat has pattered in while she is reading.

"Uh-huh," I say, and she snaps the paper down.

"Did you even listen to me? That was not an easy piece to capture in translation, you know!" Her eyes look like polished river stones, magnified by her glasses.

"Yeah, yeah," I say, "Like kissing through a veil, I get it. But I have something I need to show you."

"Aha!" She points at me. "This was all a ruse, getting me up here in the attic, pretending to be all interested in my work! You are full of agendas!"

I sit on the daybed and fire up my computer, and she drops down next to me, her cheek touching my shoulder as she positions herself to see the screen. The cat braids through our legs.

Finally the first image comes up.

Jordanna stares for a long time. I can feel the heat of her cheek through my silk blouse. "This is it, isn't it?" She looks up and I nod. "You have the whole thing?"

"Yes. And I have Yosef Schulman's translation of the first three chapters. I want you to finish the rest."

Jordanna leaps up and crosses her arms, her eyebrows pouncing on each other like predators. She looks suspicious. "Why?"

I put the laptop beside me on the bed. "Because I don't want her to belong to a group of snide academics. If I could share even a dozen chapters of her, the pressure from the public would force Norris, Itai, and the rest to finish it all. They're creating an international team to translate it. They will grind it to a halt, you know it. I wouldn't be surprised if chapter three is 'accidentally' destroyed."

"Why, what's in chapter three?"

"It talks about the discovery of the Scroll of Deuteronomy during Josiah's reign."

"It does?" Jordanna comes back to the bed, takes the computer from me, and squints at the screen. "Did you steal these?"

"No one knows that I took these photographs," I say carefully. "I rescued them. Will you help me?"

"I don't know. It's dangerous. Whatever you call it, it's still theft, and I have a reputation and a family." She squints harder. "God, I can read this; it is remarkably clear." She starts scrolling through the pictures. She stops at one. "God, it is, wait," then she peers deep into the screen. Time seems to stand still as I watch her studying. The glow of the computer exaggerates the grooves of her forehead. Ten, maybe fifteen minutes pass before she speaks, laughing. "Forget chapter three, holy sh——, wait." Jordanna thrusts herself toward her desk, snatching up pen and paper, and then dives back to the bed. "Have you tried to read—? God, no, wait." She is writing frantically, interspersing her scratching with staccato commentary. "He's not going to, oh no, oh God, he is!" she screams, and I jump backward on the bed, hitting my head hard on the slanted ceiling.

"Crap, are you okay?" she asks without looking over at me. I rub the back of my head and watch her hawkishly diving into Anatiya. She is scribbling away.

Finally I ask, "Are you gonna tell me what the hell you are screaming about? Jesus, is this how you do your work?"

"Shut up," she says. "You don't understand."

I laugh. I love her. "*I* don't understand?" I ask. "I'm the one who smuggled this out of Israel."

She turns to me. He giant eyes make me want to crack up. "Right, *you* don't understand. He is *naked*!"

"Who's naked?" I ask, scooting next to her.

She reads from her paper:

My nails dig into the ledge, and my eyes rake you, greedily sapping your life. O God, I do not want this, I do not want to peep into windows like an alley cat. My eyes are burning. My mouth is dry. The palms of my hands are sweating.

You take off your robe and stand naked. My tongue cleaves to the roof of my mouth. My bones are seized with a violent trembling. Here is my prophet, husband of my soul.

A luminance emanates from your skin.
Your thighs are smooth as the shore.
Your belly is an ivory tablet.
You stretch your arms to the ceiling,
and the whole length of you is ignited like sunlight
striking a tall waterfall.
You walk, in the dappled light,
mussing your hair with your fingers.
Your body gleams like the skin of a dolphin
and you move through the air as through water,
every muscle a dancer.
And the covenant in your lap is a delight to the eyes,
let my eyes fall out! My last image . . .

"*The covenant in your lap?*" I repeat. We look at each other, our mouths open, and then at the same time we take a deep breath and scream like schoolgirls at a rock concert. "Do you think this is Jeremiah's 'covenant' we're talking about?"

Jordanna takes off her glasses and wipes her eyes with the back of her hand. She reads, *"Give me back my dozen and one, give me that age before You stole my breath and stole my voice . . . I saw your nakedness and I am left in a spin. Utterly dazed. Jeremiah, I am a child! You mustn't overwhelm me so!"*

I gasp. Jordanna gasps too. We sit very still, our eyes unmagnified but wide as saucers staring into the space before us, shocked, as if we too had just seen a prophet of the Lord naked, as if we too were thirteen years old. "Oh no," Jordanna says slowly, shaking her head. "Oh no, oh no, oh no."

"We are going to translate this story, Jordanna," I say. "I know it, and you know it. It *has* to be done. And it has to be done faithfully."

She is pale. We hear the faint cry of the baby downstairs. She looks at me. "This is a miraculous text."

"I know," I say.

She starts manipulating the size of the photos on the screen. "The script is legible, not nearly the worst I've seen."

After a moment she says, "Yosef Schulman must have been heartbroken when the translation stopped. I am sure he hasn't slept a wink since he was pulled off the project."

I say, "This is a documented witness to a prophet's journey. It authenticates everything—even the moment Jeremiah receives prophecy for the first time."

"The religious community won't like her frolicking with trees," she says, reading an early panel. "Or a minor seeing Jeremiah naked. The text is not predictable, but there is a rhythm to it that you can immediately trust."

"What about your other work?" I say, and then tease her in a whiny voice, "Paint me! Oh, paint me! Please!"

She hauls off and hits me hard in the arm. The baby isn't crying anymore, though Jordanna has made no move to check on him. She is reading my transcription of the first three chapters. She reads softly out loud, as if reading a story to sleepy children, *"I might kiss you never, but if I could save you but once . . ."*

"Mortichai Masters sent me those words in the mail yesterday," I blurt out.

"Are you kidding me?" She shoots me her look of fury. "You are not going to talk to me about Mortichai right now. You can't possibly be thinking of him! We have here the most passionate mind of the ancient world, lifted from the trenches, and you are thinking about that creep."

"Creep?" I am startled.

"He let you think you are in love with him and never told you he is engaged! What an asshole!"

I remember wailing to her after I had learned he was engaged. "He's not that way; he's struggling."

Jordanna laughs. "Struggling! What a pompous excuse! Page, I heard you on the phone. I was having a baby and you were so devastated you didn't care, you were beside yourself with grief over him. You were livid and humiliated. He wants to link himself to you because you're now at the top of the world, and because you're hot. How selfish! You have everything right now, everything stretched out before you, and you can't just appreciate it. Instead, you look over your shoulder and dream of going back to Sodom. 'He's struggling.' Please. God should turn you into a pillar of salt!"

"You've never met him and you are judging him," I say. "What does that make you?"

"It doesn't make me an opportunist," she says. "And I am not going to meet him." She gestures furiously to the scroll on the computer screen. "I refuse to let him contaminate this. Unless he leaves his fiancée, I am not interested. And you shouldn't be either."

I have to laugh. Jordanna is such a lioness. She is the perfect translator for Anatiya, because nothing will get in her way. The baby starts crying again. She says, without looking at me, "Thaw a bottle of my milk from the freezer and feed the baby. This is incredible." I get up and head off to do as I'm told. As I walk away, I hear Jordanna say, "I am so glad you did this. I am so glad my best friend is an international thief." I turn around and she lifts her eyes to me for a moment, smiling wickedly. I know she's in it until the end. She confirms my thought with a wink.

I cradle Eli on a pillow on my lap and give him his bottle. I wonder about Mortichai's fiancée, Fruma, imagining what she must look like. In my mind, she is the embodiment of Judaism. I always felt that Israel had come between me and Itai. Mortichai will never in the end be able to choose me over his religion and heritage, I am certain. But I'm not mad, I realize. I'm not mad at Israel or Judaism, my rivals. They are regal and brave, worthy of all the best boys. Israel always holds her head high, even though she is surrounded by enemies. Most of my life, I have just been a little island with scraps of life, surrounded by nothing.

"There's no contest," I coo to the baby. "No, there isn't, right? Yes, that's right."

SITTING ON A stool in a sunlit studio in the city, I shifted my legs uncomfortably away from the cameraman while filming an interview for ABC News. Halfway through, I learn that there has been a bomb threat at the Department of Antiquities. Everyone was evacuated and the building was searched. Nothing suspicious was found.

After telling me this, the interviewer leans in and asks, "Do you agree that the skeletons, scrolls, and artifacts you discovered should be relocated out of Israel, say to France or England, or even the United States, for their own protection?"

I have not heard that there is talk of moving the skeletons to France, or anywhere for that matter. I shake my head in disgust. Then the treasure will belong to Charles de Grout and we will never see the scrolls again. It flashes through my mind that de Grout would benefit from continued bomb threats. "Perhaps a Frenchman made the threat in order to frighten people into taking them out of Israel," I say. "Or maybe it was a jealous colleague."

"You sound as if you have someone in mind," says the astute reporter.

"No one would destroy the remains of Jeremiah. No Arab, no Jew, no Christian, no one. I don't believe anyone would, and I don't believe they are in any danger. Perhaps that is the whole point of loving a prophet of the Lord. Perhaps that is why Anatiya fastened herself to him even in the grave—in order to be protected in death and in life."

"But wouldn't they be safer outside of a country as unstable as Israel?"

"When the Romans told the Jewish people they could no longer study Torah under punishment of execution, Rabbi Akiva continued to study and even to teach. His disciples said, 'Aren't you afraid?' And he responded with a fable. A clever fox said to the fish in the stream, 'Come up on land, and you will be safe from the fishermen's nets!' As dangerous as it is for fish in water, which is their natural environment, imagine how much more so if they are out of water. Israel is the natural environment for Jeremiah and Anatiya. Jeremiah even purchased land in Israel moments before the Babylonian exile. That is how much he believed in the land. He knew he'd come back. Outside of Israel, they couldn't breathe."

"Breathe?" the interviewer asks.

"They'd be fish out of water," I clarify.

The interviewer laughs. "Who knew that the poster child for Israeli PR would be a Catholic New Yorker! Let's talk about what got you started in biblical archaeology. According to your family priest, Father Charles Oren, your interest began early. He kept all your revised Bible stories in a file. He sent us a copy of his favorite. Can you tell us what you were thinking when you drew this one?"

The interviewer holds up a copy of the man rocketing out of the grave of Elisha, having been brought to life with a touch of his bones.

XXI

Open the scroll before me. It is wide and blank and it stretches like the desert before the slaves. How to take the first step?
—The Scroll of Anatiya 49:18–19

My mother lives in a two-bedroom co-op apartment directly across Central Park from mine. She lives in the same building where I grew up. We stayed in our apartment after my father died until I graduated from high school, and then she sold it, opting for a smaller place a few floors up. In the elevator I always stare at the number of our floor when Dad was alive. Seventeen. He only made it to see me blow out fourteen candles.

When I stop by my mother's apartment, I am overwhelmed by her enthusiasm. My mother is very eloquent. She's been teaching college English for thirty years. Still, I've never heard her speak so many words in a minute. She is thrilled to see me. She read the book of Jeremiah in one night and has a million questions. It is wonderful to be with her too. She has short spiky hair, darker than mine, and her neck is long and graceful. Her skin is pretty and dewy, a picture of health. I let my mother embrace me for a long while, my head on her shoulder. I love the clean smell of her clothes, the warmth of her skin, and the dab of perfume on her neck, positioned exactly for me to breathe flowers whenever she hugs me. But over her shoulder, my

eyes keep drifting to that damn Scrabble board on the wall, the suicide note I could never translate.

She feels me sigh and we pull away from each other. "You okay?"
she asks.

Tears well up in my eyes and she says, "I know that even with all
of the excitement, this is a hard year for you, being the same age that
your father—well, you could get tested, you know, and find out for
certain, instead of waiting every day and panicking any time your feet
fall asleep. You are going to be fine, honey, I know it deep inside, but
you don't know it. Do you think after September third the cloud that
clings to you will begin to dissipate?"

I blink back my tears and manage to smile. "That would be
a great birthday present," I say, sighing heavily. It is hard for me to
imagine the day after my birthday, what it means to enter the territory of time that my father never reached. I picture myself walking
beside him in the sand, and at forty, his footsteps just stopping. Mine
continue, lonely footsteps dragging. When I think of my birthday, I
imagine myself having walked alone in a great circle, reaching the very
place where his footsteps stopped, and here I am unable to go further. Maybe there is a deadly scorpion there. Maybe there is a snake.
Maybe there is just my own fear arresting me. I look into my mother's
eyes now and I see her hopes for me dancing there. A touch of her
hand on mine and for a moment I think maybe there is a day after.

When I return home, I am disappointed that there is no late-
night message from Mortichai. There are messages from Itai, Jordanna, a couple of reporters, an executive from Banana Republic, and
a colleague at Columbia wanting to set up a lecture series.

I call Banana Republic first. They want to discuss a potential
new line of clothes inspired by me. Archaeology chic. They want to
use my name in the advertising, and they want me to appear in their
ads. I sit back as I listen to the fashionista on the line, imagining
strappy silk evening gowns in bandana print, khaki business suits
with camel hair trim, fabrics inspired by the patterns in Oriental
rugs, a Star of David bikini. I imagine a Page Brookstone Peace Now

Bomber Jacket where one sleeve is an Israeli flag and the other sleeve is a Palestinian flag, and on the back are two skeletons hugging, with the caption "Better late than never."

I speak to Jordanna. Her translation is unfolding gloriously. She is enraptured but also afraid. I can hear that she understands the need to get this out, but she worries about the ramifications of stealing it and translating it. I promise to contact Jerrold March. He will be thrilled to help us find a lawyer to talk with, I am sure.

"She maps out such a precise internal landscape," Jordanna murmurs, lovestruck. "I can't believe I am the one recovering this ancient voice."

Jordanna reads a few freshly translated passages to me:

A branch switches at my legs
and I fall.
My cheek is torn against the coarse sand
and a man's foot is hard on the small of my back.
He kicks me over and I scream out:
"Jeremiah!" but no voice escapes . . .

Is my prophet foolish?
He hears the obvious blare of horns
but is deaf to my silent cry . . .

The man takes me with bruising grip
to the ravaging tent,
beats me upon my already bleeding scalp.
The branch comes down as a switch
and with each blow
I see a shock of white light.
An anger wells up in my throat,
strangely, not toward him.
No, toward him I feel profound sorrow.
I feel the need to explain

that he has made a mistake,
that I am everything good left in Fair Zion,
everything beautiful hidden underneath
and he does not realize, he thinks
I am another street rat,
he does not know that I am the keeper of a love,
a love of a prophet.
This is a mistake.
I can forgive a mistake.
But you . . .

Why should I forgive you?
You have forsaken me, Jeremiah.
How is it that you listen to God
the Most Secret
and cannot intuit my longing?

"She was raped?" I ask, feeling sick for her.
"I don't think so. But it becomes very Jobian after this."
"She is angry at him for being distant when she needed him."
"Yes. Listen," she says and reads more.

I have run like a gazelle
swiftly away from my love.
I was afraid of being consumed like firewood
in this furnace of desire.
It heats my chest and dries my throat.
It leaps and licks at my belly
in tiny tightened fists.
I cannot hold it in.

I was afraid it would pour out,
hot as the mouth of the Leviathan,
that eruptive, boiling cauldron.

Better I surrender to the cool and dank
than show my need, this monstrous thing.
My sneezes flash lightning,
firebrands stream from my mouth,
and my breath ignites coals,
eyes glimmering red as dawn.

"I want you to notice how terrified she is of love," Jordanna says. "It reminds me of you." She sounds more tender than usual. "You are terrified of love, and yet at the same time, like everyone else in the world, you want it so much. So you have found a perfect situation in which you can be in love without actually having to contend with another person."

"I thought you didn't want Mortichai contaminating the scroll," I say, surprised that the conversation has turned to this.

"I can hear you thinking about him. It is all over your breath."

I have run like a gazelle. I understand Anatiya's blaming Jeremiah for not hearing her. I understand why she felt that his not knowing her pain, not hearing her silent cry was the worst crime. I blamed my father for not heeding my cry for him to live. I blamed Itai for not knowing how I really felt, despite my being the one to split us up. I blamed Norris for not knowing that I had been falling apart for years. This time around, though, I am not going to blame Mortichai for struggling for the right reasons. And I am not going to blame myself for thinking about him. I am tired of running away from love.

She says, "Sometimes Anatiya describes love as this thing that makes her sick. She says, *I never want to be numbly healthful. Rather, let me be filled with hurt and longing.* It makes me upset. Love is not supposed to make you feel sick. It makes you healthy, vital. I think Anatiya and Jeremiah play the muse to one another's writing. Love is creative. We use so many violent terms to describe love—bombshell, breathtaking, captivating—but there is a way to look at it as a force that brings it all together, instead of blowing it all apart."

"So you are angry with her for loving that way?"

"No, I am in awe of her for recording her journey. She teaches me things. Later she says, *I surrender my being to love and at once my eyes are opened*. She is not stagnant with her feelings. She grows. That is where love should lead, not to destruction, but to awareness."

"Mortichai does make me feel aware. He opens my eyes," I think out loud. "In fact, it's deeper than that: he sparks my curiosity and *that* opens my eyes. He makes me *want* to see more."

"Mm." Jordanna sounds pensive. "Nice."

"Nice?" I say. "So he's not an asshole anymore?"

Jordanna has to think a moment. "No, I'm not saying that. He probably still is one. But you sound different. Remember when I told you it is better to be brokenhearted than depressed?"

"Yes. You said that to be depressed is to be an upside-down bowl, and to be brokenhearted is to be a broken bowl."

"When you called me to tell me he was engaged, you sounded like you wanted to die. It was nightmarish to listen to. You were up-side down, trapped, wallowingly depressed. But now, you sound a little brokenhearted, and what I mean by that is . . ."—I picture her fishing the air for a word—"dreamy."

"Dreamy," I repeat. "You think to be broken is to be dreamy?"

"*Let his heart break and begin to heal rather than this perpetual and terrible swell*, that's what Anatiya says," she answers.

"Ah, and in Psalms, *God is near to them that are of a broken heart*," I muse.

"There are two ways to live your life, Page. You can live your life swimming against the current, exhausting yourself. Or you can live your life being carried by life itself, sailing with the wind, being pulled toward every new day instead of running from every day that's past. Death-centered or life-centered. You have always been the former, but now, I don't know, you sound different."

"I feel a little different," I admit. "More peaceful."

"I am so happy," Jordanna says. "Wait." I hear her rustling papers. "I was scrolling ahead and jotted down notes, wait a minute, oh, here it is. It is in the middle of the scroll, and I think Anatiya is dying."

"Dying?" I ask, suddenly upset. How can she die in the middle of the scroll?

"Starving," she says. "Here. She says, *My body has become an upside-down ziggurat. My ribs step inward to the point of my waist.* She collapses, she can't move. *The marble floor was a pan beneath me, heat rising into my cheek. Now I, too, will be a blaze of fire.* And here's the turning point, are you ready?"

I nod, though I'm on the phone.

"*Then silence. God lifts suddenly as a storm does, leaving us calm with just a rustle of damage. Something soft presses against my mouth and I open my lips. It is a fig, a very good fig, a first-ripened fig. My eyes are soldered shut, sealed with a line of sun-blaze as with mortar. I devour the fig. Immediately another is pushed into my mouth. And another and another. The sweet honey covers my face and I rejoice and I laugh. I lose count of the number of figs I am fed. My life is restored, moving out from my belly to my fingers and toes. The marble cools. I rise up slowly and the feeding stops. The sun releases my eyes from their blindness and I look for my savior. I see, not near and not far, Jeremiah, walking away with an empty basket under his arm.*"

"He came to her. He does touch her. He fed her," I say, rapturous.

"Yes," she says. "But the turning point, that's the beauty to me. All these verses filled with the flourishment of poetry, the ecstasy of love, and then simply two words, *then silence*: there's nothing to say. She is still. The pen is still. The world is still. Silence."

"He doesn't come to her because she cried out, or because she threw herself at his feet and begged for food," I say. "He comes to her because of silence."

"She is mute, remember, so she is always silent," Jordanna says. "But here, she is also still. Not just her body, her mind. She surrendered, letting herself be carried by life's current instead of battling it."

"I see," I say, beginning to understand why Jordanna wanted to share this with me at this moment. She senses a new kind of stillness in me, and she is probably right. I think of that devouring clock that I feel I've been running from since the night I knew my father was dying. I do feel patience and generosity leaking from my broken heart. Perhaps love will alight on me someday if I remain still like this. Perhaps not. The truth is, however, I realize, that I've probably just transferred my race against my own mortality into a race to get this scroll translated. So perhaps I am still the same. But when I hear verses of Anatiya redeemed from their depths, they reach into me like nothing in all my study of the Bible before. As if her words are strewn with keys unlocking little parts of me. Each passage is a subtle elixir, a ripe fig pressed into my mouth. With each section Jordanna completes, there is another part of me that feels fed and restored.

We make plans for me to come over and bring dinner tomorrow evening.

"Keep translating, cowgirl," I cheer at the end of our call, "translate for our very lives!"

I turn on the television. PBS is running an old documentary on women in the Bible. On NPR there is a panel discussing "How Love Defines Us."

XXII

There are times when I fall into a trance, when I feel myself far away, lingering over the date tree. I look down at myself as I write in the scroll. I look down at the people who nibble baskets of berries and nuts. And I lie upon the air and float as if on water with no fear of falling. And when I return and my eyes are my own, the words I have written are not. They are lyrics from some other place, from some other hand, but I dare not discard them.
—THE SCROLL OF ANATIYA 50:60–65

I wait until one in the morning before calling Itai in Jerusalem. It is about eight a.m. in Jerusalem and am sure that by this time he is out the door, heading to the Rockefeller Museum. I imagine the morning light reflecting off the walls of the ancient City of David in pink and gold. I am in my bed, naked under my sheet. It is a warm night. The blinds on the two windows in my little bedroom are open. Through one I see the zigzag of the fire escape on the brick building across Ninety-fourth Street, lit from streetlights below and silhouetted against darkened apartment windows. Through the other, the shadowy façades across Columbus Avenue. I lie in my bed, four floors up from the street, and headlights continually scan my ceiling. They ease my sense of being alone.

Itai gives me apologetic updates about the progress of collecting nominations for an international team. He says that the scroll is shrouded in its white cloth. Yosef Schulman won't leave him alone and is behaving as if Itai has slept with his bride. Itai promises he will do his best to keep Yosef involved in the translation. The carbon dating results date the skeletons circa 575 BC, precisely when Jeremiah would have died, according to his own text. De Grout is furious with me for my snide little on-air comment suggesting that maybe a Frenchman made the bomb threats to the department for his own advancement. He has called for a public apology for such "sloppy commentary. This is exactly why the treasure must be entrusted to selected professionals rather than queers and quirks." I wonder to Itai whether I am a queer or a quirk to de Grout and Itai grows annoyed at me for taking the comment lightly. I can hear that he is under enormous pressure.

"I don't mean to make things harder for you," I say, watching bars of lights pass over me. "You sound tired. But you know as well as I do that they are going to beat all the life out of that scroll. She will become a maidservant to Matthew, Mark, Luke, and John."

"I don't know when you became so cynical. It is easier to get a scroll out of the ground than to get the story off the page."

"It shouldn't be."

Itai sighs. He sounds older and more burdened than I am used to. "At this point, I have spent more time with those skeletons than anyone," he says, "and believe me I want to do everything right by them. I have been documenting every inch of them."

"Are you okay?" I ask.

Itai is quiet for a moment. He says softly, "Do you believe in me anymore, Page?"

I sit up in my bed. My heart hurts for him that he should wonder this. There was a time when I was his constant support and encouragement. "Always," I say, though I'm not sure I believe it. I realize suddenly that my stealing pictures of the scroll could cost him his job, that the translation, when released, may impact him worst of all. But I know I can't stop. At its best, this is my calling. At its worst, it is a mad compulsion that I just can't shake. Hearing him, I feel immense guilt. Suddenly even under just a sheet, I am too warm. I kick it off.

"Listen. I understand why you are assembling a team," I tell him. I miss him. I stare out at the fire escape. I can see the shadowy presence of a small potted tree someone put there. There are so many people in love all around me. Probably behind every one of those little darkened windows is another couple in love. I look down at myself, naked and alone in my bed, and the breaks in my heart are suddenly very real.

After Itai and I disconnect, I long to call Mortichai, just to hear his voice. He can open any book and just read it to me, a recipe for bread, a dishwasher manual, with that deep resonance, and I'll be soothed. But then I worry, where is he right now? Not just physically, but emotionally? I turn on my side and look at the roll of paper towel on the bedside table. Let him be, I tell myself. Be still.

WHEN I CALL Jerrold March in the morning, he is delighted to hear from me. "Ms. Brookstone!" he gushes. "The archangel of antiquity, my darling, how proud I am of you, how lovely to see you on the telly each day."

"Thank you, Mr. March, you have always been such an important friend to me," I say.

"Friend! Ach," he says, "it is outstanding how such a well-meaning word can cause such deep pain. But sweetheart, you must be in New York. When can you tell me all about it?"

"Jerrold," I say, choosing my words.

"Yes, love, tell me," he says.

"I'm afraid I may be in a little trouble."

He practically explodes with delight. "Trouble! Oh my heart! To be young! To be free! What can I do to rescue my princess? Just tell me, and it will disappoint me completely if you are shy."

"The scroll I discovered is exquisite. It is magical."

"Tell me, yes," he says.

"And they are stalling the translation of it. They won't release pictures to the public. It is criminal," I say, my voice becoming harder.

"Yes, criminal. Delectable," he says.

"Can I tell you something confidential?"

"Of course, my dear, I swear it, upon my wife's grave and upon the lives of all my children, both known and unknown," he says.

"I stole pictures of the scroll, and I have someone translating it right now. I want to release it to the public, but I am unsure how to do it."

"Really, how profound! You have come to the right person, my dearest. I cannot tell you how many fragments and scrolls I have rescued from the black market before they are lost entirely. I've had to outbid that little prick de Grout quite a few times, I tell you. It has cost me dearly but it has been worth every penny, I assure you. Let us do this. You shall come to my penthouse this Friday, and I will have my lawyer present. You bring your translator, what is his name?"

"Her name is Jordanna Lamm," I say.

"Oh my heart!" he says. "We will open a couple of my best bottles."

"I'd like Andrew Richter to be there," I say.

"Ah yes, the editor of *Archaeology Digest*, he is a good friend of mine. Let me call him and make sure he attends our little espionage soiree. He cannot possibly say no. After I funded his Thai expedition it would be simply poor taste, wouldn't you agree, precious?"

JORDANNA PUTS THE food I brought from her favorite Indian restaurant in Manhattan into dishes. We all gather at their breakfast table in the kitchen. Jordanna and Nathaniel's older children, Sharon, who is eight, and Joshy, who is six, both armed with nan, are already diving into a palette of cashew, coconut, green mango, tomato, and pineapple chutneys. I steer them away from the ginger and tamarind. I pat down beds of curried rice on three plates and layer it with savory spinach, lentils, and tandoori chicken for Jordanna, Nathaniel, and myself.

"You owe me a wife," Nathaniel says between bites. Both children look just like him. He and Joshy have woolly black hair like the fleece of a sheep. Sharon's is longer and fuzzes out in pigtails. The three of them have the same gentle brown eyes. Jordanna and Nathaniel make a handsome couple and clearly adore each other. Jordanna seems a little weary from late-night feedings with the baby and hours withering in front of the computer screen, while Nathaniel, who manages a chain of health-food stores, looks the same as he did the day of their wedding, tall and lean, with fine, almost feminine features and cheeks rosy as if he's perpetually come back from an invigorating run.

"She's having an affair with a two-thousand-year-old prophetess, thanks to you," he continues. Baby Eli is in a bouncy seat on the floor; Nathaniel bounces it with his foot.

"Twenty-five-hundred-year-old," I correct him.

"Ah, excuse me," he says.

"I'm six!" Joshy exclaims. Each of his fingertips is a different color from a different chutney.

"Can I meet a twenty-five-hundred-year-old person?" Sharon pleads. "Please?"

Jordanna laughs. "Well, she died a long time ago. But I do want to share something about that." Jordanna gets up from the table.

"See that?" Nathaniel says. "She can't even sit through dinner! She hardly eats anything."

Jordanna comes back with some pages of printed text. She settles back into her chair and is about to read it when Nathaniel says, "Honey, you have to eat something. You're nursing. You eat, and Page will read."

I take the paper and read,

I make this covenant between you, Jeremiah son of Hilkiah, and myself, Anatiya daughter of Avigayil, in the presence of the pink

*of dawn. Because God has locked your soul in a golden cage, you
cannot court and love a woman in the way of the common man.
And so, I betroth myself to you in righteousness. I betroth myself to
you for eternity. As for you, I ask only one condition. That you not
let me die. That you sustain me through the power of your calling
from God. And only when you are near the end of your days, that
you allow my life to be released, that you let God in to gather me,
and that you yourself, prophet, you yourself with your own hands
take my body and carry me, wash me, and bury me in a white
linen robe that you have worn.*

I lower the paper and look at Jordanna. She has dutifully filled
her mouth with food but is not really interested in eating. She jabs
the air at the paper as if to say, *See that?*

"*Bury me in a robe that you have worn,*" I repeat. I picture them in
their shared coffin, arms wrapped around each other. "He knew her
desire. This is how she wanted to be buried."

She says, "I think Jeremiah buried her. I think she died first, and
then when he died, someone very close to them arranged his body
beside her."

"I want to be buried with you, Mommy," Sharon says. I look at
her and tousle her hair.

"Me too," says Joshy. "And I want to bring my trucks."

Nathaniel says, "Well, this is great dinner conversation." And
then he adds, sounding a bit bruised, "How come no one wants to be
with me?"

"You snore, Daddy," Joshy says, and we all laugh.

"Do I?" he asks Jordanna, looking worried.

Jordanna laughs and says, "Yes, honey, you snore."

"How come you never told me?"

"Because it doesn't bother me," she says. "Actually, I like it. You
know I find it hard to sleep when you're not with me, and if I wake
in the middle of the night, the sound of you is comforting. It is like a
lion growling beside me. I like it."

Nathaniel smiles and his eyes twinkle. "You two really got a good thing going," I observe.

"I like him," Jordanna admits, "from his attached earlobes to his whiskers in the sink to his funny flat feet."

"You make me sound like some kind of a freak!" Nathaniel says, self-consciously fingering one of his earlobes. But he is blushing. He says, "You dating anyone, Page?"

I shake my head. "Unfortunately, I've fallen in love with a man who is completely unattainable to me. He's Orthodox, but that's the least of my problems. He's engaged to another woman. Still, I can't stop thinking about him."

Jordanna pulls out another page of text, and after a drink of water, she reads,

Give him to me, O God! before You whittle him away into nothing, before You chisel him narrower and narrower, chip away his defenses and leave him brittle as exposed bone. Dear God, I love his flesh and his heart. I love the waves of silk that grow from his scalp. I love the pink pads of his fingertips. I love the rapid pulse in his neck. I love the perfect arch of his sole, the hollow behind his knee, the breath he heaves at day's end. Give him over to me, O God! I will cherish his humanity. I will soothe the flesh and blood of him. Perhaps You will terrify and torment the soul of Jeremiah for all eternity with Your whims. What impact have I on Your eternity? But for these few score years, while he is housed in a tender, bristling shell that ages and shivers and aches, give him to me . . . because I love him. I love him, not for what he can do for Heaven or for Israel. I love him because I am Anatiya and he is Jeremiah. Let go of Him, Father. Here am I, a frail, female mortal, laughably commanding You the Commander: You shall not murder, love.

We talk about whether she has taken too much creative license adding a comma between *murder* and *love*. The comma gives her such a keen joy, she does not want to let it go. I say, "What's the harm, one comma." She is laughing about the comma standing trial before an international court. Nathaniel is marveling at what geeks we can be.

"Who cares about a comma?" Sharon asks, leaning adoringly against her father.

Nathaniel says, "It has to do with Mommy's work. Most of the stuff Mommy translates is written in Hebrew, and old Hebrew doesn't have any punctuation, like commas or periods or exclamation points, so it is very hard sometimes for Mommy to figure out what it is supposed to be saying."

Joshy starts singing from his *Schoolhouse Rock* collection, "In-ter-jections! Show excitement! Or emotion! They're generally set apart from a sentence by an exclamation point, or by a comma when the feeling's not as strong . . ."

"You've got some damn smart kids," I compliment them.

Sharon points at me and says, "Ooooh! Page said the *d* word!"

Jordanna says, "I like that she talks about the *pink pads of his fingertips*, and his body as a *tender, bristling shell that ages and shivers and aches*. I like that she loves him as a man, not as an idea." She looks at me meaningfully.

"What are you trying to tell me between the lines?" I invite her, hesitantly.

"I don't know," she says, embarrassed. She gets up and starts clearing plates. I stand up to help her. With her back turned at the sink she says, "It's just that sometimes you talk about love as if it is this unattainable, faraway idea. You know what I think?" She shuts off the sink and swings around, her hands wet and soapy. "I think you only wanted to go on the dig in Anatot because you thought there'd be nothing there. I think no one was as surprised as you when you found that first earring. I think you love this Mortichai Masters because there are a thousand reasons he can't love you back. I think you set yourself up to be disappointed."

"Ooooh," Sharon says, pointing again. "Page is in lo-o-ove."

"Shh," Nathaniel tells her.

"There are different ways to love, Jordanna. Not everyone has what you have," I say. I can feel my neck turning red and it is not from the Indian spices. "After Mortichai marries, he will live in the Old City of Jerusalem, steps from the Western Wall. How much closer can you get to heaven? I am making peace with him getting married. There is even something beautiful about it. My relationship with him exists outside of time. He is heaven to me. The thought of him makes every place I am in feel like heaven. When he marries, I will always have that gift. I'll know what paradise is."

"You know how depressed you were after *Upon This Altar* came out and no one understood the prologue, least of all Norris?"

"Yes."

"This makes less sense."

"Jordanna, c'mon," Nathaniel tries to intercede. He tries to explain to me, "She works on this thing every night until two in the morning, and then the baby wakes up at four. I'm telling you, she is exhausted."

I listen faintly to Nathaniel and then turn to Jordanna, "How can I expect you to understand? You've never been in this situation."

"Are they fighting?" Joshy asks.

Jordanna wipes her hands on a dish towel. She rummages through the papers she brought down. "I don't choose to be in this situation. That is what you don't seem to understand. Anyone can be in your situation. And not only that, people do it all the time. People fall in love with movie stars. People fall in love with the unattainable. There is nothing unique about what you are feeling except that you choose to turn it into a philosophy about heaven. I don't understand the way you think. You are able to memorize immense amounts of material. You string together very complex concepts, but you can't understand something as simple as reciprocal love. When it comes to anything to do with relationships, you just don't get it."

"What exactly don't I get?" I ask crossly.

"If you really want him to be yours, make him yours. But I don't think you want that. I think you actually want him to marry this woman so you don't have to face your feelings for him in any real way."

This makes me very angry. I can hardly hold back, but I glance over at the kids, and the baby being bounced on his blue sling chair at Nathaniel's foot. "You're right. This is exactly like when *Upon This Altar* came out. I created a unique way of thinking, a new way of looking at the world, and everyone said it was insane. Or worse, they just skipped it! I feel good about Mortichai right now, no matter what his conclusion is, and you want to take that away from me."

"You're pretending that you feel good thinking about some imaginary scenario, but when are you going to seek happiness in real life? God, Page, the amount of energy you have to expend to construct these fantasies is maddening!"

She pulls out a page and says, "Here it is. *When I am beside you, Jeremiah, I am an astronomer and you are the sky. Here in this cave I am the queen of the mountain, grand and glorious. In your shadow I am only a speck of cinnamon dust, but the life in me is great, like the wide-leafed plant concealed within the tiny mustard seed.* Hear that? That's you. You want to be the astronomer to his sky. But you are the sky, Page! Your name is written in lights all over the planet. Yet you refuse to see that. You want it all, but when it's yours, you back into a little corner." Jordanna is pacing the kitchen now.

"Now you are mad at me *and* Anatiya?" I ask.

She stops and speaks more quietly, more seriously. "You say you are afraid of death, of nothingness, but you've chased after it. You want everyone's attention, but you refuse to engage with anyone on the level of reality. Why? Because your mother loved your father and then he died?

"You want Mortichai to be heaven? He's human, Page! He will die. He's not a god, he's human. There is no special eternity in him. Whatever soul he has is the same as the rest of us, the same in any man you might choose to love. He is human. He's a bristling, shivering shell right down to the pads of his fingertips. And if you want to love him, that's fine, I can't tell you who to love, but it would be more bearable to me if I knew you loved him for being human, because it's precisely the flaws and the brokenness that make a life poetic and beautiful. Your father was flawed, and his death didn't perfect him. He was weird. He was dramatic. He had an overbite. He was human."

I blink. My eyes are stinging. Nathaniel sends the kids into the living room with chocolate chip cookies. I hear the television snap on. I know Jordanna is exhausted and hormonal. I know she has a temper. I try to keep my heart still.

"I don't need angels to come save me," she continues. "I am not waiting for some grand, life-defining philosophy. I love my kids and I love my husband and my home, and my best friend, and I love this, what we are doing together, I love Anatiya. And I love my doubts. I don't need to think about heaven. I have a life."

I remain silent. The baby begins to stir and Nathaniel picks him up.

"You think I didn't read your prologue? I read it," she says. "I thought it was incredible. But I also thought it was inappropriate to philosophize at the beginning of a book of comparative studies. You created a philosophy about altars and then instead of lecturing on it, writing a few well-placed articles, fanning the spark until it became a book in its own right, you stuffed it in the beginning of a book where it was sure to be overlooked. You did it to yourself. You want to be successful, but you create obstacles in your own way. You want to be in love, but you distance yourself by oceans. Oceans! Why did you even leave Israel? You want to live forever, Page, but sometimes you hardly live at all."

I am angry. I look at Nathaniel. "Take me to the train," I ask him, and he nods. Even his rosy cheeks are pale.

Tears spring to Jordanna's eyes. She rushes to me and holds my arms. "I'm sorry, Page. This is just how I feel and you need to hear it."

I take a deep breath and the clouds in me start to clear. I pull away. "Jordanna," I say. "I know you're tired." She smiles and wipes tears from her eyes.

Nathaniel is getting his keys and shaking his head. "You are getting some sleep tonight," he says loudly to her, trying to sound commanding. "No Anatiya, no night-time feedings. I'll prepare the bottles. You are burning yourself out."

I pull a stack of papers out of my briefcase and give them to her.

"What is this?" she asks.

"I tried to skip ahead and do some translating on my own. I don't know if this helps you or slows you down, so feel free to disregard it. We *are* in this thing together." We hug until all the tension is crushed out of us.

XXIII

If you should forget my face someday, if you should forget the feel of my embrace, do not cry. Do not stomp. . . . When your memory of me begins to fade, it is I who is choosing to withdraw some memories, like the sea draws in the surf at low tide in order to provide the shore some relief, in order to make room for new memories.

—THE SCROLL OF ANATIYA 51:17–18

I meet Jordanna at Grand Central. She is a flurry of black when I finally see her making her way through the crowd to the information stand in the center. She is wearing a short black cotton tunic over a black silk dress, carrying a black attaché case. I am wearing a black matte crepe wrap dress and high-heeled sandals, with a new leather computer bag slung over my shoulder. We laugh when we see each other.

"We look very guilty, don't we?" I say, and she hugs me and says, "Yes, and after a month of oversized T-shirts, I love it."

Jordanna is electric with giddiness. I can tell she hasn't been sleeping, but she is wired with caffeine, tapping her fingers on her attaché case and talking a mile a minute in the cab uptown. "You painted your toes!" she notices. And I say, "I've never seen you wear stockings."

She lifts the hem of her silk dress over her knees and I see they are lacy thigh-highs. I laugh. "Why not?" she asks. "This is the adventure of my lifetime, isn't it?"

The lobby of Jerrold's building is ornate, with a chandelier that seems nearly as big as Superman's northern palace. In the mirrored elevator, Jordanna adjusts the curls around her face, and I smooth my hair around mine. We take a deep breath together and hold hands briefly.

"This could change everything," she whispers to me.

"No exaggeration," I agree.

We step out into an exquisite space whose scope and collection remind me of the Rockefeller Museum's artifact room, except that was in a basement, and here the walls seem entirely of glass, overlooking a patchwork of rooftops with silver-barreled water tanks and a jungle of pipework. I can see the silver stripe of the Hudson River in the distance. The triumph of monuments which is New York City is a fantastical contrast to the tribalistic art that dominates Jerrold's home. Giant African masks, tiny Mongol shrunken heads, gilded Sanskrit scrolls, beaded Native American headdresses, and colorful South American totems in wood and stone stand together as if attending an intercontinental summit of primitive peoples. Weapons, from Stone Age spears to Asian stars, hang together, and an authentic iron maiden stands open like a hungry Venus flytrap in the far corner. The floor is thick glass over authentic Middle Eastern mosaics, giant slabs of Aboriginal cave art, and delicate Tibetan tapestries. Above us hangs a replica of da Vinci's flying machine. The effect of everything together nearly takes our breath away.

"Ah, Ms. Brookstone!" Jerrold emotes, walking toward us. "And this must be the lovely Ms. Lamm. I am so pleased to meet you." He takes Jordanna's hand and kisses it dramatically. She smiles widely. Jerrold is in fine form, in a steel blue silk shirt with sterling cufflinks, perfectly pressed black pants. "Do come in, don't let my collection frighten you," he says, linking his arms through ours and walking us to the sitting area. "Isn't it magnificent?" he asks rhetorically and then stops for a moment before a spectacularly large African boar mask with real ivory tusks. He closes his eyes, inhales, and then exclaims, "Ah, the perfume of sophisticated women. One of you is wearing Chanel. I am putty." He continues leading us to the couches, which I am certain are pony skin. Two men put down their wine glasses and stand to greet us.

"Andrew Richter," says one, shaking our hands after Jerrold has unlinked himself. Andrew is short and quite bulky, but he presents himself well, his pants held up over his girth with a wide leather belt, and his head polished to a shine. Tufts of peppered gray grow thickly over his ears.

"And this is my indispensable lawyer," Jerrold says, "Greg Chesterfield. The best of the best. And handsome as the black obelisk of Shalmeneser the third."

Greg shakes our hands. My hand disappears into his large grip. His onyx skin far outshines his tailored English suit. His square jaw and high forehead make him kingly and magestic. An elderly woman wearing a powder blue apron and a matching cap over her neatly set gray hair brings glasses of wine to Jordanna and me. Jerrold says, "Can you believe that Anna has been tending to me since I was a wee child?"

Anna smiles and curtsies politely. "From bottles of milk to bottles of gin," she says with a Swedish accent, and we all laugh. She comes up behind Jordanna and helps her shimmy out of her tunic. Jerrold gushes to Jordanna, "You haven't nearly enough jewelry, my dear, for those perfect arms. Come, let us all sit down."

Jordanna and I sit on either side of Jerrold on the couch, and Andrew and Greg sit on lush chairs across from us.

"Thank you so much, Jerrold, for putting this together; you have always been such a friend to our field," I say.

Jerrold takes my hand. "There's that word again," he sighs. "Ah, my beauty, please share with us your dilemma."

Anna returns with a tray of rice crackers, dates halved and

stuffed with herbed cheese, caviar, and sesame sweets and lays it on the coffee table.

I open my computer bag and slip out my laptop, opening it and waiting for it to warm up.

Andrew says, "Everyone is waiting to hear more about the scroll. I can't tell you how many letters and emails I get every day wanting to know when it will be released. Have you seen it? What can you tell me about it? It is so unusual to find such an extensive new work in that region."

"Yes, I've seen it," I say, turning the computer around. "And I've taken it with me." Andrew takes a pair of spectacles out of his pocket and leans in closer.

Greg narrows his eyes at the screen and says, "Did you steal these?"

I take a breath and answer him. "Yes. Yes, I did." I look around at Jerrold and Andrew. "And if it makes anyone here uncomfortable, you can leave. Or I'll leave. In my heart of hearts, I know I have done the right thing."

Jerrold throws his hands up and exclaims, "Splendid!"

"Oh, extraordinary!" Andrew says, glued to the screen. "Oh, my Lord, it looks legible. I could print this. I could get this translated. Is it really written by a woman? Is it possible?"

Jordanna opens her attaché case and takes out a stack of papers. "I've fully translated about a third of it," she says, face flushed. "I've tried to render it accessible for the modern reader. Mr. Richter, it matches the historic and literary significance of the Dead Sea Scrolls, but if I may say, if one were to measure the finds based on condition of scrolls *as well as content*, the discovery of the complete Scroll of Anatiya might fairly be considered unrivaled."

I lean in to look around Jerrold at Jordanna. I raise my eyebrows at her, impressed. I straighten up and say, "The author is most certainly female. And she is a passionate follower of the prophet Jeremiah. As far as we can tell from an initial cursory look at the entirety, she witnessed the capture and destruction of Jerusalem in five eighty-seven, witnessed the murder of the appointed governor of Jerusalem Gedalia in five eighty-six, and survived the ensuing Chaldean attack. She joined the small number of Israelite exiles to Egypt and lived there from five eighty-six to five eighty-five, after which she returned to Anatot, where her life ended circa five eighty-three."

Andrew is in ecstasy, his face and shoulders melting as he stares into the screen. Greg is quite finished looking at the images and holds his body stiff. I say, "Readers familiar with Jeremiah will note the obvious similarities between the text of his prophecies and this text. There is a striking symmetry of structure in the outline of the chapters. The two authors frequently discuss the same historic events. Often phrases and entire verses are shared by both texts, and it is unclear whether certain phrases originate with Anatiya or with Jeremiah. Similarly, our text weaves phrases from Torah, the two Books of Samuel and two Books of Kings, Proverbs, Psalms, Song of Songs, Job, and selections from the prophets. Excepting where texts obviously predate six twenty-nine, it should be seriously considered what is the author's intentional allusion, what is original to this text, and what may have been idiom of the time."

"Listen to her speak," Jerrold purrs. "Can you imagine that such scholarship could come from such an angelic mouth?" He reaches to spoon caviar on a cracker.

Andrew says, "Would you publish this alongside Jeremiah, or alone?"

Jordanna says, "I would let her be autonomous. I wouldn't burden the initial version with extensive annotation and footnotes. The text itself does demand such scholarly study, and there is no doubt such editions will follow."

Andrew is now looking through the translation. His eyes are misting. He looks at Jordanna and says, "You have translated this beautifully."

She squirms delightedly under his gaze and says, "Well, it requires a commitment to fidelity and a burst of imagination at times. There are a number of words where I chose to use a more modern translation, where Hebraicisms were unmatched in other known texts and simpler renderings seemed to miss the leaps the author intended to make, based on the urgency of context. For example, *hazara-hazara* is literally 'repeat-repeat' and I translated it 'chant.' *Blisof* means 'without end' and I used 'infinity.'"

Andrew is looking at Jordanna. "Jordanna Lamm," he says, remembering, "I know your name. You have an excellent reputation. Well, Jerrold, I have no regret canceling my other plans for tonight. I am simply . . . in awe."

I say, "We are hoping that we can get this out, without too much trouble, because it belongs to the public, before it is sanitized to death."

"That's your cue!" Jerrold exclaims happily to Greg.

Greg takes a breath and looks only at Jerrold. It is clear he has had to extract Mr. March from many difficult brambles. His voice is no-nonsense. "Let me ask you, Ms. Brookstone. Are you the archaeologist who discovered this scroll?"

"Yes," I answer formally. Everyone knows I am.

"And you are certain that you had all the permits in order when you excavated the site?" he asks.

"Yes. I had all the paperwork in order."

Greg thinks for a moment. "I am sure you are familiar then with the legal term 'intellectual property.' If an archaeologist receives a license from the Antiquities Authority, then anything you uncover belongs to the state. However, any documentation created by the expedition is more murky territory. It belongs to the person whose name appears on the license. If the pictures had been taken before the scroll was turned over to the Antiquities archives, there would be no question about your right to translate and distribute it. Still, usually the excavator retains primary rights to the find, even after it's been archived. You are allowed to utilize data, including photographs, concerning whatever you unearth in whatever way you see fit. You are breaking no law by translating and releasing this material."

"What I am doing is pissing a lot of people off," I say.

"Yes," Greg agrees. "But you have every legal right to do it."

Relieved, I turn to Andrew. "I do not want anyone to know that this came from me. I do not want mention of my name or my friend here. Now, I am certain there will be a groundswell of protest and controversy, and I am certain that it will be clear to most that I am involved. But I would like to let them figure it out without stamping my name on the bottom. I may be prosecuted for theft but I believe that the past belongs to everyone. That's what I'm fighting for." Even as I speak, I question my own statement. Why spend your life fighting for the past? Why not fight for the future? I think about what Jordanna said. I think about Mortichai and the fact that I hesitate every time I reach to pick up the phone.

"Glorious," Jerrold says. "Whatever it takes Greg, I'll reach deep and pay it."

"It's not always about money, Jerrold," Greg says, almost exasperated, at which Jerrold laughs heartily and says, "Indeed! Whatever you say, you're the professional."

"I didn't expect to see this for years," Andrew is saying, reading with unmasked wonder. "We will print a special edition featuring only this. No commentary. No extensive annotation. Just a hunk of unpolished gemstone straight from the heart of the mountain. I want the photographed Hebrew alongside the English to authenticate it, and that is it."

"Are you ready to run this?" I ask him.

"Ms. Brookstone," he says, his brow creasing, ready for the fight, "God knows how many scrolls and scroll fragments are lost to rich fat cats who can't read a lick of ancient script and keep them crumbling in their attics. Here I have an opportunity to do this, to prove once and for all that archaeology is not for the elite but for everyone. Am I ready to run this?" He stands up and I instinctively stand up as well. He grabs my hand between his and shakes it firmly. "I have been waiting for this all my life." Then he reaches across the coffee table to where Jordanna is sitting. He grabs Jordanna's hand and shakes it too, saying, "I'm your man."

"You've got your work cut out for you," Jerrold says jovially to Greg, who nods in agreement. "Now let's have some more wine. Anna! We're dry!"

It turns out to be a lovely evening. Greg loosens up, and after a few drinks, even the totems and shrunken heads seem to take on new life, their presence participating in our party.

Andrew is still reading the translation, savoring it. He suddenly straightens up and reads,

Jeremiah smashed that belly-round jug in the sight of all the men. In the wake of its silence he charged, "So will God smash this people and this city, as one smashes a potter's vessel, which can never be mended." I watch the clay chips shatter and I think about the years. Years that can never be restored. I am no girl anymore. These hips could bear children and these breasts could nurse them. This skin is swarthier and these hands are coarser. I love you, Jeremiah. I care not about the metaphor of the shattered jug. I worry only that the shards not cut your lovely feet.

At twilight, Jeremiah rests by a rock. His eyes close and I see he is sleeping. Blessed are You, for the gift of sound sleep. I scurry in the withdrawing light to gather up the pieces of the jug. I wrap them into a bundle. In the world to come, dear God, while You are restoring living spirits to the dead, if it is not too much trouble, I pray You mend this little jug. It is most precious to me.

He addresses me, "Wasn't one of the artifacts you discovered a box containing the shattered pieces of a jug?"

I can feel the wine has warmed my whole body and softened my mind, but I snap to attention. I had not connected the passage with the fragments I had found, fragments that had been carefully and deliberately stored in a box. I had wondered at the time I found it what someone was saving it for. She was saving it for the world to come. She was hoping that when God finally resurrected the dead, He would restore this little jug that her beloved had held. The pieces had scattered around her beloved's feet. I feel myself nearly weeping with the beauty of it. I look over at Jordanna and she is weeping. Jerrold has his arm around her and offers her a handkerchief.

Jordanna says sentimentally, "We could mend it," as if she is ready to pull out some glue and tape right now. "We could put it back together for her." Her eyes grow wide. "Maybe it *is* the world to come . . ."

"What we are doing is of biblical proportions," Jerrold says.

Greg says, "We could call it the Jubilee Jug," to which Andrew applauds. His applause is infectious, and soon we are all applauding and raising toasts to the Jubilee Jug, and to this, the End, or Beginning, of Days.

XXIV

We are commanded to love. We are not commanded to befriend . . .
Whether you like the vessel or not, this is not the concern. Only
love the light that shines from within the vessel.
— THE SCROLL OF ANATIYA 51:91–95

Over the next couple of days, I narrate a short documentary
for IMAX about the discovery. I keep very busy waiting for
the *Digest* to come out. I long to call Mortichai but resist.
Still, at the end of every day, I am disappointed that he hasn't called.
Men approach me every place I go, asking to take me to dinner, inviting me for walks, but I can hardly see their hopeful faces. They
are walking skeletons to me, somehow less alive than Jeremiah and
Anatiya in their tomb.

When the first third of the Scroll of Anatiya is offered to the
world, I stand at the newsstand on the corner of my block holding *Archaeology Digest*. The verses af Anatiya are already so familiar to me.

I run my fingers gently over the text as though it is a love sonnet
in Braille, written just for me. *Her body was so faint with love that her soul*
caught in her throat.

Archaeology Digest sells more copies than ever before in its history. In my apartment I listen to news radio as I get ready to go to
Jordanna's home.

The Israeli authorities are livid that someone would take it upon themselves to bypass all process and authority by stealing the text of the newly discovered scroll and publishing it. We spoke to Charles de Grout, French antiquities specialist: "This is an unprecedented act of deceit and betrayal. It is the act of someone who is selfish and hateful. It is this kind of offensive anti-intellectualism that breeds ignorance and mistrust." The reporter said, "On the contrary, people are saying this is a Robin Hood act, redeeming precious material from the hands of the elite and distributing it to hungry minds. In that way it is seen as generous." Norris Anderson, supervisor at the ancient site of Megiddo, said, "The criminal should be brought to justice immediately. Judah sold the life of the Savior for sixty shekels, and this criminal sold this for a pretty penny, I am sure."

According to *Archaeology Digest*, the source took no money for the privilege of publishing the scroll. Says Anderson, "A thief is by definition a liar. As for the source, we all know how out of control she is. Is that who you want handling sacred material, a woman whose morals in both her personal and professional life are questionable to say the least?" And when we spoke to Itai Harani, chair of the Department of Antiquities in Israel, he had this to say: "I have no words to express my hurt."

Itai sounds deeply wounded. De Grout is correct: I am selfish. I knew this would be painful for Itai and I went ahead anyway. He will take the fall for the lack of security. I betrayed his trust. I am angry at myself, but in my heart I do not regret my decision. They will see, I assure myself; they will see that what may appear impulsive and out of control is in fact necessary. I have no question that Anatiya's story was brought out of the ground in order to be told. I have faith that Itai will be able to rise above it. I have faith that this is the right thing to do.

I take a cab to the train. I ask the driver, "Are you Hindu?" The fact that the famous guy I found was a prophet of the Bible named Jeremiah will mean very little to him, I imagine.

"Oh yes."

"What do you think of all the stories about Jeremiah?"

"Probably as much as you think of Brahma, Vishnu, and Siva."

The driver continues, "You know, the Hindu dharma accepts thousands of gods and goddesses. And my wife, she is Buddhist, and in her faith there are no gods and no goddesses, but I see no difference really. I think it is all the same, you know? I think all of her gods and goddesses are inside of her, whereas mine are all on the outside."

"How did a Hindu fall in love with a Buddhist?" I ask, finding pleasure in his crisp accent.

"That is a long story, but in a nutshell, I met her when I did my doctorate in Japan. She was my professor."

I keep listening to my story roll around on his radio every few minutes, each time with a slightly different nuance. I hear the translation called "brilliant."

Yosef Shulman is questioned and quickly cleared as the suspected translator. On the news he says, "I am unhappy about the disregard for process, and I am saddened that I could only be involved in the art of translating the first three chapters." I smile to myself. He wants the world to know he is the artist who rendered the first three. He wants credit. Then he adds, "However, I have to say, I am not displeased that the scroll of Anatiya found a way to leap into the public eye. Nor am I surprised."

"Why aren't you surprised?"

"Read her and you will understand."

My heart melts for Yosef and the romantic soul cooped up in his little bent body.

When I arrive at Jordanna's house, she is frantic. I tell her that I am with her all the way, and if it is okay with her, I am not going home until the whole thing is translated. I don't want anything getting in the way of finishing the mission and setting Anatiya free.

"They are going to come here eventually. They are going to come to this house!" Jordanna is twisting her hands. The news is on the television in her living room and Nathaniel is standing before it trying to pay attention to the report while holding the baby and coping with two rowdy children at his feet.

"This is getting out of hand!" he shouts at me, and I'm sure he isn't referring to the kids, who have forgotten he is a father and not a maypole. "The police are looking for Page Brookstone."

"And if they find me? It's not murder. It is the opposite of murder actually."

"Here we go, the savior speaks!" Nathaniel says.

"He's very stressed." Jordanna pulls me into the kitchen. "I have not been helpful at all with the kids. In fact, since you came to visit me, my milk has dried up. The others I nursed for at least a year."

"How much farther have you gotten?"

"My heart is broken for her. This love is killing her. It is making her want to kill herself. I want to reach back in time and lift her out of it, rescue her and tell her how much I love her, knowing only her bones and her words."

"Can I see?" I ask.

In the warm, bright attic, I sit on the blue and white quilt and read what Jordanna has translated. As I read, all my senses seem heightened. I am aware of the breeze sifting through the evergreens carrying a rich aroma. I am aware of the artistry of the air, scrolled with bird calls and billowing clouds. Being in Jordanna's attic, holding her translation of the scroll, feels like being in the innermost sanctum of the vast church of the world.

We sit shoulder to shoulder on the bed. I ask Jordanna if she has ever seen Anatiya, or thought she saw her, or dreamt about her. Jordanna says that she has not. I am grateful she does not yell at me for thinking about ghosts. She says, however, that at times she feels as if Anatiya is near.

My mother calls my cell phone and sounds upset. She tells me that the police came to ask her questions about my whereabouts. She had a hunch where I would be but she said she had no idea. She tells me that she hurried over to my apartment and it was being searched by police, the phone, the files, the mail, everything. They left it a mess. At first, she says, she was completely distraught seeing the two officers going through my things, but then they started talking to her. They said that they were looking for me not only because of my taking the scroll material, but for my own safety. They showed my mother some of the letters that had come in the mail for me, and they played my answering machine. There were at least six threats to halt all translation. One of them was a death threat.

"Father Chuck called me to see if I am all right," she says. "You know, he has this meditation cottage in Massachusettes, about a hundred miles from here, and he said if you need a place to finish the scroll, it would be private enough."

"He knows it's me," I say.

"Aw honey," she says, almost laughing. "Everyone knows."

The police asked her about Jordanna Lamm. They know she is a translator and that we are good friends and have been in close contact over the past few days.

Now Jordanna is completely panicked. Nathaniel is terribly worried. We gather our things quickly, packing a suitcase of her clothes for both of us. We are adamant that we are not going to turn ourselves in and end this until the scroll is complete. Nathaniel is very supportive. He understands his wife's passion, and after reading what has been translated so far, he believes the work needs to be finished. At the door of their house, he draws Jordanna into the tightest embrace and kisses her all over her face.

While I wait in Jordanna's car, I call Father Chuck. I detect no judgment in his tone, only happiness to hear from his favorite lamb. I am grateful. He says that there is a small church in Massachusetts that has shut its doors, because the rural community is too small to justify its own parish. There is a little house for the priest just behind the church, and he tells me where the key is. We can stay there. No one will know to look for us there. I think about calling Jerrold for a place to stay, but the cottage sounds so perfect. I call to let him know that we are going to be lying low for a little while, until the translation is finished. "Don't suppose you'd want to take an old man with you. I make a mean frittata," Jerrold offers.

Jordanna leaps into the driver's seat and declares of her husband, "I love that man." On the way we pass a number of churches and synagogues, many of which have signs announcing discussions of the Scroll of Anatiya. We are thrilled.

Jordanna calls Andrew Richter from the road. He says that he has already been flooded with emails and letters. Many of them enter the debate of piracy versus heroism in academia, but a good number of them are impressive scholarly commentary on the scroll so far, noting links to Jeremiah, references to Psalms, and Jobian overtones. He received a copy of a dissertation an English student had written years before on the "Productive Power of Unfulfilled Longing." It was fascinating, and Andrew plans to publish as many of these commentaries as he can. The *New York Times* is reprinting excerpts from the scroll as well. Furthermore, pictures are being released from Israel of the clay renderings of Jeremiah.

My mother says that there is a letter from Mortichai, and I ask her to read it to me.

Shalom Page,

It seems the world is healthier, doesn't it? Everyone around me seems to be in love, an international springtime. Everyone seems to want a love like Jeremiah and Anatiya, which could last for thousands of years. You probably already know that Ibrahim's clients who had trials pending for critiquing the PLO have been released and their charges have been dropped. He is home all the time now, monitoring the parade of people in his world-famous living room. Dalia and Walid are getting married on August twelfth in Jerusalem. Will you be returning by then?

I am writing you mainly to apologize for needing time to sort myself out. I hope I have not made a mess for you, but if I have, feel free to use the paper towels.

I read your books over the past week. I enjoyed Body of Water,

Body of Air, *and I found it incredible that you had already been speaking and writing about shrines being found in or around cisterns so many years ago. It struck me as I read that you could have included a whole other section, calling the book* Body of Water, Body of Air, Body of Earth. *I think you run from yourself as earth even as you've spent your career digging in it.*

Finally I read Upon This Altar. *I read the introduction three times. You wrote that in order to achieve a big life, one had to experience a little death, that in order to be fully restored, one needed to make a sacrifice. It is the sacrifice that makes the altar sacred. I wonder what sacrifice I must make in my life in order to be fully restored. I wonder if you could help me.*

In the last paragraph you wrote, "When the Temple in Jerusalem was razed and the altar of stone was demolished, the essence of that place was dispersed upon the backs of the exiles into seventy nations, and further into every home. From stone was released essence. The altar became a genie uncorked. The sacrifice of the priestly caste meant that the entire people, from woodcutter to watercarrier, were now restored to being a nation of priests. Holiness was unfettered from brick and mortar and flew out in all directions. The altar of stone became endless altars of time, ducked down and timorous between every tick and every tock."

I know what you meant when you wrote about altars of time. I experienced it sitting with you in the ambulance with Dalia between us as if she was our daughter. I experienced it many times with you.

I know I have not called. It is hard to be without your voice. I read your books, Page, because I wanted to hear you and imagine you were talking to me. Thank you for sharing the discovery in Anata with me, and every discovery since.

Mortichai Masters

After reading the letter to me, my mother says that she guesses it is true, then, what that Arab boy said on television. That I had sex with this man. I tell her that I never even touched him, and then I remember the time he threw himself over me when the brick came through the window. She says his letter makes it sound like I am running away from him.

"Mom, he's engaged to be married," I say. Jordanna glares at me out of the corner of her eye.

"You do understand the letter he wrote," she says, as if she is going over a composition with one of her students, "don't you?"

"I don't know." I don't feel like telling my mother everything I think.

"It is a long letter, but essentially it boils down to only one question, and knowing you I am concerned that you don't hear it."

"What is the question?" I ask. Then I add, "In *your* opinion."

"Wait, let me look for it." She pauses, skimming the letter. It is uncomfortable for me that such intimate words are being studied and boiled down by someone who's never met Mortichai, even if she does know me better than almost anyone. "Oh, here it is. He writes, 'I wonder what sacrifice I must make in my life in order to be fully restored.' That is the question. That is the only significant part of this letter."

"I resent that. It is all significant to me," I say, my arms crossed.

"Yes, it is all meaningful and I am sure you will stay up at night thinking about it, and wishing that you could read it over and over. But you still have to answer the question, and I'm not confident you understand it at all." She waits to give me time to prove I understand the question, and then she says, "The question he is asking you is this: If he breaks his engagement, will you be there to make a life with him? If you will not, then you are the sacrifice he has to make to have a life of wholeness. He is trying to tell you that he loves you but he is unsure whether you return those feelings, and he is afraid to ask."

"Well, A plus, Mom. Really. Brava."

"Don't be cute, Page. You have to tell him how you feel."

Then she tells me that there is also a wedding invitation from Israel. I feel my heart nearly collapse in upon itself, thinking it is for the wedding of Mortichai and Fruma. It is for the wedding of Dalia and Walid on Sunday, August 12, just over three weeks away. No reason to wait, I suppose.

After I hang up the phone I do not want to look at Jordanna at all. I press my forehead against the glass. I stare at the mirror and the sentence etched there: "Objects in mirror are closer than they appear." It is a very poorly worded, confusing sentence. Does it mean they are closer in the mirror than they appear in reality, or that they really are closer than they appear in the mirror? Moving "in mirror" to the end of the sentence would help, but even the idea behind this observation disturbs me. Objects are not actually in the mirror. Their reflection is in the mirror. Reflections in the mirror appear closer than the real objects are in reality. The sentence annoys me because it seems indicative of a much greater problem, that heaven in reality is farther than imagined.

"You okay?" Jordanna is unusually tender and I am grateful.

"I think I love him."

Without looking at me she reaches over and squeezes my hand. "I know," she says, full of understanding. We both watch the road, and I feel tears filling my eyes. The deep greens of summer spread out around us as we speed toward our hideaway.

XXV

Pursue wisdom, my child, but know first of all that this is no skip through the pasture. This is a tiresome mountain climb and the summit is far beyond your years but there are treasures along the way.

—THE SCROLL OF ANATIYA 51:97–98

After two hours we reach the little white church on the side of the road. It is in dire need of a fresh coat of paint, and weeds are overgrown all around the building. Behind the church there is a long dirt road that leads to a little house, with peeling paint like the church, and a roof covered with pinecones and leaves. I find the key behind the electrical cabinet in the back, just where Father Chuck said it would be, and we go in. The screen door slams behind us, and we both jump. It is very dark in the house, even with the lights on. It seems later than two o'clock in the afternoon because of the heavy woods that surround us, blocking the light. The furniture is sparse, and the rooms are chilly, here where the sun hardly reaches. There is a small kitchen with white metal appliances all edged with rust. The refrigerator is empty, except for an open box of baking soda. There is a little living room with a tattered couch and a fireplace, as well as a small bedroom with a metal spring cot, a stool, a cracked light beside which Jordanna puts her old-fashioned alarm clock. "I'm not here to sleep," she announces. "I'm here to translate this thing and get home."

We unpack the car, putting away the food first. I am already hungry, looking at how little we have brought. I go out the back of the house and collect some wood and sticks. The trees are towering, swaying at their distant tips as if they are playing a secret game of celestial jai alai. The air is pine-pungent. I can imagine Father Chuck strolling here intoning homilies from the sounds of the forest. I bring in an armful of wood and set about to build a fire. It is satisfying to focus on an immediate task, and to see its good and simple results as I tip newspaper with flame and watch the glowing line creep purposefully toward the stack.

Jordanna is rattling around in the kitchen making tea. The "meditation cottage" itself is pretty dreadful, and I think we both regret coming here. It is a sad place. There are water stains on the thin clapboard walls.

I spread our materials out on the floor before the fire. When Jordanna comes in and sees the fire, she says, "This is nice."

I smile weakly. I feel apologetic for getting her into this, for taking her from her adoring husband, beautiful children, snuggly cat, and bustling, warm home to come here.

Jordanna hands me a cup of vanilla chai tea and sits on the floor across from me.

Jordanna watches me for a moment. "Keep staring at the fire and thinking," she says. "Looks like it is really getting you to a good place."

I try to snap out of my mood. "I pictured rose bushes. Curtains."

"I know," she says. "But maybe it's a good canvas for Anatiya to show her colors."

I curl my fingers around the teacup and breathe in the sweet steam. I look at Jordanna sitting lotus-style on the floor holding her papers on her lap in the tent of her thick, beautiful hair. "We need a system," I say, scooting closer to her. "Why don't I do an initial rough draft of the section ahead of the one you are looking at, anticipating problem spots, and giving you a head start?" I try to sound enthusiastic.

"Sounds great," Jordanna says. She looks up. "Listen, Page, this is hard, but what we are doing is good. It is really good. I feel it deep inside."

My shoulders release their tension. I feel a gentle love for my friend. She passes me a stack of paper and a gives me a tender, motherly smile. I look at the fire again and this time it comforts me. The dappled light falling through the cheap metal-framed windows is actually pretty. I stretch my back and line up my Bible, dictionary, pens, and scratch paper. Jordanna has the laptop glowing on the floor between us. She is already writing quickly. Every now and then she holds the pencil to her mouth, looking at the empty mantel just above the fire, thinking.

I have read and reread the passage before me eight times, and my inability to understand it has nothing to do with difficulty in Hebrew vocabulary. I can read it. I just can't compute it. "Jordanna?" I ask.

"Mm-hm?" she says, not looking up.

"Can you please look at this? A cursory look? I think . . ." I can't finish. Jordanna looks at me. "What?" she asks, a little alarmed.

She takes the page from me. She puts on her glasses and studies it, and then reaches for her pen, jotting notes all over it. Then I see her eyes light up. She looks at me, full of knowing. She pulls her hair back and twists it into a rope at the nape of her neck, making a loose knot.

"Will you read it to me?" I ask, feeling small but special. I wish I could curl into her lap like a cat.

She reads,

To love a prophet is to be utterly rejected, a constant laughingstock at whom everyone jeers. For he knows you are trailing behind him. Everything is revealed to him and though you are naked to his vision, you are invisible to his eyes. He sees through the raging fire in your heart with cooling clarity and leaves you helpless and dejected

with a humiliation for all time. But if you say, "I will not think
of him, no more will I speak his name," his name reverberates off
your bones, and your sinews are as taut as Esau's bow, you quiver
with no release until you feel you are in the very throes of death.

To love a prophet is to be utterly fulfilled knowing you are close
to Vision, near to Voice, and no fire comes forth to consume you
and no angel descends to strike you. You feel radiant emanations
of the God that is in him, and it amazes you that only you, among
all people with names of renown, should gain entrance into God's
inner chamber, that your love should fit so snugly into that lock,
that hosts of angels should sympathize with you and divine beings
sustain you when you have no shekel to even purchase a morsel of
bread, that you, dark and comely and untended, should be here,
perched on the edge of Solomon's couch.

"It is lovely," I say. I feel tears roll down my face. "There's more,"
I whisper.

And she completes the passage:

If I could dig up the body of Elisha,
I would touch you with one of his bones like a wand
and bring you back to life,
to a life that I know must exist . . .

I put my hands over my heart. She takes off her glasses. "Oh
Page," she says, full of marvel. "You have been searching for Elisha all
your life. Digging and digging through countless tombs." I am surprised to see that Jordanna is crying now too. "And she was looking for him too, in her own way. And you found each other." I crawl
over to her and we wrap our arms around each other. "What are the
chances of that?" she asks.

"None," I answer into her shoulder. Suddenly the cottage seems
beautiful to me. All of its ugliness washes away as we hold each other
in front of the fire. I kiss her cheek. She kisses mine. I twist a loose

lock of her brown hair with my fingers. She strokes my hair. We pull away, each wiping our eyes and sniffling.

"If that isn't proof that you were meant to find this, I don't know what is," she says.

"*I would touch you with one of his bones like a wand,*" I say. "Like a wand, Jordanna."

"Yes," she says, and with the same tone she used when I told her I think I love Mortichai, she says, "I know."

Now we are both burning as bright as the fire, lit and determined. We are an efficient team. She is the master, and I am the able assistant. Around five o'clock, we take a walk in the forest together, just to stretch our bodies and clear our minds. We talk about our college days and she reminds me of things I haven't thought of in years.

The kitchen is narrow, with white- and gray-flecked laminate counters, pealing at the corners. The wood of the cabinets and drawers is aged and warped. Nothing opens or closes without a struggle or a creak. But the stove works, thankfully. I pour us each a glass of white wine in the glasses from a picnic basket we brought, a wedding gift Jordanna and Nathaniel received and never used. I cook chicken breasts in a pan on the stovetop with zucchini and rosemary, and put up a pot of water for quinoa. Jordanna chops lettuce and cucumber.

"Tell me what you would do," she says, leaning against the counter now that her salad is finished, "if he said he wanted to marry you."

I am turning the chicken over. It smells wonderful. "Learn to keep kosher?" I ask.

She laughs. "No, seriously, Page."

"We haven't even dated," I say.

"So? I'm just trying to imagine. What if he asked you to convert to Judaism?"

"The thing is," I say, "I don't really think that's his core. I mean, he is literally wearing this shell that just doesn't fit him."

"Do you think he'd convert?"

"No, not at all," I say. "I don't mean that. I just mean that I think he's more of a secularist underneath. I think he wants to be worldly, and he tried, but maybe it got lonely out there for him." I tuck my chin into my shoulder, acting shy, and say, "Because he hadn't met me yet."

Jordanna swirls her wine. "He was raised very traditional, right? He has a million brothers and sisters, and they all probably wear black hats or wigs. Do you picture yourself hanging out with all of them for Hanukkah? Do you think they would accept you?"

I think about that for a moment and say, "Realistically, they probably wouldn't accept me. Although his father converted to Judaism."

"Sometimes they are the most fanatic," Jordanna cautions.

"The thing is, though, when I picture being with his family, I imagine us playing whatever part we are supposed to while we are with them, and you know, they can look at me however they want, I don't really care. My whole field thought I was crazy until I found this scroll."

"Actually they still do."

I laugh. "But I imagine us visiting them. I wear whatever shell I have to, and him too, and we are very modest and proper, then we laugh about it in the car, and we tumble through the door to our happy little home, tear off each other's clothes, and make wild and wonderful love, and when we are finished, frankly, we are not thinking about his family or about world religions."

Jordanna is smiling. "What are you thinking about in bed, exactly?"

"What do you mean? It's obvious." I spoon the quinoa onto our plates and top it with the chicken and zucchini.

"Play it out for me, I want to hear," she says. I look at her to see if she is setting me up, but her face is open, her eyes receiving.

"We are thinking about how lucky we are to have unearthed each other. We are thinking about how good our skin feels against each other. We are thinking that nothing else really matters. We are thinking that we believe in each other, and we believe in God, and we believe in joy. And we are thinking about having ice cream."

Jordanna laughs hard. "Is that human enough for you?" I ask, handing her a plate, and she nods. We settle on the old couch in front of the fire and eat.

After dinner I do the dishes while Jordanna dives into the translation. When the hour is late, she creeps into the cot in the bedroom and I stretch out on the scratchy couch. I watch the fire's last sparkling and dream.

After some time I fall asleep, but I don't sleep deeply because the couch is uncomfortable. It is well before daybreak when I wake with the knowledge that I will not be able to fall back asleep. I pick up my cell phone and resolve to call Mortichai. I snap it open and realize that I get no reception here. I walk to the door and unlock it. I push it open gently and it squeaks loudly.

I walk out into the dark. It feels strange, like I am entering the territory of wolves, where the sound of my footsteps is unwelcome. The moon still sifts through the basketry of the forest's ceiling. I clutch the phone, watching to see if reception will appear. I laugh at myself. I think about what Norris yelled at me when he read my last book: "You going to start wandering around Jerusalem with the other lunatics?" I was amazed when my mother read me Mortichai's letter, when he said he read my books because it was hard to live without my voice. When I have nearly reached the church on the main road, I find my phone is working.

He answers.

"It's me," I say quietly.

"Thank God you called," he says.

I breathe deeply. I lean back against the church, looking up at the dark sky. Stars cling to the branches above me like beads of water. "I miss you," I confess.

"Page, I miss you too," he says. His voice is filled with concern. "Where are you? I know it is you translating this. There are some very angry people about this. But I think it's amazing."

"Really?" I ask.

"I think you are destined. You are remarkable."

"Thank you," I say, and we both wait on the phone for a moment, him in the sun, me in the moon.

"You sound good," I say. "It would be easy to leave it at that, but you have been thinking, and I can't help wondering where it is leading you."

The road is spookily silent around me.

"Did you get my letter?" he asks me.

"Yes," I say, my heart beginning to race. I remember how my mother had boiled it down: *If he breaks his engagement, will you be there to make a life with him? If you will not, then you are the sacrifice he has to make to have a life of wholeness.*

"Then I think you know my feelings for you are very real," he says.

I suddenly feel sad, standing here alone in the dark woods, an ocean away from someone who may or may not ever love me. Looking through the trees at the shivering branches, I feel frightened. I say softly, sadly, "You were destined for this marriage since you were a child, it seems. Maybe this friendship is a small sacrifice for that."

His voice is small and hurt. "I should sacrifice this, this friendship?"

"I don't know," I say, all my courage draining from me. *No, no, no, you should be with me.*

"I scheduled a time to meet with my rabbi to talk about this thing you call friendship," Mortichai says, his voice pleading.

I am taken aback. The same rabbi who is Fruma's father, who is going to be his father-in-law? What grown man goes to his rabbi to decide his fate? It never entered my mind to talk about my love life with Father Chuck.

I know what will happen. He will walk into his rabbi's office with the intention of seeking guidance, and he will change his mind upon seeing the rabbi's kind eyes and concerned brow. They will talk about the grandchild and the wedding. As Mortichai hears himself talk, he will relax into his decision, which, he will remind himself, isn't really a decision at all but his destiny from birth.

Or maybe he will muster the courage and confess his feeling for me to Fruma's father. What kind of father would allow this man to break his daughter's heart? What kind of rabbi would condone a Jewish Israeli lusting after an American Christian? What could the rabbi possibly advise Mortichai to do? He will defend his daughter, his people, and his country against me. If Mortichai is going to his rabbi, it means what he really wants is help getting past me.

"I don't believe you that it is only a friendship," Mortichai says.

"Well, what is it then?" I say. I am upset. "We have only known each other about six weeks. How can that be enough time to know anything?" I say this, even though, deep inside me, I do believe I know. I love him. But I love him in such a way that I don't want to kidnap him from his life. I want to love him generously. If he needs to be set free, I want to be able to set him free.

"I don't know what it is, Page," he says, "but my soul longs for you, and my heart cherishes you. The world loses all its color without you."

I look out at my dark world. I hear a small animal scamper behind a tree and I nearly jump out of my skin. "Will you be at the wedding?" I manage to ask.

"Yes," he says. He adds sadly, "Fruma will be with me; I hope that's not too uncomfortable for you. I'm meeting with Rabbi Ruskin a few days later."

I feel suddenly ashamed. His fiancée is joining him for the wedding. What kind of a person have I become? So desperate for love that I would try to steal away someone's intended. I suddenly feel unsure about the man who is hanging on the phone with me. He is making plans with the rabbi's daughter and at the same time longing for me? Suddenly he seems sleazy to me. I am unhappy, uncomfortable. We are both silent on the phone, each waiting for the other to say something. Someone has missed or misread a cue. Maybe it is me, maybe it is him, but neither of us understands the state of mind of the other. Maybe we are each waiting for the other to say more. I feel that something giant and tragic is happening to me and I can't find the words or the courage to stop it.

"I guess I'll see you in a few weeks then," I say, awkwardly.

Mortichai switches subjects and says, "Tell me about the scroll; it must be extraordinary to work with. I would love to hear what you think."

I wonder whether he deserves to hear what I think. The part of me that is physically afraid here in the suddenly ominous wood wants to hang up on him and run back to the cottage, lock the door. But there is another part of me that is also afraid, but not physically—afraid of losing him—and the piece of me that comes alive only when I am with him, and that part can't say good-bye.

"It is transporting, it is magical, it is so beautiful, Mortichai," I say, feeling myself surrender. "You know in the Book of Jeremiah that he is made to wear a yoke around his neck."

"Of course, a wooden yoke," he says.

"It is the first time she touches him." I close my eyes. I turn and press my forehead against the back of the church, and with my eyes squeezed shut I begin to recite. The words are as clear to me as if they are written inside my eyelids, and as they flow from my mouth, a well of tears inside me opens:

> It is amazing that a person can long for something her entire life, and the very power of that longing can make her afraid, frozen in fear. And then, all at once, that fear is overcome, without any strenuous effort. I dipped my fingers into the oil and I rubbed it into his neck, and my slender hand slipped under the wooden yoke and I rubbed, so gently, the oil into the skin of his neck, into the rash. And no lightning struck me, and no God intervened.

"Page, that is exquisite," he breathes. "How can words describe . . ."

I picture an invisible yoke around Mortichai, one of which he is only vaguely aware. We talk about the passage a bit more, and when the call ends, I walk quickly back along the dirt road to the cottage.

When I see the shadow of the house, it looks so flimsy and fragile in the deep woods. The walls are as of paper, floors of cardboard, panes of cellophane. I can feel the eyes of nocturnal creatures upon me. I creep into the house and lock the door quickly, folding myself up into the couch.

In the morning's first light, the forest looks like a cathedral. I make coffee and toast and wait for Jordanna to get up. When she does, she comes into the kitchen, her hair a fantastic mess of curls, wearing a long green nightshirt. She looks unhappy. I know that this is the first time she's spent even one night away from her children. I imagine she is homesick.

"Page, did you go somewhere last night?" she asks.

"I couldn't get cell phone reception, so I went for a walk. I called Mortichai." I pour coffee in two mugs.

"I woke up last night. I thought I heard a noise"—she looks very upset—"and I called for you a few times. When you didn't answer I came to look for you and you were gone."

"I'm sorry, Jordanna," I say.

"You can't leave me here alone. I felt unsafe. I have to be able to trust you that you are not just going to leave me here in the woods alone."

"I'm sorry," I tell her.

"I want to call my husband. I am worried about the kids. He is probably worried about me too. Maybe we should go home if this is how it is going to be."

Seeing her starting to spiral, I look at her and say emphatically, "I am truly sorry. I should not have gone out and left you alone. I am telling you, Jordanna, it will not happen again."

Jordanna seems appeased and sinks onto one of the two metal folding chairs in the kitchen. She receives her coffee and blows on the top. "I think we can finish this in less than a week," she says.

Twenty minutes later we are spread out on the floor again in the living room. Dusty shafts of sunlight slant over us. We are working efficiently and enjoying each other's presence and camaraderie.

It turns out to be a productive and beautiful day. Anatiya is opening to us with her smooth rhythm. At lunch, eating tuna sandwiches and drinking more vanilla chai tea, I say to Jordanna, "Forget what I said about Mortichai and heaven. *This* is heaven, being here with my closest friend, uncorking precious words that have been fermenting for centuries."

In the late afternoon, the cottage becomes chilly. I gather more wood and rekindle the fire. We sit before it, each with a blanket over our shoulders, and continue to surgically peel back the layers of this ancient story. After a couple of hours pass, we both need to get out, just to refresh ourselves. We go to the back porch with our blankets, watching the evening shadows of the forest lengthen and talking about Anatiya in the wilderness.

> *One morning I journey to the hills,*
> *to the trees who were my friends*
> *in the days of my youth;*
> *my lovers*
> *in the times of my sickness over you,*
> *those knobby fingers that broke my virgin seal.*
> *The moment I step into their lattice of branches*
> *and brush my cheek to their sweet gray moss,*
> *and watch the silver-green fringe of their leaves*
> *flutter in cedary breezes,*
> *a part of me I did not know was dying*
> *is resuscitated with a great gust of God-breath.*
> *With leaping legs I dance,*
> *with long arches and languid limbs*
> *and my hair swelling up and out in soft billows*
> *I dance as a tree whose roots are all at once*
> *unfettered.*

When suddenly a creeping comes over me, a child out of the mist;
he comes near, that he may approach me.

"She really does like trees," Jordanna says. "*Those knobby fingers that broke my virgin seal. Ouch.*" She scrunches her face and shivers as we look at the fading light through the stately pines.

"Well," I say, "I think the trees in that region were not quite as thick and robust as these." We laugh. I hug the blanket to me. Underneath I feel comfortable wearing Jordanna's leggings and one of her sweatshirts.

"She must have been *desperate* for him to throw herself upon a tree. *My lovers*, she says. There was more than one tree that bedded our little Anatiya."

The air is beautiful, its faint crispness a distant prelude to fall. I say, "Can you imagine the forest coming alive in that way, and dancing." The branches tremble around us with secret music.

"Does she really identify the child as Ezekiel?" I marvel. "It makes sense, I suppose. There is no reference to Ezekiel in Jeremiah, but he would have been alive in Jeremiah's time, and he probably would have been a boy. Where is Jeremiah when she is shaking it with the shrubbery?"

Jordanna giggles. "He is in the prison compound, remember?" She says this as if we had been there, two comfortable, old friends reminiscing about wilder days.

"Yes," I smile, thinking about the murals in the cistern. "I remember."

Jordanna reads on in our current passage:

Thus spoke the child:
"Have no fear and do not weep."
I raised my eyes to him and wondered in my heart,
"Who are you, celestial child?"
And he spoke:
"My name is Ezekiel. I am mortal."

I bolted upright, bewildered,
For he had heard and answered my unspoken thoughts.
"Yes, I do see,
And I do hear.
Far beyond what is stamped in the sky."

I half expect to see a magical elfin creature or two peep out from behind a tree. I look at Jordanna and she is deep in thought. I am certain she is thinking about her children. "Why don't you go call them and wish them good night?" I ask.

"You want to come with me?" Jordanna asks.

"No," I say. "I'm fine. Drive down to the church; there's reception there. I'll clean things up here before we have dinner."

I hear the smatter of Jordanna's tires kicking little rocks as she drives away and I patter in Jordanna's socks and my blanket-cape around the little house. The house begins to feel even more fragile without her, the woods leaning in. I go into the kitchen to make more tea to have for her when she returns. The old clock on the stove makes a metallic click with each passing second. And every second the thick silence seems to swallow up the click as soon as it sounds.

When the water is ready, I turn off the flame. I feel fidgety for her to return, and a little afraid. I wander into the bedroom carrying the blankets and pillows that had been on the floor in the living room. Her alarm clock ticks quietly in the dark. I am walking toward the cracked lamp on the stool beside the bed when my heart stops. I see something duck down swiftly just outside the bedroom window.

I gasp and drop the blankets. I am frozen for a moment. Is it an animal? No, it is definitely human. There is someone out there, and these walls are like paper. The front door is unlocked. My heart thuds in my ears. Oh God, I pray, Jordanna, come back. If only the sound of her car would come rumbling down the drive maybe he'll be frightened away. I am alone, I think, panicked. I am totally alone.

I hear footsteps crunching slowly around the side of the house and think of the crazy preacher standing on his overturned milk crate, Elias Warner, who called me a whore. Called for me to be pushed out of the window and devoured by dogs. I rush into the living room and grab the laptop and our stack of papers. My arms are trembling violently. Then I run back to the bedroom, my terror filling my throat so that I can hardly breathe. *Please let her come back, please let her come back.* I unlatch the window without noise and put one leg through. I balance the computer and stack of paper on the bed while I crook my other leg and extend it through the window. I hear the front door open. He is in the house. I pull the rest of me through with our work, and then, on sudden impulse, I reach back in and grab the alarm clock before dashing into the now dark woods, clutching everything to me. Instinct has made me grab the clock; it's hard, I can hit him with it. Behind me I can see lights being flipped on in the house. A shadowy figure climbs out the bedroom window I left open. I stand stone still behind a tree. I can hear him walking swiftly through the woods, coming in my direction. I look at the alarm clock. It is 9 p.m.

With my hands shaking and my arms desperately clutching the papers and computer to my chest, I set the clock to 9:01. I throw the alarm clock as far as I can from me and it makes a loud thump a good distance beyond me. I hear him pick up his pace and run toward the sound. Cold-sweating and shaking, I try to walk lightly but swiftly toward the dirt road, praying Jordanna will return. Whenever my feet make a noise on a branch, I freeze and wait a millisecond. Who is he? How has he located us?

From the base of a tree out of the dark, the alarm clock rings with a shrill that rattles through the black, and as if woken from sleep, I see the headlights of Jordanna's car appear and I start running with all the energy I can muster. I hear the man shout and run after me. I run with all my might between the monolithic trees. I can hear him gaining on me. I clutch our work tighter and run, tears streaming out of the corners of my eyes, and when my foot touches the road, I scream as loud as I can as I continue to run. I can see Jordanna speed up toward me. The man is almost upon me. Just as he grabs hold of the back of my shirt, I throw the papers and laptop into the car through Jordanna's open window. The man tackles me and opens my arms. Seeing nothing there, he looks toward the car and then back down at me. I can barely see in the darkness, but what I do see of him rings no bells. He pulls back a fist. I feel heat like the crack of a lightning bolt in my face, and I see a white shock of light.

I scramble my arms and legs against him and hear Jordanna screaming while she backs up the car. The car jerks forward, catching his leg and just missing mine. He falls face forward onto the dirt. While he is down, I hustle myself off the ground and rush around the car into the front seat and we take off with a screech.

"Christ!" I gasp as Jordanna careens down the road. "Who the hell was that?" I look back and see the intruder wobbling to his feet as we speed away.

"Are you okay?" Jordanna cries, patting me with her hand while she drives. "How did you get out?"

"I climbed through the bedroom window. But I got all our papers and stuff," I huff. I can't quite even out my breath.

"Your face! He hit you!" she exclaims. I touch my face and it is painfully tender and puffy.

"My eye's gonna swell up," I agree. We drive in silence for a little while as the night thickens around us. "He could have come when we were asleep," I say.

She is shaking her head. "Maybe he thought we had both left when I drove away?"

I feel a chill all over me. "I don't think so. I think he knew I was in the house."

After a moment Jordanna says, "Our house was broken into."

"Yes, and he chased me." I am breathing again. My face hurts but my heart is settling into its familiar rhythm.

"No, I mean my house. Nathaniel and the kids were out and when they got back Nathaniel noticed that the door to the attic was open even though he always keeps it closed. My office was a complete mess and my computer was stolen."

I feel tears swell in my eyes. "I thought that guy was going to kill me."

Jordanna's body is tense over the steering wheel. She looks fiercely determined. She wants to finish this translation; she doesn't want to give up. She also wants to get home to her children to protect them.

Her fingers crawl over to my seat and interlace with mine and we drive in silence for a while. I call Father Chuck and ask him if he told anyone where we were. I tell him someone broke in and tried to attack us. He is aghast. He remembers that someone called the day before, claiming to be a reporter.

"He asked me if I had been in contact with you, and I did say yes," he says. "Oh my, everyone at the church knows that I go to that little house sometimes. I am so grateful you are all right."

"We don't want to talk to the police until the translation is done," I tell him. "Should be another four days. But maybe you can call them, let them know what happened?"

"I'll call right now. Oh, thank everyone that you are all right. Thank the Father, the Son, and their good friends Jeremiah and Anatiya."

Jordanna turns on the radio. After listening to the sports report, which seems to go on inanely forever, there is an update on the pressure for the translations to continue and dueling pressure for it to stop. Study groups have formed all over the country. They are translating the scroll as it comes out into other languages. Threats are pouring into the *Digest*. There are discussions about "the Jubilee Jug," with listeners calling in to offer their opinion on whether or not it should be restored.

Once we are in Manhattan, we stop at the first newsstand we see and Jordanna runs in to buy a copy of *Archaeology Digest*. While she is there, she picks up a copy of *People*, which features the clay rendition of Jeremiah's face superimposed on the body of Michelangelo's David.

XXVI

When we say no to wisdom, we allow an entire region of ourselves
to dry up, and we allow for a hollowing of the soul. Ignorance
is blight. A desert creeps in and settles and spreads, swallowing
our soil-rich fruited plains until we feel a widening blankness, but
not a creative blankness like that of the pristine blank page, but a
feverish chalk-choked blankness that needs and needs but will not
receive. It mourns its own hunger, and laments its own void. The
soul is easily lost in this place.
—THE SCROLL OF ANATIYA 51:101–106

Jerrold March is beside himself to welcome us at 11 p.m. When
the elevator opens into his penthouse, Jerrold is standing in a
purple and black smoking jacket over silky black jacquard pants.
"Come in and take shelter, my precious refugees," he says, and then
eyes us up and down. "Darlings, you are filthy!" When he sees my
black eye, his hands come up to his aghast face. He rushes to me
and puts his arm around me. "Anna! Anna! Look at what they did to
my golden girl." Anna comes running out of the dark hall, winding
through the masks and heads. Her gray hair is set in giant rollers.
She says, "Come, let me show you where to clean up and where
you'll be sleeping."

We follow Anna and Jerrold follows us down the dark hall.

Anna pushes open a door to a magnificent bathroom that may be the size of my entire apartment. It is gleaming Jerusalem stone, the counters edged in gold leaf. Everything is highly polished, straight-edged, and modern, except for two fantastic artifacts. Over an infinity bathtub that can fit at least four extends a giant weathered sailing ship figurehead, an authentic mistress of the sea with fearsome eyes. And between the beveled glass shower and the bidet leans a massive, ten-foot-tall ship anchor with four feet of its original chain. It is covered in blooms of textured rust. There is a strip of window from floor to ceiling on either side of the counter, reminding us that we are floating just above New York at night.

Anna plops a pile of fluffy red towels between the sinks along with unopened toothbrushes, toothpaste, shaving cream, and a bag of Daisy razors. She hangs two brand-new matching pink silk robes on hooks on the back of the door and then shows us the two guest bedrooms, one Orient-themed, and one French, each one luxuriously appointed.

"I hope you find your humble boudoirs acceptable," Jerrold says with a little bow. "And should you need anything at all, my chamber is just around the corner from Anna's, with the collection of Virgin Marys on the door." He chuckles lightly. "A little harmless joke between me and the Man upstairs."

Jordanna and I go to the colossal bathroom together. She sits between the sinks while I pull my sweatshirt up over my head, careful not to touch my eye. It looks like an overripe plum that's been pecked by a bird. I turn away from the mirror and peel off my leggings. The steam from the shower begins to swirl into the room. "It's nice here," Jordanna offers.

"Yeah," I say. I step into the glass shower and the water feels amazing. The lily-scented soap is so thick and rich, it lathers me into an abominable snowman. I say to Jordanna, "Let's sleep in the same room."

"I would feel better that way," she says. "The masks and totems and shrunken heads might spook me."

All my muscles relax under the hot water. "We could go swimming in here," I hear Jordanna say.

The shower had been so weak and horrible at the cottage. I step one of my legs onto the limestone bench in the shower and daub a dollop of shaving cream along my calf. "A bag of razors, can you imagine. He thinks of *everything*."

Jordanna giggles. "He sure does like to take care of his ladies."

"What if I had brought Yosef Schulman instead of you?" I ask. Jordanna laughs as we imagine the renowned translator's drippy presence in this space.

Jordanna says, "I've heard Schulman has great legs!" I lift the razor off my leg for fear I'm going to cut myself laughing. I say, "I think Yosef and Jerrold would get along famously."

Jordanna considers for a moment and says, "I'm not sure. I think Jerrold is probably more partial to the young, lithe, and exotic."

I leave the water running when I step out of the shower. I reach for a towel just as Jordanna drops hers and steps in. While she showers, I look in the mirror at my eye for a long while. It should heal by the wedding, I tell myself. I pat myself dry and slip into one of the silk robes. It feels delicious.

I rub the towel against my hair. The terror of this evening already seems far away in this opulent place. My mind turns back to Anatiya. "The least poetic verses of the scroll so far are whenever Baruch speaks," I say.

"I know," Jordanna says from the shower. "I've been thinking about that. Anatiya uses some strange techniques when recording conversations with him. Her style becomes kind of halting. There are these stand-alone letters during Baruch's speech. Believe it or not, I am thinking of rendering them as 'um.' Sometimes the letters are smeared, and it is purposeful. Maybe she wants to let us know that he slurred."

"She also repeats syllables, as if he stutters."

"Endearing, huh?" she says.

We head in our robes to the Orient room. A serpentine paper

dragon snakes the ceiling, and the walls are covered with gorgeous painted fans and the tops of delicate paper umbrellas. We slip into the double bed, which is dressed with powder blue silk sheets printed with white orchids. We snuggle down together and Jordanna reaches behind her to snap off the light. "Sleep well," she tells me. "We have to make up for lost time tomorrow."

JERROLD DOES IN fact make a mean frittata. Jordanna and I feel about ten years younger, each wearing one of Jerrold's son's Yale Law T-shirts over our leggings. Andrew Richter has joined us for breakfast. He is dressed to impress in a black short-sleeved button-down and a thin black tie. He comes with a small bouquet of tulips for Jordanna and me. Andrew is appropriately horrified at my eye but clearly enamored with Jordanna.

"You must have been so frightened!" he exclaims to her as he settles into a chair at the table. Anna, with perfectly set hair, brings him coffee and he reaches to slice himself some frittata. "You had to be very precise to hit him with your car without hurting Page."

I am struck by Jordanna's wiggly enjoyment of the attention. Jerrold is in the same smoking jacket and pants as when he welcomed us last night. "Join me in a morning mimosa?" he proposes, and Anna brings out four fizzy flutes.

Andrew is studying the latest of our translation. "Baruch the scribe? It was his fingerprints inside the coffin. He is the artist of the murals as well, I suppose. Is he this awkward in the original? Not that I doubt your rendition, Ms. Lamm." He looks at Jordanna meaningfully.

Jordanna says, "He stumbles over himself because he is so smitten."

Andrew nods as if there are hidden layers to Jordanna's comment that only he understands. "That I understand completely," he says.

"Well, let's all have a listen, shall we?" invites Jerrold.

Andrew dabs the back of his thick neck with his napkin and then reads,

> "I, woman, I love you!" Baruch grabbed my two hands in his. I jumped back, but I did not pull them away. I was stunned. "I mean, I ache for you. I dream about you. I toss and turn over you, your curves, your hips, the gold in you, the shine. I get thirsty, I mean, my mouth gets all dry, my tongue is like a leather hide. It flops inside my mouth, a dead thing. I, I . . . my hand shakes, I drop my quill . . . your hair, uh, I mean those long twists and turns, I just . . ." He dropped my hands and looked at the ground, but not sadly, and not in shame, for there were still dimples in his cheeks from smiling.
>
> "I just . . ." Baruch lifted his eyes to mine and shrugged. "Well, I said it. How is that? You are a beautiful woman in love with a prophet of the Lord, and I am a scribe in love with you. You will never take him away from God, I will never take you away from him, and there it lies. So you and I? We may as well be friends, as we share in this unique life predicament."

Andrew has goose bumps on his meaty arms. Jerrold exclaims, "Ah! There it is! You see that, Page? For all of history good men have struggled with being thought of as 'friend.' Ancient proof of man's eternal struggle with women. Dear me, I even suspect that was the crux of the tension between you and that old rascal Norris."

"With all your flattery, you are a keen observer," I note appreciatively.

"I am full of surprises." Jerrold smiles. "As I told you, my love, half of this kingdom could be yours. But not Maximilian." Jerrold gestures to the largest of the African masks, an exquisitely beaded lion's face with an intricately woven mane. "He and I have a long history together. I have told my sons that I want to be buried in that mask and nothing else. That is how I intend to meet my Maker."

We all look at the mask in reverent quiet for a moment, until

Jordanna nearly spits out a mouthful of mimosa at the thought of Jerrold wearing the lion face and nothing else. It is impossible not to chime in.

The phone rings and Anna answers. She consults quietly with Jerrold and he says, "Indeed, send them up."

A few moments later, there is a flurry of excitement when the elevator opens and out run Joshy and Sharon followed by Nathaniel pushing a stroller with one hand and carrying a suitcase in the other.

"Mommy! Mommy!" The kids shriek, barreling past all the archaeological wonders to press into Jordanna's body. Andrew looks a little crestfallen but takes the opportunity to admire Jordanna's curvy hips as she bends over her kids to cover them with kisses.

Nathaniel has a healthy, happy glow. He has the flawless complexion of which both women and men dream. "I brought you two clothes." Nathaniel is unzipping the suitcase to show us what he packed. "I figure, four days of hiding? Hopefully less?" He is proud of himself for being so supportive, and so is Jordanna. She throws her arms around him and tears spring into her eyes.

"I'm sorry for leaving you alone," she says while they are in each other's arms. "Getting them all to bed must be so hard for you."

"Keeping them in bed is the problem," Nathaniel says.

"A good man," Jerrold says, standing to give him a hearty handshake. "If I had my life to live over, I would be a more hands-on father instead of being such a hands-on tart, if you know what I mean. Never got the hang of boy-meets-girl-and-loves-her-to-death, unfortunately. I'm more of a boy-meets-boy-and-loves-him-for-a-short-while."

Nathaniel laughs and strokes Jordanna's cheek while holding her around the waist with his other arm. The kids have disappeared into the maze of monsters and totems. Nathaniel calls, "Kids! Don't touch anything!"

Nathaniel gives me a quick hug and sits down. Jerrold serves him a slice of frittata. "What are we working on?" he asks.

Andrew says, "We were just looking at your wife's rendition of Baruch the scribe's speech patterns. Quite remarkable."

"Baruch is in a predicament," I say. "He is a regular guy in love with a gorgeous woman who is in love with a prophet of the Lord. An age-old tale."

"You yourself seem to have a thing for the people of God," Jerrold says to me. "Reaching into the earth to grasp the hand of a prophet. And this Mr. Masters, so I've heard, another man of austere and radical devotion. What do you have against robust, fabulously wealthy atheists?"

After we luxuriate too long over breakfast, and spend time with Jordanna's children, Nathaniel takes the suitcase into our bedroom. He begins taking his wife's clothing out and putting it in neat piles on the bed. He tells us. "I hope I picked the right things." He puts a neat little pile of lacy things on the bed and then another small pile, which he points to and, nearly blushing, says, "I brought the granny underwear for you, Page. I would appreciate it if you didn't wear any of these." He points to the lacy things. "And when this is all over, I want my wife back."

Jordanna can't resist and throws her arms around him, smashing her lips against his. When they pull apart I say, "Thank you, Nathaniel. You have an amazing wife, and I am so grateful that you are supporting us."

He looks at me meaningfully and says, "Don't you forget that you are amazing too, Page. You deserve to be loved madly like I love her." For this, Nathaniel is rewarded another lip smash, before he rounds up the kids to take them home.

OVER THE NEXT two days, we work on the text like zealots. Anatiya wrote in a frightening political climate, watching the Babylonian armies edging ever closer. The climate in which we translate is far more lush, with Anna's sweet pastries always at our fingertips. When we pause to catch up on world news, we learn that a ceasefire has

been called in the Middle East. The whole world seems to be taking
a deep breath. Except outside the Department of Antiquities in Jerusalem, where the Orthodox pressure has become riotous.

Andrew joins us after work each day. He doesn't know Hebrew,
so he doesn't help much, but he doesn't slow us down either. He and
Jerrold talk quietly while sipping cognac. On the second evening, Jordanna hands me a new passage and says, "If they thought Deuteronomy was a problem, wait until they read this."

"Better than Jeremiah naked?" I ask.

Jerrold strides over and takes the page from my hand. "Sit back,
relax. Why should you have to raise your voice," he says. He clears his
throat and is about to speak when Jordanna interrupts him, saying,
"Wait, wait, let me map out the context. Jeremiah has written a scroll
which he has presented to the king. The king is none too pleased
with the prophecies in the scroll."

I add, "Essentially Jeremiah is telling him to surrender to the
Babylonians."

"Right," Jordanna says. "So the king has the scroll burned. It
says so in the Book of Jeremiah. But what we have here is that
Anatiya sneaks into the palace, to the firepit, and she fills a sack
with the ashes of the scroll. She is so overwhelmed with love for
Jeremiah, and for the message he carries, that once outside, she puts
her hands in the sack and she rubs the ashes all over her body as
if they are coconut oil."

"Splendid!" Jerrold says, "Now, let us pay close attention, for we
are the very first in thousands of years to learn what actually happened next." My heart pounds with genuine thrill. He reads,

*I rubbed the ashes into my hair and into my cheeks. I smeared
them across my brow. I shook the ashes of that scroll over my arms
and rubbed them into my dress until the sack was empty and I was
covered in soot. A charred alef was smeared over my eyelid. Other
fragments of letters clung to my cool sweat like broken insect legs
and wings. I walked toward the hiding place of Jeremiah and Ba-*

ruch, with tears plowing long streaks through the soot on my face. I
arrived at the cave in which they sat quietly by a fire.

I stood at the mouth of the cave with my arms lifted from my
side, palms facing forward. Baruch leapt to his feet and cried,
"Anatiya!" but my eyes were fastened to Jeremiah. For the first
time, he seemed stunned. His eyes were wide. The whites of them
glistened in the firelight. Lips parted. Baruch rushed toward me,
when Jeremiah spoke:

"Do not touch her, Baruch. She is wearing the scroll of God."
Jeremiah rose from his place. "She immersed herself in His words."
And he walked toward me, while Baruch remained frozen in his
place. "Dear prophetess," he said, as he stood close. "You are dark
but comely, O daughter of Jerusalem . . . your locks are curled"—
he entwined one around a thin, white finger—"and black as a
raven, adorned with sapphires." Jeremiah softly stroked the side of
my face. "Ashes to ashes, dust to dust."

"Jeremiah?" Baruch inquired. "Jeremiah, what is happening?"

Jeremiah did not remove his eyes from mine, as my tears continued to well forth. Jeremiah said, "This woman is called in life
Anatiya. But the angels do call her Jerusalem. Here before me, I
see the whole city, fair Zion, fair and beautiful Zion, risen out
of the ash heap. Baruch, open a blank scroll, and dip the quill in
ink. Take down these words that I say. They shall call this scroll
'Lamentations.' "

Andrew's hands clamp over his mouth and he gasps. I grip the
side of my seat. "What?" I shout, eyes wide. I whisk the page out of
Jerrold's hand to see what follows. Indeed, what follows are verses
from the Book of Lamentations. "He is writing about her," I marvel.
"*She* is Jerusalem, covered in ash."

Jordanna's eyes are silver dollars. "Metaphor and literal have
merged into one body."

Andrew looks like he is in a trance. "It is strange," he says, "A
scroll that has been studied so thoroughly throughout the centuries,

and no one ever knew that what inspired it was this, a woman."

"A beautiful woman," Jerrold speaks as if he is narrating to a crowd, "desperately in love, her chest heaving with passion, her scantily clad body covered in ashes. Her desire for the prophet has driven her insane. The dust of his feet, the shards of a jug he's touched, even the *ashes* of the words he wrote, these are treasures to her." He looks over at the lion head mask and shakes his head. "Now, Maximilian, that's a woman."

"Can you imagine how this will be received?" Jordanna says, looking a little frightened. "Every year on the ninth of the Hebrew month of Av, people sit in sackcloth and ashes, they drape the Holy Ark in black and study the Book of Lamentations, bemoaning the destruction of the temples in Jerusalem."

"The first temple was destroyed in Jeremiah's time by the Babylonians," I say.

"Right. In fact"—she starts rifling through papers—"Jerusalem is about to be destroyed; that's why Jeremiah is trying to get his people to surrender, to survive, so that they can one day return."

"And there stands Anatiya," says Andrew, face still looking entranced, "thinking nothing of the city, the temple, the king. Only thinking about him. And yet, he says it. She *is* Jerusalem."

"He really wrote Lamentations," Jordanna says.

"And she was his muse," Jerrold adds.

"All these years," I say, "people studied this book, and no one saw her standing right in the midst of it."

"But we see her," says Jordanna.

We hang there, the four of us, while Anna clinks around in the kitchen. We have stepped outside of time, tumbling together like children down a slope, out of a dark wood and into a big bright space where all our days sprawl out like fields of Giverny gardens.

"I don't know if I should sing, laugh, or weep," admits Jerrold.

"Me too," is all I can say.

Andrew says in a whisper, "Ashes . . . ashes . . . we all . . . fall . . ."

"Down." Jordanna nods and Andrew is in rapture.

A moment later, Jerrold and Andrew return to their discussions and cognac while Jordanna and I plug on.

AT NIGHT I slip into bed with Jordanna and we look at each other from our pillows, which rise around our faces like snowy alps. Moonlight from the window makes everything seem delicate and celestial. Jordanna's dark hair spills over her pillow like silvery lace. She says, "You never told me about your call to him. You know, when you left me all alone in a gingerbread house in a wood full of witches."

I feel her hand squeeze mine under the sheet and I smile, comforted. There is a minty toothpaste aftertaste in my mouth.

"It was hard," I say. "He told me he made an appointment to speak with his rabbi. It's not for another couple of weeks. I don't know, maybe the rabbi is taking a summer holiday and doesn't realize the seriousness of this situation."

"Uh-oh," Jordanna says, squeezing my hand again. "I can guess what came next. You shut down. You wrote the story before it happens."

I nod in surrender.

Jordanna says, "Is this the same rabbi who encouraged his parents to let him join the army? And who encouraged them to let him study in America?"

I nod again. "But he's also the same rabbi who is the father of the woman he's marrying." Jordanna watches me. The paper umbrellas and fans on the wall seem to flutter and spin for a moment, and I turn onto my back. "I think that if he's made an appointment to talk to his rabbi, then it is pretty clear to me he just needs a little help to get over these nudniky feelings he has for me. Honestly, what *rabbi* would encourage his future son-in-law to pursue a heathen?" The paper dragon on the ceiling looks down on me with a wide, friendly grin.

Jordanna says quietly, "And what *father* would encourage a man who is in love with another woman to marry his daughter?" I look into the dragon's giant eyes for a long while. I never thought about that.

"Tell me more," I say. "Why then would he go to him?"

She says, "Maybe he's going to this rabbi because this rabbi has known him for his whole life. Maybe the Orthodox culture is just something you don't quite understand. The rabbi is, in many ways, the resident therapist. At the same time, he is the one whose approval makes things kosher. If Mortichai is seeking counsel with his rabbi, it means one, that he is deeply troubled by this. He is not taking his relationship with you lightly in any way. And two, he cares about his family's approval. It is clear what he wants, but the thing is, maybe he wants too much."

"What do you mean?" I ask.

"He wants you, *and* he wants everyone's blessing," she summarizes. Suddenly her accusation a week ago, that I string together very complex concepts but can't understand something as simple as reciprocal love, rings true. Jordanna continues, "Didn't you tell me that his mother was Russian and his father was Irish Catholic when they met, but he converted? That must have been some love story, don't you think? Maybe he has his mother's genes."

He wants me and he wants everyone's blessing. My heart aches. "Thank you," I whisper to Jordanna. Our hands separate and mine slip under my pillow as I turn on my stomach. Before I fall asleep, I meet Mortichai in my mind, wrap my arms around him and smile admiringly up into his face. The man I thought of as stoic and cold when I first met him I now suspect may actually be the most hopeful and naively optimistic soul I've ever known, but sewn into a disguise. He's mummified! I imagine, and I am unwrapping him.

By the morning of the fourth day, we are nearly as mute as Anatiya herself, committed to completing the mission. Andrew has joined us for the day, knowing we are near the end. By early afternoon, before Anna has a chance to warm the focaccia for lunch, Jordanna puts down her pen. She has tears in her eys. She looks like she has climbed a mountain. She is resplendent. She stands up and walks to Andrew and presents the final pages to him. He reads them reverently and then looks up at her. His eyes are filled with love. She says, "It is now up to you to bring her to light and set her free."

He stands up and says, "The translator is always the unsung hero of any work of art. When they raise up your friend as the hero, and praise the phenomenon which is Anatiya, I will be thinking of you. Intrepid, inspired, and full of grace."

Jordanna embraces him lightly and kisses him on his cheek. Jerrold breaks open a bottle of champagne and we make an exuberant toast.

Jordanna and I hold each other for a long while. "We did it," I whisper in her ear. "We have set her free." When we pull apart, Jordanna, beaming, puts down her champagne flute and says to me, "Now, my best friend, it's time to go home."

I MEET JERROLD'S lawyer Greg Chesterfield in front of Jerrold's building and we share a taxi to the police precinct. His long legs fold in sharp angles in the back seat. I roll down my window and enjoy the sun streaming in, carrying the colors and sounds of the city. Stopped in traffic I watch a mother in a flowered linen dress strolling with her daughter, who is skipping by her side so joyfully, it looks like she might become helium and take to the sky.

"Even up until college, I fantasized about being an underwater archaeologist," Greg tells me. I turn to him, and even with his rich suit and gold watch, which sits on his skin like it was designed only for him, I can picture him in scuba gear, streamlined and slick. He says, "I thought I'd dodge barracudas, punch sharks."

"Have you ever been diving?" I ask.

"The Australian reef, Hawaii, brilliant colors, the coral," he says, reminiscing. "I imagined I'd take my little submarine down through clouds of iridescent jellyfish that would sparkle like a city at night. I'd discover the underwater crater that would prove once and for all that a meteor hit the earth and destroyed the dinosaurs."

I laugh.

"Of course, there'd be sunken pirate ships. Treasure strewn all around for miles."

"And you would nobly turn it all over to the Antiquities Authority, law-abiding man that you are," I say.

"Yes, but maybe I would keep one gem for myself, not for the money, but to honor the spirits of pirates who had died in the wreck."

"But you chose law school instead of adventure under the high seas," I say.

"It was a dream that arose out of the invincibility of youth," he says. I smile because he still looks pretty invincible to me. "Now, frankly, it makes me nautilus to think about bobbing under the waves all day."

"Did you just say it makes you nautilus?"

"I said it makes me nauseous," he says, but he looks unconvinced.

"No, you didn't," I tease him. "How long is it that you've been keeping Jerrold out of trouble?"

"Listen, Jerrold isn't Jerrold unless he's in a heap of trouble."

We laugh together. At the police station they are pleased we have come and seem remarkably understanding of my decision to hide until the translation was done.

Detective Vega tells us, "As a cop, I am law-abiding. As a Christian, I am also God-fearing, and I know that God put that scroll in your hands for a reason."

I talk to the detectives for about an hour, not much time at all, and Greg makes sure everyone is aware of an archeologist's legal license to photograph and utilize data how he or she sees fit. They warn me to be careful. There are a lot of people who are furious with me. But there are more people, they say, who think I am some kind of a hero.

XXVII

There is nothing so perfect as a wall with a door and a window. A wall to shelter, a door to invite in, to leave through and come back through, to close and to open to the vast space, and a window through which to know truth.

—THE SCROLL OF ANATIYA 51:109–110

In between America and Eurasia, I look out at the dark clouds as the red wing light cuts through them, and I imagine I am on a magic carpet. The last couple of weeks have been surreal. When I returned to my apartment after days of translating on the lam, I found all my possessions slightly out of place. My mother had told me the police had rummaged through my things, and it was clear to me that my mom had tried to put everything back in its place. In a way, it looked better than I had left it, only, it didn't seem to belong to me anymore. Or I didn't belong in it. The place that had for years been to me a home base didn't feel like home at all anymore. Perhaps the stacks of mail made it feel more public than mine. The strange thing is that nothing has replaced it as home. I have no home, really. When I packed two suitcases to return to Israel, I couldn't imagine pitching my tent anywhere and calling it home. I sift through the places that might receive a wandering me, places I've slept in the past month: my stark room in the house I shared with Norris and the

Bograshovs, Ibrahim's study in the Barakats' home, the Orient guest room in Jerrold's penthouse. I think of Jordanna's serene attic. I think of my mother's apartment.

None of it is home. I press my forehead against the airplane window. We have emerged from a quiltwork of clouds. The moon creates a long aisle across the ocean. What would Anatiya and Jeremiah think about the world from up here, I wonder. They'll be on a plane someday, I like to imagine, when they do their world museum tour. They will sail, locked in each other's arms, through the sky. I think of Anatiya's prophecies. While Jeremiah was in prison, she wrote that she could feel the rhythmic pulsing of his welts and bruises, the dull pain that washed over him like the surf lapping over the white shore. She had quilled, *Someday we too, darling, will slide across the sapphire pavement, two graceful, long-necked cranes skimming the waters. This day I feel myself aging. This day I want so much to hate the men who flogged you, but I can only love, more deeply, more purely. Know, Jeremiah, how much joy for you is in me. How I serve you adoringly, and on account of you, your God I do forgive.*

I think of the last time I visited my father's grave in Long Island, about twenty years ago. My parents would have been married twenty years, and my mother wanted to honor their anniversary. If anything, that is my true home, I realize. There, in our small family plot. That is my home on earth. But here, in the sky, I am rootless, a feeling that would make most people anxious. This moment, it makes me feel free. I realize, I am grounded in something more eternal than earth. I am grounded in purpose. I see that purpose in the eyes of everyone I meet, everyone who sees me. I read it in the stacks of mail that waited for me when I returned to my apartment, most of it supportive, some aggressive. It didn't frighten me. My name, my soul, will always be woven into the life of the prophet Jeremiah and the beauty of the woman who loved him. That's my home. There are stars winking from Anatiya's "sapphire pavement." The lights of another airplane far in the distance move steadily in the other direction. I envision archaeologists thousands of years from now opening the

grave of Jerrold March and finding a giant African mask, and I laugh
out loud. It's what we do, I think. We look for legacy whether it's
in lunacy, children, great or small deeds. Mostly it's countless small
deeds strung together in an effort to survive and live earnestly. I think
of the thousands of infant Canaanite tombs I've uncovered, and look
at the now thousands of stars. They are related, I feel. Each star ema-
nated one of those souls, who inspired a little more love, if only for a
day, a couple of days, or years. Then comes grief, which is always the
price for loving. But thank God for loving. And the stars keep shining
their light to dispel the gloom, orient the troops, chart the wanderers,
on and on and on. I marvel at the night.

I took care of everything I had left outstanding. I told Banana
Republic I wasn't interested. I finished with IMAX. I am free. I am
different. Dalia asked that I say something at the wedding. I open the
latest issue of the *Digest*, scanning Anatiya for inspiration.

I turn to the time when she and Jeremiah are at the feast of
the Rechabites, and he kisses her for the first time. She is mute the
entire scroll but for here, when she speaks one word, "I . . . ," and then
stops.

*My love spoke to me: "When Jacob saw Rachel, he rolled the stone
off the mouth of the well and watered the flock and then he kissed
her. I have now seen the stone move off the well. I have now looked
into the well. It is filled with the tears of Rachel's weeping. I have
now seen the waters that will water the flock. The living waters are
your love. I was born with the stone on my soul, a dislodged jewel
that seals my spirit as a pent-up fountain. I cannot love, for this
stone. I cannot marry, for this stone. I cannot surrender, for this
stone . . . though with everything in me, as God, my God lives, I
want . . . And no shepherd's strength, and no king's command, and
no foreign force could shift this stone. Even so, I have now seen the
stone move off the well, by the tiny splash of a woman's tear, and
for a moment, with you, I am Jacob . . ."*

My love rose from the table, and his words were a net cast around my body, lifting me. I moved to him. In an instant his arms locked around me, and he whispered and I felt the sweet breeze of his breath, "I have never kissed, for this stone . . ." and I felt my lips press against my love. I held tightly around his wide back and my tears streamed into our joined mouths. All of the blood in me rushed in frenzy and every thought, every thought in the world, was silenced, every breath held, every wave on the sea, every tumbling rock, every star in its path stilled until . . . My love pulled away, and his sweep of white hair smoothed over my neck, and he pressed his forehead to mine, and a white light pounded through the place our heads touched, and this light flooded my eyes. I opened my mouth and said softly, but audibly, "I," and I could not go on and he said, "Hush, now, my bride. God returns."

I put down the *Digest*, thinking back to the day we removed the stone slab from the step, uncovering a small trove of jewelry and cherished belongings, including the large brass cuff bracelet with a small stone imbedded in the center with the Hebrew words, "I love you." I imagine Anatiya scattering these stones throughout the downtrodden people like a celestial farmer scattering starry seeds.

I think of Mortichai, and a sudden sweetness envelops me as if I've been candied. *Someday we too, darling, will slide across the sapphire pavement . . .*

IBRAHIM AND NAIMA knew I was returning to them. Still, when I arrive, they are as ecstatic as if I've come up the walk with chariots and dancing troops. The house looks entirely different from the front. The living room and the entranceway have been extended into one large protruding room, which is neatly stacked with equipment. In what was once the living room, a smaller room has been constructed over the entrance to the cistern in order to control the temperature and maintain the murals. It looks odd there, like an army bunker in the middle of a house. Inside, I see that the entrance to the cistern has been expanded into a polished square, and a set of stable wooden steps have been built going down. The colors of the murals are even more vibrant than I remember. I stand in the little room looking down. I am tempted to throw in a coin as if this is the world's wishing well. The colors are all drawn of rainbows and dust. The rest of the house is the same, for now. Ibrahim tells me that they have purchased the lot next door, and he shows me the construction that has begun on their new home, as it ultimately won't be possible to live atop an international treasure.

A cornucopia of savory delights is heaped on brass trays on the dining room table. Naima piles a plate for me with cubes of lamb snowcapped with goat milk yogurt. The cucumber salad is sliced so thin it is nearly transparent. Ibrahim is waving his arms as he updates me on the pressure from the Orthodox to rebury the skeletons, while there are some on the Christian Right calling to separate them first. Three of the members of Israel's parliament, the Knesset, have had their houses burned down and the arsonist has not been caught. The Barakats are grateful for the guards posted around their home, and Naima keeps them very well fed.

My mouth is stuffed with milk and meat when Mortichai arrives. I stand up, trying to swallow and wipe the juices off my lips, but the evidence is right there in the spicy lamb juices spiraled in white yogurt on my plate. He doesn't seem to notice the table but embraces Ibrahim, bows cordially to Naima, and then stands before me. It is an awkward moment for each of us. I want to throw my arms around him, and his hands seem pinioned to his hips in order not to touch, or invite touching. Still his smile lassos me tight and we both laugh, looking at one another and smiling. He takes off his black jacket, slinging it onto a chair, and he pushes up the sleeves of his white shirt. He sits down beside me. He is not wearing his hat, and his hair is a little longer, thick and that color I love, yellow fields made pink by dawn. His lids seem heavy over his blue sky eyes. He looks sleepy, pensive, and relieved to see me. I find myself looking at him the way I looked at the murals, hypothesizing from where these colors came:

What spice routes did the lapis lazuli have to travel to make such a blue? What trades had to be made to acquire such a gold? I think about his parents and their heritage and imagine a paintbrush dipped into the slopes and seas of Ireland, and then swirled with the sun over Russian forests full of legends.

"I have something for you," he is saying, and he puts a small white box on the table. It is unwrapped. "I don't know . . . ," he begins. His face reddens and he glances down at his hands, which are on his knees. He takes a short, deep breath and continues, "if it is appropriate or not to bring you a gift. Probably not." He looks at me and smiles meekly. I find his struggle endearing. "But I want you to have this."

I open the box. It is a hair clip, beautifully adorned. I stare down at it. "Where did you get this?" I ask quietly.

"It's a butterfly," he points out, avoiding my question. Ibrahim is putting a plate of food in front of Mortichai. He takes it and nods his appreciation, and then holds the dish awkwardly for a moment. He puts it on the table.

I laugh and look at him. "No, it's not," I correct him. "It's a luna moth."

I hold it up. It is four inches across, laquered a luminescent lime green. "A *moth?*" he says, embarrassed. "Are you sure? I thought it was so pretty."

"It will be so beautiful in your hair," Naima says.

I laugh. "Luna moths are beautiful. I've seen them in New York a couple of times. When you see one, it takes your breath away. They are ghostly and exquisite. They are miraculous, tragic, delicate creatures." I hold the clip to my chest. "I love it. Where did you get this?" I ask again. I know there are no luna moths in Israel.

His face reddens again. "Actually, if you have to know the truth, I bought it when I was a college student. I got it in Bloomington. I had been living there for three years already. It is so funny, originally I had bought it thinking I'd send it to my mother, and it wasn't until I got back to my dorm that it struck me that my mother would never wear something like this in her hair. Her hair is always covered with a scarf."

Something clicks in Ibrahim and he jumps up and takes Mortichai's plate away, returning apologetically with a glass of water, an unpeeled orange, and a bowl of sunflower seeds.

Mortichai thanks him and continues, "Then I thought, well, I'll save it and I'll give it to my wife one day." He looks at the clip in my hands and then at me. "Then I remembered that no married woman in my community wears her hair exposed." He laughs. "That's how far removed I was from it all. That's how far I had strayed. That I would buy a barrette thinking I'd give it one day to a woman I loved." He suddenly coughs and looks terribly uncomfortable. He drinks some of the water.

I rub the clip between my fingers. It is heavy and smooth. My heart is so full, I feel as though all my seams are unraveling. He says, "I wanted to give you something, Page, but it felt strange to go out and buy something, given, you know, the circumstances, and then I remembered I had this. I hope it's okay," and then he adds, "I'm sorry."

I look at it and it is full of meaning to me. Whatever happens between us. Even if he marries and disappears into a world where spicy lamb never mixes with cooling yogurt, I will treasure this gift, a gift from his past, from his former self, shed of his chrysalis of custom and commitment. He had bought this for me, I am certain in my heart, long before he knew me. And he knows that I will wear it out loud, my hair exposed and shining, and it will be beautiful. And he likes that. He doesn't like that his mother is always covered by a scarf. He bought her something beautiful for her hair!

"Why are they tragic?" Naima asks.

"What?" I say, shaking myself out of my euphoria.

"You said that they are tragic," she reminds me about the luna moths.

"Oh"—I jolt into the present—"they are. As caterpillars they are fine, but when they come out of their cocoons, for some reason there is something flawed in their design. They have no mouths. And so they live for only about a week before they starve to death."

"How could they have no mouths?" Ibrahim asks.

"That is so sad," Naima says.

Mortichai is staring at me as if he is looking into a kaleidoscope. "It's not tragic," he says. "It would be tragic if they never got to spread their wings at all."

I gather my hair and twist it up, fastening it with the clip. I am deeply aware of the nakedness of my neck, and of Mortichai watching me and turning away. Naima clears the table except for the orange and the sunflower seeds and we open my copy of the *Digest* and talk about Anatiya with animated excitement, like a family sharing stories about a sister or daughter who's finally, after hope was nearly lost, returned.

I GIVE MYSELF plenty of time to prepare for the wedding. After I shower, wash and comb my hair, I want to pamper myself more. I fill the bath, swirling it with the bath salts that were here my first visit, and immerse myself. Afterward I dust myself with baby powder and wrap myself in a soft towel, twisting another over my head like a turban. I lean into the mirror, smoothing coconut cream on my face. I look younger than my years, I think happily to myself. Or maybe it is that I am happy and relaxed. In my room I slip a dress I bought in New York over my head, and it falls over me in airy ripples of silk down to my ankles. As simple as the dress is, it is fancier than anything else I own, a gray moiré sleeveless sheath dress with gentle ruching that comes together with a braided silver cord at my neck. In the mirror, I can see the outline of my body through the thin fabric, the peaks of my breasts, and the gentle curve of my hips. The fabric spills like water over the muscles in my thighs and down around my calves. I sweep my hair up and fasten the luna moth clip so it sparkles at the crown of my head. Wisps of daffodil blond stick straight out, like little rays from my shining face. I put on the small diamond studs my father gave me, post-mortem, at my confirmation. Lastly I slip into silver sandals with a three-inch heel. When I come downstairs, Ibrahim and Naima are by the door looking handsome and radiant. Naima is in an emerald green long-sleeved dress. "You are going to be cold!" she exclaims when she sees me. "I'll bring a shawl in case you need it," she says and hurries past me upstairs.

Ibrahim is eyeing me carefully. "He'd be a fool," he says slowly. "You are a lighthouse . . ."

"A lighthouse!" I laugh.

"All your brilliance is up here," he says, pointing to his head. Then he repeats, "He'd be a real fool."

I climb into the back of their car, despite Naima's sincere protests that I should ride in the front. The wedding takes place in West Jerusalem at the Sultan's Pool, a Herodian reservoir that acquired its name from Suleiman the Magnificent, who restored the site in the sixteenth century. As we park the car I feel a slight tremble in my bones, knowing I'll be seeing Mortichai and Fruma soon. I walk a little uneasily down the antique stone steps. There is already a significant crowd gathered below. Though he conquered Iraq, Hungary, Albania, and the Mediterranean sea, I am certain Suleiman never saw such a bounty of sequined and beaded women. Muslims with checked kaffiyehs and white robes move through the crowd with soft stealth. Orthodox Jewish men in elegant black suits and dark halo hats skim the outskirts with wives in regal crowns of cloth braided around their heads. Among the descendants of ancient feuds glint earrings and crystal Vs of martini glasses. I can see them all laughing, looking about with black Semitic eyes, and somewhere down there among them is Mortichai, with eyes of sky.

I pause on the steps. Ibrahim and Naima have walked ahead. Tiny moths are flitting about high in the night sky, and behind them looms the floodlit walls of the Old City and the Tower of David, stony witness to the clash of centuries. I wish to be among the moths. I shiver and draw Naima's black shawl around my bare arms, trying to steady myself on my high heels. Suleiman gave Jews, Armenian Christians, and Greek Orthodox Christians religious autonomy. He would have been delighted with the international gathering in his pool, the beautiful blending of all his guilds.

When I reach the bottom of the steps, dozens of people descend upon me talking excitedly. A videographer with a microphone cuts through the crowd, heading straight toward me. In my imagination, he is an aquanaut here at the bottom of the Sultan's Pool, and his microphone cord is his air tube. The piercing light on the video camera toted behind him is the nose of his deep-diving sub. Just before the light zeroes into my eyes, I catch a glimpse of Mortichai. He is wearing, as always, a black hat and suit. I am vaguely disappointed that he seems to be wearing a hat that actually fits his head. He is leaning down to talk with a woman. My eyes run over her before the videographer obscures my view. She is in a navy tweed jacket, a long matching pleated skirt, and sensibly flat closed-toe shoes. She has straight brown hair parted in the middle and pulled into a tight, long braid. For a terrible moment, in all her ordinariness, she is to me the most ominously beautiful fish in the pool.

I offer a blessing for Dalia and Walid and wave the camera away to look again toward Fruma. She is petite. Her ivory skin is scrubbed brightly: there is no blemish, no sun crease on her uplifted face. Her brown hair parted over her high forehead is like curtains swept open. Her little earlobes are snowbells peeking out from underneath. She wears no earrings. No makeup. When her mouth smiles, her eyes smile too, leaping into half moons. The walls of the Old City rise up behind her, and only she seems to belong to them. A rabbi's daughter. A pure soul. A good and loyal mother. A psalm at the ready upon her tongue.

Before Fruma, with his back to me, stands Mortichai, his new black jacket fitting properly over his shoulders. His black hat tilts toward her as he leans in to her to absorb her speech. I feel poison rising into my chest. *How could I try to tear him from her? Who am I?* I turn around and press through the circle of people waiting to grab a piece of me. I exist for them because of the discovery. I myself am nothing more than the bones that I found.

Mortichai turns and sees me. He smiles and raises his hand to wave. I am faint with sadness but trying to recover, to respond amicably. He reads my posture, and his smile instantly evaporates. In the time it takes for him to come to me, I find my center. I clutch the shawl around me and smile to him.

"You look beautiful," he says, and then adds quickly, "You okay?"

I nod, afraid to speak.

"The clip looks nice," he says. "I knew it would."

I breathe deep and try to be courageous, and honest. "We need to talk at some point, not tonight, but soon. I have feelings for you, and I am happy to celebrate your wedding, if that's what makes you happy. But I can also picture myself walking down that aisle with you. And that's a fantasy full of all sorts of holes, I know. But you support it, with your gaze, you know you do. You have to tell me what you feel. Clearly. And then we can face a flawed but beautiful future together, or we can let each other go with a blessing. That too is a kind of love, I suppose. Either way is good, Mortichai. But I need to know what you want."

I barely finish when Meirav comes up beside us. She expresses her excitement to see me with an abandon that I've never seen from her. Her hair is no longer red but midnight blue. It is still spiky, but long enough for her to have tied little red bows throughout it. She wears an off-the-shoulder black rayon top that looks painted on her body, and a cherry red crinoline skirt that poofs out at her hips and looks like she took a scissors to it while drunk.

"Page Brookstone," she says, peeling away from me, "meet my boyfriend, Shrag. Shrag, this is my boss, Page Brookstone." I have to laugh when she calls me her boss, knowing there's little likelihood we'll work together again. But who knows anything, really?

Shrag is strapping, having dressed up his army uniform with the cummerbund and bow tie from a tuxedo. He has the classic army buzz cut, but what sets him apart from his comrades all over the country are the multiple piercings in his face and giant holes in his earlobes rimmed with black plastic. These two look fantastic together, I have to admit.

"How have you been?" I ask Meirav. I notice that she has buffed her cheeks with circles of rouge like a rag doll.

"Everything has changed in my life since our time in the underground together," she says. "Get this, I've been invited to give presentations on the discovery. Can you picture this? Me standing in front of a group of yeshiva girls teaching about finding Jeremiah. Ever since we came up from underneath, the world has been upside down."

"She rocks it as a teacher," Shrag says supportively. "Hey, that is crazy what you did, stealing those photos."

"Isn't she awesome?" Meirav gushes. "It all started because she believed some Arabs telling ghost stories."

"Is that what you tell the yeshiva girls?"

"Of course," Meirav says, thrusting out her hip with her hand on it in her classic petulant pose. "I tell them everything, and I don't stop until I see their little ears get red and the teacher starts to sweat, even if I have to make stuff up. It's not about the discovery for me anymore. It's about trying to blast those little slaves out of their cages and teach them about self-expression."

"My baby's on a mission to liberate women," Shrag says. "You can't be with this one if you want to be on top."

Meirav tries to sock him in the chest but he catches her arm and twists it roughly behind her, which makes her laugh even as she struggles to get away. "Unless you cuff her," he says, and growls in her ear.

"I thought women were already liberated," I say.

Meirav says, "Maybe where you're from. But I'm gonna tear the burka off the rest of this spaceship." She stomps on the toe of his combat boot and he releases her.

When the ceremony begins, I sit with Ibrahim and Naima toward the front. As Walid practically skips down the aisle, the women in his family trill in celebration. His grin is contagious. He glows and waves ecstatically at all the people. Dalia comes down the aisle in a sleeveless black dress with leather trim lined with silver studs. It erupts over her knees into a foam of black lace and shredded fishnet. Rising up from her black dress, her pale skin looks phantasmic. Her hair is her natural brown but frosted with pink and topped with a tiara. Her makeup has been applied professionally, in shades of peacock all around her eyes.

I think about Fruma. She probably puts her sponges and drain plugs through the dishwasher every week. She can probably bone a fish. She can probably call songbirds to her sill by singing up and down the music scale. Above the ceremony, the moths are flirting with the moon. As if the moon cares a thimble about them. Naima puts her arm through mine and cradles her head into my shoulder, and her touch is comforting. I remind myself that I am happy, and when I watch Walid and Dalia kiss at the end of the ceremony, I genuinely am for them. Naima says to me, "Maybe he's a terrible kisser."

"Walid?" I ask.

"No," she says. "Mortichai." I just look at her for a moment, considering. She continues, "For all you know he could still be a virgin."

I laugh. "No, I don't think so," I say.

"Based on what?" she asks.

"He said when he was in college he dated and experimented," I say. Suddenly I doubt myself.

Naima tucks her chin down and looks at me from under a creased forehead. "Pretty flimsy evidence," she says. "For all you know, 'dating' to him might mean coffee and a walk, and 'experimenting' might be wearing a color."

I roll my eyes at myself. She's right. I've connected all the clues I've gathered about him in my mind as if he is a dot-to-dot. I kiss her on her warm cheek.

After dinner, it is my turn to offer a toast. I go to the center of the dance floor, biting my lip and holding the microphone limply. I stand listening to Suleiman's crickets, then I offer, "In a cistern deep under the ground, a prophet and his beloved took their love to their grave. And in that same cistern deep under ground, Walid and Dalia brought their love to the world." And here my voice breaks in two. I try to continue but find I can't go on. The moment grows tense, uncomfortable, the silence deepening with each heavy pound of pulse. I lift my glass and take a deep breath. I remember what I read on the plane and rely on that, reciting, "*I was born with the stone on my soul, a dislodged jewel that seals my spirit as a pent-up fountain . . . Even so, I have now seen the stone move off the well, by the tiny splash of a woman's tear . . .* When Dalia was hospitalized, a stone became dislodged in the heart of the world, and in the heart of Walid, and through the prism of their love, all that was opposite merged, all that once clashed . . ." I see Mortichai looking quite small where he is sitting. I remember him speaking to me at the Colony bar. I remember him saying, *In the world of paint, it all may come from three. But in the world of light, the whole spectrum's refracted from only one . . .* I clear my throat and finish, "all that once clashed becomes one." I hold up one finger, as he did. I lift my glass with the other hand and announce, "To life. And more to life."

The guests stand up and applaud. I'm not sure if they are applauding anything I just said, or if they are applauding the bones to which I am inextricably linked and to which this wedding is indebted. When they applaud me, I have a vision of my own funeral. Fireworks are exploding over the Sultan's Pool.

Soon after the fireworks, the dance floor is filled. The music alternates between Hebrew and Arabic, and Ibrahim stands up and invites his wife to join him. A moment later, I am transfixed watching them, each one gracing the other.

"They are a great team," Mortichai says, and I turn toward him, both pleased and a little nervous that he has come to sit with me. I am worried I laid it all on the table too soon, too suddenly. But he is here, and he looks peaceful.

"Hi," I say. "Having fun?"

He shrugs. There are colorful blinking lights rimming the dance floor, and they change his hat from black to red to purple to yellow to green. He looks at me steadily.

"Do you people even dance?" I ask, a little too curtly.

He seems to bristle, but then sighs and leans forward. "I was raised to dance with my brothers, to dance with my male friends." He touches his hands together and brings his fingertips to his lips. After a pause he looks at me and speaks, "I want to address what you asked me. You asked me to tell you how I feel, and I'm sorry if I've been ambiguous."

"I don't know if it is appropriate to talk about it here," I say, glancing over to his table to see if Fruma is there. The truth is, his complexion seems darker, and I'm not sure I want to hear what he's going to say.

"I'm talking about it," he says, and I am surprised at how forceful his voice suddenly sounds. He touches his fingertips to his lips again and then softens his tone. "Listen, you ask me if 'you people even dance.' You say you can imagine walking down an aisle with me, but I have no idea what you really think of my life. I have no idea what you think of the tradition in which I was raised. I have no idea whether you respect my struggle or think it's petty, whether you even understand it."

I am stunned. I am handing him my heart and he sounds like he is reprimanding me.

He continues. "Sometimes I get the feeling that you are more a person of faith than I am. I am, at my heart, an anthropologist. That is what I love. And because of that I love the complexity of culture and faith and tribalism; it fascinates me. But even though I am comfortable being immersed in it, I think I keep myself removed. As if my very life is a kind of field study, but for no one. Do you understand? But with you, I find it impossible to remain objective. My heart is in it, despite myself. I'm not collecting data on human nature, I'm living."

"Thank you," I eke out, unsure.

"As an anthropologist, I can honestly say that I totally respect you for your faith. I really do. I admire it. However, I don't quite have a handle on what your commitment is. I don't know if you are a devotee of the Catholic Church or the chapel of Page Brookstone. It doesn't matter, whatever it is, it is beautiful. I like it. I like people with history and devotion. I veered away from the traditions of my family for a long time. It was very painful for them. Some of them were very openly disappointed in me. If it wasn't for our rabbi's intervention, I would have been cut off. Mourned. And despite feeling called from the outside, I do care about my family. I don't want them to mourn me. Do you understand?"

"I think so," I say. "Why did you come back from 'the outside'?"

"I came back because I was tired. I had my heart broken out there by a woman I thought I loved. We had been living together, though my family doesn't know that. When it ended I didn't feel I had a home. I was lonely."

"Are you a virgin?" I blurt out, and then feel ashamed.

He laughs, but not kindly. "You are not listening to me! You have no idea about so much of my life, and yet you say you can imagine marrying me. I am not talking about sex. This," he gestures angrily between us, "is not about sex. Listen, I am not a teenager. I am a man. Yes, I've made love before, if that makes you happy. But I've only dated Jewish women. I've never even had feelings like this for someone like you. And the first woman I dated, it was very hard for me. I had to overcome a lot of guilt for not marrying first, the way all my siblings, hell, the way all my community growing up did. My guilt was a big part of why that first relationship ended. And my last relationship, with Dafne—she said she loved me but she couldn't help cheating. She begged me to stay, months of tears, but I couldn't get past the infidelity. It was a fault in her, but it was a fault in me too, Page. To me it was symbolic of everything empty about secularism. I'm as guilty as she is for destroying our home." He waits and watches me for a moment. "You are very attractive, Page, but I've been attracted to women before and it's never kept me up at night the way you do. It's never haunted me. It's not about sex. It would be easy if it were."

He goes on. "I came back to my family because I was tired, and

I was ready to settle down. You haven't even been to my home. There is so much you don't know about me."

"You haven't invited me," I say. "Where do you live anyway?"

"I live on Ushiskin Street, it doesn't matter. The question is why I haven't invited you. I live in an apartment complex with six of my siblings and their families. I am the adventurous and oddly clean-shaven uncle. My nieces and nephews always fill the courtyard between our apartments. Fruma lives on the same block. I thought about inviting you, I would have loved to, but then I worried about what my sisters would say, and their fanatical husbands. It's more complicated than you think."

"Maybe," I say sadly, "maybe not."

"No, it is. Listen, when we first talked in the Rockefeller library, you spilled your soul to me, and you didn't even know me, and I still to this day don't know why. Was it because there was this connection between us? Or was I just at the right place and the right time, when you needed to talk? Did my *costume* make me anonymous enough for you to feel I was safe?"

"I don't know," I say. "I think you shared first."

"You trouble me, Page. And it's awkward for Fruma too, after Walid announced live on television that you and I had had sex. Of course she understood it wasn't true, but it's hard. She's not stupid. She must know that I'm troubled by you."

"Well, I didn't intend to *trouble* you," I say, feeling a little cross myself. Hurt, as well.

"When you were away, everyone around me was riding into sunsets, while for me, everything was gray. I missed you terribly, but the distance, honestly, was good for me. It helped me to think. It helped me to better know what I feel." He pauses, weighing words in his mind while he looks at the dance floor. He looks back at me and says, "When I meet with the rabbi—"

I interrupt him. "The rabbi. Will you consult the rabbi whenever you have to make a big decision? When you and Fruma have to decide what's for dinner?"

"Don't mock me," he says, his eyes narrowing. Then his shoulders drop and he seems to surrender. "You really don't understand, or maybe I'm not making myself clear enough. I don't trouble easily, but I am afraid that I might be in love with you. And at the same time, I have to ask myself, what is it that I really know about you? And how much of me do you really know? When you say you can picture walking down the aisle with me, what exactly does that mean in your mind? I don't know how you see me. I don't know if you've in some way invented me, and you'd be disappointed to live with me a week. I don't know your whole history, and you are ignorant of so much of mine. And yet, ever since we first spoke in the library, I have been plagued by you. Plagued and"—he turns his palms turn up as they rest on his knees as if he is offering me something—"happier than I've ever been."

"Happier than with Dafne?" I ask.

He shakes his head and laughs. "Sometimes you can be such a child, *Geveret*."

Naima comes sweeping over to the table from the dance floor, falling into her seat with an air of exhilaration. She is followed closely by Ibrahim, who stands behind her chair, leaning on it and breathing hard. The bride and groom come over to us. Walid looks so much more mature than the seventeen-year-old I met on my first visit to Anata. I remember him bolstering his courage in the cistern to challenge Meirav. I feel that I have seen him grow up. I stand, and Dalia hugs me tightly. "I am so glad you are here," she says. "You are my hero. I am the luckiest girl in the world that I met you." I look into her petite face. She is beaming. She looks like an intergalactic princess. She squeezes both my hands. "You saved my life," she says, "in so many ways. You saved my body from falling into the pit, and you saved my heart by bringing me Walid. I love you so much."

Walid takes my face in his warm hands and kisses me on each cheek. "You have made us a new world," he says, his brown eyes dancing, "a world I was never creative enough to even imagine."

"You are very creative," I say.

"I pretend to be, to win Miss Imagination." He puts his arm around Dalia's neck and draws her into a light kiss. She does three quick little jumps for joy, and he leads her to the next table. Walid looks back and calls over his shoulder to us, "Get on that dance floor, you nerds, it's a party!"

Naima waves her hands in the air, letting us know she is too exhausted for any more right now, so Ibrahim puts his hand out to me. I glance at Mortichai and he smiles meekly. Ibrahim pulls me up into his strong arms, and in a moment we are swept into the current of people swirling on the dance floor. The music is now Arabic, the versatile band switching to electric oud, steady strong drums and a male vocalist whose vowels punch holes into the air above us. It has been so long since I've danced, and it feels so good. Ibrahim is a strong leader, and in his arms I feel as sheer as the fabric of my dress. Meirav and Shrag bump their way toward us. They both look a little drunk, and I laugh thinking it must take a special talent for them both to be so out of step. Everyone has their hands in the air, hips thumping from side to side. Ibrahim's arms make an open circle around me without actually touching me and I dance in the small center, my hands too reaching for the moon. I imagine that we are not too different from Suleiman's belly dancers, their veils lined with jangling coins, who probably danced here hundreds of years ago. The circle of Ibrahim's arms is broken when Dalia's father breaks in and invites me to dance, and soon I lose track of the number of people I dance with, lose track of myself, and get swept up in the celebration of what Walid called a new world. I see them in the middle. Dalia is spinning in his arms, and her dress is rippling with light.

XXVIII

⚜

I am tired. I shall soon lay down my quill.
—THE SCROLL OF ANATIYA 51:III

Seventy Anatiyas were born last week in America, I read in the paper. She belongs to the public now, I think to myself, and she can never be taken back.

I visit with Itai at a café we used to frequent. He looks tired, his olive skin looks washed out and bristly, and he has faint circles under his deep eyes. We sit at a table on the sidewalk. We once sat in this same place holding hands under the table. Across the street is a jewelry store, and I am aware of couples going in and out while Itai sits stewing. He is angry with me.

"You almost cost me my job," he says, his eyes practically drilling mine.

"What about 'intellectual property'?" I ask, trying to make it okay.

"What about friendship?" he retorts. "What about keeping the people who care about you in the loop? What about respect?"

I reach across the table to touch his sleeve but he pulls it away. Tears well up in my eyes. "Itai, I am so sorry I didn't tell you. Please look at me. I loved you, I still do, I never wanted to hurt you. I *had* to do this. I am not sure how to explain it, but I knew in my soul that it was the only decision I could make. It felt bigger than me or than you. It was about Anatiya. I was rushing to get her translated and I was thinking of nothing else. I wasn't thinking about how it would hurt you, and I am so sorry about that."

He stares at me for a moment and I can see him struggling not to forgive me. He wants me to suffer a little, as this is the first time we are seeing each other since the complete translation has been released. "You should have included me, Page. You may have loved me but you ran away from those feelings. *You* ended our relationship, if you remember. I have never given you any reason not to trust me."

"I know," I say, feeling genuinely defeated. "I am sorry. I was afraid you would stop me, and I didn't want to be stopped."

"Clearly." A couple come out of the jewelry store with their arms interwoven. The girl is practically sailing on sunshine, like one of Chagall's floating brides.

"I'm sorry, Itai," I say again. "It would be a tragedy for me to lose your friendship."

He nods in agreement. By the time we've swept up all the hummus in silence and my salad and his Saint Peter's fish arrive, I can see him becoming more relaxed.

"Can't we just bury the hatchet?" I suggest hopefully.

"Any archaeologist worth his salt would never bury a hatchet," he says, with the barest note of whimsy.

I can see that he's forgiven me. He confides in me that Jeremiah and Anatiya are going to be taken out of the department secretly for fear of heavier riots. The pressure to rebury the remains have been growing more intense. He's even had protesters outside his home, pelting the cars in his driveway. The remains are going to be moved to a more secure location on an army base.

"How do Jeremiah and Anatiya feel about moving?" I ask jokingly.

"Well," he says, playing along, "Anatiya was just telling Jeremiah that she had been hoping to go scuba diving in Eilat."

I laugh. I am so grateful to be able to recover his lightness and friendship. Dalia and Walid's wedding was on Sunday and it is now

Friday afternoon. I haven't heard from Mortichai, and I am certain he must have met with his rabbi by now. I try not to think about it, yet it is a constant static fuzzing all my thoughts. It is nice to sit with a man in whose arms I remember being, with whom I shared the warmth of flesh and not just the illusion of fantasy.

Itai continues, "I am actually very sorry they are leaving my dominion, even though respite from the Orthodox will be welcome."

"I heard rumors," I say, "that the Knesset has received threats. I heard about the arson, and I've heard that individual members of the parliament have received death threats."

"I heard you've received death threats," he says.

"I've been living with the threat of death for a long time," I say, spearing a mushroom and a tomato and dipping them in dill vinaigrette. "Rumor has it that someone at the top is getting freaked out and wants the skeletons out of the country."

His voice becomes stern. "Don't ever believe rumors about Israel," he chastises. "The Israeli government doesn't spook easily." He chips off a crispy forkful of fish and savors it slowly. He closes his eyes and I feel that he and Israel are sharing a private moment. When he reopens his eyes he is with me again. "But it is strange. I'm sharing a building with these two, and maybe I'm losing it, but sometimes I suspect it's them pulling the strings. It feels as if they are making things happen. As if they wanted to be found, want to be relocated, and they are weaving some intricate design of which we are all just a small part. Even you running off with her story seems, well, determined by them somehow. We extricated them out of their coffin to prepare for the move, and they were so light, it was almost as if . . ."

I am angry to hear they have been removed from their bed. I can't fathom a group of scientists touching them, handling them. "You kept them together, right?" I demand, suddenly fearful that they were separated for easier transport.

"Of course." He looks surprised. "Page, we are not some backward band of amateurs and mobsters, as you seem to think." We are *Israel*, I can imagine him saying, but he doesn't. I glance over at the jewelry store. He and I went in there together once. I tried on a white gold filigreed ring with a princess cut diamond. We were just testing what it felt like. When he learned that the setting was made in Austria, he said, "There is no way we would buy rings made outside Israel," and I knew we would never really marry. I notice he is also looking across the street. "I'm sorry," I say, "what were you saying about moving them?"

"Never mind," he backs off, locking eyes with his fish instead of me. "It's stupid."

"C'mon, Itai," I plead.

He busies himself with a lemon wedge. "All right, I was going to say it was almost as if they themselves were helping. I remember lifting them with the team. But it is as if I have two simultaneous memories—one possible and one impossible. One, moving them with a team precisely, professionally. The correct memory. And another memory in which, crazy as it seems, I lift Anatiya and she puts her arm around my shoulders. And I remember the incorrect memory as vividly as the correct one. This has been happening to me ever since they came here. Once I was watching them, and I was eating a sandwich, and I was just considering the way they had been arranged in the tomb. But I also remember having the same sandwich, the same sequence of bites, but I was watching her walk out the door, toss a mischievous smile over her shoulder, and leave. A true memory and a false memory." He shakes his head. "I must be exhausted."

"Memory is always twofold," I say, trying to protect his sanity. "There is what happened, and then there is the story we tell ourselves about what happened. Everyone does that. You're not crazy." At the same time, I am filled with wonderment for the skeletons. I remember seeing Anatiya and Jeremiah sit up as if they were rising from a bed, in the flesh, radiant. The memory is still crisp and real.

When I return to the Barakats, I find that they have jammed the living room furniture into the dining room, making it an incredibly crowded space. The couch is pressed into the far corner, and the television sits on the edge of the dining room table with wires crossing the room. The Barakats are not home. Ibrahim has told me that they will build an extra wing in the new house for me to live in, and I know they are serious. But I know it is not right for me to stay much longer. I will close the apartment in New York and rent a place of my own, maybe outside of Jerusalem. Start another project, maybe work for Jerrold.

Itai won't tell me when the skeletons will be moved, but I feel it necessary to stay very still. I curl on the couch, my legs tucked under me mermaid style, steady and motionless before CNN, as if any gross movement of mine might result in turbulence and the rattling of fragile bones. I fall asleep on the couch.

A gentle squeeze on my shoulder wakes me up. It is dark, and my eyes adjust to see Ibrahim standing over me, his eyes so intense they nearly glow. I sit up, feeling my hair nested on one side of my head. "What time is it?" I say, rubbing my eyes. He hands me the phone and says, "It's Itai."

I realize that Ibrahim looks angry and I wonder what I've done. I see Naima standing on the other side of the room, partially blocked by the television. "What happened?" I say, as I take the phone.

"They've been stolen, Page." Itai's voice trembles. "They're gone."

"Who's gone?" I say, my heart thumping, though I know he is talking about Anatiya and Jeremiah.

"Someone came up through the floor. They went in through the reflecting pool in the courtyard. They went through the underground cistern right below the scrollery and blasted their way up. By the time the guards came down, they and the skeletons were gone." Itai's voice breaks and I can hear his heavy breathing. I imagine he is pacing quickly.

"They blasted through the scrollery?" I ask, real panic now seizing my chest. Ibrahim turns up the news and I can see images of the Rockefeller, swarming with soldiers. Naima sinks down on the couch next to me.

"Oh God," Itai cries. "I am sorry. It is as if you knew, you had to get her story out of there, and you did, you did."

"Did they destroy it?" I ask. I feel nausea in my throat, my veins swelling with something blacker than blood.

I can hear him sobbing. "Half of it is gone. Half of it is dust and ash. The rest is charred, barely salvageable. I don't think they intended to destroy it. Even the pictures are destroyed. They were just after the skeletons. I'm at the museum. They are questioning the guards and they'll question me next."

My blood is drumming loudly in my ears. I feel dizzy. I lean on Naima. She has tear streaks on her cheeks. Ibrahim is watching the news, hands balled into fists.

"What should I do?" I say, my stomach sick.

"Okay, calm down," Itai says, clearly commanding himself as well as me. "There is no one better than the Israeli army at this. No one in the world. The skeletons will be found." When I hang up the phone, Naima and I collapse into each other and weep. When I look up, I see on the television that it is five-thirty in the morning.

I need to talk to Mortichai. I try to call him on his cell phone but he doesn't answer. He is probably sleeping, I imagine. "I'm going to the museum," I tell Ibrahim and Naima, and Ibrahim says, "I am going with you."

Ibrahim's car cuts through the darkness and I comb through my hair with my fingers, my chest heaving with worry. I call Jordanna as we begin the ascent into Jerusalem. I hold the phone away from me when she screams. Ibrahim's hands tighten around the steering wheel, his knuckles like the white peaks of a brown mountain range.

"Who authorized their being shipped in the first place? How could they remove them from their coffin—they were safe in there! They are going to kill her! They are going to tear them apart!" Jordanna is shouting through her tears.

"They can't kill her, Jordanna," I say, trying to calm her. I can imagine her children being frightened, if they are home. "She is already dead." But my comment only makes her weep harder.

"Oh, Page," she sobs into the phone. "No one knows her like we do. We did everything we could to set her free, and now they are going to grind her into dust and scatter her in the wind." Jordanna is practically wheezing. "Do you remember what she says in chapter ten? *Let my darkness reunite with his light! Though the world be unborn, though we return to the void, though we become unformed, at least unformed we cannot bear your yoke.* She might be dead already, but they can still kill her, they can unform her. And poor Jeremiah! Ridiculed and abused his whole life, and now in his death—it is unforgivable!" I decide not to tell her about the scroll just yet.

"They are together," I say tentatively, but my tears are rolling freely now. "Maybe Jeremiah promised her a honeymoon."

Jordanna sucks in her breath. "I am going to throw up," she says. "They didn't take the scroll, did they?" I think about being with Jordanna in Jerrold's penthouse when we were reading about the scroll Jeremiah had written that had been burned by the king. We were learning how Anatiya had filled her sack with the ashes and had thrust her hands in, rubbing the charred flakes of her prophet's words and warnings all over her hair and skin. And now her own scroll, half incinerated. I start shaking. I answer her, "Jordanna, I love you. Anatiya has Jeremiah, and you and I have each other. We will get through this. I have to go. We are almost at the museum. I will call you later."

A woman soldier with a high black ponytail and a machine gun strapped over her back recognizes me. "*Geveret* Brookstone," she says, taking me by the arm, "come with me, we would like to ask you some questions."

"This is Ibrahim Barakat," I say, reaching out for Ibrahim.

"*Ken,*" she says, addressing him in Hebrew, "yes, I am sorry I did not recognize you. Please, come with me as well."

The grounds are filled with Israeli police. She leads us to the library where Mortichai and I spoke not more than three months ago. It is just after six, and the morning light seeps through the arched windows. There on one of the large tables is a recording device, and two Israeli policemen are interviewing a guard.

The soldier asks us to take a seat and wait to be interviewed. I want to find Itai, but I obey. I take out my phone and call Mortichai again, but there is no answer. Suddenly I remember that it is Shab-bat, and he wouldn't have his phone or his television on in observance of the day of rest. He probably doesn't know. Tears spill from my eyes and Ibrahim cradles me. I cry into his shirt and breathe in his woodsy musk. It comforts a deep place in me.

The female soldier returns and asks to take our cell phones to screen them, and without questioning it, we turn them over. We wait for nearly two hours before I am interviewed.

I sit in the chair where the guard had been. The policeman is younger than I am. He wears a blue beret and has a neatly trimmed mustache and goatee that look like black metal shavings. He takes a little satchel of tissues out of his pocket and offers me one, and I swab my whole face.

"Do you speak Hebrew?" he asks. "My English is so-so."

"Yes," I sniff.

He begins talking to me in Hebrew. "Good. You may be able to help us. Our primary suspect is the ultra-Orthodox community here. The same group that has been pressuring the administration to rebury the bodies and has been threatening to do this from the beginning. We already have some leads. We are also exploring some local faith groups that have centers abroad. What you can do for me is just try to remember anything unusual that happened concerning the excavation and transport of those skeletons. Any questionable people, strange occurrences, overly interested observers. Anything unusual might be of some help to us."

"I keep thinking of that evangelist, Elias Warner, with whom I had a screaming match," I say. I dab at my eyes and can feel the red-ness burning in them.

"Warner wasn't involved," the detective replies dismissively. "We checked into him already." I think to ask him a question about that but his expression prevents it. He continues, "Tell me about Morti-chai Masters. Did he have access to this building?"

I am surprised for a moment. "Is he a suspect? You know he is a scientist first. Religion is more of an anthropological thing for him."

I sound stupid even to myself. I can imagine Mortichai telling me how much more complicated it all is and that I am sometimes such a child. Still, I believe my words.

Then I remember something. "Do you know anything about an organization called CROSS, the Christian Remains Salvation Society? It is led by someone named Yeshu Abraham. Mortichai works for them." The detective makes a note.

Ibrahim is waiting for me, leaning against a pillar. He reminds me for a moment of my father, leaning against the lockers outside the gym, waiting for me while I was at my cousins' school dance. An invisible weight upon him. Ibrahim just needs a cigarette.

Our cell phones have been returned. We get permission to go downstairs to the basement. We can smell the smoke as we descend the steps, and inside the artifacts room the scene is overwhelming. The empty coffin as strange and alluring as a grand piano with no keys and nothing inside. I feel chilled. I recognize Itai from the back through the door of the scrollery. I rush to him. When he turns and sees me, he clutches me into a painful embrace. He holds the back of my head so my face is pressed into his shoulder as if he doesn't want me to see. When he releases me, I am stunned to see the room. There is a hole in the ground, about the same size as the hole in the Barakats' living room when I first visited them. There is black dust in rays across the floor around it. It looks like something cosmic, a black hole, a collapsed star. And there is half of Anatiya's scroll, still on its table but blackened; the glass that had been protecting it has been shattered. Throughout the room there are fragments, some Anatiya and some other parchments. Even on the ceiling, they stick. All over the room, like a massacre of insects in a bug lantern, fragile wings shorn and fried. I restrain myself from gasping and sobbing, and instead center myself. I look at Itai and say, "No international team now. I want to be in charge of cleaning this up."

"You are in charge," he says. "Tell me what to do." The people who have already begun working stop. I take a deep breath and tell Itai the tools I need and I assign him, Ibrahim, and the others who are there sections to clean with strict instructions not to discard a single speck. As I crouch picking flakes out of the grooves in the floor with a toothpick, I think suddenly of Mortichai and his work with ZAKA. I look at the specks of ash on my tray. That is all they are. Specks of ash. There is nothing left to reassemble. And yet, I think of the verse *Dust to dust, ashes to ashes*, and it means something new to me. I think of Anatiya saving the shattered pieces of the jug Jeremiah had smashed, loving the very shards because they were part of something he had touched. I think of the mural in our cistern of Jeremiah's scroll being burned, how there were Hebrew letters rising on the smoke above the flames, as if they could not be extinguished. I realize the dust we return to is not the same dust from which we come. It is not that we come from ashes and nothingness and return to the same ashes and nothingness. The dust we return to has history. The ashes we become were touched, inscribed, detailed, adorned. They glowed. I pick up a fragment with my tweezers and can read the Hebrew word *anochi* on it. It means simply, "I am." Tears roll down my face and I set the fragment carefully on my tray.

We organize the fragments as best we can so that they can be studied, tested, and resorted. It is seven in the evening before we are ready to stop for the day. I think of Anatiya rubbing the ash of Jeremiah's scroll over her body. I quietly dip my finger into a small pile of ash and touch it, when I am sure no one is looking, behind my ears like perfume. When I touch it to me, a strange sensation overwhelms me. It rushes through my blood, like thousands of sparks of light. I feel her, I think to myself. I feel her becoming a part of me. Then I take a breath and the sensation subsides. I thank everyone for working so hard and everyone, including Itai, applauds. We have done a tremendous job salvaging.

"Do you know where Ushiskin Street is?" I ask Ibrahim when we get outside, and he agrees to drop me off. The sun is low in the sky, but it is at least an hour from sunset. Sabbath or no Sabbath, I think to myself, I have to see Mortichai. Ibrahim agrees to drop me off.

XXIX

The sparrow rests on the eagle's back and when the eagle, from fatigue, can carry her no more, the rested sparrow jumps up and flies even higher. Fly even higher, my child, even higher than I.
—THE SCROLL OF ANATIYA 51:114–115

We drive slowly up the narrow street, and I look for what might be an apartment complex with a courtyard, as he described. I see a four-story building that wraps around a garden, and from my car window I can see numerous children playing. Young boys dressed like miniature Mortichais, and girls with long, warm-looking dresses and long braided hair run in and out of sight, chasing a ball. I tell Ibrahim that this must be the place. He wishes me luck.

I rush into the courtyard. I am wearing jeans and a white T-shirt, which hardly looks white, as it is streaked with dust and ash. I can't even imagine what my face looks like. I didn't think to check my face in Ibrahim's car. I stop short in the center of the courtyard, feeling the eyes of all the children upon me, all looking like little adults in their mature clothes, except for their sweaty faces, rosy cheeks, and white button-down shirts half untucked. I ask a little girl with the same golden strawberry hair as Mortichai if she knows him.

Her eyes look me up and down as if I am something new and strange. A friendly yeti who has wandered a little too far south. She points to a door. I stand before it, all their eyes on my back. Just before I knock, I notice the little brass mezuzah on the doorframe to my right. I reach up and touch it lightly and then kiss my finger. I look over my shoulder and the girl smiles at me and suddenly one of them kicks a ball and the bevy of them are up and after it.

I knock. Mortichai opens the door. He sees me standing here and his eyes widen in surprise, his mouth breaking into a grin. For a moment I forget why I came as I realize that he is pleased to see me.

"Do you know?" I ask him.

"The police left here about an hour ago," he says. "I was going to call you as soon as Shabbat ended."

"When is that?" I ask, and he looks up to the sky above the courtyard. He says, "About forty minutes." He looks at my shirt and then at my face. He says, *"Do not touch her, Baruch. She is wearing the scroll of God."* His face drops as we both move from a feeling of relief in seeing one another and into the reality that the skeletons are gone. So much of the scroll destroyed.

We stand for a moment, breathing. The sound of children echoes behind us. I feel a chill suddenly. "Am I allowed in?" I ask. The tears begin welling over my eyes.

"Of course," he says, "please." He stands aside and I hear him sigh heavily. "I can't believe it," he says. "The police were here for an hour and a half. I'm not sure I had anything helpful to offer." Amid my sorrow I almost laugh when I step into his apartment, and I am grateful he doesn't see. The front door opens into a large living room. The walls are a soft taupe, and there is a long chocolate Ultrasuede couch with matching love seat and large, tufted square ottoman. Upon it is a heavy-looking iron plate serving as a tray for a tall glass carafe of what looks like brandy and a silver bowl of rock candy. The back wall is floor-to-ceiling bookcases, stuffed with books and papers. There is an oak desk by the bookshelves with a closed laptop with what looks like a nickel table lamp with a rectangular black shade. On the ceiling there is a fan with large tropical-looking rattan blades and frosted amber glass. Above the couch are six different desert photographs in rustic frames. On the wall across from the couch there is a small flat-screened television. There is a rattan wing chair with red jacquard cushions and a braided jute rug. All of this would be classic and comforting if it wasn't for the mess of toys littered over everything. Stacking boxes, rainbow-colored blocks, a half-finished dinosaur-shaped wooden Hebrew alphabet puzzle, at least three rattles, a Slinky, teddy bears, two modestly dressed dolls sitting at a toy table, a tipped-over bin of plastic food, an Othello game, Trouble, and a takeoff on Chutes and Ladders involving characters such as Judah Maccabee. There is even a little teddy bear hanging in a parachute from one of the blades of the ceiling fan.

"Are you a suspect?" I manage to ask, muffling my surprise at the explosion of toys in a bachelor pad.

"Goodness, no," he says. I turn to look at him as he closes the door. He is wearing that same white buttoned-down shirt, but it is hanging open, and I can see his broad chest rise and fall under a thin white undershirt tucked into his black pants. I want so much for him to embrace me, to kiss my neck, to love me. A few seconds in his home and I feel I know him so much better. I can imagine his door is always open when he is home, and his nephews and nieces run in and out to play. He really loves them, I think as I look at him. He was so lonely out there, and his heart was broken, and here he is surrounded constantly by children who adore him. Fruma's grandchild as well. He wants family. As complicated as he likes to think he is, he returned home because he wants family. It's as simple, and as painfully precious, as that.

"Please, come in, sit down," he says awkwardly, although I am already in. He quickly moves the iron plate carrying the brandy carafe and bowl of sweets. He opens the top of the ottoman and begins throwing toys inside it.

"Don't, Mortichai, don't clean up," I say. "I don't mind, really. I like it, actually." I sit on the rattan chair. He laughs and surrenders onto the love seat. "It keeps them visiting me," he says of the toys. "I let them make more of a mess here than they can at their homes."

"Clearly," I say, smiling through pressed lips.

"Whew," he suddenly exhales. "It is so good to see you." His eyes are steady on my face and I feel my cheeks become warm. "Were you at the museum? Was it awful? Can I get you some ice water?"

I tell him about the scrollery and the process of cleaning it. He tells me that the police do have a very strong lead, and they're visiting the homes of the other members of ZAKA, who are generally among the fiercest when it comes to the sanctity of the dead.

"How could it be the Orthodox?" I ask. "They had to have real equipment to go in through the reflecting pool—oxygen, flashlights—and then they blasted up through the basement floor. Then they barricaded the door to the artifacts room, and by the time the guards shot through, they were gone. God knows how they transported the skeletons. Giant Ziploc. Some sort of waterproof bag, I hope." The tears now spill over. "But I'm sorry, I don't imagine your long-bearded ZAKA comrades shuttling underground in wetsuits carrying explosives on Shabbat. It all sounds wrong to me."

"No," Mortichai says. "You are right. They wouldn't do it on Shabbat. They would consider it a desecration. I've been thinking the same thing."

"They had to partner with someone, someone non-Orthodox," I say, and add apologetically, "I mentioned to the police that you worked for CROSS."

"I had a feeling you did. They talked to me about that, but only for a minute or two. There are a thousand fundamentalist organizations that all like to hone in on Israel. CROSS is banal in comparison."

"This is devastating," I say, tugging up the dirty sleeve of my T-shirt to wipe my eyes.

"Oh no, don't do that, hold on." Mortichai springs up and returns with a soft brown hand towel. I blot my whole face in it.

"What can we do?" I say miserably. "There must be something

we can do. I feel her in me. I feel her in my veins." I feel a wellspring of tears burst in my head, my eyes and nose running. I rub my nose with the towel. "Maybe we weren't supposed to find them? Maybe we weren't supposed to disturb them?"

"Page, this has nothing to do with you or anything you did; you can't go down that road," he tries to comfort me.

"But you know these people. Where are they taking them? Mount of Olives? Where? Can we look for them?"

He is thinking for a moment. "These people. Page," he says gently, "there is no 'these people.' We are all different. You would like my family, and I think they would like you, once everyone got past their preconceptions. They wouldn't any longer be 'these people,' and you wouldn't be one of 'those people.' " I am not honestly in the mood for a lesson. But there is tenderness in his tone, which comforts me. I wonder, maybe he is not teaching me, but inviting me. "Sabbath ends in about half an hour. After that we can do whatever you want, but I don't know how we can help. Whoever did this is highly organized, highly motivated. It is not a job for individuals like us. It's for military intelligence."

Through tears I hear myself complain, "But you were a soldier," and then I see him looking at me with his eyes almost smiling and I have to laugh at myself. "I am a child sometimes, I know."

He nods. "I'll bet you haven't eaten. I have eggplant parmigiana on a warming plate in the kitchen. Can I bring you some?" He gets up and I get up as well, following him.

"But why involve the army? It's not like it's a terrorist cell," I say, trailing him.

"No, but they've stolen a national treasure," he says. His kitchen is not much bigger than Naima's but far less cluttered with pots and pans. The cabinets are all cherry wood and the counters are dark gray soapstone. He spatulas a slab of layered eggplant onto a glass plate. Off the kitchen is a small dining area with a wooden table with iron scrollwork legs. I sit down and he sits across from me. The warm, heavy food feels life-affirming and regenerative.

"I think I met some of your nephews and nieces out there," I say with my mouth full. "I don't think they hated me."

He laughs. "I'm sure they didn't. Who could hate you?" He watches me eat for a moment. The silence begins to make me uncomfortable. I swallow a big mouthful and ask him, "Are you worried about what they're going to say, your sisters and brothers, because I'm here? I'm sure it's not proper." I feel my cheeks warming again.

"I'm not worried. They already saw the police coming in and out, so they know there is something big going on. Soon Shabbat will end and they'll all flip on their televisions and probably swarm over here."

"Does that worry you?" I ask.

He shakes his head slowly. His eyes look heavy and tired. He says in a low voice, "Page, I spoke with Rabbi Ruskin."

I sigh heavily and then wipe my mouth with a napkin. "You know, it is all I've been thinking about since the wedding, wondering when you were going to speak with him and what it would mean for me. But"—I fold the napkin, then unfold it and return it to my lap—"I just don't feel like now is the right time to talk about it. Nothing feels stable or safe. My body is here, but my heart is running all over the country looking for Anatiya. I don't think I can really hear with justice what he said."

"I understand that," he says. "I respect that."

A basil leaf bursts flavor in my mouth and compels me to ask, "Did Fruma make this?" I feel a knot in my stomach.

He shakes his head no. "But one of my sisters did."

I shake a finger at him. "You know, I am learning that you are something of a mooch, mister."

"What is a mooch?" he asks. I forget sometimes that he wasn't born in America.

"Someone who gets things for free. You seem to mooch your siblings' children. In a way, you mooched your way onto my dig."

He smiles a little sadly. "I don't want to be a mooch. I want something of my own."

After a few more minutes, Mortichai gets up and returns with a cup of wine, a braided candle, and a satchel of cloves and dried orange rind. He dims the light and sparks the candle, and its multiple wicks ignite into a torchlike flame. "It is a short ceremony," he says. "Three minutes. It's called *havdalah*, and it marks the end of the Sabbath." I join him standing up. He opens a small gilded prayer book and recites the prayers too quickly and quietly for me to understand.

I stare into the flame. I see the mural with the Hebrew letters rising in the smoke. I see the hole in the middle of the scrollery. The ash as delicate as snow crystals. I think of Anatiya, one of the first passages I read, when she had run up the altar's ramp in the Temple. *I slammed the shovel into the flames to extinguish them. To put an end to this burning. Smoke collected in my eyes, lifted the tresses of my hair* . . . And then it is as if a fire seizes my mind. Heat throbs through my head and my spine feels soldered. I feel as if my skin is cracking, branching out in a maze of rifts and splits, revealing something lava-hot beneath the surface. I feel the points behind my ears where I touched myself with ash and they sear. I feel I am about to combust, and despite myself, I suddenly cry out, hot tears singeing my eyelashes, and Mortichai drops his prayer book onto the table. "What happened?" he asks. I cough and I taste smoke in my mouth. I grasp the back of the chair in front of me and suck in air. "Panic attack? What is it?" Mortichai demands. "She's burning," I say. "They are going to burn her." I feel as if there is ash in my throat, and I cough deeply. Mortichai approaches me, his arm out, his angular hand, and he reaches for me, hesitates for a split second, and then I feel his hand on my arm, then on my back, and he pats me hard, thinking I'm choking. My cough becomes productive and I spit into a napkin, face streaked with tears. I am frightened, and a little embarrassed. I sink into a chair. His hand still rests on my back. "They are going to burn her," I repeat. "She is burning. I know it. I *feel* her."

"Mortichai!" we hear. "*Shavua tov!* Turn on the news!"

"My sister Rachel," he says. I try to wipe my face off, my forehead.

"It's insane out there," we hear.

"And her husband Hayim," he says. His hand slides off my back. He gets up. I whisper, "She's burning, Mortichai. I saw her in the candle. She's burning."

I hear him greet Rachel and Hayim in the living room and soon after, I hear a parade of children. I stand up, close my eyes, and breathe deep. I am alive, I tell myself. I am not burning. The fever has broken as quickly as it arose. I pick up my plate and bring it into the kitchen. I put it in the sink. I turn on the faucet and splash cool water on my face. I see my reflection in the window over the sink, ghostly upon the night like a swath of silk upon dark water.

I collect myself—all the little pieces—and enter the living room. There are already sixteen people in there, seven adults including Mortichai, seven children under ten years old, and two teenage boys. Mortichai is standing amid them, buttoning his shirt. The front door is open and through it I can see more children playing in the courtyard. A platter of moist lemon bars and thin, lacy sesame cookies has appeared.

The black hats of his brothers or brothers-in-law lift when I walk into the room, as do the open faces of their wives. They all look strangely regal to me, crowded into Mortichai's home. Each women has her own unique crown over her hair. I feel a little naked. I feel my dirty shirt is too thin over my breasts. I almost step back into the kitchen when one of the women says, "Page Brookstone! You are here! We can't believe they've been stolen!"

"A prophet of the Lord should be in the ground," one of the teenage boys says.

"Yes," says one of the women, "but to be stolen? With acts of destruction?"

To my surprise one of the men whacks the teenager on the back of his head, but not too hard. The boy's hat sits askew on his head. "We do not condone violence," the father scolds. Mortichai begins introducing me, but my mind is too weak to retain all the names. I cross my arms in front of my chest because I feel vulnerable. When

Mortichai introduces me to one sister, a beautiful young woman with creamy skin and a full mouth, her thin chiseled face framed with a crown of deep violet fabric, a matching shawl around her shoulders over a boxy black dress far too roomy for her small frame, I sense deep kindness in her eyes. I ask her would it be okay if I borrowed her shawl to wrap it around me. "I feel a little strange," I confess to her. She lights up and sweeps it off, putting it around me herself. She adjusts it over my shoulders and I sense the seeds of a friendship between us. "Cochava." I repeat her name to be able to remember.

"I have heard a lot about you," she says to me. "I have read some but also heard from my brother what an amazing scholar you are."

"He is generous," I say.

"Ah yes," she agrees. "Just look at the toys here! He is indeed very generous. He is a good man, even if his path is obscured at times. I am sorry we haven't met before."

The television is turned on to the BBC; a reporter is standing before a building in London where a disgruntled lover has just fire-bombed his girlfriend's apartment building.

"They wouldn't have done it on Shabbat," one of the men is arguing. "They wouldn't desecrate one mitzvah in pursuit of another."

"They could have partnered with an Islamic group; they are masters at tunneling," another proposes.

I am sitting on the couch between Cochava and one of the other sisters or sisters-in-law. Two girls are playing with the dolls on the ottoman in front of me. "Where would they bury them?" I ask, and they begin discussing it.

"Where do you take the bodies after a bombing, Mortichai? Isn't it a big pit?" one says.

"I think they'd go to the Judean Hills," Mortichai says. "Maybe into the mountains. I don't think they'd want an obvious place."

I feel panic returning to me, my stomach turning.

The news rolls on. A shooting in a diner in Chicago. They are all talking while I watch the screen across from me. We are watching each other, the screen and I. Disasters scroll along the bottom of the television. I am trying to piece something together but can't find the parts that fit, until like a gong the answer strikes and vibrates through me. I instinctively grab Cochava by the knee. She startles, and I say, "They've been separated."

Everyone looks at me. "They've been separated, the skeletons. That's what's happening. There was a partnership." I stand up. "There was a partnership between an Orthodox sect and a Christian one, and the deal was that the Jews got to rebury the prophet, and the others got Anatiya." I think of the words of the preacher Elias. *Let her fate be the same as the Jezebel who tormented the prophet Elijah. Let her fall from her window and be devoured by dogs.* I stand up. "They will burn her."

"Not possible," says one of the men. "It is against *halacha* for any body to be burned. It is a violence to the human vessel."

"It's also just a bitter idea," one woman says. "Millions of our people were massacred and disposed of like trash in the Nazi crematoriums. The idea of allowing a Jewish woman who some say is a prophetess to be burned, it is chilling."

"But maybe they had to make a trade," Mortichai says. "So one group took Jeremiah and the other took Anatiya."

The television keeps scrolling, keeps telling me that there is a great and terrible fissure that has happened, and it is felt at the cellular level, everywhere. My phone rings. It is Jordanna. "They've been separated," she says. She is crying. "The house is out of control. I am having a breakdown."

"I know they are separated; I don't know what to do," I sympathize. "I can't really talk now, Jordanna. I'm sorry. Love Nathaniel. He is your soul mate." I click my phone closed.

A man who may be Cochava's husband is talking. "A couple of years ago the first crematorium was opened in Israel, just outside Hadera. There was huge protest against it. Because of Jewish law. Because of the Holocaust. It's the only one in the whole country."

"Who funds it?" I ask.

One of the teenage boys pops open Mortichai's laptop. The men are pouring themselves some brandy and saying blessings over their glasses. "Hadera has had a rough history," says Cochava. "They've had Islamic Jihad terrorism. They've had long-range missiles hit them from Lebanon. Such a nice city."

"River of Dreams Mortuary," the teenager reads. "It says that because of protests, the incinerator is in a secret place. No one really knows where it is."

"I can't stand this conversation," a woman says.

"It's interesting," the teenager continues. "I did a name match with their website, and there are links between them and this—"

"What?" I ask, walking over to him.

"The Church of Armageddon." I look over his shoulder at the computer screen. I am careful not to touch him.

"The Church of Armageddon," someone repeats behind me.

"Doesn't Armageddon mean Mount Megiddo?" one of them asks, but I don't know who. I don't even know if the voices are male or female.

"That preacher," I say, turning around to seek out Mortichai, "he called me the mistress of Megiddo." Mortichai is perched on the edge of the love seat.

"I remember that," a man with a wide girth sitting in the love seat says. "You can recite some good Torah for an American."

"I don't get it," whines a child.

Someone explains, "In certain branches of Christianity there is a belief that leading up to a battle at Armageddon there are dark signs, earthquakes and eclipses, hail and firestorms, a plague of locusts, blood flowing for hundreds of miles."

Another says, "Megiddo was where the just King Josiah was slain in six oh nine BC, the last of the rulers descended from the messianic line of David. Zealots envision avenging Josiah's death in the same place he died, restoring the Kingdom of David and the Kingdom of God, ushering in the era which will culminate in the restoration of Jesus, resurrection of the dead, and the judgment of souls."

"I still don't get it," says the child, diving into the dinosaur puzzle.

"Me neither, to be honest," says the man on the love seat.

I think of the Book of Revelation, where it is written, *Then I saw heaven opened and there was a white horse. Its rider is called Faithful and True and in righteousness he judges and makes war . . .* and I remember the white car that was sent into the Rockefeller. Its bumper sticker had said Faithful and True. I look at Mortichai and he looks nervous.

"So you are suggesting," says Cochava, "that they would want to destroy Anatiya? Why?"

"Maybe," I say, "to find her, winding her leg like a serpent around the prophet's leg, sapping his life even in death—maybe they see her that way, see her as representing all that is lustful. A leech on a saint." I suddenly clutch Cochava's shawl tighter around me. I look at Mortichai, who is pale, and then at the rest of them, paused in their thinking. "But she isn't any of those things. She simply loves him. She *loves* him. She . . ." I feel faint. I hardly know where I am. I whisper, "She loves him."

I excuse myself to go to the bathroom. It is through Mortichai's bedroom. I pass through quickly. I don't want to look at myself. I wash my face in the sink for the second time, and I lean over the sink on my elbows with my head in my hands. "I'm crazy," I tell myself. "I am crazy. I am talking about lust and love, Jesus Christ, in front of Mortichai's family." I wish I can rewind the last half hour and rewrite all my words. Rewind it back to when I asked Cochava for her scarf and she looked at me with respect and friendship. I feel humiliated. I dry my face, careful to avoid the mirror, and step out of the bathroom. I stand still for a moment in Mortichai's bedroom. The unmade double bed. There is a single bedside table, and on the other side is a tall fern with fronds that arch over his pillows. I see the sliding doors to his closet and I walk to them. I don't want to go back into the living room. I stand before the closet and watch my hand reach out. I open the door and run my hand over his clothes hanging there. At first they look the same, the same as the clothes he is wearing now. The same as the clothing his brothers and brothers-in-law wear. The same as even the male children wear. I open the closet more and all the colors swim in my teary eyes. College sweatshirts. Colorful T-shirts. Jeans. I clutch a handful of the denim and nearly cry out loud for joy. My courage returns. I close the closet door and step back into the living room.

There is commotion. "There was a bombing outside of Tel Aviv," Mortichai explains to me. "I'm going."

"What about Anatiya?" I say.

"Listen," he says. "The people from ZAKA will be there. Maybe they know something. There is nothing that can be done from here except to talk and argue."

"I'm going with you," I say. Cochava is beside me. She puts her arms around me and embraces me and it feels beautiful. It feels like home. She says, "You make sure my brother drives carefully."

Mortichai goes into his bedroom, and I spy after him through the open door from where I stand in the living room. He disappears from my view when he goes to his closet. When he comes back into view, he has on his hat and a jacket. He then goes to his bed and kneels beside it. I am momentarily confused. I remember kneeling and praying this way when I was a child. Then I realize he is not praying. Rather he reaches under his bed and pulls out a metal case. He unlocks it with a key and takes out a handgun, putting it under his jacket in the back of his pants. When he stands up he sees me watching him.

"Is that—" I begin to ask and he says, "I *was* a soldier, you know," and winks at me with tired, bloodshot eyes.

We leave his family, which is animated with conversation, everyone talking over everyone else. I can see how a man who felt lonely, misunderstood, angry, betrayed, would find comfort immersing himself in the center of this bustle. Mortichai's pager is going off. We pause in the courtyard as he checks it. There are kids all around us. A small huddle of kids pull apart excitedly, holding just-lit sparklers. They run around, little sparks falling from their wands.

XXX

I am tired. I have had a lovely swim in a large, freshwater foun-
tain, long gulps of clean water, and now I shall dive down to the
depths, and now I shall burst up to the heights. I am tired . . .
—THE SCROLL OF ANATIYA 51: 116–117

In the car I call Itai. I tell him that they've been separated, but he already knows. He tells me that he has heard the army is zeroing in on the site where they are planning reburial.

"Anatiya won't be there, I am telling you," I beg him.

I call the detective who interviewed me in the library and leave him a message. Mortichai silently tolerates my frantic calling.

"Let's go to Hadera," I say to him. "Let's go to River of Dreams. That's where she is, Mortichai."

"No," Mortichai says. "We don't really know anything. Let's entertain for a moment that she is there. That they are planning to incinerate her. Can you imagine how armed these people would be? You are going to risk your life to protect a skeleton?"

I look at him fondly. "Says the man speeding to scrape up the flesh of the dead."

He rolls his eyes at me. The detective calls me back and I tell him my theory. He tells me they think they know where the burial site is, and they are preparing to go in. My words sound incoherent as I try to impress upon him what I know inside. After the call I tell Mortichai, "For Christ's sake, we found a prophet because I listened to a ghost story. And now I am telling you I am more certain about this than anything else. I had a vision. She is going to burn. I know it."

Mortichai is silent as he drives. I am exasperated and tired. I lean my seat back and watch the sky. I feel my mind start to sink before I can muster the energy to reel it back to the surface. Mortichai wakes me and says we've arrived. I can see barricades and a Magen David Adom ambulance up the hill from where we are parked. I tell him I just don't have the strength to come with him. I don't want to see it. I can't bear it now. I'm sorry. He says, you just rest. Here are the keys. Just rest. I'll be just two blocks north of here if you need me. "Thank you," I say and close my eyes again as he gets out. He shuts the door and I am glad to be alone. I feel my mind sinking again but I wake screaming, thinking the car is engulfed in flames. It is not. I lie still for a number of minutes breathing and staring at the roof of the car, turning Mortichai's keys over and over in my hand.

HADERA IS ABOUT twenty-five miles north of Tel Aviv. As I drive I remember the feeling I had when we began to chisel the inner wall of the cistern. At the time, my mind kept repeating, *I am here. Don't worry. I am here. I am coming for you.* The same feeling motivates me now. *I am coming for you.*

Ibrahim calls me while I am driving. "They have been separated," he says, in the same way Jordanna did when she called. "I can feel it."

"Me too," I say.

"The world is a mess. There was a bombing outside Tel Aviv. Imagine this? Six people died. All of them Israeli Arab. This guy thinks he is walking into a crowd of Israeli Jews and instead it is his own kin."

"We are all kin," I say flatly.

"Naima is sick," he says. "She has a terrible fever and I have tried everything to cool her down."

"A fever?" I feel hot tears in my own eyes and the dark road warps in front of me.

"She is seeing things, screaming about fire."

"I have had the same vision," I say, my voice uncharacteristically flat. "I think I know where she is, Ibrahim. I can't explain why I know, but I just know. I am going there now."

"Tell me, Page. Let me help. She has been a guest in my house, or I in hers."

"I am going to River of Dreams Mortuary, in Hadera. They have the only crematorium in the country."

"Why couldn't it just be a bonfire? A firepit? Why there?"

"Like I said. I can't explain why I know, but I just know."

"River of Dreams. Right, there was a lot of controversy about that place."

"You could help me," I say. "You could tell me where they have their incinerator hidden. I would imagine they have Arabs who work there. An Arab gardener. I don't know."

"And we all know each other. All two million Arabs living in Israel," he says with a hint of humor.

I blink my eyes clear. "You don't?"

"I will find where it is," he promises me, "and I will call you back. Don't get hurt, Page."

Somewhere in the Promised Land, someone is planning to burn the prophetess, the only confirmed female Jewish scribe. Crush her and feed her to the dogs, if they haven't already. I wonder if I am in danger myself, and then I think, how much more noble to be sacrificial than suicidal, to offer your life instead of taking it. I want to offer myself up for Anatiya. I feel I was born to do this.

Then I think of Mortichai and my eyes overflow. He loves me. I am sure of it.

I veer off the highway down an exit ramp. I stop at a red light dangling over the intersection. It is eleven at night, and there is no one around me. This is the loneliest spot in the world right now, I think. I drop my head against the steering wheel, my eyes burning.

My forehead hits the horn and the car starts blaring its warning. I lift my head, peeling it off the vinyl and looking again in both directions. Hadera town center is to the right. I begin to drive, though my body is shaking and I can barely hold the wheel. I drive a quarter mile to the right and then I do a quick U-turn and head west. My eyes are glazed. Why hasn't Ibrahim called? I check my phone. I call information for the address of River of Dreams. I ask the operator for directions from where I am, something one can do in a country as small and intimate as Israel.

Ten minutes later I turn on the street the operator gave me. It is quiet and tree-lined. I am supposed to follow this road for three miles to the end. The moon is the white face of a clock above me. To my left I approach a beautiful old olive tree growing up and over the road, a little canopy of green leaves crowning the twisted gray trunk. From the deep creases of its bark it is telling me, *I've been around a long time. I've seen a lot of things and I'll see a lot more.* Its wispier branches lift in a billow of wind, and the slender leaves fan their silver undersides. It appears to be beckoning.

There is a dirt road behind the olive tree. I turn onto it and drive slowly, trying to inch the car so as not to spit pebbles. The road winds through a thick orchard. I pull off the road and park my car in a thicket. When I shut off my headlights, darkness swallows the car. I get out, quietly closing my door. A step toward the road and the moon untangles from the branches and peers down on me with its benevolent face. I begin to walk. The air is dense and humid. Through the trees I see a low building with three cars parked in front of it. One is a hearse. I whisper a prayer of gratitude. She has led me here. I press myself against the trunk of a tree and watch the building. There is no sign on it.

I know she is in there. I am paces from a cult of fanatics with their substantial arsenal. I look through the orchard trees to the moon and take a deep breath from that faraway place. I am so eerily alone, and yet the trees seem to welcome me. Their branches are quick black brushstrokes. Descendants of Anatiya's trees, I imagine. They say *shush, shush*, with their branches in the warm desert wind, and they lean all together in a gust toward the building, as if pointing, *go, go.*

I peer around the tree. A gust of warm wind picks up a scattering of leaves from the ground and they tumble and cartwheel toward the building. I tiptoe close. At the place where the leaves come to rest against the side of the mortuary, there is a dark little window, covered with silver threads of spider webs and fuzzy white cocoons. I watch my own hand as if my true self is safe elsewhere, watching my actions. I push the window inward, lightly tearing the thick web, and slide myself through, into a black basement.

I stand in darkness, perfectly still. Then I lift myself back to peek out the window. I see four figures, four men, leaving the building. I pull my head back in. I stand, my eyes adjusting to the darkness. I am in a large storage room filled with coffins. The cars aren't moving outside. The men haven't left. A square of light suddenly appears midair, and I realize it is the frosted glass of a window in the door. I crouch down with my hand on a coffin handle to steady myself as footsteps pass through a hall. Under the door I see three pairs of shoes pass. They are speaking in English. "They should be here in ten minutes," I hear one say. And, "Let's heat it up."

I crawl quietly behind the coffin and peer over its lid at the square of light. I wait. My mind is unusually empty save for one thing. Find Anatiya. Get her out. Or at least, hold her in her death the way she is accustomed to being held. She shouldn't be alone.

I see the shadow of two heads cloud the square of light. They are walking back from where they came. A moment later, I see the third. I walk lightly back to the window, lift myself up, and look out. One man is standing before the front door. Then the other three emerge into the night air. I go to the door and open it into the hall. Out of the dark and into the light, the fear that I'd been strangely immune to now grips me, but my life now is on a projectory toward her. I have no direction but forward. At the end of the hall, I enter a large room, in the center of which there is a deep oven whose mouth is open wide with flame. There is also a pine coffin on a metal gurney.

I open the lid like a mother peeking at her child. By the light of the oven I see her inside. She is alone and her bones are bent. Parts of her have crumbled off. Her skull is tilted down rather than up into the eyes of Jeremiah. *I'm sorry*, I tell her in my mind. "Our day and age is no less violent than yours." I look around. I cannot wheel this whole thing out. I could reach in and just take her skull, snap it off her spine and escape with it. I could paint it with flowers and return it to Jeremiah when he is found. Or take off my jeans and stuff her bones in the pant legs, smuggle her out in my underwear. The fire warms my left side. I hear cars smattering gravel as they pull up to the building, and footsteps coming down the hall. A lot of them. I look around and realize there is nowhere for me to go. I look down at Anatiya, and I shift her bones gently. I lift my leg and touch my foot to the bottom of her coffin, careful to avoid touching her. The footsteps and voices are nearly at the door. I pull myself in and lie on my side beside her, lowering the lid. The moment the lid touches closed, I hear the door open and a number of men come in. I realize suddenly that my cell phone is in my pocket. Gently as I can I crook my arm to reach in and slowly slip it out, praying that Ibrahim doesn't call now. I flip it open and the coffin fills with gentle light. I see Anatiya's eyes, and they don't seem empty to me. Her forehead touches mine. I turn off the phone and lay it behind her neck. My body starts to quiver. I am afraid the coffin is rattling. I rest my arm over her waist. One day I too will live in this place. I too will be underground. Why on earth aren't mourners compelled to dig their loved one out? I silently kiss her forehead.

I hear them talking. I am certain they will find me. They will riddle my body with bullets and I will bleed to death in this coffin, staining Anatiya with my blood. Or they will not find me but push me along with her into the incinerator. Ashes to ashes.

I squeeze my eyes shut. I try to imagine I am in the subway with my father, racing home to bed before midnight. "We made it," I said. I was safe and loved. And then I think of Mortichai. He loves me. My heart starts to pound so that I can almost hear it. He loves me, and suddenly I want desperately to get out. Desperately to live.

What have I done? I walked into this place. I walked into this with eyes open. My own fear put me here. Running away from life, now I am Jonah, in the belly of a fish at the bottom of the sea.

All my life I've been digging through the graves, for what? For this, to finally bury myself where no one will ever find me. To prove to myself that I'm as valueless as I always suspected. Isn't that right? Or maybe it is not death that I've been chasing. Maybe it is love. I feel the coffin jolt. Someone is leaning against it. I am terrified. My throat starts to constrict and I feel myself running out of air. I struggle not to panic. I am going to asphyxiate here, just like my father. I feel her cold bones against mine. My breath is quick and shallow. I am disappearing, like a reflection fogging in the mirror.

Out of the pitch black of my coffin, there appears something soft and pale, a twinkling far, far away, like stars poking through the thickest night. Little by little, as I lie still beneath them, they come into focus, and I am able to see that they are letters, white letters written on the black, and they shimmer as if they are floating on a black sea.

The verses are from her scroll. I remember translating them myself. They are a gift from her to me. I start to smile. *At that time, Jeremiah, I am going to stand from my place. I am going to ascend before your eyes, and your ears will be filled with the sound of mirth and gladness. And your voice shall be the rejoicing of the bridegroom, lifted in song. And my voice shall shake off its yoke of silence, and carol you, with the perfumed tones of the happiest bride.* With these words, I remember what I told Jordanna about Mortichai's being my heaven. Yes, Anatiya, the grave will open, as you say, and we will emerge winged creatures, dazzling and free. I will come out of this cocoon, and my wings will be a monarch gold. I will not resign myself to my father's destiny. I will not let Mortichai resign himself. The grave will open. I will ascend before his eyes. He shall be my bridegroom, and I the happiest bride. In this world, perhaps, or in some future world, long after the extinguishing of the sun.

Some people say that when they near death they see a light, white and feathery, lulling them at the end of a tunnel. This moment, I am near death. But after spending a lifetime dying, I am alive.

My blood beats vigorously through my body. My mind races. In this place, I too see lights, but not at the end of a tunnel. The lights I see are tiny iridescent letters, as if someone has spilled the contents of a dictionary all over the night sky. Some of the words grasp hands and form constellations. Her words to me. Her lullaby.

I have found my altar, and here I lay my sadness and all my fears upon it to die. I am ready to live fully now. I am ready to be discovered and reborn. Either now, or my ash will write poetry in the air.

Here I lie, in the place I've feared most of all. I have spent my life opening tombs, and now I am sealed with the ancients. But no tears fall. My eyes are dry. My thoughts clear. Love is stronger than death, and I am in love.

I want to share with Mortichai what I've learned here. What she's taught me. That life and death are not enemies. In fact, they are not even opposites. They are partners in a dance. There is something that links one to the other, and I see it. It is stories. In the basement of the Department of Antiquities, I sensed that there was a key hidden in the golden quill carved into Jeremiah and Anatiya's coffin, and now I know what it is: story is the one thing that moves between death and life. The soul of a person is made from stories. Stories that keep telling themselves over countless ages, and when man no longer listens, they become the lyrics to the music of galaxies. Someone listens. We are so small. We are so tragically finite. And yet, fragile as we are, we are the only ones in the infinity of universes who have ever looked at the stars and thought, *How magnificent,* who have ever wondered, *How does it all work?* That is why we are here, if only for a short while. To see. To bear witness to how beautiful it all is. Here in the dark, I see. For the first time in my life, I see.

I hear gunshots, and the person leaning on the coffin pushes off saying, "What the hell is going on?"

"Fuck," another says. I hear a rush of running to the door, and someone shouts, "Burn the whore now, before they get in here." I feel the coffin being wheeled. I squeeze my eyes and gently link a finger around Anatiya's hand. It doesn't feel like bone but like the tender hand of a child. "I am going with you," I whisper. "You will not be alone." I have never been less afraid of death than right now.

We are moving, rolling across the room. There is a great commotion outside, and suddenly we come to a stop. There is an explosion of gunfire—this time it is in the room, very close—and it is followed by an eruption of Arabic shouting. Two bodies crash into the coffin, and I feel us wobble and roll to the side.

I hear shouting in Hebrew, fierce arguing and scuffling. After a moment there is a stretch of silence and the battle is over. There are voices talking, and they are calm now. The coffin is thrown open by a young soldier. He is Ethiopian Israeli, with delicate features. "Page Brookstone," he says with surprise, reaching his hands under my arms. I feel limp. He has a willowy build but is sinewy and strong, and he lifts me. I bend my knees and try to help extract myself without crushing Anatiya any further. When I am out I throw my arms around him and he strokes my hair. He might be eighteen or nineteen years old. "Thank you," I say, and he holds me. I nestle my head into his shoulder, rubbing my tears onto his uniform. I'm alive. It is beautiful. To be held. I lift my eyes and scan the room. There are four soldiers. Three Arab men stand in the corner talking with one of them while the others are looking around. I see the mouth of the giant oven, its fire dying down. Over his shoulder something else bright and red catches my eyes. On the wall across from me is a LED digital clock. It reads 12:12.

The other soldiers come, along with the Arab men. One of the soldiers looks into the coffin and says, "We recovered Jeremiah. We will bring them together again."

"You did?" I want to cry with relief. I look around the room. "What happened here? How did you know to come?"

One of the Arab men says, "You think Arabs don't care about Jeremiah and Anatiya as well?"

"I didn't—" I start, but he interrupts with a smile and says, "Ibrahim said you were looking for this place. He worried it might be dangerous for you and asked us to come and check."

"Did Ibrahim call the army too?"

The soldier who lifted me out says, "After they found Jeremiah and found him alone, we learned that you had reported that you thought you knew where she was."

Another says, "It was good you came here, Ms. Brookstone. The Church of Armageddon is a group we were aware of, but haven't been able to identify its leadership or headquarters. They have quite an arsenal here. Thanks to you we now have a good number in custody and will be able to learn their true intentions. We had put a homing device in your cell phone. You led us right to Anatiya."

Ibrahim rushes into the room, and I am so happy to see him, we run to each other and he embraces me tightly. "You didn't call me," I say.

"Of course not," he says. "Why would I call you and tell you where you might get killed?" He leans his shoulders away from me and looks into my face. "How did you find this little unmarked road anyway?"

"She brought me here," I say, wiping my eyes. I can say this to him and know he'll believe me. He and Naima. Jordanna too. Maybe Itai.

"They'll put them back together?" I ask. "She's in bad shape." I laugh when I say this, realizing how funny it is, considering she died well over two thousand years ago.

"Where is she?" I hear someone call in the hall, and I assume someone is looking for Anatiya, when Mortichai pushes through the door. Ibrahim lets me go. Mortichai stands, framed by the doorway.

"She's in bad shape," I repeat to him. He shakes his head. I take a step toward him and see that he has been crying. He stares at me and smiles. He says, "She looks fine to me." I smile and we look at each other. He keeps looking at me and finally responds, "Ibrahim called me. He told me where this was. I didn't believe him that you would find it. I went to River of Dreams first, but there was no one there. We turned around. And then I saw army trucks turning down this road."

"How did you get here without your car? Did you fly?"

"I had a cab driver who didn't have to be asked twice to drive like the wind. He is outside with the soldiers having the time of his life. How did you . . ."

I open my mouth to answer. "I . . ."

"No, stop," he says. "I don't want to know. I don't want to talk. I want to know that you are alive. I want to know that I'm alive." He steps toward me and all at once I can feel the spin of the world around me. I am in his arms and I feel like a ballerina spinning on a magnet in the toy store. How fast it all turns! How quickly it rolls from day to night to endless day!

His fingers dig into my back. His mouth moves against the top of my head. "*I have put before you life and death, blessing and curse.* Page, I choose life . . ."

I run my hands over his shoulders and back, the sweep of his spine, the swell of the muscles in his arms. I feel every part of me coming to life. I kiss him under his ear and his arms tighten around me. He says, "If you show me where my car is, I can take you out of here."

After I give a statement, we leave. We walk through the dark orchard. Moonlight sifts through the weave of branches above us. Tears roll from my eyes as we step gingerly through the night.

We reach his car. "Huh," he says. "Nice parking job."

I laugh. We get in and the car bumps and crunches over branches out onto the dirt road. It isn't long before we are at the same intersection where I had felt a stab of despair, the red light dangling in the night. I reach out with my hand open and he looks at it, then takes it in his own.

"Where are we going?" I ask.

"You must be so tired. I know I am," he says. "We can go to a hotel in Tel Aviv. We could be alone. Rest." I smile. I look at his hand in mine and trace his knuckles with my other hand.

"What did your rabbi say?" I ask. I think about asking him if

I can put my head on his shoulder. But I decide not to ask, to do it anyway.

"He told me that a very important aspect of Judaism is honoring the dead."

"No one knows that more than you," I say, as we pick up speed on the quiet highway.

"That is what I said. I've devoted my life to honoring the long and recent dead. Then he said that Judaism's *essence*, however, is not about honoring the dead. Its essence is about the triumph of life. Then he got angry. He told me I had shown too much honor for the dead and not enough celebration of life. He told me that I was trying to win my mother's affection by adhering to the path of my dead brother. That I always had a sense that my brother was better than me because his death had perfected him. I went to the dead to honor them the same way my mother honored Menachem. He said that I was taking my mission so far that I was willing to forgo my life and step into a dead man's family, take a dead man's wife. He said that what I thought was love for his daughter was actually my devotion to the dead."

My eyes are wide as I listen to him. I think of Fruma. She is radiant and warm and pure, as life-giving as a fountain.

"And then he stood up and he said with all the power and fury of a prophet, 'I sent you to the graves, and now I command you to get out! You will not marry my daughter!'"

"He really said that?" I say.

"He did," Mortichai says. "Now I don't want you to ever think that you took me away from her, Page. You saved me from a life that I thought I was destined to have, but that was not my own. And you saved Fruma too. She doesn't deserve to live out her days with someone who is unhappy. She should have laughter, devotion. And she will. You are not a destructive person. You saved us." Mortichai stops. He takes his hand out of mine and pulls over to the shoulder of the road, slowing to a stop. He turns to me and then reaches up and holds my face in his big warm, hands. "I love you, *Geveret* Brookstone, *with all my heart, with all my soul, and with all my might.*"

XXXI

~❧~

My handwriting is slow and the letters are dropping and slanting
downward toward the corner of the parchment. I find my thought,
my thought is somewhere else. I have wearied myself for fire. I have
wearied myself for fire. Now comes the quenching . . .
—THE SCROLL OF ANATIYA 51:118–121

When the door to our room clicks closed at the Dan Hotel
on the Mediterranean shore, Mortichai looks down
into my eyes. Heat spreads all throughout me and I feel
healthier than I ever have before. With Mortichai's smile and his soft
step toward me, I know that I am no longer digging in the dirt, in the
dust of the long, long dead. Now I am planted in a rich, nourishing
soil, rooted in joy, lifting my face to the beautiful sun. I say, "How do
you feel about this?"

He looks at me for a long while. "I feel lit," he says slowly, "like
a Christmas tree." We both laugh and I throw my arms around him.
My body vibrates with exaltation. He kisses my neck, presses his
lips into my temples, returns to my lips. I am melting into maple
syrup. He holds my face. Kisses me again. Quickly, and then again,
and then deeper. "You must be so tired," he says, twirling a piece
of my hair.

"We should go to bed," I say dreamily.

He keeps looking at me. "You are so beautiful, Page," he says. He runs his thumbs over my eyebrows. He kisses my mouth again. Then he says, "We should take it slow until we are married, don't you think?"

Tears roll from my eyes. "Yes," I say. "But can we marry in the next five minutes?"

He laughs. "We could fly to Cyprus tomorrow, get married there." I see that he is serious. "I want a life I can call my own. I want you to be my wife, and I want to be your husband. I want to hold you and love you until we are nothing but dust and ash. I want what we have now, but every day. I want forever with you, Page."

"Where will we live?" I ask, not sure I care where, only that we are together.

"We can stay in Greece for all I care," he says. "We can find a project to join. We can do a worldwide lecture circuit on the discovery and its implications. We can mop floors in India. I don't care."

"You want to run away from your family?"

"No," he says, "no, don't think that. It's not about running away. It's about running toward. But it might be nice to spend some time somewhere else. So we can build ourselves together, just you and I. We could return to Israel. Buy a house in Netanya. I don't care. I just want the right to adore you always, wherever we are."

I take a shower, the water pelting me with heat. The dirt of the long day, of many long days, rolls off me. I scrub myself with sweet-smelling Ahava body soap. Fill my hair with suds. When I come out of the shower in a white robe, Mortichai is sitting on the edge of the bed. He is wearing a T-shirt and black boxers. I hug the robe to me and can't help giggling. He says, "I picked this up in the lobby," and holds up a copy of *Archaeology Digest*.

I sit down next to him and we kiss for a long while. While he is in the shower, I pick up the *Digest* and it falls open in my hands.

One night, as I burrowed into my sheepskin mats, Jeremiah came to me for the first time. He sat beside me and started to speak. The

words, it seemed, were difficult for him to form, they had been pent
up for so long:

"I always knew, Jerusalem,
that you were there,
peering into my window,
lurking in the shadow.
I could smell the tangy sweetness of your skin,
I could feel the heat in your hair,
in its wonderful waves.
I stole a glimpse of you.
Your crimson lips shone like olive oil,
and your eyes were the only eyes,
the only eyes that saw everything,
they drank in visions like quills drinking ink.
I saw the swell of your breasts
and the fullness of your hips.
I watched you age with me,
as a wine growing richer and riper each season.
And I could not turn to you,
for my soul was attached to God,
my spirit in the grip of His right hand.
He held me on the brink of Sheol
and afflicted me with His breakers.
But His hand has lifted from me,
and at last I am unfettered
to fulfill a mortal gladness,
to drink from my own cistern
and find joy in the wife of my youth,
a loving doe.
and behold,
you are still here!
You have never left my side,
a loyal and faithful bride

to the very end.
How I feared I would lose you,
your presence is a healing salve.
Many women have done well,
but you, Jerusalem, surpass them all."

Jeremiah gathered me in his arms. He bent his face toward me and
I lifted mine to his, but before he kissed me, there arose a need in
him to add:

"I love God,
I do.
With all my heart
and all my soul
and all my might.
But let me, this once,
love God through you."

He kissed me and a fire consumed me. I felt the blood drain completely from my face only to return in a burning rush. He pulled
me into his lap and we pressed into each other, and banners were
raised in my thought declaring: This is the body of my prophet!
This is his taste and his touch! This is the Garden of Eden, hanging with luscious fruits and brilliant with ever-flowing streams!
This is the one my heart has sought through every city square and
every sand-strewn path, here in my arms, in his arms, this is the
prophet Jeremiah, this is Jeremiah the man—a part of me, and I a
part of him. His sealed eyelids were dewy and pearlescent. His hair
was a curtain of white silk that fell over my shoulders in cool cas-
cades. His kisses upon my neck were prayers of gratitude, offerings
of thanksgiving, his embrace worshipful. This was the love that I
knew lay dormant, hidden at the core of his volcanic God-fervor,
the love that I prayed to blossom. My careful tending. He kissed
and caressed and clung to me, and I cried and quivered until there

was no border between my tears and his, no boundary between trembling, no fence between reverence and rapture, life and death and resurrection and death again to which the choirs of Heaven and earth cry, "Amen, selah!" for rebirth which is certain as dawn is to break. And we lay, gleaming and wet in each other's arms, soft and warm as melted wax, and the breath of my prophet was deep and even and easy, and the child I carried turned in my womb.

EPILOGUE

The joy of flowers is never quiet ... There is one fountain which nourishes all and this fountain is called love. Just as a fountain never runs dry no matter how many buckets are filled, so too does love regenerate itself, ever-flowing, spilling from one heart to another. The waters of this hidden fountain are love and its garden is lush with passion fruit. Love itself cannot be seen, but its effects on the ones who feel themselves loved are bountiful.
—THE SCROLL OF ANATIYA 51:69–76

I have spent my professional life digging through graves, up to my neck in the dust of the long dead. Like any archaeologist, I used to fantasize about what I would find, but after a decade it all began to look the same—so many bones, pieces of pottery, and coins sapped of all color. At some point I realized I was no longer digging to find relics. Instead, I was testing the world the way a child tests her father. I was burying myself in the darkest caverns to see if anyone would ever find me there, if anyone would come looking and discover me living, as I had discovered so many of the dead.

On the morning of my forty-first birthday, I wake early, as usual. I take a cup of coffee to our balcony so I can watch the dawn spill over the Mediterranean Sea. I sink into the jacquard pillows on the rattan chair. When Mor wakes we will walk to our new site, winding through the great arches of a Roman aqueduct. We'll continue documenting the thousand fallen pillars of Caesarea. The sky is scrolled with purple clouds. I feel his hands caress my shoulders, massaging my neck. I look up. "Good morning," I say.

"Happy birthday," he says, leaning down to kiss me on the cheek. "A person can do a lot of things in forty-one years."

"The best thing this person did was discover you," I say. He sits in a chair beside me. I blow on my coffee while he twirls my hair and strokes my neck. He still makes me giddy. His touch always amazes me. He looks at me now the same way he looked at me the night we married, leaning into me and kissing me under a Grecian sky crowded with stars.

AUTHOR'S NOTE

I have been asked by readers whether Anatiya is a historic figure or a work of pure fiction. While the answer is clear—she is fictional—I cringe a little in saying so. Before writing *Drawing in the Dust*, I wrote *The Scroll of Anatiya*, a fifty-two-chapter book in the style of the ancient prophets that parallels the JPS rendition of Jeremiah. Of all the great works I studied in seminary and beyond, I fell most deeply in love with Jeremiah. I envisioned Anatiya's narrative as a creative commentary on his journey. Perhaps writing Anatiya was also my attempt to adhere myself to such a towering ancient spirit. Jeremiah suffered so greatly throughout his life. I wanted to reach back into his world and give to him the way his words and visions have given to me. I wanted to weave an enduring love into his terror-filled days. There is a concept called "ongoing revelation," which teaches that revelation did not occur only at one time in one place, to Moses on Mount Sinai, but continually happens to each of us, at every time, in every age. I love that there is poetry, music, and art that continue to unfurl messages over generations in all sorts of unexpected blooms. We fall in love with these teachings and sometimes call them sacred. In sharing these texts, whether in private or from pulpits, I have seen people discover their own personal story, stitched like a gold thread throughout ancient scrolls, recognizing their own faces reflected there in the mysterious text. Is Anatiya a historic figure? No. Is she real? How does one answer such a question?

For more about *Drawing in the Dust* and Anatiya please visit my website, www.zoeklein.com.

READER'S GROUP GUIDE

Summary

When called upon by a young Arab couple to investigate a cistern that lies beneath their home, Page Brookstone discovers more than she bargained for. The couple believes the cistern is the reason that the spirits of two lovers keep appearing in their home, while Page's colleagues believe that the young couple are all but insane and that she should stay away. Page, however, takes the opportunity to investigate the site and discovers that, in fact, it is not a cistern, but a tomb. In it are the remains of an ancient Israelite, the prophet Jeremiah, buried alongside a woman who may have been his lover, and a set of scrolls that tell of their great love. In uncovering the mystery of a centuries-old romance that defies convention, Page could be on to the archaeological discovery of a lifetime. The finding also sets Page on a path of self-discovery, where she is forced to dig into long-buried issues from her own past, which along with a new and unexpected romance, reawaken her from the stupor in which she's been living. Author Zoe Klein, who is also the youngest female congregational rabbi in the United States, elegantly blends fact and fiction with two appealing love stories; however, the novel also engages powerful questions of identity, family, discovery, politics, and sexuality with originality and subtlety.

Questions and Topics for Discussion

1. The Barakats believe the ground beneath their house is haunted and claim to have seen spirits in their home. How does their faith contribute to this belief? Do you think that Page begins believing in ghosts and the paranormal as the book progresses? Who are the skeptics and who are the cynics of the novel?

2. Discuss the various aspects of faith as they relate to the novel. Do not limit yourself to strictly religious faith, but also discuss everyday matters of faith, i.e., the hope and belief that things will always work out for the best, etc.

3. What parts of the book made you reflect upon your own feelings and beliefs about religion? How do you feel about the religious restrictions placed on Page and Mortichai's relationship? What was your reaction to the destruction of the archaeological finds in the name of religion?

4. Water makes several appearances in the novel, from the cistern below the Barakats' home, to baths, to ritual cleansing. What is the symbolism of water throughout the book as it relates to worship and faith?

5. The author is a congregational rabbi, a position that has been traditionally held by men. How are traditional gender roles subverted in this story? What is Klein saying by giving Anatiya as much agency as she does? How would the story have been different if Jeremiah had written the scrolls instead?

6. The passages from the scrolls that appear at the beginning of each chapter tell of the love story between Jeremiah and Anatiya. How do those passages mirror what happens to the characters in each of those chapters?

7. Early in the book Page's friend points out the difference between a broken heart and a depressed heart. How would you describe the status of Page's heart at the beginning of the novel? Where is it at the end? How does her relationship with Mortichai change it?

8. Page is accused of being able to string together complex concepts, but of being unable to understand simple things such as love. How true do you think this is and why? How does her emotional growth progress throughout the novel?

9. The conventional definition of archaeology is the scientific study of historic or prehistoric people and their cultures. Beyond Page's search into the history of Jeremiah, what else is she searching for in her past as it relates to her family and relationships? What does she discover that she wasn't searching for?

10. Page has chosen a career that isolates her and places her within a small contained group of people. What is she avoiding? Do you see symbolism in her choice of a career in archaeology? Part of the process of archaeology is the constant search for things long hidden, things in the past that will help us better understand the present. What are the various characters searching for? Norris? Page? Itai? The Barakats? Who is more successful in finding what they seek, and why?

Tips for Enhancing Your Book Club

Learn more about some of the themes addressed in this novel. Try reading one of the following books about the experience of Jews in the Middle East or stories that deal with displacement.

- *The Yacoubian Building,* by Alaa Al Aswany
- *Out of Egypt: A Memoir,* by Andre Aciman
- *Moonlight on the Avenue of Faith,* by Gina B. Nahai
- *House of Sand and Fog,* by Andre Dubus III
- *The Septembers of Shiraz,* by Dalia Sofer

Israel is known as the land of "milk and honey," so this is the perfect opportunity to bring a different type of food into your group the night you discuss *Drawing in the Dust.* Do some research on traditional Israeli food and prepare some special dishes to share with your group.

For any members of your group who are not familiar with the Jewish faith, do some research on some of the more traditional Jewish Holidays—Hanukkah, Yom Kippur, and Rosh Hashanah—and create some cards for members of your group that describe the holiday, the history of it, and the traditions of how they're celebrated. If you are able, try to make a visit to a local synagogue.

Questions for the Author

Discuss the title *Drawing in the Dust*. The use of "drawing" implies continuous creation. In your mind, what creation is happening throughout the novel?

There is a dance that begins in the first sentence of the novel. The opening describes a young Page sitting slumped at a school social staring at a clock across a swarm of dancing students. Page observes in the first paragraph, "The clock was my only partner at the dance." The rest of the novel is a continuation of this dance between Page and the clock. Time, which was once benevolent and generous, becomes monstrous and devouring with her father's illness. It stalks her the way the ticking crocodile stalked an aging Captain Hook while Peter Pan flew about forever and tauntingly young. Page spends her life trying to figure out the steps to this dance, but her own terror robs her of any grace. She cannot reconcile time as her partner, and instead tries to run by burying herself in the sand.

The creation that is happening throughout the novel is the choreography of a dance between mortal and eternal. Toward the end of the novel Page realizes, "Story is the one thing that moves between death and life. The soul of a person is made from stories. Stories that keep telling themselves over countless ages, and when man no longer listens, they become the lyrics to the music of galaxies." She finally begins to transform the battle into dance.

The phrase, "drawing in the dust," of course means different things. It is what a vacuum does. It is also what a child does. Page is a little bit of both. She has childishness to her as well as emotional vacancy. She struggles with impermanence. Drawings in the dust, castles in the sand, flesh and blood that become bleached bone. But one could argue that impermanence is the essential quality of beautiful. Fleetingness lends to enchantment rather than detracts.

You are one of the youngest female senior rabbis in the United States. How did that influence your writing?

I think that when one assumes the title of rabbi, one steps out of age and gender. A rabbi needs to be able to be as genuinely connected to the elderly widower who is taking off his wedding ring for the first time as she is to the young parent bringing a child to the podium for a blessing.

That being said, I do remember this private moment I had in my apartment when I was living in Jerusalem. I had been studying Kabbalah, Jewish mysticism, and I had a passionate fire in me about it. After a few months, however, I began to become frustrated and even despondent. I felt myself excluded from the texts. It seemed that woman was just a vessel for man's further enlightenment. A sage was to make love to his wife on the sixth day in order to arouse harmony in the cosmos. In other words, sleeping with his wife was all about affecting something in the universe, she was just some vessel for *his* ultimate, heroic, heaven-altering purpose. That is how I read it then, young and tutorless. But just as quickly, out of my sorrow something broke through. I realized that because I wasn't written into the story, I was entirely free. I wasn't fettered by lettering. Kabbalah, Torah, Talmud were all mine to learn and play with and tease and mold and own and dance through. I was outside the grain, so I didn't have to follow the grain. I was female and under forty, so I wasn't even supposed to be here, which meant that no one was looking for me. I could be wind or water, fluid enough to move around and in and throughout every looping letter. No one could see me, I felt, because I wasn't written in. I felt as if I was, all at once, invisible, and instead of sadness this filled me with elation, with a surge of joy and ownership and freedom. I could spook into the Holy of Holies where no one but the High Priest ventured, and no one could find me. I could join Moses on Sinai, and crouch by the ram on the top of Mount Moria. And though I've grown and my learning has been deepened with spectacular teachers through Seminary along the way, when I write I still experience that pure and solitary joy of being bodiless, moving undetected through time and space. In a way, age and gender did contribute to that.

My mentor, Rabbi Jerome Malino, used to tell me that being a rabbi is about seeing the unshed tear and hearing the unasked question. I think that writing is not too different. The private wrestling that writing requires and the public presence that is the rabbinate symphonize with each other for me. I think without the writing, I would be fragile as an empty shell. My stories are my substance. They are my soul, and allow me to listen with greater depth. So as much as my rabbinate influences my writing, I think my writing influences my rabbinate more.

Though the two are not mutually exclusive, what do you consider yourself most to be? A religious figure— a rabbi—who has written a novel, or a novelist who is also a rabbi?

While the answer to this question is clear in my heart, it is hard to answer it in words, but I will try. I consider myself a novelist first, but this takes a bit of explaining. While God is often referred to as the Author of All Life, I like to relate to God as the Reader of All Life as well. Life is a love letter, written in logos deeper than language. I am a novelist first, but I don't always compose with pen and ink, or keyboard and monitor. Rather, as a rabbi I help people compose with heartbeats and breath, identifying the myths and truths in their lives. A community is a library of timeless tales and adventures, of grief that poeticizes, often darkly, and of redemptions that fill the air with song. When I officiate life cycle ceremonies, I always feel as if I am trying to weave something strong out of delicate fibers. At weddings, I try to help build a solid foundation out of very feathery dreams. At births, I try to infuse joy and light into an entirely mysterious future. At death, I take the tiny strands of an infinitely complex life and try to thread them into something sacred. Writing and serving as a rabbi are not too different to me. In the end, it is about crafting stories, and helping people discover their grand themes and subtler metaphors. It is about offering these stories skyward to the Reader of All Life.

Throughout the history of Judaism, women have had many different roles and have been treated very differently in regard to the faith, at times very well, and in some instances, not so well. How did this affect you in creating the book's characters?

It is interesting to me that most people, when they imagine a pious, God-fearing woman, imagine someone very modest, soft-spoken, and dutiful. However, women rarely make it into the Bible unless they use a little sass. Eve's desire for wisdom causes her to transgress. Sarah, afraid people might kill her husband, Abraham, in order to take her, pretends she is single and even allows herself to be married off to two different kings. Yael seduced Sisera before driving a tent peg through his head. Look at the only women outside of Mary mentioned in the Gospel's genealogy of Jesus: Tamar, Ruth, Rahab, and Bathsheba. Tamar disguised herself as a prostitute to seduce her father-in-law. Ruth sneaked up to a sleeping landowner, Boaz, in the middle of the night and lay at his feet. Rahab was a prostitute who lived in the wall of Jericho. Bathsheba slept with King David while her husband Uriah was at war. Biblical women were very strong, and they used what little power they had to influence history and protect their families' futures, and that power was primarily sexuality. I wanted to recast what it means to be a God-fearing, God-wrestling woman and to lift the sanitizing veil and let the raw faces, with flushed cheeks, of Page and her ancient soul-sister Anatiya shine.

Judaism is a home-based rather than a church-based religion, which means that most of the rituals are centered around the home. For that reason, woman has traditionally been a pillar of the house of Israel. A Jewish marriage contract is ultimately concerned with the happiness and protection of the wife in the household.

When I was in Israel, I studied everything. I was so hungry to learn, and since I did not have a bat mitzvah I was really starting from the beginning. I took a class at a very orthodox yeshiva for girls. I was learning Ein Yaakov, ethical teachings, in a class with other girls. I was always very careful about what I wore so I would fit in—closed-toe shoes, no shoulder blade peeking out. The teacher was a middle-aged man in a black coat and hat who had spent most of his life teaching girls. The last day of class, after a full year, I decided to "come out," and I revealed that I was applying to rabbinical school. The teacher laughed so hard that his hat popped off his head and fell on the floor! I couldn't help laughing too! But then the most amazing thing happened . . . now, mind you, I *know* that he deeply disapproved of my decision but . . . for the first time that entire year he taught a phenomenal class that included Jewish law . . . he had never taught any Jewish law to us, and now he went all out. I mean he was on fire. I realized that here was this man who had spent his life teaching girls only certain ethical "easy" things, and then, for the first time in his life, he had a rabbinical student in one of his classes; how she got there, who she was, that she was a woman or a heretic, didn't matter at the moment. He became for the next hour a teacher to rabbis, and it was remarkable. The girls wouldn't talk to me on the bus back to Jerusalem, but I felt glowing. I felt that I had given them something that might deepen them even if just the littlest bit, for the rest of their lives. They would never forget.

How did you research *Drawing in the Dust*? Was your knowledge of Jeremiah something that you brought with you from your rabbinical training and you framed the story around it, or was there some other inspiration?

It is interesting. We didn't spend an inordinate amount of time studying prophets in rabbinical school, but those were the texts that captivated me the most. I read them again and again, turning their words over, trying to refract every meaning. I fell in love with Jeremiah instantly, the courage of his furious poetry. The bones of *Drawing in the Dust* is definitely my fascination with Jeremiah, but the book gained sinews and flesh with every wedding or funeral I officiated, with every bedside I sat beside. There are so many hats a clergyperson wears in a day, from teaching songs to preschoolers to walking loved ones through tragedy to handling personnel and politicking. At some point you find yourself in danger of becoming completely fragmented, pieces of you deposited in other people's lives. You have to learn to turn a thousand stories into one story that you tell yourself, to turn a community with all its diversity into one spinning galaxy, one living organism, lest you fall apart. And when you learn to do this, there starts to appear little fingerprints of creation. When the Hebrew name the young couple chooses happens to be the same name as the man whose funeral you officiated that morning, it becomes evidence of one story, all of us like dew on one trembling web. It becomes beautiful rather than burdensome, and I am grateful any moment I get to catch a tiny glimpse.

So how did I research this novel? Monday is my day off, and Monday is the day I sit and write. Every day in between I was immersed in people's stories and teaching Torah. That is how I did my research.

What do you see as the role of fiction, as opposed to non-fiction, in addressing change and reaching the hearts and minds of people who may be inflexible in their beliefs?
I have always believed in the power of fiction. Many semanticists, linguists, and language purists claim that metaphor is a parasite on language, that when we say, "My love is a red, red rose," what we are really saying is that there is no word to express what I mean and so I will take words out of context and abuse them to express myself.

But what they call untrue, I call revelation. To me, metaphor says, "I have no other means in my language to combine the depth of my feelings and fears, my creativity and my intellect, my sense of spiritual connectedness . . . I have a million thoughts and ideas and questions that I could unload over hours and hours, or I can simply *admit* the shortcomings and futility of language, and in my *desperation* to communicate simply say all of that in one easy breath, 'My love is a red, red rose.'"

In nonfiction, there is little need for relationship, but with metaphor and story, we have to trust each other. We have to assume an intricate, deep understanding. Metaphor *relies* on the ability for any two people to immediately strike up a relationship.

The definition of metaphor is the conditional relationship of two concepts, a relationship that is reciprocal, where both concepts influence and redefine each other. Think about that. Isn't that covenantal? Isn't that beautiful? Isn't that the revelation we seek? To me, story reaches more deeply into hearts and minds because unlike nonfiction, which demands the attention of a fraction of our selves, fiction invites our presence wholly: mind, body, spirit. It sweeps up and away and returns us renewed with keener vision. We do not *live* objectively. We live in metaphor. Poetry, to me, is not just something that "makes pretty." It reveals and it redeems.

As many people read, they "cast" the movie of the book in their minds to help the story play out. In your perfect world, who would you cast to play some of the main characters— Page, Mortichai, Itai, and Norris?
I would love to see how differently this movie looks in different people's minds! Who would I cast? I guess I want to say that I want a woman who is reading this book to imagine herself in really good shape, and tanned, and to put herself in it. And stick the guy you have a secret crush on in a black hat and cast him as well. I'm not sure I can say who I would ideally cast because I live in Los Angeles and I don't want any of my friends who are aspiring actors to get mad at me!

Who are writers you admire? What books or authors inspire you?
I tend to admire books based on how much I admire the person who recommended them to me. I recently read Nathan Englander's collection, *For the Relief of Unbearable Urges,* and found it haunting and exquisite. I love Mary Doria Russell's writing. My Milan Kundera books are covered in my highlighting and scribbles. *As a Driven Leaf* by Milton Steinberg was a great influence to me as well. Abraham Joshua Heschel's work endlessly astounds, especially *The Sabbath.* I find irrational joy in Billy Collins's poem "Taking Off Emily Dickinson's Clothes." I love K. C. Cole's book *The Hole in the Universe,* which is

actually a nonfiction physics book for laypeople, and it explores, basically, the mathematical concept of nothing. It has a permanent place on my bedside table and I draw strange comfort from this elegant biography of the zero. I think I have been most inspired, however, by the often anonymous language I find in prayer books. I used to read them cover to cover like novels. And the book that taught me the most and without which I would be lost would have to be *The Book of Legends: Sefer Ha-Aggadah: Legends from the Talmud and Midrash* by Hayyim Nahman Bialik and Yehoshua Hana Ravnitzky, which is really a masterful treasury of ancient stories and teachings from which I could derive nourishment for a hundred lifetimes.

Stephen King once compared his writing process to archaeology, writing, "Stories are relics, part of an undiscovered pre-existing world. The writer's job is to use the tools in his or her toolbox to get as much of each one out of the ground intact as possible." Do you agree? Share with readers a bit about your writing process. Did the novel take a different turn once you began writing, or did you know how everything would play out from the beginning? How long did the research take you, and then the actual writing?

I love Stephen King's description. When I write, I can only maintain the self-discipline if I put myself in a very corporate mind-set. I actually have a terribly mean imaginary boss who often stands behind me looking over my shoulder and yelling at me. I don't know what he looks like—I imagine him kind of wiry—but I know his voice well. "I'm not paying you to sit here making up names!" "I'm not paying you to sit here eating pretzels and grapes staring at a blank screen!" Of course, he's not paying me at all, but his prodding helps me push forward.

For me, it is important to have the entire book well-outlined from the start, with dates alongside each section that serve as deadlines. These deadlines are never ever met until months later (something that doesn't make my wiry boss happy!), but I think they help keep me in that business mind-set, which keeps me focused. It is also a lot more believable and manageable to say to yourself, "I am going to write a scene" than to say "I am writing a novel." I like having the whole book outlined because then you can plant allusions in the beginning that can carry through to the end. The end of the book is written in my mind long before it is reached because I have been working toward it deliberately from the beginning.

I first wrote *The Scroll of Anatiya*, which was Anatiya's own story. This part of the work didn't require as much research as it did long immersion in biblical text, and a lot of genuine love.

I feel that sometimes because the research never really ends, the research itself becomes a dangerous excuse for not writing. For *Drawing in the Dust*, I did do a lot of research. I had stacks of books on Megiddo, lots of articles and essays on archaeology in the Middle East, and pages of notes. But at a certain point, I (encouraged by my imaginary boss: "I'm not paying you to look at pictures of digs!") said enough. I had the book outlined, and I sat down to aim for that first deadline, with the knowledge that once the manuscript was finished, I could take the time to do further research and fill it in.

In many ways, the hardest research came after the first draft was complete. Understanding the story through the eyes of excellent and insightful readers demanded countless revisits. Giant two-hundred-page portions were removed and rewritten. The order was played with again and again. Characters were deepened with more and more layers. For me, once the manuscript is complete, the careful and painstaking transformation from writing to storytelling really begins.

Are you working on another novel? If so, will it feature Page, or an entirely different cast of characters?
I wrote a book called *The Goat-Keeper* before writing *Drawing in the Dust*, which I then put aside. I am currently revising it. *The Goat-Keeper* is a biblical novel that is about a tribe of people called Edge who witnessed God at Sinai from afar, but never actually received the Law. There is a purification ritual described in the book of Leviticus (6:6–10) in which once a year the High Priest would take

two goats and mark one to be offered on the altar as a sacrifice to God, and the other to be driven into the wilderness of Azazel carrying the sins of the people. The modern term "scapegoat" is derived from this ancient ritual. In *The Goat-Keeper*, each year the sin-laden scapegoat finds its way into the herd of one of the daughters of Edge, the matriarchal shepherdess of these mystical Panlike creatures. It is different from *Drawing in the Dust*, but shares the notion of love as a messianic value.

Currently, I am also in the process of completing another novel, *Whish*. *Whish* is about a modern girl, named Whish, who develops the ability to understand *Shome 'ah*, the language of the entire natural world. Once her ability is awakened, she quickly realizes that the natural world is at vicious war with itself, a war of which humankind is unaware, where the pretty plants and docile pets we love the best in fact may be plotting our demise. Whish finds herself dangerously in the middle of this secret war that has been raging since Jurassic times.

I know *Whish* sounds completely different from *Drawing in the Dust*, but to me there is a subtle golden thread that connects them. Both Page and Whish are convinced of their own worthlessness. Page spent most of her career in Megiddo, where enormous historical battles have taken place over hundreds of years. Her own battles, however, were all internal, struggling with her own fear and morbidity. Whish's battles are all external, struggling to survive brutal attacks. While Page allows herself to be consumed from within, Whish is in danger of being consumed from without. The characters of both books are seeking psychological ceasefire. I think all of my characters want to transcend their limited allotments of time and space. Page seeks the tranquillity of her own wholeness and inadvertently gifts the world with the same. Whish, on the other hand, seeks to mend a planet and inadvertently may find herself mended.